I0583063

PETER THORN

HAND OF GOD

WOLF'S MOUNT

If you purchased this book without a cover
You should be aware that it is stolen property.
It was reported as "unsold and destroyed" to the publisher
And neither the author nor the publisher
Has received any payment for this "stripped book."

This is a work of fiction. The characters and events here portrayed are fictitious.
If real, they are being used fictitiously and should not be taken otherwise.
The use of names of actual persons and places are incidental to the purposes of the
plot and are not intended to change the entirely fictional character of the work.

WOLF'S MOUNT

Copyright © 2016 by George Stratigakis
Cover, Colophon, and Peter Thorn are Trademarks of Wolf's Mount®
All rights reserved.
www.HandofGodBook.net

No part of this book may be reproduced or transmitted in any form or by any means,
electronic or mechanical, including photocopying, recording, or by any information
storage and retrieval system, without the written permission of the Publisher.

Publisher's Cataloging-in-Publication Data
Thorn, Peter.
Hand of God/ Peter Thorn.
    Summary: An American diplomat in Cyprus uncovers a terror plot against
    America and is assassinated so the attack can proceed and benefit Israel. Former
    Marine Ben Huntley pursues the killers who begin an Impact Event landslide on
    La Palma and create a mega-tsunami to cripple America.
ISBN-13: 978-1533152046
ISBN-10: 1533152047
Description: Wolf's Mount Paperback Edition. | New York: 2016.
    Subjects: BISAC: FICTION / Action & Adventure. | Terror—Fiction. | Tsunami—
    Fiction. | La Palma Landslide—Fiction. | Cyprus—Fiction. | Morocco—Fiction. |
    Drones—Fiction. | Lituya Bay Tsunami—Non-Fiction. | Author's Note. |
Glossary and Characters

Printed in the United States of America
Palatino Linotype

PETER THORN

HAND OF GOD

WOLF'S MOUNT

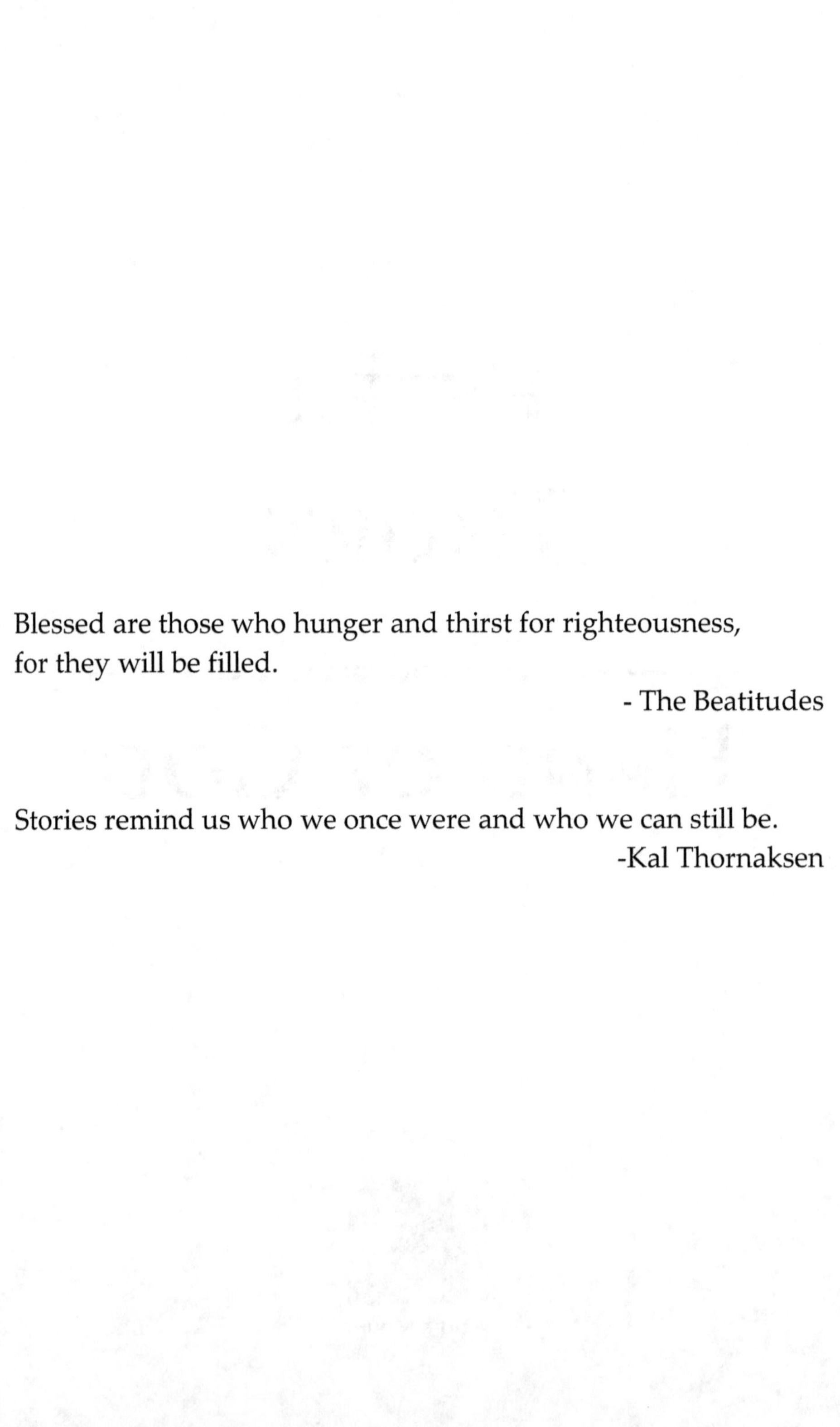

Blessed are those who hunger and thirst for righteousness,
for they will be filled.

- The Beatitudes

Stories remind us who we once were and who we can still be.

-Kal Thornaksen

Prologue

Keryneia, Turkish Occupied Northern Cyprus

Nivit and Yarden, both young women in their early twenties, appeared at the top of the yacht's gangway. With lithe bodies and buoyant steps, they descended to the stone dock. Their easy interaction suggested the familiarity that comes with a long friendship. It was late afternoon, and behind them, the sun was dropping into the horizon. They walked with the energy of young bodies, and their sparkling eyes and animated faces bubbled in anticipation of the coming excitement of the evening.

The boat at their back was reserved and emphasized function over ostentatiousness. It was one of several large pleasure craft anchored at the port's edges during this the height of the tourist season and was secured alongside Keryneia's ancient castle by the harbor's narrow inlet/outlet. People strolling in the evening breeze under the fortress's battlements would think the owners wealthy and on summer tour of various Mediterranean ports. They might even be envious of its 39 feet and consider the owner standoffish for anchoring far from local vessels.

The entry to the harbor, at the boat's port side, was a 30-meter wide waterway. The thin seawall jutted out into the bay like a long crooked finger to protect the port. Only a well-trained eye might notice that the boat faced the ocean and could be in open water in under a minute. The boat's interior had been designed with three staterooms, but on this mission, the master was crammed with several bunk beds, and the other two were filled with computers, communication equipment and an array of gear and armaments.

The women headed towards port center. They had maybe 300 meters to walk on the quay and then they'd turn right to enter the esplanade. The few locals they passed admired their svelte physiques and short form-hugging evening dresses. They'd be thought of as wealthy outsiders—likely the daughters or escorts of foreigners heading to a waterfront cafe and later to the city's nightspots.

The women turned and entered the port's esplanade. Awnings and restaurant tables ringed the water's edge. Two and three story stone waterfront buildings lined the left. Most had been warehouses during the times of the carob bean industry but now had been turned into restaurants, cafes, and gift shops to serve the tourist trade.

The young women stopped, unlocked elbows, faced each other, and feigned a surprised exchange. After this flit of enthusiasm, they interlocked elbows again and resumed their walk. Their banter and bit of shallowness was meant to conceal covert operative training. Their steps were light over the 40-cm white cement squares that were etched to resemble street tiles. A few meters below the esplanade, small skiffs bobbed in the water.

Nivit and Yarden became Saturday sundown strollers going nowhere. Their conversation slowed and they blended with the ambling pedestrians. Four teenage boys walked side-by-side chewing and dropping pumpkin seeds onto the chalky pavement while they eyed a group of similarly aged girls approaching from the opposite direction. Two young men on Yamaha dirt bikes revved their engines but cruised so slowly that they zigzagged the width of the street to keep balance. They stopped next to another group of girls holding cellphones.

The night's activity had started; the next three hours would consist of sitting, snacking, conversing, and watching the world go by while locals and visitors crossed back and forth between shops and promenade. The two Israeli women found a table, ordered coffee, and chatted over cigarettes. Waiters standing at shop entrances enticed customers or carried trays of pastries and frappe coffees back and forth. A young couple pushing a stroller met another couple. The women greeted each other with kisses on both cheeks, the men clasped hands and then all moved to sit at a table under the awning. A group of tourists, the men in white slacks and polo shirts and the women in aquamarine and pink sweaters draped over their shoulders, examined a restaurant menu.

No one noticed when after several cigarettes, the women placed some currency under the ashtray for their coffees and moved towards a side street.

########################

Why hadn't Nivit come? Yarden wondered. *Question everything,* she heard Major Doyan demanding at the academy. Did she have a reason not to go with her to the ladies' room? Yarden proceeded alone but in the hallway slipped behind the stage and peeked back. Nivit was scanning the room. The large bass speaker shook Yarden's body but provided her with cover to watch the room. Nivit was up and walking; she paused next to a man, wrote on a napkin and placed it and the pen in his chest pocket. She started back for her table glancing all the while towards the restroom. *I was right,* Yarden thought with dread. *I knew she was up to something.* Nivit had passed a note to an American!

1
Sam

Keryneia, Turkish Occupied Northern Cyprus

The Russian yacht cut through the oily smooth water and slowed as it approached the dock. It slid quietly next to the stone structure as if snuggling safely home.

The speaker in Sam's ear came alive, "Confirming two men." There's the Israelis, Sam's mind registered.

"Understood," he replied. "Observe only, as agreed."

Two men, one tall and bulky and the other shorter and wider, stepped ashore. Three dark masses followed closely behind. Each consisted of a man holding onto a woman by the arm. They might have been revelers returning after a day's pleasure cruise, but the women walked oddly as if not quite in control of themselves. The men held them closely and occasionally tugged at them. When the entourage reached two black Mercedes cars, the men gave up pretenses and brusquely tossed the women into the back seat.

The cars drove off. Spotters from three different agencies monitored their course through Keryneia's streets. Minutes later, the cars reached the *White Caucasus* nightclub on Erdal Aksa Street. One driver managed to get one foot out before men in dark military fatigues with automatic weapons surrounded the car. The Russians could do nothing. The white slavers were caught in an indefensible position and Turkish Cypriot Special Forces arrested them without firing a shot.

The operation had gone as planned. The coordination and the negotiations with the Israelis—meticulous to the point of almost driving him mad—looped over and over in Sam's mind. He thought of the girls. Three saved from a life of prostitution, drugs, and anything else that made the Russians money. It was cause for celebration and Sam felt a satisfaction that was very soothing.

He, Sam Johnston, CIA Case Officer at the U.S. Embassy in Cyprus, had not only witnessed the arrests—he'd arranged the whole thing. *Man, he felt good!* Three months of maneuverings had brought Russian gangsters, victims, Mossad, Turkish-Cypriot Police, and American Intelligence to a thrilling and satisfying conclusion.

He'd brought the Israelis in at the very last minute when all the details were in place and they had no choice but to stay on the sidelines. He knew better. They had played safety, watched the events play out, and stayed out of the actual arrest. That had taken some arm-twisting. The Cypriots had watched the Russians, the Israelis had watched the Cypriots, and Sam had watched everyone. The evening's prize, Yevgeny Malinovsky the old émigré smuggler turned human trafficker, had been wanted man by Israel for 30 years. He would finally pay for promising the Jewish refuseniks safe passage out of Russia but never delivering. *He deserves whatever he gets,* Sam thought. No qualms about handing him over. He'd restored some vague equilibrium that had been off kilter for 30 years.

The Turkish-Cypriots would get the rest of the gangsters. Sam would get the women. He had a van from a local shelter waiting; barring major health issues, they'd be handed to American Relief where they'd be interviewed and their ordeals catalogued. Their information on trafficking networks in the Eastern Mediterranean would be valuable. Sam scored points with the Israelis, the Turkish-Cypriots, the Embassy, and Washington. Best of all, he had stayed out of the Russians' radar. All this, on the same night he was to meet the Israeli whistleblower. A high point to end his career. So far so good.

Time to meet the young woman. He got up from the coffee shop, made the slight corner and several doors down entered the boîte.

A hell of a night, indeed.

2
Goodbye to Keryneia

Keryneia, Turkish Occupied Northern Cyprus

Embassy staff were always told they were targets. The words no longer registered with Sam because he'd been hearing the warning for decades—only the words changed. He'd grown up in Istanbul the child of State Department employees, had served in Turkey, and was in the 15th year of his Cyprus posting. Things were familiar and safe here. The difference, now, was that he'd finally set a retirement date. This last bit of business remained. *Was angst getting the best of him?*

He'd been apprehensive since morning. *Was it the Malinovsky operation or the anxiety of returning to Cathy in Connecticut?*

He stepped into the Impala and reached for the slip in his pocket. He read:

"Islamic militants plan to kill millions of Americans in operation called 'Palm of God or Hand of God.' Not sure of details. Info on memory stick in pen. Need your help with Mossad agents recently arrested."

He pushed the gas pedal into the floor. The car's 214 horses roared in response and the engine swelled under him. The sound and power were consoling and would be used to the fullest over the next two of hours. Now at night with pedestrians around, the port's streets seemed more like alleys. He slowed to pass a crowd of teens loitering outside a nightclub. The next block consisted of modest working class homes and was quieter; empty road beckoned beyond. *Calm down,* he told himself and consciously took a few long slow breaths.

He passed the ancient buildings of Old Keryneia oblivious to the fraying stone facades. He entered a roundabout and shifted to the outside lane. A three-quarter mile straightaway—the quickest route out of the city—stretched in front.

He approached a larger second roundabout. The car screeched around half of it and exited to the right. He entered the divided four-lane Ecevit Caddesi highway that headed for the pass through the mountains. Taking advantage of the modern road built to European specs, Sam pushed the Impala to its limit.

He climbed the hilltops above Keryneia. He passed the homes of prosperous Turkish-Cypriots and tourist enclaves that took advantage of the elevation for a picturesque view over city and ocean. Hours before on his descent, he'd noticed the number of swimming pools had increased. Amidst the sparse vegetation and yellowed dry landscape of the mountainside, the aquamarine water resembled turquoise squares against the deep background of blue sea that stretched to the horizon.

The car responded to his foot but strained with the climb. Looming behind him, the Mediterranean Sea went on for 40 miles to the Turkish mainland. No cars in front or behind. The unlit highway and car forced a slower pace than he wished. The incline steepened. He shifted the automatic transmission into Low trying to eke more speed. The engine's whine increased but gave little in return. He moved back to Drive. He'd have make up time in the flat central plateau after he crested the pass.

He imagined he saw Keryneia behind him. From this distance, its lights would be compacting into a haze and hovering over the port. The vastness of the black ocean would be overwhelming as if trying to drown out whatever glitter the city managed. On either side of the port, the lights of the coastal roads would be shriveling to irregular necklaces until they reached the next small glittering pearl.

Then he remembered the moon as it had been the last time he'd been here. Dick, Ben, and he had come to send-off Dick who was being transferred to Italy. Rather than the trip or the night's kebab and beer, the blemished but very bright moon had stayed with Sam. It had been a pure and elemental evening. The mountain range had towered empty of trees but with thickets of Spanish grass and cactus shrubs. Bare mountain, quiet, sky, moonlight. The moon was as bright as a pale cool sun. He remembered everything: the road, the mountains, the sky, the crisp air. It had been a fitting end to an era.

He'd traveled the world and was prepared for cultural differences. New places and experiences no longer intimidated him. He tried to be pragmatic and add new information to his inventory. He thought of his father and the large lump of bone on his ankle where the horse had kicked him and scarred him for life. *It gives me character*, he had said. For a time now, Sam had known exactly what his father meant.

During that night's drive home from Keryneia, he'd stocked up on the scene and the moon. He still thought of its clarity fondly. He held onto it as a salve against day-to-day doldrums. The image of that night's moon over the ridgeline near St. Hilarion's Castle was permanently etched in his mind.

In contrast, now in the dark, his agitation and speeding car devoured the miles. The road and spruce trees flew by and did not register.

'Millions,' she said. *Was it possible? Did the Israelis know they had a whistleblower? They'd treat her as a traitor. She was in danger and she must know it. Or, was it a false flag? Why would they set him up? They'd expect him to rush to the Embassy. He'd stack the deck and head for the Brits instead.*

It was past midnight; Lefkosia was a half-hour away, Golf Section maybe an hour-and-a-half. *How many hairpin curves?* His hands were clammy. The ascent to RAF Troodos on Mt. Olympus began at the end of the Solea valley; the switchbacks were nasty. He'd have to stay alert, slow to pass through farming villages, and be wary of dew-slickened pavement.

He had to learn the rest of the message.

3
Execution

On the Road to the Greek Sector, Cyprus

Sam crested the pass. Cyprus's inner plain stretched to the horizon. Thousands of flickering lights indicated the capital, Lefkosia. On the outskirts of the city, he'd take the B9 peripheral road to the southwest to bypass local streets and cross into the Greek sector. The sight of the Impala and his diplomatic plates would grant him quick entry from the Turkish border guards.

The world drove four-cylinder European and Asian gas misers but politicians still legislated that federal employees drive American cars—as if there was such a thing anymore. He snickered. Permitting U.S. Government personnel to drive "foreign" cars was political suicide and undermined U.S. workers, the logic went. Lobbyists kept tabs and careers were on the line. End result? Washington dictated that Government employees drive American-made cars. Never mind that a 17 mpg V-6 Detroit automobile in a foreign country looked odd, gulped expensive gas, and might as well have an imaginary inscription on its door saying, "Hit here with Molotov." Sam shook his head. *Terrorists are everywhere and Americans are prime targets,* he thought. At least the

Impala was a few generations beyond the old boats of the 1960's. He thought of his father's '72 Galaxie. *Thank God for small favors.*

He entered the plain, and the Impala hit 85 mph. The foothills of Olympus and the climb to the RAF station were half an hour away.

#########################

Ten kilometers back, a short exchange over secure mobile phones ended. A lone rider mounted a rented Yamaha 230 off-road motorcycle. Meticulously, he tugged black leather gloves tight against his fingers and put on a helmet with a visor. He kicked the engine to life and revved it several times. Satisfied with the smooth burn of the gasoline, he started after Sam.

##########################

The light flooded the inside of the Impala before Sam realized someone was behind him. He'd come out of a turn and in the dark was gauging when he'd brake again. The floodlight's glare hit the rear view mirror, filled the interior, and blinded him. He waited for what must be the high beam to dim. Instead, the vehicle blasted past him inches from his outside mirror and disappeared to the right into a tight turn.

Seconds later, a panicked Sam braked hard to avoid a blinding light unnaturally low on the road. Dust and smoke particles swirled in the beam. He noticed a splash of white paint, which, as he approached, turned into a motorcycle's rear fender. The machine was sprawled on the pavement at an odd angle and its front wheel was spinning. Sam looked around for the driver having visions of his son's chest gasping for air. The next thing he knew, his rear door was open and someone had entered behind him.

It took less than three seconds but the onslaught of unexpected stimuli numbed Sam's cerebral cortex. Before he could make sense of the scene or of the intruder, the most important fact of Sam's life became the sharp pain digging into his neck.

"Park. There," a voice said by his ear. A warm waft of garlic reached him. Sam looked at the dark mass of bushes and felt the pain of the blade between his neck bones. He inched the car off the road onto the dirt and into a mound of overhanging vines.

He tried to place the accent but two words were not enough for a good guess.

Then he heard, rather than felt, the slicing of his windpipe. For an eternal moment, nothing; he entered a timeless plane. The door opening behind him did not register but he felt the force of it slamming shut. Curiously, the sound was muffled and far away.

He lifted his left hand to his throat. He felt a gap in his skin and a hot moistness on his fingers. The roar of an engine crashed into a reality that was now foreign. The noise violated a precious and sacred moment. The frothy waters of a waterfall bubbled over rocks down a wooded hill over a shallow streambed that cut through a green meadow. Cathy was radiant in a sundress. They were in love and it was joyous. He felt a chill. How can such communion, such bonding fade? *Cathy, what happened?*

Anger swelled in him and the image faded. Desperate now, Sam searched for strength. With his right hand, he reached for his shirt pocket, but the hand collided and fumbled against his left, which had somehow gotten in the way. *Why was he so clumsy?* He managed to reach the pen in his shirt pocket and got his thumb and two fingers around it. Trembling with the demand for stamina no longer there, he tossed the pen at the passenger window but was dumbfounded when it bounced back in a downward angle and disappeared under the passenger seat. The unnatural clatter of the pen on the glass stunned his mind and froze the expression on his face like a hit from a sledgehammer.

Blood gushed from his neck. His hand felt heavy and dragged down his chest. It came to rest on his thigh, but Sam did not notice. His eyes were open and locked on the window. He felt a faint surge of anger but there was no response from his body. His mind slammed into a massive gray wall that reached high up into a charcoal sky—the logical and emotional dead end of the closed window.

4
How Far Have We Fallen?

Foothills of Mount Olympus, Cyprus

Thanasis walked around his ancient Mazda B1500 pick-up truck that he'd loaded the night before with two new beehives, the smoker, and the dented tin containers. Now preparing to drive to Ampelokipo, he was struck by the age of the tins. He'd first seen them as a five year old when he had watched his father under the balcony empty the honey. When had his father gotten them? As a nine-year old, he'd carried them a few doors down to the ruin with the caved-in roof to leave with the travelling tinker. Assorted metal shiny pots littered the man's temporary workshop. Two days later, the canisters sparkled like new silvery jewels. How long ago was that? Twenty…twenty-four years? That long! Thanasis marveled. The dents, gray streaks, and the off-kilter spouts stared back. He felt how they looked. *How far we've fallen*, he thought.

For three days he had measured, re-measured, meticulously trimmed wood and assembled the new hives. Measuring, marking, and nailing the thin moldings to the boxes had taken the bulk of that time. The spaces had to be correct. Bees were fickle and built honeycombs to store their honey only if the gaps were of a certain width. If the distance was off, they'd bridge the spaces shut and that would make inspection, honey collection, and reuse of the combs a mess. But, if the spaces were exact, the bees navigated the frames and deposited their nectar with the industry bees were known for. He had checked and double-checked that the gap was his preferred 6.35 millimeters. His father came to mind saying repeatedly, *"A hundred times measure, cut only once."* Wanting to put his own stamp on things, he learned the hard way after many do-overs. How could he have argued with that advice? Ah, youth.

When he finished the hives, Thanasis had tested the frames by sliding them back and forth to ensure they moved freely. It was a technical problem, and if he took proper care, he'd get it right the first time. Having to fix an error meant he'd been too hasty the first time and this he took as a personal failure. *Who wants to clean and re-build hives a second time?* he thought. He wanted functional honeycombs and an easy harvest. *It's all about having a system,* he thought. The rewards were ease, speed, and time saved. Fixing mistakes was frustrating and boring and most of all, annoying. The faster he took in the honey, the calmer the bees, the faster they were back producing and he bottling and selling. Care up front meant no propolis buildup to deal with, no hive damage, no disease, no swarming, and no risk of colony death.

At Ampelokipo, he'd put on the mask, calm the bees with the smoker, and move two colonies over. He'd proceed slowly so they'd remain calm. He'd exchange two old frames for two new ones. He had already lined the bottom of the new hives with wax. The rest of the day, he'd harvest honey from the other twelve. He'd bring it home to can and sell and come another day when he had a few hours. That's what he'd do. That way he'd check on the health of the bees he moved today. If all were well, he'd save that honey for the kids when they came up from Lemesos.

He slowed to enter the access road and downshifted into second gear to drive the dirt path to the terraces where his hives were laid out in a line. He maneuvered to pass the thorny rosebush that towered over his pickup and got annoyed at the height and thickness of the overgrowth. *Just like the olive growers,* he muttered. *Why can't they keep the path clear? How do they expect tractors loaded with olives to get through?*

That's when they'd cut the vines? Why can't people do something because it's the right thing? He didn't understand it. *Wasn't anyone meticulous anymore? Don't they crave the satisfaction?* He'd take a look at how each pruned his trees and that would tell him about the man.

The Mazda inched forward and scraped the brush. A passenger car blocked his way. Probably some tourist stopping for the night. Then Thanasis noticed the peculiar plates. He got out, walked past his hood and avoided the bramble vines. He looked into the car.

Three seconds later he was crossing himself and exclaiming in Greek the equivalent of "Christ and Holy-Mother-of-God" followed by "God forgive him." He scuffled back to the pick-up. With no coordination, he bungled the gear into reverse. The little truck jerked backwards onto the main road and screeched to a halt as the tires caught on the pavement. His new hives no longer on his mind, Thanasis raced back towards the town of Galata to report the dead man.

5

Ben Huntley

American Embassy, Lefkosia, Cyprus, Monday, July 21

Seventy analysts in the building and I'm at it alone, Ben Huntley said to himself. He thought the words consciously and slowly and felt as if he actually spoke them. *Maybe I was in the Marines too long—around here, everyone's selling and negotiating. And, most are working on the Middle East.*

The U.S. Embassy in Cyprus has the most varied role of all State Department facilities. It has evacuated Americans from Middle East trouble spots and supported armed missions to Iraq, Afghanistan, or other hotspot of the moment. While Israeli bombings played out on the internet and on front pages of newspapers during the Lebanese Civil War, Embassy staffers were in overdrive chartering ships and airplanes and evacuating thousands. Countries the world over praised their humanitarian efforts giving the U.S. a much-needed popularity boost.

The participants were now called ISIS and Syria but they were still in the Middle East. Cypriot matters were left to Ben. To make matters worse, Dick Higgins, the Drug Enforcement Officer, had been sent to Italy and no one had replaced him. Only Ben and Sam were left to gist criminal and strategic intel to Virginia. Thank God for Sam.

Where the hell was Sam? The Trafficking in Persons Report had to be sent out and Sam was AWOL. The man had an encyclopedic knowledge of Cyprus. His instinct for intelligence and the local mood matched only his pursuit of doner kebab all over the island.

When Ben had appeared before him all decked out and deferential the first time, Sam had simply said, "C'mon. We're going for doner."

"Now?" Ben had asked expecting a formal Q and A on his service and background. An hour later, they were having beers in Northern Cyprus, in Keryneia.

"You need to come up to speed fast and we might as well eat. Heard you had some trouble in Afghanistan. Regardless of the details, I'm sure you blame yourself. No matter. We all have our skeletons. Point is, what are you going to do about it? I'll tell you what…face the next thing that needs doing and do it better than last time. Think of it as making amends, if you have to."

"Thanks…I think," Ben answered unsure thanking Sam was the proper response.

"Now, the most basic thing to keep in mind here is that Arabs, Jews, Christians, Greeks, Turks—every group—has memories and rivalries going back thousands of years. They never forget. That's the Middle East."

"Memory—history—creates problems?" Ben had asked slyly.

Sam wasn't fazed. "You know what I mean. You need sources, but they have their own angles. Figure how far you can trust each, where the human intel is, and who are only poseurs."

Ben listened and learned. Sam saved him months of legwork. He knew recent and ancient history, religious wars, ethnic animosities, and powerbrokers. He provided Ben with a map of the ebbs, offshoots, branches and undercurrents. Obstacles would always be there, he said, but all Ben needed was to adjust perspective and follow the trends. Soon, Ben's analyses back to Washington had enough insight to deem him a worthy successor to Dick and that earned him the leeway to operate without having to account for every sneeze. Life was much easier when he didn't need to justify every minute detail. After Afghanistan, Ben had no patience to explain himself to technocrats who knew jack.

6
The Russians

American Embassy, Lefkosia, Cyprus, Monday, July 21

Cyprus came with hundreds of miles of coastline, two major airports, more than ten times as many visitors a year than residents, Lebanese profiteers, drug runners, Western businessmen, foreigners on buying trips, and the Russians. Plenty of opportunity, anything for a price, and lots of transactions. In the quarterly Trafficking in Persons Report, the Russians were again front and center. Sam had been present when the Russians first showed up. When the Soviet Union collapsed, they starting coming on "buying trips" with wads of cash from looting state assets. From the beginning, there was no way to tell legitimate from gang money apart. Ben could only hope that the reports he sent to Washington would make their way back through high enough channels to get the Cypriots to listen.

Ever since Dick left, the stakes had gotten higher and the criminals more ruthless. Sam had warned about lax banking regulations, the 16,000 Russian companies on the books as operating locally, and cautioned against the elimination of visa requirements.

But, Cyprus had remade itself for thousands of years in order to survive. From the time of the Knights Templar, its location at the crossroads of Middle East, Europe, and Africa made it an ideal middleman. Its current iteration as a business hub rendered Sam and Ben's warnings lone voices in the wilderness.

Money flowed; hotels, vacation homes and luxury cars were everywhere. Complaints and pressure to change Cyprus's tax haven status were years in the future. The U.S. had to balance Greeks, Turks, local and regional issues. The Russian weekend junketeers were loud and obnoxious. Big money kept a lower profile. Cypriot authorities didn't have the willpower or staff to deal with white-collar crime. Russian criminal enterprises fell into a gray zone between American involvement and Cypriot independence.

Then too, Cyprus still blamed the U.S. and considered Kissinger the 'arch conspirator' of the troubles that began in 1974 and continued still. So the U.S. walked a fine line between criticizing the Cypriots and securing their cooperation against money laundering and drug trafficking. At the top of the list was the worst of all international scourges: human trafficking. The Cypriots didn't look too deeply to locate Russian criminal enterprises except for the occasional scandal.

Then again, connecting the Russians to American-Cypriot relations was not easy; the U. S. could not appear to interfere in domestic affairs. Cypriot politicians listened but acted only occasionally. American Diplomats could warn about trends, but policy makers assessed interests, informed the Cypriots and coordinated joint actions. The tiny Cypriot government had the final say on responding, if at all.

Ben would not hold his breath.

The Russians controlled the nightclubs, the women, and the drugs. The Cypriots—Greek or Turkish—didn't have the stomach for human suffering like the Russians. "Barmaids" and "artistes" were the capital of the entertainment industry and the Russians had an inexhaustible supply from the former Soviet states complete with ethnic varieties to suit every taste. After decades of communist rule, the brutal and insatiable Russian gangster had been let loose on the world.

"The Mafia," Sam had said, "is all Hollywood; the Italians are outdated, outgunned, and outnumbered. Only the Mexican cartels are as ruthless as the Russians. Soon the Russians will control all criminal activity. I'm serious."

\#########################

I don't have 15 years like Sam. The world's moving too fast and people are more expendable than ever. I may as well be back in Afghanistan, Ben thought. Sam was Defense Attaché. With Syria and Afghanistan still raging, he and Sam kept tabs on security, criminal, and terrorist issues. That left no time for street work. Between visiting Navy vessels, the comings and goings of personnel and aircraft, and the listening stations, the two of them had their hands full.

Ben stared at the figures sent him by Police Chief George Petrou. They confirmed what he already knew. Reality was probably worse. He'd be frank in his report: police abuse was minimal as were cases of degrading treatment of persons in custody; violence against women, including spousal abuse, was on the upswing, and there were seven incidents of violence against children. Cases of discrimination against asylum seekers were up. The Cypriots were doing the best they could, as were other Southern Europeans for that matter. Syrians, Northern Africans and Southeast Asian migrants were infiltrating Europe's borders and overwhelming the security forces of every Mediterranean country.

Trafficking of women for sexual exploitation was the biggy. He'd mention the recent Cypriot law on trafficking and the new shelter for victims. He would end with recommendations for changes in law enforcement, victim protection, and trafficking prevention.

Time for the report. He typed two lines and stopped. *Where the hell was Sam? He should sign off on the report before he sent it off.* He picked up the phone.

"Hey Scott, anything new on Sam?"

"Was just calling you. He's missed his second check in. His cell won't take any more messages. Same thing at his home number."

"Last sighting still Friday afternoon?"

"Yup. We've checked with everyone we can think of."

"O.K. You and I are going to his place, right now."

Half an hour later, Ben placed two calls—one to his nominal superior in Cyprus, U.S. Ambassador Thomas Milhaus, and the other to CIA headquarters in Langley, Virginia.

7
Andreas and Demos

Amiantos Mine, Mount Olympus, Cyprus

A small Mazda pick-up approached the small security shack and stopped. The two guards playing cards inside looked up.

"Your turn. Might be another tour," Andreas made an effort to sound upbeat to give the other man hope. He had taken a look at the pick-up truck and decided otherwise for it was old and not likely the vehicle of a tourist.

"Yeah, right. Listen, I think we should take turns with tours—not vehicles," grumbled the younger man.

"You never know who's coming," replied Andreas effecting a knowledgeable voice regarding visitors. *The new guy was questioning the way things were done? He'd put a stop to that.*

Demos wasn't sure if Andreas just wanted the final say in the arrangement or a larger cut for himself. Probably both. He decided he'd speak his mind even if it meant standing up to older man. He'd watch the other's reaction and back down only if he sensed the senior guard took insult or would not budge.

"You're toying with me, right? You think I'm an idiot?" Demos said mounting a strong offense. "When was the last time a pick-up asked for a tour?"

"Obviously, you didn't notice, as I did, that they're foreigners. Are you going to talk to them or not?"

"I'm going. If we're going to give unauthorized tours, we should work together…" he lowered his voice "and not attract attention," he concluded.

"Exactly," Andreas pounced. "So learn how it's done."

Demos glared but turned and walked to the pickup.

When he stood at the window and chatted for a bit too long, Andreas knew something was up. Just as he decided he'd look for himself, the other man started back. He was smiling.

"Egyptians," he said, "at the university for a week. They want to see the geology," he snickered. The idea of being interested in the ground was far removed from his thinking. He'd suffer the foreigners for a while since they were paying and cut it short when he tired of them. He'd be careful—not like his sister who overcharged for a gold chain once and bragged to her husband while the tourists were still in the store. She'd never live down the scolding she got from the two women who turned out to be Cypriot natives and understood every word. To this day if business dipped, Lydia worried that gossip about the incident had resurfaced.

"Thirty euros," Demos continued, "but if a bus pulls up, we're splitting the pot equally. I don't care if you know the driver or not. Equal risk; equal take. Not every man for himself."

"Now is that fair? The system's been in place since you were a kid. The drivers come for me. Take the 30 and say thanks."

8

Theft

Amiantos Mine, Mount Olympus, Cyprus

Abu Nur al Deen and Mahmud Mahduni again looked at the crude map of the mine that identified nine different buildings. A few had been added to the layout as some were on switchbacks and had been missed on the first day. The complex was over 100 years old and a mile-and-a-half in diameter. Half of the large hill had been sheared off by blasting and the remaining point looked a lot like Mount Blanc. Several hillside basins emptied into the large pit. Terraces lined the perimeter and some were planted with uniformly arranged saplings that looked artificial and new. The two men had watched for two nights, but still had no idea where the detonators were stored and how they'd remove them.

The original plan had been to break in and steal the detonators at night. Sneaking into the mine and identifying the right building presented difficulties. It would take all night—assuming it proved easy to get into the sheds and check them. Then they'd need to load the truck and escape. Once they took the guards out, they had only one chance to find the detonators. Blue metallic residue from the mine littered the barren hillsides and reflected so much light that the site was bright even at night. That added risk.

Scuttling that plan, they decided to take the guards hostage and force them to reveal the location of the detonators. But now Demos approached with a welcoming look and inquired if they wanted to see the mine. Abu Nur al-Deen, 'the Doctor,' almost lost control of his facial muscles. He fell into the cover of Egyptian geologists in Cyprus for a conference and chatted Demos up.

"We are at the University for the Tectonic Plate Conference. Five days only and we came to see the famous geology of the mountain."

"The geology?" Demos asked puzzled. "What about the old miners' town and the mine?"

Yes, the geology. Many doctoral students write dissertations on the geology of Troodos. The mine was situated atop the juncture of the Eurasian and Afro-Arabian plates. Strata that had once been miles underground was now on the surface. Ophiolite sequences preserved as oceanic crystal fragments that were millions of years old were visible here. Very unique place. The tectonic plates subducted at this very spot. In fact, Cyprus itself was a creation of these incredible forces. If fortunate, they might identify fragments of the Mesozoic or even the older metamorphic basement of the Paleozoic and its underlying carbonate sequences.

Demos's eyes glazed over at the indecipherable language and he was immediately convinced the two men were scientists. The two 'Egyptians' even protested the 40 euro fee he asked. They haggled a bit and settled on 30.

While Demos recounted to Andreas what the 'Egyptians' wanted, Abu Nur al-Deen, known to Mahmud as 'The Doctor,' smiled and waved at the guards. Under his breath, he whispered, "Using the right words can achieve what we wish. We locate the detonators and leave. We come back tonight. Follow my lead."

Demos waved them through the gate into the mine.

An hour later, Demos had lost his enthusiasm for the tour but it the Doctor had found what he needed and was ready to leave.

That night a supply of detonator cords, electronic initiation units and cast boosters were stolen from the mine. By 3 a.m., the pick-up with the booty arrived at a deserted location on Cyprus's southern coast and several men transferred the cargo onto an inflatable boat. It took two trips to ferry the men and material to the larger boat that waited a kilometer out at sea.

The next morning, Andreas and Demos arrived for their shift and found the night guards gagged and bound but alive. The victims would never know of Demos and Andreas's role in their brush with death.

9

The Patriot

Zygi, Southern Coast of Cyprus

The white apron covering Tolis Apostolou's waist made it only halfway around his substantial midsection. In a trimmer person, the long butcher's apron would have slenderized the wearer and hung three-four inches above his shoes. On Tolis, the apron bulged in the center and its cuff slanted diagonally from front to back two feet off the ground giving him an immense presence.

He walked outside into what had been the front yard of his small ancestral home that his father had built in the 1920's. Each spring he whitewashed the exterior wall that now served as the restaurant's façade. He used a Tyrian purple to freshen the door's plain architrave, which turned to a light indigo when the whitewash seeped through. The courtyard's floor was made up of uneven natural stone slates. Tolis had filled the gaps between the slabs with cement and white pebbles and outlined the edges with whitewash giving the courtyard a cared-for and clean appearance. Around the perimeter, his wife, Tasia, maintained a garden of flowers. There was no order. Yellow and orange marigolds were next to geraniums while lilies sprouted from among green leafy plants. Tolis's favorite, cyclamen, was everywhere but dormant now for the summer. The roof was made from long stalks of dried bamboo tied into three-by-six foot sections for shade from the sun.

Now in the afternoon Tolis swung a broom that seemed a thin flimsy stick in his large hands. He swept the day's dust off his stones preparing for the night's business. His baldhead and salt-and-pepper mustache gave his torso nobility and hinted at the slenderness and toughness of his youth. Years of sitting with friends on the off hours with a liter of Xynisteri wine and *mezedes* had softened his body, but his passion for work, for his wine groves, and for his country continued unabated.

Zygi was a tiny town known for its simple seafood restaurants—including Tolis's which served whatever the few remaining fishermen brought in. Situated on the southern coast of Cyprus halfway between Larnaka and Lemesos the little town was proud of its traditions and remained an unspoiled spot between the two modern and lively cities on either side. The nearby naval base strengthened the town's nationalistic sentiments. In the 1950's, Tolis's father had run with EOKA on campaigns against the British. Tolis, in his turn, had faced Turkish forces invading from the mainland in '74. Once a week in the afternoon when the sun cooled, Tolis and a few similarly aged men sat with wine. Frequently the conversation turned to captured and disappeared comrades-in-arms. Families still sought clues to their sons' fate. Tolis had survived but was haunted by the memory of stolen friends, lost youth, and derailed dreams. Cyprus remained divided, property and homes in the North were squatted on, and justice had not come from the diplo-politico nonsense that continued for more than four decades now.

Then the government announced its purchase of a Russian missile system to defend against Turkish aggression. It'd be installed in the nearby base and Tolis could hardly contain himself. Forty years of promises and diplomacy had amounted to nothing, but a new missile system was something. His hair had turned gray and his pace had slowed but he'd also not learned anything new regarding Vaggelis, Kyriakos and Demetris. The Turks avoided the topic since disclosing graves and executions amounted to admitting they'd committed atrocities. By remaining silent, they avoided culpability and doubts as to whether they were ready to join a civilized and transparent Europe. But for Tolis, events were not in doubt. He would not move past what he'd seen and trudged through. Friends had been killed and never been found. His Aunt Froso, old now, shuffled along wearing black from head to toe forever broken by the loss of her son, Vaggeli. She knew in her heart, as did everyone in Zygi, that Vaggeli was dead. God rest his soul.

There had been a funeral but no body. Vaggeli's black suit was laid out in a coffin and a wedding crown placed where his head would have been. Laments and dirges had been wailed, but that was nothing compared to seeing Aunt Froso, the aunt who sang when she fed the two boys their fried potatoes and hoisted them under her arms, fall silent, dead to the world. Whenever Tolis saw her, it was one more instance of "salt tossed on a wound," as his father used to say.

Tolis lifted his chin to indicate the two men walking past his shop and looked at Kosta who was reading the newspaper, "What's with those two?"

10
Once in Intelligence

Zygi, Southern Coast of Cyprus

"Them? They've gone back and forth for two-three days now."

"In those clothes?"

"What's the problem?" Kostas snickered.

"And you say nothing? Did they go to the beach? Those are cases for lenses."

"So they're photographers," Kosta said. "Tourists. What? Forty years later, you're still in Intelligence? Give it a rest."

"I have eyes and I see. Who comes here and doesn't go swimming? They should be in bathing suits, tired and walking slow after a day in the sun. They should have towels and mats and be sunburnt, not carry knapsacks and cameras. I know the English; they're not English. Did you think about the Naval Station?" Tolis said considering the angles.

"Tasia!" he yelled over the wooden tables with the checkered plastic tablecloths tied below with string. He looked towards the door and the interior of the taverna and called again.

"Tasia!"

"What is it now?" Tasia's annoyed voice came from deep in the kitchen.

"Call your sister. I have to talk to that cop husband of hers."

The next day the movements of the two men were monitored. The day after that, Cypriot Police raided their flat at Holiday Bungalows.

The items found and the police operation were detailed on the front pages of the island's several dailies and made Tolis and his taverna famous. They were Israelis, teachers they claimed, gathering historical data on the area. The trove of photographic equipment, frequency scanners, recorded military communiqués, logs of recent naval exercises, and maps identifying military installations proved otherwise.

The "Israeli Affair" became the cause célèbre of the next several weeks; media coverage and speculation riveted the nation. Newspapers were quick to identify Israel as pro-Turkish to the detriment of the Greek side. The incident was eerily reminiscent of the Mossad agents arrested in Jordan six months back who had bungled the assassination of Palestinian leader Abdel Mashal. Cypriots demanded long prison sentences for what were clearly Israeli spies. It was time to take a stand: the Turks hadn't cooperated on the missing for 40 years; they'd defiled Cypriot cultural heritage; destroyed religious and historical sites; disregarded international law and turned confiscated property to imported hardened nationalists and collaborated with the Americans on a new base in the north. Now they were using Israelis against the Cypriots? Israelis and Americans were warned that any pressure to release the two men would be seen as biased support for the Turkish side.

A crusade was born: punish the Israeli agents with life in prison and pressure the Turkish-Israeli-American alliance to accept the newly negotiated Russian missile system.

11

Missing No More

American Embassy, Lefkosia, Cyprus

"Mr. Hantley, you sit too much. Go outside for the sun to see you."

This was Maria Andrikou. Only she held the first syllable of his name and flattened the *u* into an *a*. It irritated him at first but three years later either Maria's pronunciation had improved or he'd made peace with it. Her habit was to move past his name—her de facto greeting—and into pleasantries like the day's heat, her son in London, or some culinary treat that she'd brought from home.

"*Kalimera*, Maria," he answered. Today, Sam's disappearance was on his mind.

"Look," Maria said.

He allowed himself a lapse and looked up. She was pointing out the window. The branches of several palm trees were barely nodding up and down as if they'd been lulled by the scalding midday sun.

"What is it, Maria?" he heard the exasperation in his voice. He caught himself. *The back and forth exchange is therapy. It will last only a minute. It's Cyprus. The Mediterraneans consider one-word greetings cold.*

Don't snap at the woman, though God knew, with Sam missing, today, he was entitled.

"The light, the sun. Do you see a cloud in the sky?" she was saying.

"It is very bright and very blue."

"Ex*a*ctly," she declared triumphantly. There was that *a* again. "Go out for five minutes for the day to see you a *leettle*."

Maria had a knack for granting a moment's respite from work. Even now with the Embassy in an uproar and Washington and Langley all over him, she shifted his viewpoint. It was a Cypriot trait and a characteristic of frequent reversals of personal and national fortune.

Sam, and maybe even Maria, had forced Ben to consider the big picture—to strip information down to its essence. A few times, Ben had asked Maria how she could be philosophical and practical at the same time.

Her responses had ranged from "Days come and days go," to "My children need to eat," and "That is life," as if these remarks explained everything. Finally, he just accepted that her view of the world was as valid as his own.

Today she was saying, "The life is outside, not only inside." On other occasions it was, "I bring *koupekia*" and held the stuffed grape leaves in a plastic container in front of his nose, or "I make *sheftalia*," or "Today you taste the *haloumi*." Now he accepted these pronouncements. How much English she'd learned in school and how much from working at the Embassy was another mystery.

"Mr. Hantley, yesterday, I talk to my son. London is too cold, he say. Too much rain; no sun. Not like Kipros. You go outside and see the day. If no now, later."

The phone rang.

"I will, Maria. *Kalimera*," he dismissed her.

Maria moved on to dusting and emptying trashcans into her cart.

Ben lifted the receiver and listened. His face froze. He stared at the palm tree outside the window and his eyes did not move.

He hung up and picked up his secure line. He pushed a preprogrammed button.

"Ambassador? It's Ben. You'd better return to the Embassy, Sir. The Cypriots have found Sam. He's dead, Sir. They're hinting at suicide."

12

Between Earth and Sky

Outskirts of Larnaka, Southern Cyprus

Ben pulled into the parking lot of the Hala Sultan Tekke mosque on the shores of Larnaka's Aliki Lake. The mosque's grounds were lined with pebble-sized crushed white rock. Myrtle, palm, and cypress trees were planted all around the limestone edifice. Two trees challenged the height of the single minaret that towered over the mosque's dome. Below the minaret's point was the balcony used by the muezzin to call the faithful to prayer. Several mausoleums, a cemetery, and living quarters for men and women made up the rest of the complex.

Beyond the mosque grounds, sparse cane and low willows indicated the lake edge. A light breeze came in and stirred the grass. Ben felt the salty dust in his eyes. Farther along the silt, flamingos plucked the tiny local shrimp from shallow waters.

A jet took off on the right a couple miles away. Ben turned and followed the plane's dirty exhaust as it stained the sky. Larnaka Airport was a waypoint between Europe and the Middle East. Cyprus had about 900,000 residents but 7 million visitors a year. Agent Nelson would be added to that number any moment.

Ben glanced back at the minaret and the tomb and then caught himself checking the mosque's security. There was none. The Hala Sultan Tekke Mosque was the burial site of the Prophet's nurse and a holy shrine for Muslims. Cyprus was replete with antiquities and religious sites central to Islam and Christianity but few were secured. The tomb of Saint Lazarus, who had found 30 years of refuge on Cyprus, was a few miles to the east. Ruins everywhere. Locals didn't need lessons on national identity or a sell job on their culture. Sure the British were still here, the Turks had invaded, International peacekeepers patrolled, the Green Line divided the capital, and, once again, Cyprus was a staging ground for Western incursions into the Middle East.

His mind went into a tangent: *Cypriot youth were indistinguishable from the youth of any other place. Did the stones speak to them? Did they know the monuments and ruins? Maria knew, but she had reached adulthood before the internet. Cypriot history was as much a part of her as America the righteous was a part of his dad and every G.I. that had served in WWII.*

######################

Maybe if Sam had taken the damn Fiat he'd be alive. Again, Ben caught himself. *Stop thinking that way.* His emotions returned to where the logical part of his mind was saying they shouldn't go. He relented. *It's therapy. 'What if's' are analysis and, yes, punishment. Sam's dead and, once more I'm facing the unknown. I need information, I need control, I need to increase the certainty around me.*

All my obsessing didn't prevent Parnell and Parente from getting killed in Afghanistan. Maybe I didn't obsess enough back then.

His foot sank into a dip in the pebbled ground and he caught himself before his ankle buckled. Sam's death was throwing him for a loop. He nearly sprained the ankle just walking the *tekkesi* grounds. *Jeesus, I'm a mess; I have to concentrate to walk,* he muttered shaking his head. *Think: evidence, culprits, motives.*

If he didn't get a hold of his thoughts, he'd be facing the old bottomless pit again. He could second guess and torment his conscience a thousand ways to Sunday, and nothing would change. He couldn't enter that abyss again. *I'm debating if Sam's choice in cars would have made a difference! Really? He was dead. That's it. Move on. The only thing that mattered was what the living did next. The mess on his desk has been there for three days. Deal with his absence and death.*

What the hell did that mean? Years of therapy? Going through the stages of the mourning process? What were they anyway? Did knowing them make it easier to get through them? He was back in his Intro to Psychology class in college; he remembered that there were definite stages with names but didn't remember what they were. *Never imagined I'd have use for that bit of information.*

Sam's death—the death of anyone as good as Sam—scarred the survivor and changed his outlook on life. *I'll function, but I'll never be the same. I have work.* Death numbed, sometimes confused, and sometimes brought wisdom.

I have to find out how Sam died and why. Prepare for the gruesome details and don't dwell on them. Look for closure. Another freaking fairy tale, he snickered. *Try telling Sam's kids they should find 'closure.' Or his own father. Or the thousands of cripples returning from Iraq, Afghanistan and every other God forsaken place in pieces but still breathing. No, too early to think about closure.*

He faced a plaque that read 'Rose Garden of Enlightenment.' He entered. *They'd have to hurry; Sam's murder would become public in a day or two.* The Cypriots had seen no sign of struggle and suggested suicide. Ben knew better. *Sam, if you'd taken the damn Fiat instead of the Impala maybe another sequence events would have been set in motion.*

He drifted back to Dick. *Wrinkled hands, which really meant wise hands, taught you things you never knew you needed. You learned their value only if lucky enough or if you suffered enough. The Fiat was handy. It was older, nondescript and blended into Cypriot traffic. The two of them had used it to travel anonymously on the island. Sam, why didn't you take it?*

He hit a wall.

13
Artemis Nelson

Outskirts of Larnaka, Southern Cyprus

His shoulder bounced back and his mind snapped to the present. He was stunned from the collision and braced himself. His first thought was to wonder why he hadn't sensed danger. Instinctively he blurted out, "Oh, I'm sorry. I didn't see you."

A dark haired composed woman was smiling at him. Her eyes were dark—wondrously large eyes and hair that reached to her shoulders in long serene waves. She was signaling she was not a threat.

"I see meeting here was the right move."

"Excuse me?"

"I said, meeting here was best instead of at the airport. I'm Artemis Nelson."

"Agent Nelson?"

"Yup. Artemis Nelson. Nice to meet you."

He glanced at the short feminine jacket that barely reached her waist. It featured narrow lapels while a skintight leotard type under-blouse concealed her cleavage.

At his silence, she asked, "Expecting a dress uniform?"

Then she spread her hands at her side, rested her palms on her hips, and, Ben swore, pivoted slightly on her heels while her eyes sparkled. The action was coy, controlled and subdued yet hinted at other attributes. She seemed genuine and delighted to see him. Ben was confused. One more airplane rumbling and seeking altitude above them did not help.

"Relax, Huntley. CIA training—basic stuff—catch the opponent off guard, flatter, and manipulate assets to gain the edge. Sound familiar?"

She was pleasant to look at and she knew it. He was not sure how to respond. It was safer not to engage in banter laced with innuendo so he responded with the most neutral question he could think of, "How did you know who I was?"

"I've watched you for a few minutes. You were off somewhere so I gave you some time. And, you told me."

"When?"

"Now, with your reaction."

"You're early."

"Always like to arrive on my own terms—do a little recon, find out what I'm getting into. Bumping into you was the simple way. It *is an investigation*," she emphasized the phrase as if he needed reminding she was here on assignment.

"I expected an Alex or Arthur or something like that."

"It's O.K. I won't hold it against you."

He panicked, "Artemis is a fantastic name."

"Trying to score points? People have no idea what or who 'Artemis' is…or was."

She paused to let this register. Before Huntley could respond, she smiled deliciously and added, "Someday I'll tell you about my sister, Aphrodite."

Ben was speechless. Was she being flippant or just truthful? He'd reserve judgment for now and find out later.

"Another time," she cut that line short. "Right now, we've got a missing diplomat to locate." She turned and started for the parking lot.

Ben did not budge.

"You haven't heard," he said slowly and gravely. Artemis caught the change in his voice and turned around.

"The Cypriots found Sam dead this morning. We're investigating cause of death now."

"Oh," she said. A far way look came over her eyes and her tone became solemn. Circumstances had changed.

"We'd better get started then," she responded.

Ben started the car. Artemis stared at the gearshift, which hung midair below the dash with a void underneath it. She said nothing.

They headed north. Soon they were skirting the shore of the salt lake. After two kilometers, Ben took the larger Leoforos Apriliou, which followed the lake edge towards Larnaka to the south. Then he took a left onto Leoforos Griva Digeni and two blocks later entered the A2 highway heading north to Lefkosia, 22 miles away.

14

Sideshow

Press Room, American Embassy, Lefkosia, Cyprus

Artemis, Ben, and Scott Bailey, the Assistant Army Attaché, slipped into the Embassy pressroom from the back and took seats near the rear door.

State Public Affairs Officer Len Blinkman stepped out of the side of the front of the room and walked like a performer towards the dais. His easy gait exuded confidence and resolve. This was American domain. Make no mistake, the U.S. was efficient and on top of things.

He did not acknowledge the reporters sitting in the front rows, as was his practice in the past. This was a somber occasion. He'd been in Cyprus for a year and was had become familiar with the idiosyncrasies of this State Department posting. The Diplomatic circuit reporters had entered Len's world. They needed him and, when he called, they came. It was a mutually self-aggrandizing arrangement but he had the starring role as choreographer of the U.S. Government's unleashings on Cyprus, nay the Middle East.

"Good morning, everyone," he started. "I know you have questions regarding this morning's sad events. First, I have a statement to read from the Ambassador. A copy will be made available if you wish an accurate transcript. Afterwards, I will take your questions.

'After notification of his family and with deep sadness, we here at the American Embassy in Cyprus mourn the loss of LTC Sam Johnston who served his country with distinction as Defense Attaché. Sam was a friend to all and we will miss him dearly. The investigation is ongoing and cause of death has not yet been determined. Americans in Cyprus should remain vigilant and exercise caution, as always. I must emphasize that no threat has been made against Americans—being aware of your surroundings is just common sense. As soon as the Embassy has further information, we will make it available. Local authorities and the Cypriot people have shown extraordinary support and sympathy during this difficult time. Please remember Lieutenant Colonel Sam Johnston and his family in your prayers.
Ambassador Thomas Milhaus

'I add my own condolences to those of the Ambassador's. The Department of State assures LTC Sam Johnston's family, as well as the Cypriot people, that the United States will conduct a thorough investigation into the circumstances of his death.

'Now, I will do my best to provide answers to any questions you may have."

"*Phileleftheros* is reporting cause of death as suicide. Can you confirm this?" a journalist in the front row asked with a familiarity and brusqueness that said he was a fixture at press conferences but a skeptic of American pronouncements.

"The Cypriot coroner's office is in the process of turning the body over to American representatives. Chief Coroner Pavlos Pavlou will report preliminary findings in a day or two. The U.S. Diplomatic Service will conduct its own investigation as is customary under international law. We are also in contact with Justice Minister Ioannis Hatzioannou. As of this moment, nothing points to foul play or an act of terror.

'Let me emphasize that local media reports are speculative at best. There is little evidence as yet and no cause for alarm. Any conclusions arrived at by the Cypriot authorities in the conduct of their own investigations are entirely their own. The Embassy only confirms that on becoming aware of LTC Johnston's disappearance, a heightened state of security was initiated and precautionary procedures were put in place. This is a normal response, which will continue until the U.S. Government is satisfied that no terrorism connection exists. I want specifically to assure those Americans visiting Cyprus that the country remains safe. U.S. Embassy personnel are available to address any individual concerns."

"How long has the Colonel been missing? Any connection to his work in the North?"

"He failed to appear for work Monday morning. Embassy staffers tried to locate him at his home and cell phone. As those efforts proved fruitless, we asked Cypriot authorities for their assistance. Colonel Johnston was recently in the North investigating human trafficking."

Artemis leaned closer to Ben and whispered, "Do we have his cell?"

Ben whispered back, "Later."

Artemis nodded in acknowledgment.

Another reporter, this one apparently Turkish-Cypriot was asking:

"But he was found in the South? Is the Greek press suggesting Turks were involved?"

Lennie had to deflect this comment.

"His car was spotted by a farmer in the foothills of the Troodos Mountains 60 kilometers west of Lefkosia. The area is rugged and exact circumstances are not known as we await further investigation. Dr. Pavlou at the Lefkosia coroner's office will have a more detailed description of LTC Johnston's condition on discovery. I simply do not have it nor am I an authority on medical issues."

"Mr. Blinkman, is the United States going to respond to what is clearly a provocation from Turkey and the illegal regime it supports here on Cyprus?"

"Now, gentlemen of the press, you know I cannot speak for the Turkish press or comment on rumors and speculations. The U.S. is an ally and friend of both…"

"Maybe the two Israelis arrested two weeks ago are involved? They were spying for Turkey," Savvas Savva of the Cypriot Post interrupted.

"Are you asking me, Mr. Savva, or informing me? If you have information that suggests that LTC Johnston was killed by Turkish-

Cypriots, or anyone else, or any connection to alleged Israeli spying activity, I am certain my government would listen and investigate."

Reporters jumped in blaming each other and order was lost. Some shouted about conspiracies while others went on about the Israelis.

"The Greeks always blame the Turks," the Turkish journalist tried to be heard but his voice was lost in the noise.

"Here we go," Ben said in a voice barely audible above the commotion in the room. "Back into the Greek-Turkish quagmire." He turned to Artemis. Her face was full of questions. Her unfocused look betrayed her strain in trying to follow the characters and positions.

"Len will go into a shuffling act for a while and then close the press conference before it deteriorates any further," Ben explained. "I have to give him credit for the way he dodges and parries."

From a few inches away, Artemis looked at him squarely in the eyes and asked, "What Israeli spies are they talking about?"

"Come on," he said. "I'll fill you in on the drive the crime scene."

Ben motioned to Scott Bailey, the 26-year-old Assistant Army Attaché, who acknowledged he'd see the end of the press conference. There were benefits to having junior assistants. Over the din of the room, Ben and Artemis slipped out unnoticed.

15
Loss

Lefkosia, Cyprus

Ben and Artemis came out into the Embassy parking lot and headed for the Fiat. The press conference was a delay, but Ben had insisted they attend telling Artemis:

"The press has viewpoints we don't, and they'll have heard all the rumors. Saves us some time and it's good background."

"I need to get up to speed as soon as possible," Artemis had responded.

They stepped into another cloudless bright Cypriot day and energy quickened through Ben's body. Finally, he had a puzzle, a mission, a hunt. Answers waited at the end of the trail; it felt primal.

She's smart and willing to listen and learn. To be a good team, we have to complement each other. Let's get to the scene and see what we can learn.

His chest tightened. Guilt was there next to his grief—guilt that Sam's death was giving him purpose. Sam would appreciate the irony.

Was it Iranian retaliation for the ambush of their "diplomats" by U.S. Forces on the Iran-Iraq border last week? Or, was it Russian white slavers? A connection to the Israelis jailed two weeks ago, as the Cypriot press assumed?

They turned south heading towards the spot they'd entered the city the day before. After a few miles, Ben turned right and entered the A9 highway, which skirted Lefkosia's abandoned airport. A blue UN flag fluttered over the control tower that now served as an observation post for the international peacekeepers. The eerily quiet airport baffled first time visitors. There were no airplanes. The control towers were used to monitor no man's land between North and South.

Dick had brought Ben for coffee one Sunday morning. The noise coming from the runways was high pitched and peculiar. To Ben's amazement, go-carts were racing around the tarmac. The British contingent of U. N. Forces Cyprus was using the runway as a racetrack. The post 1974 Greek-Turkish border, known as the Green Line, split the runway in half and the airport could no longer function as an airport. The U.N. set up its base on the grounds and the British put the tarmac to use.

Dick and Ben sat and watched the races while Dick filled Ben in on the British. They'd been in Cyprus for over 100 years and had the run of the island: water sports, skiing and climbing in Olympus, auto races, bike races, tennis courts, television stations, supermarkets, and 15,000 of their countrymen in a 254 square kilometer sovereign territory. They lacked for nothing. Not surprisingly, a posting to Cyprus was highly sought after.

Ben kept his speed at a reasonable 80 kph. The Fiat had a small 1.3 cylinder engine, small wheels, and a stub of a hatch. But, it also boasted full-time four-wheel drive, ABS, and a turbo diesel engine. The gearlever, mounted halfway between floor and dash on its own mini-parapet, had taken some getting used to. In his initial errands around Lefkosia, Ben had stayed in one gear too long, bringing a grin to Dick's face.

"Just imagine sitting in a kitchen chair rather than driving," Dick had instructed. It was a simple city car but its four-wheel drive would come in handy today when the A9 highway ended and the rural B9 began. The road paralleled the Green Line separating the Turkish north and the Greek south and led to the Solea Valley and Mount Olympus. Cypriot roads had been built to connect towns already in existence for hundreds of years. Highways had appeared only recently.

The tit-for-tat between Greeks and Turks was constant but neither would ever assassinate an American—too much to lose. No. Someone with a different agenda had killed Sam. Cyprus just happened to be the location. Al-Qaida? ISIS sympathizers?

His mind went from one possibility to another. His pulse quickened —this wasn't gists going to Washington, or probability analyses, but a murder site with evidence to sift through. He thought of Sam dead on the morgue's table. *I'm disgusted with myself for not controlling my feelings. Sam was dead, damn it. How quickly I've latched onto the grisly details!*

He had to focus on Sam. He had to! He had live sinewy bad guys to go after. He had spent too much time on theoretical exercises. He'd lost Sam, like he'd lost Ortega, "Saddle," Parnell, and Parente in Afghanistan. It hurt like it had then. Loss never stopped hurting no matter what anyone said. He'd sort things out. He'd find out what happened and assess repercussions for Americans in Cyprus.

He glanced at Artemis. Was she lost in her own thoughts? Or, was she taking in the Cypriot neighborhood they were driving through? He was glad she was here. She'd keep him in check. Never mind that the hunt was partly his motivation. The endgame was the same—find Sam's killers. He looked at the mountains in the distance and tried to clear his head.

The central Cypriot plateau was dominated by sandy countryside with little green. As they moved into the hills of the west, the air changed. He was eager, then felt guilty for feeling eager, and then angry. *Keep it simple. One step at a time. Leave politics and the city behind. Think of an illuminated art book—let color, landscape and imagination take over. Keep your eyes on the road, the trees, the countryside, the crime scene— simple one to one relationships. Investigate the murder.*

"I think it's time you filled me in," Artemis broke in.

16
Mass Casualty Event

Cypriot Countryside

She had expected he'd start briefing her as soon as they got to the car. Then, as his face stayed dead ahead and he seemed lost, she left him alone.

Now he looked like she caught him off guard.

"Sam was our liaison to Turkey and was fluent in the language. He was negotiating the new listening stations in the north; this weekend he was taking down a Russian slave ring in Keryneia. Can't be them—they haven't had time to recover. You asked about his cell—he had it with a Turkish company."

"Why is that?"

"He was born in Turkey and lived there for years. Part of the problem with the wife. She thought he was consumed with work; he thought her self-absorbed. But, they reached an understanding years back: she'd stay with the kids in Connecticut and he'd work in Cyprus. We're waiting on Ankara for phone records, so that'll be a while. Last contact was from Keryneia confirming the women were on their way, then nothing."

"You think there's any truth to the suicide theory?"

"No. He was retiring so that was a bit stressful, but no. I'd know. Who cuts his own neck? Besides, the angle of the cut was off."

"Really? You saw it? How?"

"Right before I met you, yesterday."

He reached over with his free hand and demonstrated on Artemis's neck his eyes darting back and forth to the road that continued flat ahead.

"The cut I saw was too horizontal. If he'd cut his own neck the angle would've slanted down. He was cut from behind by a left-handed attacker. Sam was right handed. Knife entry is clean on the right side of the neck and tapers off to the left."

"He could've used his left."

"He was on his way somewhere. And, why use a blade? He had a gun — that's what a man would use to off himself. We'll check the blood flow in the car. That'll confirm it one way or the other."

"How much time do we have?"

"The Embassy will keep a lid on things for a few days. The locals are another matter. The police are cooperating and the coroner is under pressure to delay his report so we can investigate. The longer we take, the bigger the chance for leaks. Some reporter will blow the story. Couple of days at most."

"Any idea where he was going? I mean why go up a mountain?" Artemis asked.

"That's puzzling. I'd think he'd come and finish off the smuggling case before running off somewhere."

"Why go up there? Anything there?"

"There's the Amiantos mine, the ski club — but it's closed now. What else…Cypriot commando training grounds. He and I went on a day trip to the Kykos monastery and on a tour of the RAF station."

"What RAF station? You said the British were on the coast."

"They are. Two separate installations — Sovereign Bases they call them — thousands of troops, listening stations, aircraft squadrons, you name it."

"Then what's on the mountain?"

"Troodos Station. British Signal Unit. Everyone calls it Golf Section, as in large white dome radars that look like giant golf balls. Operations are 24/7 with 12-hour shifts. That's where all the intel on Russia and the Middle East comes from."

"And on the coast?"

"Over the Horizon Radar, numbers stations, a T101 Commander System, BBC Monitoring. Back in the day, U-2's and AWAC's flew out of there. Now, they're supplying Iraq, Syria and Afghanistan. For listening and e-chatter, nothing compares to Golf Section. Top Signals Intelligence station in the world. Direct feed to the supercomputers at Menwith Hill and Langley."

"That's got to be it. Unless he was sightseeing. Nothing else makes sense."

"He had no reason to go to Golf Section. He had an encrypted cell phone, the Embassy scrambler, FBIS Nicosia. He could have called me."

Silence. Finally, Ben uttered, "Unless he was being overly cautious or couldn't wait…"

"What does that mean?" Artemis faced him exasperated.

"If he had something major, something off the charts, then I can see him heading to Golf Section."

"Such as?" Artemis asked with panic in her voice.

"Nonsense. Speculation. World War III or a 9/11 type event. Something big enough to bypass normal channels and set off every alarm in the UKUSA intelligence network."

Artemis stared at him with eyes so large that Ben just stared back. Ben's brow slowly turned into a frown. His facial muscles tightened and the strain was evident. They considered the possibilities quietly.

Finally, Artemis said, "What do you say we get a look at the crime scene and the car before we jump to conclusions?"

Ben responded by gripping the steering wheel and shifting to a lower gear. The Fiat's engine wound up.

"I don't know. He's been missing for three days and nothing's happened. We're still here," Ben finally broke the silence but with little confidence in his voice.

"That might mean we're running out of time," Artemis said. Her pleasant features froze and her eyes locked in the distance oblivious to the olive tree covered hills they were entering.

17
Dust to Dust

Foothills of Mount Olympus, Cyprus

After a switchback, the roof tiles of a town appeared in the distance. The terracotta was reddish and stained with age and Ben and Artemis got no more than a glimpse before the car headed into the inside of a hillside. The rooftops reappeared for another moment but were blocked this time by holm oaks and cypresses towering 10 to 20 meters above the roadbed. As the car moved, the white houses checkered through the gaps between trees and shrubbery.

They approached from below and now noticed an elongated black mass resembling a black oozing stain seeping out of the town. It took a few moments and a turn or two before Ben and Artemis came face to face with a funeral procession.

A priest was in the lead in a stovetop hat and white vestments with gold trim and swinging a smoking censer. Off to his side and slightly behind, another man moved his mouth—obviously chanting. Farther back, three altar boys held a cross and two round gold standards. All walked ceremoniously. Next, four men, visibly struggling, carried a casket on their shoulders. The men were in tieless white shirts and black jackets. The bulk of the procession followed slowly behind with most women wearing black scarves and charcoal dresses.

About 50 meters away, Ben slowed the car and pulled to the side. He came to a stop half on pavement half on dirt and shut off the engine. The priest's chant reached them followed by the cantor's response. A minute later incense wafted in through the window.

The four pallbearers strained and teetered with every step. No one offered help. Their bare heads were sunburnt and reflected the sun. Their weathered appearance testified to working with the land and their hands. The procession's pace was dictated by the four men. When the head finally passed, chants gave way to the crowd's murmurs and shuffling of feet.

An occasional mourner came face-to-face with the Fiat and moved to the right to walk past. The pallbearers' faces showed the strain of their work. The casket dipped occasionally towards one corner and then rose as the man responded to the weight bearing down. They'd obviously been carrying the casket a while. If they ever had a rhythm, it was now lost to exhaustion.

An old shrunken woman supported by two women in their fifties was behind the casket. Other women, with arms entwined, walked beside them. Several younger couples carried babies or held young children by the hand.

"Must be the family patriarch," said Ben bringing Artemis's attention back to the four men and the casket. "Four sons. Large family."

"Going to the cemetery?" Artemis she asked.

"They're usually outside of town here."

Quiet fell on the car.

Ben thought about the dead man. *He'd lived a full life, built a home, filled it with children, celebrated marriages, baptized, held, and enjoyed his grandchildren. A better life could not be had. Sam would never get those things. Not even close.*

And, what about me? How much of what I'm ascribing to the dead man will I ever get?

The crowd brushed the Fiat and quick glances met Ben's eyes. The shuffling drowned out other sounds. In the background, whitewashed stone houses were scattered in no particular order around town with some appearing to sit atop others. On closer look, lichen and mold blemished the red-brown roofs. Except for the grieving townspeople, the scene would have been picturesque.

He continued watching the procession until it thinned. He gently turned the engine on, shifted to first and the car peacefully rolled through the stragglers.

In the passenger seat, Artemis was looking off beyond the ravine by the road at the hills in the distance where a small white chapel next to a tall cypress tree stood atop one hill. Ben could not see the single tear that ran down her face.

18
Journey's End

Mount Olympus, Cyprus

A giant round shape came into view atop Mount Olympus. Its roundness and unnatural whiteness among the forest of green pine made it visible from miles away. It came in and out of view as the car drove the mountain road.

Up close, the forest appeared sparse. Aromas of catmint, sage, and cyclamen wafted in and out of the car. The lavender and rose blossoms of the cyclamen on the roadside were twisted and resembled tiny butterfly wings as a response to the coolness of the altitude.

Ben fell into a routine of slowing, downshifting to second gear, entering a turn, shifting to third to exit powerfully, and then picking up speed until the next curve. Coming around one bend, they came to a blue and white Cypriot police car on the side of the road.

They stopped a distance away. They got out and walked towards the policeman who came out and waited for them. They presented their I.D.'s and introduced themselves. The man pointed to the location of the car in decent but accented English. He said the car was barely visible from the road and was buried inside a thicket of thorny rosebushes. He made to bring them to the car but Ben told him not yet.

Ben and Artemis backtracked about 75 yards down the road they had just traveled. Ben studied the approach and the asphalt surface. Then they headed past the yellow tape of the crime scene and did the same from the other direction. No skid marks or anything out of the ordinary. They came back to the yellow tape.

Ben now indicated their readiness, ducked underneath the tape and, with the policeman beside them, all three headed for the car.

"You can see here," the policeman offered pointing to the driver's seat.

Again Ben and Artemis ignored him but slowly circled around considering the surroundings and checking the entryway into the thicket.

"The window was open?" Ben asked about the driver's window.

"Open, yes. I ask the bee farmer. He no touch it. The American was driver." He raised his hands, spread his fingers next to his face, and puffed his cheeks to indicate the body was swollen. "The farmer sees he is dead so he no touch nothing."

Ben walked around inspecting the car. Its tire edges were dark and raw.

"He was speeding," he said, not bothering to check if Artemis could hear him.

Artemis peered into the car careful not to touch the exterior or the window. A swath of blood, caked and blackened, stained the driver's seat. Flies buzzed about. The seat cloth was dark and soaked through. Black gook had run down between the console and the seat.

"Blood flow confirms cut on right side of neck," she volunteered.

Ben nodded.

"The Criminalistic Service will be here in one, maybe two hours," the Cypriot said. Artemis looked puzzled and the man explained, "The forensic laboratory."

Ben used a handkerchief to open the door behind the driver and stuck his head in to study the interior. The back was clean and empty. He walked around the trunk of the car and opened the right rear passenger door the same way. Again nothing out of the ordinary.

Artemis chatted with the officer and led him towards the trunk wanting to know if it had been opened. Ben opened the front passenger door and looked inside. Keys still in the slot. He looked at the seat and the floor. Holding a handkerchief, he bent to the floor and lifted what looked like a black and silver pen. He put it in his pocket.

Minutes later, they told the policeman they were done. They drove a bit up the mountain but when out of sight, Ben pulled to the side.

"This I don't recognize," he said. "Never seen it in the car or on Sam."

He turned and examined the pen looking at it from all angles. Seeing no click on top, he carefully wrapped the handkerchief around it and twisted. A point appeared. Not done fiddling, he spread his elbows slightly and pulled. It separated into two sections revealing not an ink cartridge but a small squared off chrome projection. Ben did not have to say a word as both recognized the USB plug of a flash drive.

"Might as well go see the Brits," he pointed to the globe atop the mountain now about 20 minutes away. "Looks like that's where he was going."

19

Golf Section

Troodos British Intelligence Station, Mount Olympus

The Fiat sped through the narrow streets of the little town of Pedoulas in the early afternoon. Ben slowed for several pedestrians who were obviously non-Greeks. Signs for ski rentals, lodgings, and food marts were hawking their wares in English. The awning of the green grocer was rolled up and the shop closed for the afternoon. Pedoulas was near the top of Mt. Olympus and its few shops catered to skiers and the English personnel of Troodos Station.

A coffee shop with a large number of director type wooden chairs under its awning was open. It doubled as a beeraria as evidenced by the three Englishmen in their twenties sprawled and resting their legs on nearby chairs. Ben reached the town's outskirts and passed a tiny garish shop covered in posters of well-known cell company logos.

As the Fiat left the town, a panoramic view of the island below came in and out of view. To the east, the central Pitsilia plain faded into a haze of undulating heat waves and culminated in the capital, Lefkosia. To the northwest, the Solea Valley was sprawled out. Beyond that, Morphou Bay and the Mediterranean were a mere blue sliver near the horizon.

Paphos was off to the southwest while directly south, the Akrotiri SBA peninsula separated Episkopi and Akrotiri Bays. The cosmopolitan cities of Lemesos and Larnaka lay further east along the coast.

Below to the southeast in the foothills of Olympus, the blueish Amiantos open pit mine consisted of rings of strap-like terraces that radiated outward in expanding circles. At about a mile and a half in diameter, the blue-green streaks so contrasted with the natural green of the surrounding vegetation that the mine was truly an open sore on the earth's surface.

Cyprus was a dry yellow landscape that suffered perennial water shortages. The Troodos mountain range was an exception as it was made up of green forests, picturesque villages, and ancient churches. Looking down from Olympus, a distinct line was visible in the landscape where cultivated fields and regularly spaced olive trees ended and the tree line of cypress and pines of the higher elevations began.

The car came to a branch in the road. Signs in English indicated the radar installation to the left and residences to the right. Ben selected the left and entered the last mile to Golf Section.

"What do we tell the British?" Artemis asked.

"Honesty is a good policy," Ben answered.

"You're kidding, right?" Artemis squared off with Ben trying to read his face. She continued, "We should stick to the accident or suicide story."

"There's no reason to hide. They're an intelligence station. Trust me, it's secure—more secure than any other place. We're on the same side and we need info, motives, suspects."

"We don't have much to tell them," Artemis said.

"Exactly. All the more reason to share. We have a lot of ground to cover. It's pretty clear that Sam had a reason for coming here and it probably concerned the U.S. and Britain. Our only other choice is to go back to the Embassy and work through channels. We don't need that delay. We're here, let's use them."

"It's your call," she relented.

She looked out at the facility looming ahead. "There's more than one golf ball," she said.

They were at the summit. In the foreground, a fence and guardhouse surrounded the complex. In the middle, at the highest point, three golf balls stood. Their round whiteness against the void of the blue sky transformed the scene into an exotic architectural wonder.

The globes were not strictly spheres but geodesic domes that resembled golf balls down to the indentations. Each dome's surface was made up of thousands of small rigid triangles that distributed stresses evenly over the entire structure. Domes were ideal antenna covers because their enclosed space was free of supports, which allowed the radar dish inside unobstructed movement. They were aerodynamic and could withstand hurricane force winds—especially useful on a mountain top location like Mount Olympus. The cover hid the antenna's direction and had the peculiar characteristic of being the only architectural structure whose strength increased the larger it got. A geodesic radome at the secret base of Menwith Hill in England boasted an unobstructed diameter of 200 feet.

The main large radome, like a perfectly round bunion on the ridgeline, had been visible five miles out. Now, up close, it was immense. Two other radomes were a short distance away. The three radars, sitting atop stone foundations, resembled giant beige and white gumball machines. Each lay atop its own stonework foundation and had windows and ventilation ducts. Their bases housed workstations where personnel monitored directional targeting and managed the inflow and outflow of information to Menwith Hill. A couple of oil-well type metal antennas with assorted tip configurations, a two-story building, and a fence with guardhouse completed the complex.

The guard was on the phone authorizing entry. After a two minute wait, the station commander drove up in a Rover. He opened the door with energy nobody his age should have and slid off the seat.

20

Any Man's Death Diminishes Me

Troodos British Intelligence Station, Mount Olympus

"Ah, Huntley, it is you. Welcome back." The two men shook hands.

"Thank you, Captain. This is Agent Nelson, from the Office of Investigations and Counterintelligence, Bureau of Diplomatic Security," Ben said. Then looking at Artemis, "This is Group Captain Evan Bishops, Commander RAF Troodos."

"Welcome to our tip of the world, Miss Nelson," Bishops saluted and then shook her hand. He turned to Ben. "You have my sympathies on your man Johnston. Sorry business that. Terrible thing losing a man that you've served with. Nothing's the same after; we lose an irreplaceable piece of ourselves. '*No man is an island…every man is a piece of the continent, a part of the main…Any man's death diminishes me, because I am involved in mankind.*'" Bishops took on a distant and stoic demeanor that made the moment at the top of the island a poignant and fitting memorial to Sam. Obviously, Bishops had had losses of his own.

"So you've heard?" Artemis asked giving Ben some time to get a hold of his emotions.

"Yes. We're a bit remote here but communications are excellent," Bishops pointed to the domes with his thumb and a twinkle in his eye. "We learned of his absence on Sunday last and then yesterday late came the news of the discovery of the car. It was on CyBC. Local chaps are always first. He was a gentleman."

He said this solemnly devoid of any hint of snobbery. He was acknowledging a man's accomplishments and the obstacles he often overcomes to lift himself from whatever gutter fate had tossed him into.

Ben wasn't sure how well Captain Bishops knew Sam but his sympathy was genuine, and that was an admirable quality in any man.

"Thank you," Ben said. "He was a good man and my friend. An altruist who took pride in his work. He and I toured your command back in March—the snow and wind were brutal that day."

"It does get fierce at times. Shall we?" Bishops motioned to the Rover.

"Commander, we believe Sam was on his way here when he was killed—that possibly he was killed to prevent him getting here."

The Captain looked surprised. "So he didn't perish by his own hand, then?"

"Absolutely not."

"Why would he come here? We're Signals Intelligence. Everything we collect, we send off to the Hill; we don't do analysis. You've considered circumvention of protocol? Embassy collection?"

"Yes, and microwave interception, and secure channels, and any number of Embassy personnel he could have turned to, including me."

"A personal visit, then?"

"No indication of that—no clothes, no bag, no hiking supplies, not even a bottle of water, nothing. His coming here wasn't planned," Artemis volunteered.

"We think he was deliberately bypassing established channels," Ben continued. "That it was safer to come here. We're following a lead, but first would like to speak to Fort Meade."

"Intelligence leaving Golf Section goes through Menwith Hill." He looked at Ben and his face changed, "I'll see what I can do. Nothing like talking face to face with a chap, I say."

They reached and entered the medium radome. Banks of computer screens lined the inside walls. Bishops continued, "What's this lead you have?"

Ben pulled out the pen, and Artemis answered, "A flash drive we need to look at."

Bishops now looked at Artemis with new awareness, "You're sure he was assassinated?"

"We're convinced," Artemis said.

Bishops turned and called, "Potsbury!"

"Sir," answered a young man who perked up from a monitor. He proceeded to come over sharp.

"Take our guests to the canteen and locate a PC, if you please."

"Sir," Potsbury answered. He released a quantity of air from his chest and let his shoulders fall an inch or two and left.

"Seeing as I was to receive this from Johnston, perhaps I should accompany you," Bishops said.

Artemis answered before Ben had a chance, "We're in your debt, Commander, but it may concern the U.S. only. Sorry. Can we get a look first?"

Ben added, "Let us get a preview. If it concerns both our countries, we'll share. I promise."

"As you wish. I'll look into Fort Meade for you." He turned and scanned the computer terminals taking in the activity of the stations.

Potsbury led Ben and Artemis outside.

"You got your way," Ben said.

"I stepped on your turf, didn't I?" Artemis asked.

"Don't like to be told what to do, do you? It's all right. It's not like Bishops has a choice—the NSA runs F83. The Brits run administration and logistics, but we do the real work."

"F83?"

"Menwith Hill in England. The NSA's been running it since 1966. Bishops collects and sends intel, but it's American equipment here and there. Our people from DIA, CIA and NSA staff the computers. Those domes there? Maybe another three over there..." he pointed to a hillside about a mile away, "Menwith Hill has 26 and five acres of buildings. Two-thirds of the 2000 analysts are U.S. Army and Air Intelligence."

Potsbury had led them inside a building. "You may use this room," he said.

21
The Peacemaker

Troodos British Intelligence Station, Mount Olympus

Ben inserted the USB end of the pen into the laptop and a moment later, a young pretty face with dark hair was on the screen speaking.

'Since 2nd July, my Mossad unit on Cyprus has tracked 4 Islamic radicals who, based on LPD profiles and electronic intercepts, plan an attack with 'thousands of deaths.' They refer to the attack as 'Palm and Hand of God.' Reference may be to Dubai Palm but that is only me speculating.

Mossad has allowed terror to proceed in the past if there is benefit to Mossad. Mossad has committed terror in the name of state security with and without the authority of the Prime Minister. I have been a part of Metsada false flag operations and Kidon assassinations. Mossad's justification is that it is eliminating threats to Israel.

I am asking for your help in releasing Ari Ben Amin and Ido Wietzman two members of my unit arrested by the Cypriots in June, and in return, I provide the last report filed with our katsa:

1.   We verified four men gathering detonation supplies at the Amiantos mine on Cyprus.

2.   We identified one as Mahmud Mahduni, a Palestinian, with training in explosives at a South African mining company in the Sudan.

3.   We confirmed the men left Cyprus by sea for an unknown destination.

After the arrest of our two agents, my unit was deactivated and recalled to Herzliya. IDF Air Force and Lamdan Technical Assistance Unit will now likely assume surveillance.

I know of two previous occasions that information was kept from European and American governments to allow terrorist attacks to succeed. The same may happen here. Zionists believe that Israel benefits when Arabs and Palestinians are blamed for bloodshed and for derailing peace. Mossad has even sanctioned sniper killings of American soldiers to secure continued U. S. military presence in the Middle East.

I love my country but I believe Israel and Jews can live in peace with other cultures and not at Israel's expense. I don't believe that assassinations, bulldozing Palestinian homes, and false flag operations lead to peace. Hostilities will continue as long as Mossad uses car bombs, kills protesters in the occupied territories, and denies trials to the arrested. These methods have not worked but continue still. Israeli character suffers when Mossad uses the tactics of Islamic fundamentalists. And so, the cycle of violence continues.

If Israel helps stop a terror attack like the "Hand of God," the world will be grateful and maybe attitudes towards Israel will change.

In return, ask the Cypriots for leniency for Ari and Ido. All Ari did, all any of us did, was observe the terrorists. If Ari serves the eight-year prison sentence given yesterday, I will be 28 on his release. I only wish the two of us to live private lives in a better world.

I love my country, yet Mossad and Israel's defenders condemn Jews who question their self-righteous tactics. They consider us anti-Semites, but I am a Jew and I stand for peace.

Stop this attack and spare our families accusations and blacklisting. Bring Ari back to me.

Shalom.'

Ben remained quiet.

Artemis spoke first, "What is this Dubai Palm?"

"I don't know. Principled young lady, huh?"

"She's young and idealistic. Do we believe her?"

"Yes, we do," Ben answered.

"Why?"

"She's got too much to lose. She's risking prison and treason."

"Possible double agent? A set up?"

"I don't think so."

"Why not?"

"The two Israelis arrested two weeks ago. It's personal for her."

"So she turned whistleblower on Friday or Saturday," Artemis added.

"Sam goes missing immediately after. The split inside Hawks and Doves in Israel is accurate, but what's more convincing is Mossad killing American troops. Nobody knows about it and revealing it will ostracize her family for years. It's not related to this threat and she didn't have to mention it. She doesn't agree with Mossad tactics and reached her limit with the boyfriend going to jail. So she's trading."

"Israel can get its spies back without us."

"Sure. But if there's an attack any time soon, they'll be forgotten and rot in jail—especially if it gets out that Israel knew beforehand. The young lady is getting in front of all of that."

"The days of my country right or wrong are gone, eh?" Artemis said.

"You know what they say, *'Love and war conquer all.'*"

"I thought it was, *'Love conquers all.'*"

"Yeah? That's a fantasy," Ben said sharply.

His look was strange as if he'd just been challenged and didn't like it. If he believed what he'd said, he was jaded. And, jaded men were abrupt and cruel.

"I guess we'll see," Artemis coldly.

"We will," he answered not letting go.

"She's right about one thing—violence just affirms humanity's failures," Artemis said and walked out into the mountain air.

Ben didn't have a chance to respond but stared at the door long after it closed.

22

The Taking of the *Pytheas*

Coast of Northern Mauritania, Atlantic Ocean

The heavy anchor chain stretched at an angle from the ship and disappeared into the ocean. Ahmed gauged the distance from the water to the ship's anchor-well to be 15 meters. Then he thought of a long skinny walnut tree branch until the chain and the branch became one in his mind. He noted the length, the smoothness of the links, their size, the thickness, the incline. Now he knew how to hold the chain, how long it'd take to climb, and the stamina he'd need. He was ready. Rafiq had asked about gloves. The thought had never crossed Ahmed's mind. It was another testament to Rafiq's wisdom.

A doubt nagged at him. How similar would climbing the chain be to climbing the walnut tree? Then, like a scroll being unfolded, a tendon tingled. It alerted the next and the next until all were awake throughout his body. His experiences coalesced. He felt energy that he'd not felt since he was eighteen. The ocean, vast and empty around him, was a peripheral thing; the metal ship that blotted out the stars was a mystery. His comrades ceased to exist; the chain, inches from his face, was all he saw. He understood it; he mastered it.

He grabbed the chain and his body absorbed the effort. He accepted its tautness and weight. Solid. The links made no sound—too large and too heavy to clang. Now he'd climb. He might be spotted by a deck patrol but that was incidental to his clarity and purpose.

He was on the outskirts of Ateret in the ravine and in the walnut tree that he'd stared into from infancy. He had a vague recollection of his mother hanging a basket from a branch but he was not sure if he was in it or his sister. He just remembered looking up at thick limbs coming off the main trunk and becoming thinner and web-like towards the edge and the vast interior space they created. The canopy of large green leaves created an interior void as large as a house. Smaller secondary branches led to limbs and twigs. Shoots of assorted sizes divided and ended in fruit buds and in leaves that hid walnuts. The tree dominated the ravine—immense, proud, and indomitable. Unlike other vegetation that only eked an existence from the arid Palestinian soil, the tree found water and protection in the ravine. Enough out of the way not to interfere with the olive trees, it towered 16 meters high and 12 meters wide. It had given his family walnuts for generations.

Lapping ocean water forced Ahmed's attention back to the chain. He moved hand over hand to climb. Time to harvest the walnuts. He grabbed an impossibly long branch. For an instant, he sought the stick he'd use to knock the fruit loose. On the tree, his one hand held the 3-meter long pole to smack the branches and the other hand held onto the tree. He jammed elbows and knees into crotches and spread his feet for balance or wrapped them around limbs. His hips and shoulders abraded onto branches for more support. Three fingers slipped into a link to pull himself up. Nothing to worry about—knowing one link meant he knew them all. No fluctuation, no judgment—all exact, all equal. In the tree, he held on as best he could. He raised the pole, sought the counter-force, held the stick at weightlessness, and, as gravity took effect, brought it down hard on the branch to jar the green nuts loose. The added force bent the branches and sometimes cracking was heard. The chain was strong, predictable, and impervious to such concerns.

Ahmed moved higher and higher—in two minutes he was at the opening in the ship's side. The anchor was large and the opening to the ship spacious. He jumped in and looked around. It was an odd shaped space smothered in thick waterproof white paint. He secured the cable he'd brought and tossed it over the side.

Someone caught it, attached it to the boat and hooked the winch. In less than eight minutes, everyone had boarded.

The oil exploration ship *Pytheas* was anchored off the West coast of Africa. The petrochemists aboard had another three weeks to examine the current tract. Then the ship would return to Accra to be turned over to BP Shell. The *Pytheas* was booked years in advance. Oil companies searched for new gas and oil sources, and, with the changing market, now reconsidered fields not economically feasible before.

The *Pytheas* boasted a variety of cutting edge ocean surveying equipment—magnetometers, Ifremer Sabrina noise and vibration measurement units, sediment extractors, echo-sounders, bathy-thermographs, and Sabrina-Ifremer temperature, noise, and vibration sensors. It used multi-beam and side-scan sonar to collect bathymetry and seabed texture data that it assembled into detailed pictures of the seabed. It towed multiple seismic cables called streamers for deep-water surveys and recorded and interpreted data, which it projected three-dimensionally on a video screen.

Its specialty was seismic reflection surveys. Being a new ship, it was equipped with the latest acoustic technologies. It penetrated the seabed searching for anomalies like reservoirs, seals, and traps—sure signs of hydrocarbon deposits. If it any hints were identified, the specialists aboard conducted more detailed seismic surveys to profile the area. Finally, if that evidence was promising, they classified the coordinates a potential drill site and included it in the weekly reports to their corporate offices. Company scientists, officers, and cost analysis experts evaluated further before committing to drilling cores and exploratory wells to verify gas and carbon layers.

The *Pytheas's* seismic reflection technology was comprised of air guns, mechanical thumpers, Plasma sound sources and an enhanced long-range acoustic device. Most stored and released electric or mechanical charges in an arc across electrodes. The high-pressure plasma, vapor, or kinetic energy created direct sound waves in single or continuous seismic waves, which traveled in water and sediment and reflected back to geophonic or hydrophonic receivers that turned them into images.

The 4:00 a.m. boarding of the *Pytheas* was chosen for minimal resistance from crew and scientific personnel. A dark tarp had covered the skiff so it could approach unobserved. The night was dark and no moon was out. The raiding party's leader had chosen well. Out of the 12 crewmembers, two were on guard—one patrolling the deck and the other keeping a bird's eye view from the bridge. Of the 19 scientists, three had pored over that day's data deciding whether a feature on grid 15°55N, 19°32W was worth a closer look. They quit at 2:00 a.m. The following day they'd move five kilometers northwest to map their final quadrant. They'd be up early for a full day of data analysis.

23

Absolution

Coast of Northern Mauritania, Atlantic Ocean

On realizing his ship had been boarded, Captain Willem De Vondel was caught off guard. The thought of pirates was a stretch because his ship was nowhere near pirate territory. His next thought was fear for the researchers and crew. They'd face threats, ransom demands, and violence. If lucky, lengthy negotiations with the ship's owners. *Pytheas* security had been minimal because the ship had been in deep waters and pirates operated hundreds of nautical miles to the south and, on the coast of Western Africa, focused primarily on stealing and selling oil. They avoided kidnaping or taking vessels that only brought unwanted foreign attention and disrupted operations. Kidnapping for ransom was a Somali specialty but Somalia was on the other side of Africa.

The attack on the *Pytheas* did not neatly fit into the pirate profile for another reason; the pirates were not the blacks of coastal Central Africa. They looked Muslim rather than Creole. *They look Mauritanian,* the Captain thought, *perhaps a new group.*

A slim wiry man with intense eyes and two shiny patches of skin on either side of a triangle of white hair still on his head scanned the assembled crew and scientists. Most were disheveled, in various stages of undress or sleepwear, and in shock; some had withdrawn into themselves to wrestle individual versions of the ordeal that was coming.

Before Rafiq finished his scan, a man spoke, "I am Captain Vondel. The ship's owners will negotiate. There is no need to harm anyone."

"Ah, yes, Captain." Rafiq's gaze turned to Vondel and a look of recognition came over his face.

The Captain continued, "There's no need for violence; we will not resist."

"Whether anyone is harmed or not depends on your cooperation," Rafiq said. "There is no negotiation. No one will be harmed unless you refuse my demands. I have no interest in your ship or in prisoners."

This surprised the Captain. The Arab was composed, in control, with no panic in his voice. His eyes were strong but not cruel. He was calm, focused and determined.

He looked around and addressed the gathered men slowly.

"You will stay here on deck." He pointed to two men with AK-47's. "We expect your cooperation. My men will shoot you if move or get up. Is this clear?"

He then turned and faced the Captain, "This way."

The two moved off but remained in sight of the others. Rafiq lowered his voice so that only the Captain could hear him.

"I came for your long range acoustic device, nothing more. I have no interest in money, your ship, or your men. Give me that, and I will leave. You will not mind losing it. Your American insurance will pay for another. A life, you will agree, is different. Once lost, it is lost forever. Believe me; I have killed many; I know. Today, there is no need to kill, but I will not hesitate. If you doubt me, I can demonstrate."

He scanned the crew and scientists lined and sitting on the deck. He approached the youngest and prettiest woman on the ship, twenty-four year old graduate student "Vi" Revelley. With everyone staring, Rafiq took out a pistol. With her dark and long curly hair tied behind her neck, and full eyebrows and dark eyes, Vi was a striking figure and a magnet for the males on board. Rafiq aimed the pistol at her. Cries of alarm and shouts rose as the captives saw Rafiq's intent; some cowered, some covered their eyes and others stood immobilized by raw abhorrence for the act of killing.

Rafiq aimed the gun. "It is simple—no one is killed and in return, you give me the sonic device. Help will arrive much too late to change anything. You agree or you do not."

Not waiting for an answer, he continued, "My vessel will be here in a few minutes. You will move this acoustic device to my ship. You have one hour. Captain, your crew will follow your lead and your decision. Make it a wise one."

He looked at the dull glass of a watch on his hand, then returned his gaze to the Captain and said, "I can begin by shooting this woman."

In his 28 years at sea, and 11 of these as Captain, this was the first time Willem De Vondel had had such an offer. An acquiescent look came over his eyes and then everyone saw his body sag.

"Yes, yes. You can have it," Vondel said.

"Thank you. Someone needs to operate the crane."

"Sjaak," the Captain motioned to a man in overalls.

The deckhand, Sjaak, rose. Ahmed escorted him and they approached Rafiq and Vondel.

The Captain faced his crewmember, "Sjaak, unfasten the eLRAD and load it on this man's boat. Full cooperation, please."

Sjaak nodded, "I need two men." Rafiq nodded 'yes.' Sjaak got two men out of the group.

"Now, let's see this machine of yours," Rafiq said. He motioned to Ahmed, Faruq the technician, Sjaak, and Captain Vondel. Ahmed held an AK-47 and walked behind Sjaak and the others. Vondel and Rafiq walked behind side by side.

"Faruq tells me that this machine beaches whales and dolphins—that the sound waves damage their reproduction and hearing and that it kills many. That, whales do not approach within 50 kilometers when it's in use. You show more concern for one woman when there are 4 billion on earth, but kill many whales when so few are left. Thousands of Muslims have likewise been killed and suffer at the hands of America. Surely, you see the hypocrisy?

'The prophet, peace be upon Him, said: *Those who do righteous deeds are destined for paradise. On the day of resurrection, Allah will grasp the whole earth in His palm; glory be to Him, and may He be exalted.* Perhaps you regret the deaths you cause; perhaps by taking the machine, I relieve you of a burden and provide absolution," Rafiq finished. "It does not matter."

Two hours later the eLRAD was safely aboard the terrorist boat and Rafiq and his crew were heading north.

24
Hand of God

Troodos British Intelligence Station, Mount Olympus

Ben and Artemis returned to the mid-sized radome atop Mt. Olympus. They passed through the metal door and were back in the sprawling command center. Bishops was pacing and talking into his headset behind a partition of aluminum and glass. He spotted them and motioned for them to join him. He continued his conversation, and then tapped the side of his headset to close the connection.

Ben explained, "The Israelis have been tracking a terror cell on Cyprus who are about to stage an attack—possible target is Dubai. They're talking thousands of casualties…should definitely be taken seriously. We need to alert the USAUK network ASAP. Captain, how many men under your command?"

"Twenty seven."

"Can you help us assess the situation? Maybe check Cyprus chatter over the last two weeks? I don't want to step on your toes…but we're ground zero. We sound the alarm, but do some poking around as well. We know Cyprus best and we may come up with something."

"We can set up some vocabularies...conduct data probes...at least look into it," Bishops responded.

"Are you able to check marine transmissions? Off the southern coast—last seventy-two hours—and the route from Keryneia to here?" Artemis asked.

Bishops gave a look of understanding and nodded. He poked his head out of his office and called out a few names, including Potsbury's. Four men got up from their stations and entered the office.

Bishops introduced Huntley, "This is RSO Ben Huntley from the American Embassy and Artemis Nelson from Diplomatic Security. Proceed, Colonel."

Ben addressed the small crowd, "As you probably know LTC Sam Johnston of the U.S. Embassy in Lefkosia has been missing for several days. He was Military Attaché and a friend. Really the brother I never had..."

He stopped and swallowed. The men saw the emotion and remained quiet.

"Ms. Nelson and I just arrived from...I can confirm to you that Sam has been found murdered..."

Spontaneous groans arose from the men. Others shifted posture as their bodies absorbed the information and reacted to the gravity of Ben's news but also to his obvious connection to Sam.

"...we believe that LTC Sam Johnston died bringing intelligence to this station about a terrorist attack by Islamic fundamentalists recently on Cyprus. Details are sketchy. We need your help...possible target may be Dubai. We'd like to confirm and ascertain the credibility of the information. Check any high profile targets—Dubai Palm, Burj Tower, Coalition Forces, and any relevant chatter."

He looked at Bishops, "Maybe rank Western vulnerabilities? If we can offer a lead like what, where, when...We don't need another *U.S.S. Cole*, or Beirut Embassy bombing on our watch. Check visiting dignitaries, media events, civilian, military, the U.S. Soccer team, a rugby match, an OPEC ministers meeting. If more than 50 Westerners are involved, consider them a target...the attack has been referred to as 'Palm of God and Hand of God.'"

Bishops added to his analysts, "Bear in mind that Arabian Peninsula nations are ruled by conservative royal families whom fundamentalists consider corrupt. Osama bin Laden was a Saudi radical. Ruling families are under tremendous pressure and a tough go in maintaining order. The stereotype of jet-setting sheiks and Arab opulence applies most closely to the Emirates. An attack on Dubai would be a major success for any terrorist organization."

"The men we're looking for were on Cyprus as late as Saturday a week ago," Ben added. "At least one explosives expert is amongst them. Let's give Intelligence something. The source of the info is Israeli so check that connection…maybe even 'Mossad.'"

"How is the Mossad involved?" a man asked with a perplexed look.

Artemis answered, "The Mossad has had this cell in their sights for a while. Their surveillance ended with the arrest of two of their agents two weeks ago. However, the IDF or their Lambdan Technical Unit will still have eyes on them—worth checking out."

Ben continued, "We should request a Mobile Tactical Support Unit from somebody. Once we have a location, they can be on scene quick. Anything I've missed? Now's the time to speak up."

"Sir?" Potsbury was looking at Bishops for permission to speak.

"Proceed," said Bishops.

"Given the lack of distractions at sea, a subject vessel can be sought using GEOINT's Maritime Safety Unit. We use satellite imagery to compile a list of craft recently in Cypriot waters. We electronically tag the vessels entering or departing the area over a given time period that will provide arrival and departure coordinates and may even extrapolate destination. We will effectively identify the craft of interest before it reaches its staging area. I might add, if the craft makes land, prospects for discovery diminish greatly."

"Excellent. Right. Grab yourself a man and see to it," Bishops said a bit in awe.

"Sir, one additional item. The Standing NATO Maritime Group 2 is currently stationed the Eastern Mediterranean. Lead vessel is the *Northumberland* with, I believe, an escort of two Royal Navy frigates, which are equipped with two Lynx choppers. Current assignment is Operation Active Endeavour targeting international terrorism, which is to say not active in Iraq or Afghanistan. They have a Rapid Reaction Force on board."

"Farnsworth, you handle that. Alert the *Northumberland* and get readiness specifics."

"Sir."

"Potsbury, you and I need to talk," Artemis said appreciating the young Flying Officer's performance.

Bishops added, "Right. Ames, ring the canteen and bring in the next shift. We've work. I'll call the SBA Commander after I talk to the Hill. Off you go, chaps."

Then in explanation to Ben and Artemis, "We'll put the Royal Navy's P2000's on alert. Your boat may still be close by."

25

Tragic Lives

Troodos British Intelligence Station, Mount Olympus

The buzz increased in the room as the RAF made inquiries and connected to governmental agencies in Britain and the United States. Ames, Farnsworth, and Potsbury doled out work, asked for follow-up, re-directed inquiries and delegated to others. Questions were asked aloud of nobody in particular but someone invariably answered. Others reported progress and then returned to their monitors.

Artemis and Ben were called on to enter passwords or to confirm their identities to people and service agencies on the other end of the communications links. The threat was relayed to Langley, Washington, Vauxhall Cross, and the several Middle East Intelligence Desks of the U.S. and Britain. Ben briefed Ambassador Milhaus in Lefkosia on Sam and the new threat. An hour passed faster than Ben ever remembered. He still wanted to talk to several Security Officers he knew in the Middle East.

Artemis was working at a terminal with one of Bishops' men standing over her and occasionally pointing at the screen as they talked. Ben stole a few glances at her; she was in control, composed, deliberate.

She was handling things. He could depend on her. He knew the two of them would do everything they could to stop this thing. That was a calming thought.

He realized that he'd crossed a threshold. Her calm made her more appealing and energized parts of him that had been dormant for a long time. His faculties sharpened and brought him to an enticing but vague precipice.

His next thought was realizing that from the minute he'd met her, he had watched her with a critical eye. She was an unknown and he'd gone back to his old habit of not trusting anyone. Her manner and face were inviting but her dark eyes darted and were unknowable.

Had she noticed his wariness?

Of course, she'd noticed. She knew men and how they'd behave long before she touched Cypriot soil or any other soil. Women always knew. Some attracted men like nectar summoned bees. Women always knew.

What they did with the knowledge revealed their character. Men always circled women, and some women got lost in all the attention. They enjoyed it and sought to repeat the process with suitor after suitor. But not this woman; her identity did not depend on others. She operated without regard to anyone's approval—she was equal parts moral strength and physical beauty.

Some people live tragic lives. They never know themselves well enough and squander their short sojourn on earth fighting the white whales that torment them. But not this woman. His prejudices hadn't fazed her. She'd stayed the course. She had a moral center; and with him or without him, she'd continue on that course. He was the unknown variable here. He had expected her to let him down ever since she'd toyed with him at the mosque. He had judged her every move expecting her to bitch and whine, but she hadn't. Definitely a good thing.

########################

At some point, the sound of the wind outside increased and reminded Ben he was atop a mountain. No one else seemed to notice the rising and undulating din. A half-hour later, the noise was deafening. Air currents hit passed through cypress pines or around mountain outcroppings and resulted in a background of screaming wails. The whistling and surging air toyed with the auditory scale, reached deep lows and crested in highs as air streamed over the ridgelines. Incredible crescendos rode atop the constant rumble.

The radomes' aerodynamic roundness reduced drag but allowed low frequency reverberations to saturate the building until the noise seemed to be coming from the very core of the earth below them. The vibrating walls of the golf ball seemed to worry only Ben.

A young officer approached Commander Bishops and spoke to him. He in turn looked at Ben and said, "The chopper can't make it up here in this wind. You'll have to get to Akrotiri on your own. I'll ring ahead."

"It's no problem, Commander."

"Follow the signs outside the perimeter and bear right at Pano Platres. The left goes to Limassol; the right to Akrotiri."

"Thanks. We'd better head out."

"Akrotiri will be more useful than Golf Section. I'll let you know what we find."

"Thanks for your help."

Bishops's face softened and the wrinkles on his forehead relaxed while his eyes glinted in agreement. "I'd like to know how it turns out, from the inside, as it were. I'll spring for a taverna and we'll make a night of it on your successful return."

"My treat," replied Ben.

Bishops laughed heartily, "We shall see about that."

26
Torment

On the Road to Episkopi, British Sovereign Base Area, Cyprus

Since the debacle in Afghanistan, Ben put everyone to the test telling himself he was gauging competence and ability. But, that was only half of it. When someone let him down or proved too superficial, depression came. It was his punishment and possibly his atonement.

Maybe he was being unfair. What about those who didn't have a choice, who inherited bad situations or unforgiving genes and struggled to lead semblances of normal lives? Was he making allowances for them? Who was he to judge, to condemn? Had he walked in their shoes, faced their demons, their hunger, their disillusionment?

It was a holier than thou attitude—a character flaw that tormented him. So, he was thrilled to know in his gut that Artemis would fight death and destruction because it was her nature. She valued work, honesty, and the improvement of the human condition. It was a kinder approach. No nuances, no debates, no moral dilemmas to get lost in.

Evil and misguided creatures (what else were they?) created misery. My job is to stop them. They are stagnant, lost. People are put on earth to learn, to improve, to spread the innocence they knew as babes. What better ambition than that? It took work and education. Terrorists must want the same thing—they'd just lost their way and justified destruction and death. Good people in the Middle East, Christians and Muslims, were mostly concerned with feeding, educating, and improving their kids' lives.

It was the 21ˢᵗ century. Satellites, video, and computers laid bare the lives of everyone across the planet. Their preoccupations weren't all that different; furtive glances at their struggles brought everyone close and made the world smaller. Too many lived in injustice. See a drone destroy a house, the video go black, and accept it? Forsake family and choose death over life? The destroyers were wrecking what they had worked for. Didn't they know how hard it was to build? How easy to destroy?

He answered his own question. They thought they *were* grabbing opportunities. Maybe that's why he'd been so down lately. America had betrayed the ideals and principles it cited in creating itself. Its corporations were stripping resources and humanity bare across the globe. It supported dictators and pint-sized colonels who imposed their will with America's help. It had overthrown elected governments to suit its moneyed agenda and monopolized morality while begrudging it to others. Nameless American institutions run by biased twits bought senators, influenced policy and set selfish agendas.

Those whose agenda is not aligned with America's, we call terrorists. We support nations and corporations that profit us. It's O.K. for the CIA to bring drugs to the U.S. and ruin millions of families for cash to finance a war banned by American law. Just call it "cowboy mentality" and "America First" when, in fact, it's just doublespeak for terrorism. Arabs, Israelis, and Christians want American ideas and institutions, but we send them 'shock and awe.' They want Coca Cola, jeans, and an education for their kids but we send their infrastructure to the stone ages and relegate their aspirations to promises. Then we pay for the damage we cause. Double whammy; pay for it twice. Bishops and he were on Cyprus due to British and American 'enlightened' attitudes. Britain had colonized Cyprus and still controlled more than 200 square miles of the country. America had stood by while the country was divided in half. Never mind the lives, and cultural treasures lost in the process.

I must be getting old. That Israeli whistleblower, Nivit, she's betraying the Mossad, and risking it all for love and a better tomorrow.

Was anything more worthwhile? Was anything more necessary?

27
Yes-Men and Critics

On the Road to Episkopi, British Sovereign Base Area, Cyprus

The car negotiated the inside turn of a ravine and then moved to the outside, rounded the arc of the hillside, reached a short straightaway and slowed to enter the next turn. They were moving steadily down the mountain, feet from the unprotected edge of the road on one side and the fraying rock on the other. They passed through a quiet and picturesque village and olive tree covered hillsides. In the distance, the Akrotiri peninsula crept closer while the hazy blue sea in the distance grew larger.

"Eh…Artemis, I've not been exactly fair to you."

"I almost messed it up."

"No, you didn't."

"I shouldn't have barged ahead back there. This is your turf—you knew Bishops, I didn't. He could have shut us down. I should've followed your lead."

"It worked out. I don't have all the answers. Nothing wrong with another viewpoint."

"But you know the lay of the land—I shouldn't have said anything."

"I've not exactly trusted you."

"We just met. Your friend is dead—and a bunch of terrorists are trying to kill who knows how many others. That's the focus."

"Sam was a hell of a nice guy, completely selfless and my only friend the past three years. You and I need to have an understanding so we don't fall apart at the first sign of stress. The Marines taught me that and I believe it.

'Let me finish. I had to see what you were made of. I lost my team in Afghanistan. And, I saw men do things to other men that shouldn't be done to anybody—not today. The War changed me. I don't believe in my country right or wrong any more…and I know I'm supposed to believe it.

'But I *am* here to make the world a better place. The only way I know to do that is to speak my mind and criticize whatever's wrong. Now, I decide what's right and wrong. You know why there are 30,000 lobbyists in Washington but only 3,000 politicians? Lots of demand for yes-men and no demand for critics.

'One day I'll piss off someone high up and they'll sack me. But while anyone will still listen, I'm fighting evil my way. A lone voice in the wilderness," he snickered. "Critical voices and minority opinions need protecting, not political correctness. That's the country I want. What I'm saying is, I didn't know where you stood before but I do now."

"Sounds good to me. I got no problem with any of it," Artemis said seriously. Then deciding to lighten the mood and with a glint in her eyes, she added with good-natured sarcasm, "At least I passed your little test."

"I told you, I'm the skeptic, the misanthrope, but I…"

"The what?"

"The misanthrope. The cynic. I expect too much from people. Everyone seems to ignore the shit the U.S. is into. I hold people to a higher standard—it's thrilling when somebody rises to the occasion. I don't like slouches. I'm glad you're on my side."

"Colonel, are you flirting with me? You actually like me?"

There was a momentary pause as Ben looked distraught. Finally, he blurted, "I'm tying myself up in knots…I've spilled my guts…I'm just glad you're here."

It was time she let him off the hook. His honesty was refreshing. She couldn't help but feel for him. Her chest felt light.

"As long as we're sharing, let me tell you about my sister, Aph. I love her to death but she's so beautiful and such a softy that she attracts every man that does her absolutely no good. You talk of seeing things through…she married a parasitic leech and instead of getting rid of him, all she can think about is her commitment and her vows. She'd rather stick it out and work herself to death. I can't decide if she's a noble soul trying to lift up the unfortunate or enabling the unworthy. How's that for a paradox?"

She stopped and looked off in the distance. A quiet descended on the small space of the car.

Ben finally said, "Sounds like you're just worried about her. She sounds kind and so do you."

"Thank you," she said graciously looking straight ahead. A feeling of camaraderie came over her. It had been hard for him but he'd explained himself and had done it with deference. Her misgivings about the investigation and her contribution had gotten mixed up with her insecurities about men and her sister. He had buoyed her and affirmed her convictions when she'd felt vulnerable. She was ready for whatever the next few days would bring. She was comfortable next to the man beside her.

She looked off over the ocean at the horizon. Had Ben been able to, he'd have seen her facial muscles relax and a faint smile appear. Her eyes softened and complemented her dark wavy hair. Unconsciously, her lips swelled while the two tiny sparks in her eyes remained hers for a bit longer.

28

Meron Ran

Tel Nof Air Force Base, Israel

Meron Ran pulled on the controls of his Beechcraft 200 King Air and the plane's nose lifted sharply into the sky. This RC-12K Electronic Intelligence version of the aircraft used a turboprop configuration and was equipped with the world's most efficient turbines. A fierce and solid whine shot out of the engines as Meron pushed them close to their limit. The result was an abrupt but exemplary take-off honed by eight years of flying combat missions on F15I's. In contrast to the agile but fickle F15's built to order for the Israeli Air Force, the King Air was so stable that Meron frequently breached the design threshold without realizing it. When the plane teetered on the brink of failure, Meron had the skill to recover. Only the most knowledgeable pilot knew how close and how often Meron came to disaster.

He half-expected the tower to break in with some snotty comment. But whatever the controllers felt, they kept their mouths shut. As a decorated military pilot, he and his flying decisions rated deference and quiet acquiescence. The two-mile long runways of Tel Nof Air Force Base faded behind him and the blue Mediterranean beckoned a few miles ahead. He radioed the all clear to the tower. He was leaving mundane cares behind and could now focus on non-controversial tasks like flying, checking instruments, and feeling the movement of air currents that buoyed his heart whenever they nudged the plane. His body felt free of shackles and his innards hummed with adrenaline. Here he was in control and the skies would be as forgiving or as judgmental as he made them. If he opened his mind, he found solace and celebration.

"You O.K. back there?" he asked Ziki.

"Sure," Ziki's tense voice answered. "Just waiting for my stomach to catch up. I'm not touching nothing until you reach altitude. Let me know. Then I'll get to work. I know you by now."

Meron laughed. "Give me ten minutes," he replied.

"How far to target?"

"Last position was about 420km southwest of Cyprus."

"That tells me nothing."

"Two hundred twenty klicks southwest of Crete, 600 klicks west of Base 8…two hours. Then we find them."

"I've got plenty of time then."

Minutes later the port city of Ashdod was many miles behind. Clear blue skies stretched ahead to the horizon. The sea below was an immense canvas of ruffled navy blue. As far as Meron could see, the earth was blue rippled water and light blue sky. He lived for such moments.

He reached 28,000 feet and gave the all clear to Ziki. Here it was easy and peaceful. No enemy, no orders, no dilemmas, no missiles, no civilians, no death. Ferry the FLIR operators to location and bring them home. Today, easier still: only Ziki, reconnaissance and thermal imaging over international waters. Nothing to worry about.

They'd find the target, make several runs at preset altitudes, record position, note the boat's heading, record images and data and head home—two hours out, 40 minutes for intelligence gathering, and two hours back. The extra fuel tanks in the wingtips had been switched for electronic monitoring pods. That meant less fuel but still left an extra hour over mission requirements not counting the 45-minute emergency tank.

At 28, Meron Ran had seen all he wanted of armed conflict. Strafing homes from the air had taken its toll. In the beginning, when young, he'd focused on following orders and completing each mission. Soon he heard rumblings from pilots about the accuracy of the intelligence and target choices: Palestinian police installations, terrorist compounds and weapons' workshops; rockets against homes and cars and targeted raids against 140 men. Who knew how many more had died in the collateral damage? Meron and the other pilots felt the missions change. The rationale had been to kill militants, but now they were eliminating anyone that might consider violence. Death ensured plans never materialized. It didn't take long to figure out that people were being assassinated before they'd done anything—it was death at the military's discretion but at a pilot's hands.

Killing women and children in pursuit of suspects in these 'focused foiling' missions exacted a huge psychological price from the pilots. Eitan, his buddy and a natural helicopter gunship pilot, was reduced to nightmares after strafing a 10-year-old girl running out of a house crumbling from his rockets. On the next mission, Eitan missed every home he was to bomb. Others started doing the same. Finally, Meron and a few others wrote a letter of protest to superiors and to a TV station condemning their own actions as illegal and immoral.

Sixty years after its creation, Israel still considered itself a country at war. These preemptive strikes caused a backlash that almost brought the government and the military to its knees. In the pushback, pilots were labeled embarrassments and accused of dereliction of duty. Some who had lived through Israel's birth and wars even called them traitors. Meron's eight years of exemplary service couldn't compete; his own family looked at him differently. The public accepted the fodder it was fed never seeing houses explode and civilians littering the streets shredded by his rockets. Few cared about the morality or legality of the attacks. Meron had killed and he'd had enough. He moved to Electronic Intelligence as soon as he could manage the transfer.

Ziki broke in, "HISAR, Electro-optical, and infrared sensors ready. Let's do the mosaic first and the targeted beam next."

"I don't have a target yet."

"I still have the FLIR fairing to calibrate and to sync things with GPS coordinates. How long?"

"Thirty minutes."

"The HISAR's high-resolution MMR covers a wide area and will discriminate targets on water. Put us in the general area and it'll find the boat for us. Then I'll adjust sector parameters and focus the radar. Why are we tracking a boat 700 km from our coastline anyway? You believe it's really an exercise? That they want to see long it takes us to locate the target?"

"Sure. You're logging in surveillance hours, right?"

"I'm serious, Meron. We're way past normal monitoring limits. I'm not complaining—just wondering."

"We're tracking a target. You think finding a boat in the middle of the ocean is easy? The coordinates are twenty hours old, maybe older."

"Get me in the general area and we'll see."

Forty minutes later the turboprop aircraft slowed and went to surveillance mode. The forward-looking infrared sensors and the medium to long-range opticals recorded everything. At 28,000-feet, the Beechcraft remained undetected. Its enhanced com-links sent real time data to ground stations back in Israel.

As the electronic flow came into Israeli intelligence, a young analyst got up and approached an older man in uniform. He handed him a digital printout, "Course heading continues to be the Western Mediterranean, sir."

"Present location?" he asked.

"Two hundred thirty-five kilometers south of Crete. Same heading as yesterday, confirming no deviation from course of six hours ago."

"Likely landfall?"

"Too early to predict. Could be Europe, could be North Africa. No way of knowing."

"Thank you, Samal," the older man said, dismissing the young intelligence officer.

29

British Forces Cyprus

Episkopi, British Sovereign Base Area, Cyprus

"Colonel, I'm Air Vice-Marshal Stanwell. This is Flight Lieutenant Barnes. In my dual capacity as Administrator of the Sovereign Area Bases and Commander British Forces Cyprus, I am at your service."

"Thank you, Commander. This is Agent Nelson from Diplomatic Security. We're grateful for any assistance you can give us."

"Sorry about the chopper, but the winds at Golf Section were uncooperative, although, Barnes here wanted to give it a go. He's had a spat of inactivity of late, apart from rescuing some locals caught in a gale. But I couldn't risk losing a chopper with the wind at 8-9 Beaufort. Sorry that."

"Quite all right. Commander, any updates? Anything from the intelligence services?"

Rick Barnes answered, "Only Sergeant Potsbury from Golf Section. He's been most anxious to speak with Ms. Nelson. If you'd accompany Sergeant Priestly here. Something about the theft at the mine. He was quite agitated."

A now alert Artemis left with Priestly. Behind her, she heard the SBA Commander saying, "Colonel, I have this past hour spoken to your Deputy Secretary of State Campbell and some Undersecretary for International Security from the Department of Defence, didn't quite get his name..." Then Artemis was out of range.

"...both men felt it necessary to speak personally to me and this, after a chat with Whitehall and my own Chief of Defence. All wish to impress on me the urgency of this threat you've identified. Hearing from the Home Office boys comes with the territory..."

Huntley made to speak but the Commander was having his say.

"And, of course Bishops from Golf Section. I'll make it brief: you have my attention and the attention of Her Majesty's Government on Cyprus."

"Bishops is examining Dubai as a possible target. We could use some help in threat analysis and scenarios..." He hesitated and then added, "I'd consider a British viewpoint extremely valuable."

"London and Washington are a bit removed from our little corner of the world—perspective of field officers and so on. Let's chat with my staff, shall we? I understand you were personally acquainted with the Defense Attaché recently lost. Please accept my own condolences."

"Thank you. We're pressed for time...the terrorists likely killed Sam to prevent the attack from being found out. Our Israeli source has the terrorists off Cyprus probably heading to target location. So we assume killing Sam was incidental to the larger operation."

"My command consists of units from all three British services. We seldom operate as an independent entity but rather as part of a 'Comprehensive Approach'—most often your country. At the moment, American presence is mostly layovers. Our Tornados are engaged in reconnaissance and support of Iraqi forces, but we're also equipped with two Chinooks, four HARs and a Globemaster. Point is, British Forces Cyprus can direct and deploy an operation if that target boat is found."

Stanwell paused and faced Huntley with a look that indicated reassurance and the camaraderie of men of action.

"...I'd be happy to arrange for you to be present if that happens."

Commander Stanwell was offering him the coup de grâce against his enemy. Very gentlemanly of him. He finished with a glint in his eye, looked at Barnes and said, "I don't think Barnes, here, would mind that jig one bit."

Barnes smiled. Ben said, "That would make me a happy man."

The grin on the Sovereign Base Area Commander's face widened and looked conspiratorial.

"Now, let's get you a line to Washington."

The three moved down the hall. Ben gazed out the long windows that looked at the southern ocean. A huge curtain array antenna in the distance stretched for a quarter mile on the shore of the salt lake and towered 300 feet into the air but Ben did not really see it. Rather, the antenna's massive metallic latticework was an annoyance as he focused past it on the dull orange sun looming large on the horizon and approaching its haven behind the distant edge of the sea. On the water, a wide shimmer extended from the horizon to the rocky gray-sanded beach. Above, the few small clouds that an hour earlier had been white now glowed with hues ranging from purple to yellow and every shade in between.

30
Anarchist

Episkopi, British Sovereign Base Area, Cyprus

Either jet lag was catching up with Artemis or too many things were up in the air, which discombobulated her. The past twenty-four hours had been a whirlwind. She'd gone from Larnaka Airport in the south to the capital, Lefkosia, in the center, then up to Cyprus's highest peak and now was back on the coast a few miles from where she'd landed. She'd been thrown into a foreign land, was facing a threat that, if to be believed, promised death to more people than any other and had cost Sam his life. And, she had too little information to make sense of it all.

Ben was in his own world. He knew the British and Cyprus. It would take months for Artemis to become aware of the nuances. He was stoic and had shared a few tidbits but she still had no idea what made him so cynical and wary. He was military and answered to the CIA. She didn't have the facts to judge him one way or the other, just a sense that he was decent and lived by a code. She had no time to delve into those details now. She'd stick to her role and the basics. He was genuine, he was concerned and, in a twisted sort of way, noble. He'd expressed misgivings and opinions that bordered on treason considering his job was to enforce American policies. He was quiet for long stretches in what seemed like stoic attempts to balance, even to satiate, a tortured conscience. Would he act when action was called for?

She'd have to wait and see.

Her only option was to rely on Ben. She'd help and do what she did best and he'd handle the things he knew. When she got her bearings, maybe the haze would lift and she'd reappraise the situation. He said he had no qualms about going at it alone. That was something. He was in the wrong profession to be a freethinker. She imagined him standing alone as whirlwinds spun fiercely around him.

She felt helpless and wanted to protect him. He needed an ally and she was it.

She brought herself back. Figuring out Huntley would have to wait. She picked up the phone that Priestley handed her. Finding Johnston's killers and saving–how many lives? A hundred? A thousand? That was the goal. Maybe one of the innocents they saved would cure cancer. That was the way to think. Trying to make sense of Huntley, the murdered Sam, Cyprus, the British, and the terrorist threat in a less than a lucid brain was too much for now. *Stick to the basics*, she told herself again, *and connect the pieces*.

On the phone, Potsbury was excited.

"…you gave me the idea," he said. "We run Project Anarchist out of Golf Section. Essentially, we tap into Israeli drone and F-16 networks. If they have a visual on the boat, we'll pick it up. We're in process of locating imagery right now."

"Sergeant, get down to Akrotiri ASAP. We could use your help," she told him. Potsbury was a wonder and she wanted him on this.

The line went quiet for a long second.

"Don't worry," she said sensing his hesitation. "I'll get it approved."

31
Status Report

Episkopi, British Sovereign Base Area, Cyprus

The table was long and its sides bulged in the center in tapered arcs reminiscent of the sides of a ship. The short ends were chopped off to accommodate a single seat. Vice-Marshall Stanwell sat at its head. Every other seat was occupied and several men in uniform stood at various points around the situation room. Potsbury was at the wall pointing on a huge map of Cyprus, "It was an unusual theft, by Cypriot standards," he was saying.

"Explain," Commander Stanwell prompted him.

"Thefts at National Guard sites in Cyprus are more common than one would think. However, the items most often taken are small arms, grenades, and light explosives."

Barnes added, "Grenades are popular with older fishermen, though illegal for some time. The culprits are often recently released conscripts. Nothing organized."

Potsbury nodded and continued, "This theft occurred at the recently shuttered Amiantos mine on Troodos. The government is arranging for environmental cleanup and the only security consists of two guards per eight-hour shift. Secondly, despite the presence of explosives on site only detonators, cords, and boosters were taken."

"Let me guess, the Cypriots have made no headway tracking the culprits nor do they have any theories on motives," Commander Stanwell commented.

"It's not a high priority case. No one was harmed and the items are not in themselves dangerous. No Interpol report was filed."

"Thank you, Captain."

"Conclusions?" Ben asked.

Potsbury answered, "Likely means the thieves are either already in possession of explosives or will procure them closer to target."

"The M.O. fits in with the boat mentioned by our informant," Artemis volunteered. "Explosives are harder to transport and may already be in place closer to the target. We could use intel from Geospatial or Anarchist on that boat."

"Let me remind everyone," Stanwell paused and looked over the table, "notwithstanding your conviction that Cyprus is not a target, my concern is the protection of British and American personnel on Her Majesty's territories. And let's not forget the number of tourists on the island from both nations."

He glanced around—the firm eyes of a career soldier pinning each man in place. He waited for his no-nonsense look to communicate what he expected of the men under his command. He was asking them to be accountable and do their utmost. They responded with a loud "Sir!" in acceptance of their duties.

After this perfunctory ritual, which only took about ten seconds, Ben asked, "Commander, pursuing Colonel Johnston's killers is the only lead we have and it points to Dubai. There is little point in Agent Nelson and me staying in Cyprus. I could use a few men, including Potsbury here, if you don't mind."

Potsbury's eyes danced at the compliment.

Commander Stanwell turned to his second in command, "Barnes prep a Rapid Reaction Force to accompany Colonel Huntley. Readiness report within the hour, if you please. You need a long-range plane. Take the Globemaster, a CLV, a Seahawk…and an explosives man. Combat readiness, Flight Lieutenant."

Barnes lit up like a youngster who'd been given the toy he thought he'd never get. He jumped up as if flung from a spring, "Sir!"

32
Dubai

Airspace Over Saudi Arabia

Ben steadied himself as he walked in the cavernous interior of the Globemaster. He came up behind Potsbury and Artemis who did not notice him over the noise of the plane.

"Okay, you two. What do you have?"

Artemis looked up from the screen and leaned back. Potsbury was reluctant to take his eyes off the screen. On boarding the massive C-17 military plane, the two had buried themselves in computer terminals.

Potsbury glanced at Artemis and began, "Dubai is the second largest of the seven sheikdoms comprising the United Arab Emirates. All are run by family monarchies who are vested in keeping the status quo and are allied with the West. Publically they support Arab agendas but far from fundamentalists. Missions against ISIL, Syria, and Afghanistan fly out of AL Dhafra Air Base. Dubai has a large ex-pat community and is the leading destination for troop R and R. Population is approximately two million, but three-quarters of that is the service sector—mostly Indians and Pakistanis."

Potsbury, now fully engaged in Artemis' synopsis, could no longer contain himself.

"Dubai's top commodity is capital, real estate, trade, and finance and is home to several international conglomerates. The country is in the midst of a building boom financed by Sheikh Al Maktoum who, at last count has several wives, 21 children, and is the fifth wealthiest man on the planet. He controls most of the world's horse operations and has made the Dubai Cup the most prestigious prize in racing. He's also been accused of enslaving boys for use as camel jockeys. He recently donated 10 billion, that's with a *b*, to bridging the educational gap between Arabs and the developed world. Current projects include a theme park twice the size of Disneyland and Dubai Sports City, which is being groomed as a future Olympic site. The recent economic downturn has forced reorganization; however, given the pockets involved, it's likely temporary."

"Some of the world's wealthiest men may be in Dubai at any time. We're putting together a list of scheduled events and evaluating target values," said Artemis.

"The Dubai RSO mentioned the Burj…"

"Burj is Arabic for 'tower.' Dubai is known for dream buildings like the Emirates Towers, the Rose Tower, and the Diamond Tower whose 74 floors are devoted to diamond cutting. There are two buildings called Burj—the al Arab and the Burj Khalifa. The al Arab is the one shaped like a ship's sail and sits on its own island. The other, the Burj Khalifa, and is the world's tallest building with 163 stories. Anniversary celebrations are two weeks from today with dignitaries expected from across the world. That's our best candidate for a target."

"Any connections to 'Palm or Hand of God'?" Ben asked.

"May refer to the Palm Islands which is a massive land reclamation project shaped like a palm tree. The sheik is pulling sand out of the ocean, which will double the size of the country and add 520 kilometers of beaches to Dubai City. Not likely our target, however."

"Why is that?"

"It's mostly mansions atop of sand. The size of the islands makes an attack impractical—it will damage access ways, service conduits, and the homes of the super wealthy. Hardly a crippling blow; symbolic possibly but nothing more. The Burj, on the other hand, is a monolithic structure that would rival the World Trade Center disaster. It'd be an attack on the established order and the West. Here's an image."

Ben took the computer printout from Potsbury and examined the tower.

"Tall and narrow. Do you have the Palm Islands?"

"I'll pull them up on the screen." Potsbury turned to the monitor and struck a few keystrokes bringing up an image of the Dubai coastline.

"There's the Burj," he pointed.

After examining the images for a few seconds, Ben said, "It would take a nuke to impact the islands. The Burj is a better target."

"What else could they attack?" Artemis asked.

"'Palm' as in palm tree is only one possibility…" Potsbury added.

"Sorry to barge in," Barnes's voice came from the cockpit, "but you'll want to see this."

33
Abu Nur-al Deen and Abdellatif Ferroukhi

Moroccan Coast Several Miles from Alhuceima

"As-salaam Alaikum."

"Wa' Alaikum As-salaam. Allah will reward those that labor on his behalf."

"A reward soon to be ours. It has been a long time, my brother, and it is good to be by your side again. I hope your journey over the sea has been without trouble."

"Nothing like your troubles in Casablanca…and yet, you are here. I had no reason to worry. As always, you are true to your word. Tell me your news."

"We only failed to communicate. *Kafirs* are everywhere around us; the misguided and weak of heart increase by the day; but it is also the time that reveals the strong of faith. You have heard of the martyrdom of the brothers Houssaini? Their faith was with them until the end. Surrounded by *kufr*, they did not waver; truly they are *shahid* and rejoice in Allah's bounty."

"Were they found out? Do we need to worry about security?"

"There was no breach—that, we are sure of. They were at an internet café to post a message for you. The café owner became suspicious and stopped them from leaving. Fearing capture and questioning, they detonated their belts and sent forty-two *kafirs* to their judgment. They are with Allah; we are the unfortunate for we are still here."

"Our duty is to be His Hand. All will be as He wishes."

"May we be worthy of the task. All that can be done, we have done. We are prepared for the ultimate sacrifice."

"And you are certain that we will not be prevented from the victory we've dreamed of for so many years?"

"I stand witness to my faith and my resolve. That is my assurance. As Abdelfattah and Mohammed Houssaini showed no hesitation in Casablanca, we also will not hesitate. Only you and I know every aspect of the operation. The Houssainis knew your internet address but not of your arrival, the target, or other details. They performed righteously and reside in paradise. Ten others of my cell rejoice that the Houssainis have no cause to grieve."

"*'Allah has purchased of the believers their persons and their goods; paradise will be theirs; they fight in His Cause, and slay and are slain.'*"

"As we agreed in Madrid, I am prepared and rejoice in the bargain."

"I commend you on the belts. Your men did not wait for the *jahiliyya* to judge them. Their *shahid* is an example to all. May we be worthy of the glory that comes to those that find sustenance in the presence of their Lord."

"Our faith brought us victory in the past. The magnitude of that victory has sustained and strengthened me. We will succeed here as well and our *istishhad* will live for 10,000 years. Believers will emulate our martyrdom. I have accumulated 80,000 kilos. But, we will not go through Casablanca as previously planned; no reason to take the risk. Instead, we avoid the coast and go south to Fes. Fewer eyes in the interior. At Marrakech, we take Highway N8 to Agadir and from there, N1 to Laayoune. No other changes. We will be the Hand of Allah and begin the new golden age for Islam."

Abu Nur al-Deen finally relaxed. He was on a path of certainty and no retreat. Only the next step remained.

"As you put your life in my hands in Madrid, I now place mine in yours," he responded in a reverent and slow drawl that was contractual acquiescence.

"Welcome, brother. The time has come and is most welcome."

The two embraced. The ritual was elaborate and deferential. Each man kissed the other's cheeks three times.

"New York, London, Madrid—victories, yes, but granules of sand compared to the Hand of Allah. I submit to his will. *La illaha ill Allah, Muhammadur Rasul Allah.*"

"He is our protector.' The controls are with you?"

The other man's eyes sparkled and he smiled, "Only *jihad* remains. Now, I have been too long at sea and, over a cup of *kahwamazboot,* you can tell me about the trucks, the ANFO, the containers, everything."

The two men walked on the sandy beach past thickets of sea grass. Three hundred meters off the coast, a Spanish Sovereign Area, the Peñón de Alhuceimas, stood stoically in the sea. A garish stone garrison sat atop the small isle overwhelming and covering every meter of rock.

The two conspirators walked side by side until they reached a wooden shack eatery that faced the beach. Its roof consisted of thatch reeds laid atop bamboo. An overhang provided shade over a small tarrazza. They stepped onto the cement slab that held three wooden tables covered with faded checkered blue and white plastic tablecloths. In low voices, they talked and ate for the next three hours.

34
Morocco

Airspace Over Saudi Arabia

The C-17 Globemaster banked to the right and an airport came into view below.

"We're about fifteen clicks out of Dubai," Barnes came in over Ben's headphones. "That's a Canadian airfield; doesn't exist officially. Ever see anything so desolate?"

The airport slid diagonally past them on the left as the huge aircraft continued forward.

Barnes continued, "There's the Burj," he pointed above the plane's controls.

The air was sandy-colored and hazy. Ben made out a lone spire that narrowed to an antenna at the top. It was slender and its tip vanished in the haze. He recognized the image from the computer printout of a few minutes ago. Circular towers clad in reflective aluminum and stainless steel glazing were bound together and ended in setbacks; the building's core emerged from the setbacks and became the narrow central spire. It was an elegant monster and out of place among the sand colors of the desert—an obscene affront on the landscape but also a testament to human will.

Sandy flat emptiness stretched below; no shrubbery, little variation. They passed several tiny settlements that consisted of one-story sandy squares, which were almost indistinguishable from the desert around them.

Barnes was saying something. Ben caught the tail end. "...he wants to speak to you personally."

He turned to face Barnes, "Who did you say?"

"Vice-Marshall Stanwell, British Forces Cyprus."

Stanwell wasted no time, "Huntley, I wanted to tell you personally. Anarchist came through and Geospatial just confirmed the location of your boat. The coordinates are en route as we speak."

Ben tensed. "Where are they?"

"You're not going to like it—Morocco."

"Morocco?" Ben blurted out in shock. "What's it doing in Morocco?"

He was nowhere. *We could've stopped this thing in Dubai. The Burj was on lock down, its perimeter monitored and contained. There was a chance with a building! Maybe even catch the bastards. Morocco! They had nothing!*

"All of Western intelligence is asking that question. My staff and I had a go around—that's why I called."

"Do we know if those detonators are on board?"

"No confirmation yet."

"I've heard nothing from Langley—no doubt preparing situation reports," Ben said sarcastically. He was aligning himself with the British since he had their aircraft and a commander that could shut him down at any moment.

"Morocco is in the midst of similar unrest as the rest of the Arab world—fundamentalists versus monarchists. Casablanca had 42 dead in one bombing last week."

"Any link to our boat?"

"We're checking...If the provisions on that boat enter the fray, it will get more chaotic. Of course, Morocco may not be the final destination; the terrorists may have gone ashore to avoid Gibraltar."

"How's that?"

"Her Majesty's Navy inspects vessels passing through Gibraltar. A supertanker or container ship sunk in the Straits would affect world markets and possibly bring several Western nations to their knees. Same goes for Suez and Panama. What the public doesn't know…"

"The consequences would be that severe?"

"Gibraltar shutting down may lead to a world-wide economic tailspin—not to mention keep our navies from entering or leaving the Mediterranean."

"So they come ashore in Morocco and head to target by land."

"It's one option. Take your pick. Listen, you're in transit with my men and my plane. Dubai or Morocco—makes no difference to me—proceed as you see fit. I'll keep Langley apprised. Good luck and good hunting."

A minute later, Ben was filling Artemis, Potsbury and Barnes in on his conversation with Stanwell.

"The two have to be linked," Potsbury was saying. "There's an attack on Morocco and a boat laden with explosives materiel arrives days later? Too closely connected geographically and chronologically."

"But why *after* an attack that's paralyzed the country?" Artemis asked.

Ben looked grim, his jaw set firmly and his gaze unfocused indicating that he had not yet settled on a direction. Finally, he broke the silence, "To intensify the chaos—it could be an offensive to make Morocco another Syria or Afghanistan," Ben concluded.

"Morocco is not high priority for the West. Libya turned into a full-scale civil war and the U.S. did nothing. Fanatics running Morocco will be a nuisance but at the end of the day, the U. S. and Britain are more vulnerable from an attack on the Straits."

"All speculation," said Ben. "An attack is coming from a cell that likely killed Sam. Now we know where they are and that's more than we knew a few minutes ago. Yesterday, we were a week behind them; now, less than a day. Our mandate remains. We're going to Morocco."

He tried to appear confident and resolute. The conversation with Stanwell reverberated in his mind. Morocco as a way station to another location nagged at him. His quarry could vanish into the countryside or into some impenetrable shantytown in any of several large cities in Morocco.

I'd better close the gap before I lose the trail or before Langley calls me off.

35
Terror of the Rash

Airspace Over the Mediterranean

The plane banked sharply until the right wing pointed at the sandy ground below. Then the Globemaster pulled out of the arc and leveled facing west. It was a behemoth of a plane with four huge Pratt and Whitney engines, and now it was heading for Morocco.

Ben dumped his body into one of the minimally padded plastic seats fused into the plane's outer skin. Every muscle cried for attention. He felt raw and exposed as if stripped of the layers of training, experience, and willpower that had protected him to this point. His reserves were gone and it seemed as if only fragile skin remained. The mental and physical strain of the past few days had caught up with him. From the minute Sam went missing, Ben had gone tense and had thought of little else. Then the devastation of Sam's death. The shock of the cut on his throat in the morgue and the caked blood on the car seat had taken its toll.

He'd been caught off guard when Artemis crashed into him at the mosque. That first encounter had been mesmerizing. For her part, she'd been non-judgmental. A door had opened as if Maria, the cleaning woman, had thrown open a window and the air had filled with the scent of fresh orange blossoms.

His interest had been piqued; Artemis's exterior appearance was pleasant and her personality hinted at an equally wonderful interior. She had field experience, which had honed her skills and confidence. She did not appear fazed. Whatever she'd been through, she was still an optimist. He imagined her waltzing through threats, unfazed by temptation, composed, devoted to truth. He was romanticizing. Few had the discipline to live by a code. Some morphed into selfish and intolerant bitches. She wasn't one.

Did he dare to imagine happy years with her? She was decent and kind—and attractive, well, that was icing on the proverbial cake.

Energy seeped back into him. He put thoughts of Artemis the woman aside and tried to think of her as his team. His final thought on the matter was, "For now."

I thought I had a lead, that the whole mess would start to crystalize. Another pipe dream. Things are always more complicated, take more time, and cost more and, like a pebble dropped into a still pool, everything affects everything else.

Morocco. What a sideswipe that was. Time to regroup.

He looked off into the light blue sky. After Afghanistan, he spent more time taking stock of unknowns, weighing information, and sifting through crap trying to get a grip on situations. Only then, he was confident enough for action.

It takes time but I gotta do it. Doesn't apply to women though; I still don't understand them. Seems like they're into instant satisfaction and complain a hell of a lot. They're able to handle many stimuli at once. They go to a store, feel twenty fabrics, and keep track of all of them. Just give me the bottom line. I don't need anything else. Except with Sam's death; I don't have enough info to make sense of it. Damn.

Maybe I'm wrong. Maybe the job is action, snap decisions and for the young and foolish. I lost my buddies in Afghanistan because proper gisting of intel wasn't done. The 'golden boys' can do no wrong and are promoted past their competence levels. Then they set the world back generations because they turn out not to be so golden after all. How many supported the Shah, Saddam Hussein, Pinochet and were threatened by Mossadegh, Allende, and other legitimate leaders? They never deal with genocide, the misery of millions, and the day-to-day work that progress needs. Dulles, Kissinger, and Col. North are named, but countless others work secure in their self-righteousness. They promise salvation to local populations but instead decimate them and ply them into fodder for the warped delusions of demagogues. No. I'll think first, and act later.

36
Charlie Fui

Wright-Patterson Air Force Base, Ohio

"We'll talk on the way," Randall pointed down the hall.

"Hank, tranquilizers are the best option. They won't know what hit them. The SEALs can get it done." This was Frank Foley, the Navy man.

"Carstens?" Lt. Col. Henry Randall turned and asked another man.

"Sir, no disrespect to the Navy but this enemy is too unpredictable. We're talking open ocean—anybody trying to approach will be seen a mile away. Then they have to board and bring the hostiles back alive …the margin for error is too high."

"We're talking SEALs," Foley said the annoyance in his voice quite evident. "There is no margin of error. It's what they do."

Randall asked, "With darts? Are you guaranteeing two perfect shots simultaneously? What if they're wearing suicide belts? Two already blew themselves up to keep this thing secret. Seem way too trigger-happy to me. If we lose the boat, we have nothing. You understand that? We need to get to the bottom of this."

He looked at the men. Silence.

Finally, Frank Foley, the Navy man, said, "We'll have surprise on our side. We monitor the boat, and commit when we have clean shots. A team from Spain can stage in less than six hours."

"Sir, Huntley has a Rapid Reaction Force with him and will be there in three hours."

"Hank, c'mon! That unit is British."

"With Huntley in charge."

"Huntley hasn't been in the field in years. Do we really want the British handling this? I say we send in the SEALs."

"The Rapid Reaction Force is trained for terror response."

"Hank, the SEALs can do it. They'll get close from underwater."

"Divers? They'll get on board without getting the boat blown up?"

"We don't even know if Westerners are the target! It's Morocco! Could be an Arab on Arab attack," Frank Foley, the Navy man said.

Hank stopped as they were entered the large open hangar and stared hard at Foley.

"There's Fui," Randall's aide said. Randall stopped and looked. Worktables were spread out over the hangar. Young techs were bent over each. One group was staring at a tiny drone buzzing in the air. Randall turned and faced Foley with a hard look.

"I'm going to pretend I didn't hear that. We've got a dead diplomat and the trail getting colder by the minute, an RSO with a planeload of special forces crisscrossing the Mediterranean, Morocco about to blow wide open, and God knows what else and you make a comment like that. Frank, we're not playing politics. If we get these guys and stop the attack—everybody wins. That's what we're going to do. Let's go."

They approached an oriental man in his forties with a roundish face and a bit of white above the ears.

"Charlie, we need your expertise. We have two men on a boat approximately a mile off shore that we need to take alive. Can your nanos handle this?"

"Yes, sir. No problem."

"Walk us through it, Charlie. Gentlemen, Charlie Fui, currently on loan to the Air Force from DARPA, where he's been miniaturizing drones."

"Managing Biologic Systems and Platforms, actually. My team provides real time combat capability as a Forward Cell (DFC)...that's DARPA-speak for full-time forward presence in a combat zone. We adapt capabilities found in nature to military applications and use them in the field. Biologics can detect and surpass a multitude of stimuli— changes in temperature, pressure, flow—and do so with inexpensive conformal materials in high noise backgrounds. Several DARPA programs are currently attempting to emulate the unique locomotive, chemical, visual, and aural sensing abilities of animals. Two examples: first, we are adapting the vacillating foil approach of fish and aquatic birds to a human-powered device to convert human motion to propulsion and increase swimming efficiency from the current 15 to over 70 percent. Second, we're emulating insects, specifically the common water-strider, to develop suits and footwear allowing for human buoyancy."

"Doc? Hold on. Are you saying you're working on getting soldiers to walk on water?"

37

MAV's

Wright-Patterson Air Force Base, Ohio

"With the proper footwear, yes. Thousands of microscopic hair properly oriented and layered allow tiny air bubbles to be trapped and to increase water resistance to the point of buoyancy. Suits and shoes paired with enhanced physical and cognitive peak performance of human subjects have a very promising future."

"Walk on water?" said Frank Foley the Navy man.

"Absolutely. Within the decade, I believe. The science is valid; however, human subjects have yet to reach necessary performance levels."

"Charlie, the MAVs, please," Randall interrupted with a firm voice bringing the discussion back to the issue of the boat.

"Micro Aerial Vehicles are microscopic versions of unmanned aerial vehicles but as tiny as dragonflies or bumblebees. Their advantage is they can fly undetected and photograph, record, and attack the enemy using advanced nanotechnology. My team uses a hybrid approach—biological macromolecules within synthetic sensors. We've streamlined several animal models with significant advances. For example, we've adapted the flight properties of insects, notably bats and birds, using biomechanical sensor engineering, motor system neurophysiologies and hybrid bio-molecular devices. We've achieved outstanding capabilities in wind, rain, and snow—which are the most challenging environments. Our current models can hover and move forward with respectable performance emulations compared to their biological counterparts. They react satisfactorily in real-world situations when confronted with unpredictable wind gusts. I'm pleased to say, the Dragonfly has surpassed our expectations."

"Charlie, the short version, please," Randall said.

Charlie was confounded for a moment. Then as his mental synapses came back on track, he continued.

"For a long time, the most vexing issue has been developing a nano-sized energy source to render the MAVs practicable in the field. Your request, as described, is well within parameters. Per Department of Defense specs, we can leech power and recharge using transmission lines. Guidelines require that MAVs return to base for reuse, as the expenditure for each at this early stage, is in the many thousands. The standard configuration D-fly is adequate."

"Last report had range at two miles?" Randall said.

"We've made progress," Charlie paused in glory. "Beginning in the 1960's, vehicle propulsion systems faced the performance-to-power paradox: massive amounts of fuel were needed to reach space, but the required fuel added weight requiring even more fuel to offset the weight of the fuel. Rockets were so heavy they almost never got off the ground. The power source itself was the problem. Our program specs require us to keep our drones at less than six inches so our power-to-weight challenge is analogous. Of course, we have options not available in the '60's."

"What does that mean, for us now, Charlie?"

"Current range is 6 miles. Each system uses two D-flies to conduct reconnaissance; next we engage the targets; boots perform clean up."

"Hank, do you really want to use untested and unproven technologies on this? I'd rather have men on the ground making split second decisions."

Charlie Fui recoiled; the bite in his voice was unmistakable, "Operators *are* on site calling the shots—but they're out of harm's way. We're a Forward Combat Cell. We use real time video to make informed decisions with more data than otherwise available. I have the test data to prove it."

"Frank, we've been using drones in combat for 20 years now. The D-fly is smaller, more advanced and more agile. Charlie, how would you incapacitate the hostiles? Nerve agents?"

"That's the beauty of the D-fly. Each system is customizable with a ground control station and interchangeable payloads. It can be outfitted with aerosols, miniature bombs, and a variety of sensors—GPS, IR, and optic flow collision-avoidance systems. It'll even take cBASS canisters."

"And those are?" Carstens asked.

"Compact Bead Array Sensor Systems...they detect and identify biological warfare agents using biotechnology. Magnetic nanotech identifies the molecules. Again the approach is hybrid: microfluidics synthesize biologics and technologics into a single compact chip."

Randall looked from one man to the other looking for objections. Finally, his eyes settled on Charlie Fui.

"Get your team ready. You leave within the hour."

38
The Sentinel of Henry Street

Airspace Over the Mediterranean

Ben looked at Artemis. Her arms were bare to her shoulders and the deceptively small muscles flexed with every movement. For all he knew she exercised two hours a day and had twice his stamina. He imagined her as the archetypical female—sensual, shapely, with hints of fertility and immortality. Her dark chestnut hair and features were disarmingly balanced and her cheekbones firm but subdued. A smoothly contoured chin finished the face in a classic oval. A lot to be said for good genes.

He returned to and savored the satisfaction that he'd first felt in Cyprus. She was an altruist and it was refreshing. Henry Street came back to mind. He was twelve. He, his sister, and her girlfriend were walking on Henry Street to get to after-school at the church all the while stared at by adults and harassed by black kids. No idea why. One day the bullies got brazen and closed in. There had been no question; in a firm voice Ben said, "You go on," and the girls knew. They held each other's hand and hurried out of harm's way. Ben turned to face the pack. A swell rose in him and he stood braver and taller than ever before ready to hold his ground and keep the girls safe. They would not, could not, pass. The punks stopped their approach surprised he hadn't run. They moved in and started jeering. Ben kicked out a tall and long foot and caught the closest one in the groin. He bent over and retreated with his hands between his legs. The other two rushed in, but their hits felt puny and, strangely, did not hurt. Ben felt power leaving his attackers and seeping into him. The one he'd hurt teetered and picked up stones to pelt Ben. His two accomplices followed suit. He dodged, and, the ones that hit did not hurt. They threw a few more rocks and yelled obscenities. He advanced; they retreated. Sensing the fight was over and that the girls were safe ahead, Ben stood as a sentinel impervious to anything they could do. Finally, he turned his back and walked away unafraid in his heart but fearing a rock would crack his head open and he'd be incapacitated. None did.

Artemis would see the mission to its end. She could have stayed in Cyprus to tie up loose ends but hadn't. She'd followed his lead and trusted him. It felt good to have a partner whose loyalty and priorities were beyond question. Now she was working communications until she got results so they could hit the ground running in Morocco. He had seen the dedication in her eyes then and he saw it again, now, on the plane—calm, methodical, and determined to uncover the impending attack.

The answers lay in the intelligence. It was a matter of looking until something connected. The effort mattered—but in the final analysis, one always competed with oneself. Nothing was more vital than that.

He'd known Jolene and Cindy a hell of a lot better than he knew Artemis and it still hadn't worked out with either one. Let the past lie, he told himself.

He thought of Sam; he'd lost his kids because he'd chosen the wrong woman. He'd told Ben how Kathy drove the kids to school in the morning and then entered the netherworld of daytime soaps, on-line shopping for vacuuming gadgets, and diet swindles. "The parasites are leeching her dry," a bitter Sam complained. "I feel like shit most of the time. I'll be useless in the States. There's no saving her; she's gone. Maybe I can save the kids before they're lost to consumerism. I'm not saying we're doing a great job here but at least we're trying. Do I go back and try to save my kids or stay here and fight shysters and bring a hope and truth to the deluded?"

If Sam expected an answer, Ben had none for him. Then, "It's just guilt talking. I made my choice years ago. In Connecticut, I'd be strolling the mall in loafers with a cup of Starbucks while she woos and ahhhs at display windows. The suburbs. La di da. You know why I'm here? A skinny nine-year-old I met in a one-room school in Somalia. I was there verifying powdered milk was reaching the school and this kid just broke my heart. Eyes like I've never seen. There are 30 to 40 kids around me and all I see is this one kid—his life teetering between retribution and contribution. His soul is in his eyes, yearning, forcing me to decide for him. I never felt so naked in my life. I don't know too many things, but I know those few minutes in that rundown shack changed his life and mine. He'll be somebody someday because I gave him one stinking minute of my time—not a bad return, eh?"

What had Bishops said back on Troodos?

"Any man's death diminishes me, because I am involved in mankind." Yeah, that was it. Goddamn it, Sam, life's not fair. It'd be so much better if you were here. The world is less for losing you.

39
Enrique Alcretan

Paseo Tunnel, La Palma, Canary Islands

Enrique grabbed the padlock and turned it upside down to insert his key. He was in front of a metal gate of galvanized wire fencing which guarded an opening in the tunnel wall. Four round pipes came off the sides and entered the rock where they were secured by cement patches. The opening extended twelve feet up the wall to the curved tunnel ceiling. A separate fence panel blocked the four feet above the door.

To a motorist crossing to the other side of the island, the gate appeared as an entryway into the tunnel's service area. Older residents remembered the discovery of the caverns during tunnel construction. Engineers had entered and investigated the caverns for structural repercussions to the roadway. They'd been satisfied that the schisms and shafts were not a threat. Residents already knew the mountains were porous; this was just one more system.

Runoff culverts were added to the roadside to capture the water and bring it to the reservoirs that dotted the island. The "gallerias," as the locals called them, had supplied water for hundreds of years. More water meant more vineyards on the hillsides and more banana plantations at the coast. Good news for farmers.

But, the caverns could also serve the rear of the cement shields. They were a readymade solution to tunnel maintenance, but as an entryway into the mountain's labyrinthine caverns, they were quickly forgotten.

A few cars sped by. A voice yelled out a greeting and Enrique looked up to see the dented back of a blue Nissan pick-up moving past him in the tunnel. The hand waving out the window and a glance at the license plate confirmed that his cousin, Miguel, was at the wheel. Enrique lifted his hand in response and held it aloft until he saw Miguel glance at his rear view mirror and acknowledge him. The pick-up sped towards the coin-sized sunlit opening and was quickly lost in the chiaroscuro shadows of the tunnel.

Enrique returned to the gate and his annoyance. He should think of it as a safety precaution. When he'd been a child, few strangers and cars came to Puerto Naos. He and friends followed the lumbering trucks that struggled through the dirt roads and the banana fields. They climbed onto stone boundary walls for vantage points mesmerized by the old Mercedes. They lived for the mechanical groans and stared at the flattened leaf suspensions wondering if they'd snap. They watched the metal sheaths bend and strain as they passed over mounds and rocks. Now trucks moved effortlessly on pneumatic systems and didn't seem to impress today's kids. Thank you, television and internet.

Everyone seemed to have a Japanese car or pickup. Conveniences and modernity felt oddly out of place on the quiet rural home he'd left as an 18-year-old. Things felt cheaper.

Small Yamaha motorcycles had first appeared when he was in elementary school. Teens cruised the squares and crossed to Santa Cruz or rode the mountain trails to the calderas for thrills. No one ventured into the openings behind the tunnels; they did not have the appeal of calderas, beaches, or discotheques.

La Palma's pristine natural wonders, volcanic morphology and clear sky caught the attention of scientists, surfers, and eco-tourists. European universities built observatories to look into the heavens. While Enrique was absent at university, the gate was installed to keep trespassers and thrill seekers out.

As kids, they had just walked in. Now, on his return, he'd been forced to apply to the Ministerio de Fomento for access. He moved the key nervously twinging with anger at having to follow rules not meant for him. He'd been at school eight years and back for three months. He found a row of facilities ringing Taburiente and two new radio telescopes about to go on line; more were planned. The quiet and out-of-the-way home he'd left behind had been taken over by new agendas. UNESCO had declared La Palma a World Biosphere Reserve. That was a good thing. It might keep out the frenzy and commercialism of Europe and America.

After university, Enrique returned to Madrid and, as soon as he could manage, joined the new Volcanological Station on La Palma, which monitored Canary Island Volcanos. The Teide-Pico Viejo complex on Tenerife and the Cumbre Vieja on La Palma were the most worrisome. Teide was a stratovolcano that had created the third largest volcanic island in the world and had become the tallest volcano in the Atlantic. It was highly unstable, in an advanced stage of deformation, and went through an eruptive cycle on average every 90 years. Cumbre Vieja on La Palma was a volcanic ridge whose series of craters crawled further south with every eruption. The monitoring station had been built along the active rift zones known as "dorsales." It collected radio telemetered (UHF) analog signals of seismic activity, measured surface temperatures at fumaroles and water gallerias, and monitored the release of geochemical gases.

Enrique, now a geologist, had gone into the caverns. He took data gathering instruments deeper then they'd ever been before. He'd gotten three sets of readings and they were worrisome. Now he was back and this fourth set would verify the increases in temperature and gas emissions.

Then he could panic.

40
Isabella

Volcanological Station, La Palma

Isabella's khaki pants hung loosely about her hips. It stopped a few inches above her canvas shoes leaving her ankles exposed. Her sandy blond hair dipped and touched her face with every jostle of her body. A straw colored linen blouse with pockets over each breast and straps holding the rolled up sleeves at the upper arms tied the whole look together harmoniously. Certain people are exceptional and exude energy and confidence that draws others to them. Isabella had that effect on people. Too bad the Station and the *Observatorios* were mostly filled with older men who thought too much of themselves.

One side pocket contained a notebook and an iPad. The extra weight increased the swing of her trousers making her more attractive. The look was a cross between disheveled and functional and added to well-balanced features while accentuating the roundness of her hips. Enrique's imagination had lingered over the silky feel of the worn and soft cotton brushing against warm legs and buttocks.

Enrique first saw Isabella when Director Carlos Mendoza gave him a tour of the Station. She was engrossed in instruments and gave no indication that she saw them. Enrique couldn't help but notice her.

While Carlos explained the Station and described each machine's function, Enrique stole several glances at her.

Later when the two geologists moved towards the spectrometers and the data displays near her, she paused for introductions. Carlos didn't mention Enrique was a La Palma native and for some reason Enrique was relieved. Her unfettered look caused flutters in his heart. The scientists came from all over Europe and the U.S. There were even several Chinese research fellows from western universities. Enrique worried his personal connection to the island would obscure his scientific credentials. He resolved to separate the first 18 years of his life from his scientific work. It kept things simple.

His imagined that Isabella was not averse to him and thought that her eyes lingered an extra second in his. For days afterwards, he wondered if it was simply her character or if she might be interested in him. Then, he realized he'd spent so much time trying to interpret the nuances that he was no longer sure what he remembered. Finally, his memory of the moment was so compromised that he doubted everything. The only option? Spend more time together.

41

Omens

Inside Cumbre Vieja, La Palma, Canary Islands

Enrique closed the gate behind him and entered the service tunnel. He veered off the paved passageway used by the Highway Department and past a sign that warned he was leaving the service area. He turned on his helmet light and gave a reassuring tug on the straps of his backpack. With some residual lighting behind him, his eyes adjusted to the darkness. He spotted his markers and began to descend.

He was walking on porous volcanic rock. The softer sediments had eroded long ago leaving the rock pockmarked and hard. The caverns were only crevices in places—tight, sharp and dangerous. Some shafts were vertical schisms of scoriaceous rock. Water ran down the sides almost everywhere. The terrain was abrasive and intimidating. *That's just fine,* thought Enrique. *It keeps people out. If they only knew what lay beyond.* He turned his head and the light from his torch hit the walls. He tugged again at his straps and felt the pressure of his back-up digging into his back.

His destination was 700-800 meters diagonally down from the entrance. The additional weight of the backpack shifted his center of gravity and threw his balance and sense of security off. The knowledge that he should not be entering alone gnawed at him and he vowed to be extra cautious. He decided he would consciously test for solid footing before committing his weight to the next step.

Ten minutes later, he'd gone down 165 meters. He stopped and lowered himself a few inches so that his buttocks rested on a rock. He sat for a minute to quiet his breathing. The air was humid and he caught a scent of sulfur. His anxiety spiked and his hands tensed as he pushed on the rock to lift himself. Another descent lay ahead.

His route angled and brought him towards the western side of the mountain. *Was there a magma shaft nearby? Perhaps a vent? Readings could have stabilized. The caverns might extend far into the mountain—maybe even reach the ocean over 1200 meters below. Anything was possible. Heat and gasses from a single volcanic vent could inundate and affect the whole system.*

His instruments would have the final say.

He hugged the wall and continued to descend. He tested his footing again. He went down another 35 meters. On his first entry, he had rappelled down this section. Afterwards he'd tested the route with a backpack. Each time after that, the trip had been easier.

He reached a boulder that towered over him. He veered to one side, went almost completely around it, and stepped first on one outcropping then another until he reached a level section. Easy walk from this point on. He stepped over a water gulley whose water flowed quickly in the direction he was headed. He moved off to the right and went past an ancient hardened bastion of a rock that looked like it supported the ceiling and resembled a massive tree trunk. It was known as an igneous intrusion, and, high up, it blended with the wall. Basically, it was crystallized molten magma. It was dense, dark, and granular and aroused his suspicions that a lava tube might be nearby. He was right.

He stepped over jagged outcroppings and mounds getting ever closer to his destination. He finally reached the sill and felt a bit of his original excitement. This intrusion between older layers of sedimentary rock and beds of volcanic lava wasn't large but it was nearly horizontal and different from the surrounding rock. Erosion had stripped away the earth leaving a smooth and walkable tunnel. He climbed over debris and reached the lava tube.

The hard part was over. He checked himself. His boots were caked with mud and his sleeves had wet blotches. He hadn't noticed. He reached the instruments and took out a pod. Temperature was up; gases had spiked. He'd compare detailed data later, but definitely worrisome data. He downloaded the memory banks to his portable reader and replaced battery packs. He put the old batteries in his backpack, replaced the battery in the torch, tightened the straps and started back. He left the lava tube by sliding down over a pile of eroded debris.

The previous Tuesday he had followed this cavern all the way to the ancient Guanche cave of Belmaco a kilometer below. The scientist had triumphed over his grandfather's superstitions. Geology had revealed shafts and tributaries and told the island's history from its volcanic birth, to the eruptions, to the devastating collapses into the sea. The rocks were excellent guides because their information was undeniable. Still, he'd come to dead ends until, finally, the chamber looked vaguely familiar. His inner radar buzzed at a particular section. It was dry and lined with gravel, which meant it was close to the exterior of the mountain. He noted the vaulted ceiling and how it carried echoes—perfect for Guanche ceremonies. He examined the walls and then spotted the petroglyphs. Stacks of stones held together by mud and guano were nearby—the final resting place of a pre-Spanish native. The Guanches had reached this point from the opposite direction—from outside the mountain.

He exited. He savored the slopping landscape stretching in front of him, the familiar coastal towns below, and the ocean in the distance. A journey that began in the wrinkled palms of Abuelo Theo 20 years ago had come full circle. He was elated and, strangely, felt confident and secure. He belonged; the island's mysteries were neatly arrayed in front and threats no longer. The adult scientist had connected the tunnels and caverns to the cave he'd visited with Abuelo as a child. He had no need or reason to share the discovery with anyone.

Until now.

He'd go back to the Volcanological Station. He had work. He'd get exact figures of the changes to compare with those of the monitoring stations. The seismic network was made up of five analog 3-component and four 1-component short-period recorders. Computer systems processed the UHF analog signals relying on U.S. Geological Survey specs. Upgrades were planned to portable 3-component digital stations, which would tie in to the permanent seismic network.

He needed Isabella. Over the past month, he'd noticed some escalations in gaseous emissions and fluctuations in temperatures.

La Palma's 30-year eruptive cycle was nine years overdue. If today's preliminary observations confirmed a further jump, he'd have to sound the alarm. He had to quantify the changes. If the temperature and gas discharges were real, others would notice soon. He didn't have much time.

First, he'd talk to Isabella.

42
Avner Kishon

The International Hotel, Washington D.C.

"Wonderful trip. Every time I visit, I return energized and hopeful. Israel is a paradox; its existence is always in doubt but also a dream come true. So, I return to Washington an optimist, convinced that in pursuit of worthwhile ideals any obstacle can be overcome. Of course, optimism requires men of vision. In our profession, we do have the opportunity to befriend extraordinary individuals—a privilege really."

Avner Kishon lifted his glass of Carmel 1984 Cabernet Sauvignon (*a very good year*), paused, and looked directly into the eyes of his companion. Then he nodded ever so slightly to ensure his compliment was recognized. He continued, "Anna and Leah are thrilled to be back. My daughter considers Washington home. Three weeks in Israel were a monumental catastrophe for Leah. Spent every free moment on her mobile texting friends."

"With two daughters of my own, I know exactly what you mean. The young are connected the way we never were," Andrew Hansen replied while scanning the room ready to move on.

Kishon continued, "Leah is entering Georgetown next month. Anna and I are thrilled, of course, though her motives may not be purely academic. Several friends are already enrolled."

"The decisions and relationships made now will likely shape the rest of her life," Hansen was being perfunctory now.

Avner's mind, too, was beyond this parry and ready for a new front on his assault on the secretary. He barely heard the Secretary's comments.

"Yes. A good choice. That she attend is paramount regardless of the motivation. Eh, Mr. Secretary, I must broach a matter that I've recently been made aware of."

"Here, Ambassador?" A hint of irritation crept into the U.S. Secretary of State's voice. He did not relish a 15 minute canned speech in support of the latest Israeli incursion or its campaign to soften American objections. The Ambassador was expected to promote the Israeli agenda. After all, these gatherings facilitated one person's access to another. The larger an official's circle, the larger his cachet; as for lobbyists, it confirmed their access to the VIP. It was an exclusive club. Power and influence were the engines of the world but spoken of only behind closed doors.

The credo of "it's who you know" always applied. It had gotten Leah into Georgetown and Avner his ambassadorial posting. And now his access to Secretary of State Hansen for 10 precious minutes would elevate Avner Kishon even further. It would oblige the Secretary to him and catapult him into Washington's top echelon. Avner Kishon had dreamed of this opportunity since his posting three years ago.

In Washington, lobbyists, influence peddlers, and all those hoping to get anywhere were only as valuable as the ware they had to trade. Wooing the powerful and getting an audience were difficult. Suitors peddled their currency. Everyone strutted among crystals, jewelry, designer wardrobes, old and new money; deals were made; it wasn't very different from a bazaar.

Positioning was as intricate as the naval battles that had been fought in the flooded Roman Coliseum. There was little predictability, many unknowns, lots of contestants and spectacle galore. Thrills for everyone. If there was value, a feeding frenzy followed.

Timing and skill were everything. The surroundings were opulent, the Grecian columns stately and delicacies indispensable. Champagne, eveningwear, exquisitely sculpted hair on barebacked women were the trappings and larger than life. The occasional celebrity was fodder for those easily distracted by glitter and appearance. West Coast moguls were the biggest whales due to the media attention they commanded.

The currency of the evening was power. It was an aphrodisiac to men that dealt in capital and influence. The attendants, the women, and the supplicants were décor to pay homage to the movers and shakers. The wannabes thrust and parried. Sides and allegiances were fluid. Losing access or being left off an invitation list was as deadly as announcing cancer or one's impending funeral.

The pecking order in the room, the rush of adrenaline, the implied results, the maneuverings, and the unknown were factors bringing victory to the agile of mind. When a topic was raised, verbal acrobatics, feigned interest and jousting for position followed. Holding reserves and committing little was at the other end. Avner's goal tonight was simply to introduce an idea. The brief face-to-face moment was not to convince or debate. That would come later. Negotiations could begin only once the rules were laid out.

Secretary Hansen braced himself. *Here it comes*, he thought.

"My government in its fight against world terror has information of an impending attack on the United States. In view of our joint commitment to battling the scourge, Prime Minister Neharin is prepared to cooperate in the hope that American lives may be saved."

43

Tête-à-Tête

The International Hotel, Washington D.C.

"We are grateful for your country's anti-terror efforts. It affirms Israel as an ally of the United States and critical to the security of the entire Middle East. Surely there is a more appropriate venue for this discussion."

"In the interest of the lives at stake, I am not sure this should wait. Prime Minister Neharin knows that doubts exist regarding Israel's cooperation in intelligence matters and is determined to share all information with the United States as soon as possible."

"Not much to ask, Ambassador, for the $3 billion per year and 60 years of unwavering support we provide Israel. Every member of Congress publicly declares his commitment to the State of Israel. I'm sure you're also aware of my own efforts on Israel's behalf during my years at the U. N. Not an easy position, I assure you, considering the number of anti-Israeli resolutions I had to veto. If this is a pressing matter, you have my attention. Otherwise, I must make the rounds—protocol and pleasantries, you understand."

"Certainly, Mr. Secretary. Minister Talmi believes the threat is on the scale of Madrid or London."

The Secretary gave Kishon a direct and serious gaze. It was put up or shut up time.

Kishon knew he had the Secretary. He'd obsessed how to broach the topic. There was no going back. It was simple really. Once he mentioned a terrorist attack and that Israel had intelligence the U.S. did not, the Secretary had no choice but to listen. Kishon purposely did not mention the World Trade Center. That attack was larger than Madrid or London but had become cliché and alluding to it was rash given Kishon's lack of facts. Hansen would make that connection on his own. The 2001 terror attack influenced every decision America now made. Andrew Hansen, who had been U.S. representative to the U.N. during 9/11 could not but have it as a reference point.

The specifics of this attack pointed to a large operation, but Mossad had few details and no target. Lots of Muslim groups called for *jihad* against the U.S. With current security, most took the form of suicide bombings on airports, restaurants and other soft targets. But, this group felt different. They'd been in Palestine, in Cyprus, were making their way west, and had spoken of a new age for Islam with thousands of dead. Israel's cooperation was the smart move. The pro-Israeli lobby would pick up the cause and keep the matter in the public eye as long as they could. Avner's timely warning would reap him dividends for many years to come.

"Perhaps we should take a moment," Hansen said. He had to listen. If it were a ploy, he'd ostracize Kishon for a few months.

"Mr. Secretary, I would not mention this tonight…but my Ministry has in its possession a recording of several Muslim militants who are discussing an attack on the United States. Israel is prepared to make this recording available to you."

Hansen took a good look at Avner Kishon as if deciding how to respond. Then he looked at the men and women in tuxedos and glittering formal dresses and said, "In the hallway, second door on the left. We can speak there."

The two men separated. Kishon made his way to a group that included Senator Thursland. After a few pleasantries, he expressed appreciation for the Senator's recent votes in support of the President's initiative in the Middle East.

Hansen nodded to a few guests and made his way to the bar. He set his glass on the counter.

"Louis," he said, "I am ready for the Bowmore."

"Certainly, Sir." The bartender bent behind the deeply veneered oak bar and brought up a half-empty bottle of liquor.

"Looks like I need to replenish your stock, Louis. Henry will drop off a couple of bottles on Tuesday. Would that be all right?"

"Yes, Sir, Mr. Hansen. Henry and I will take care of it. No need to concern yourself."

Andrew Hansen had discovered the drink in the summer of 1972 when making his way through Scotland. He'd gone off route and ended up in the isle of Islay in the Hebrides. He had walked the last few miles to the bare Beinn Bheigier hilltop in howling wind. On his way, he'd identified the isles of Mull, Colonsay, and Jura to the north and Gigha and the Cinn Tire peninsula to the east. Off to the west, on the edge of Loch Indail lay the village of Bowmore. He'd been seduced by the bleak landscape and the equally austere streets of the tiny community. He stayed for a month. He had intended to be reckless, but the solemnity of the town and the earnestness of the residents placed extreme significance on every little thing. There was little time for foolishness; survival was a fulltime preoccupation. During his stay, a WWII veteran died. He remembered the funeral procession to the round whitewashed Kilarrow Parish Church at the cross of Main and High Streets. He left a week later a confused young man but deeply aware and appreciative of his own parents' sacrifices. In Bowmore, he'd gained the willingness to consider viewpoints other than his own. A year later, he was no longer the self-centered esthete he had been.

The rich Islay peat flavor of the whisky had become an island of solace. He had sought it out in his thirties as a connection to that critical summer. He stayed in contact with Mag Raith and his supply was assured direct. He pictured rows of barrels resting in the damp earthen vaults below sea level just as he'd seen them. Water poured into the distillery from the hills above the Village. Peat fed the fires under the kilns that dried the malt. He savored the smoky flavor of the Bowmore

Islay Single Malt. This particular batch had come unannounced and unordered. When he opened the case, he understood why. The past had caught up with him; it was the 36-year-old 1980 vintage.

While Louis refilled his glass, Hanson pulled out a cigar. Holding the glass and the unlit cigar in one hand, he made his way to the door as if to locate a smoking area. Outside, he turned left and moved down the hall until he faced a door. Once inside, he headed for a couch bound in worn burgundy leather and sat. He lit the cigar and crossed his legs. He rested his elbow on the arm of the chair and held the cigar several inches from his face while the smoke streamed towards the ceiling 14 feet above. He took a slow and long drag and exhaled peacefully. He moved the whisky glass close. Slowly and deliberately, he sent his senses out in search of its aroma and of the solace of days gone by.

44
Quid Pro Quo

The International Hotel, Washington D.C.

After the second drag, Hansen looked around for an ashtray. He found it next to the Tiffany lamp on his left. He picked it up, moved it to the coffee table in front of him, and tapped ashes into it. After what seemed too short a time of tranquility, the door opened and Avner Kishon put his head in as if ensuring he had the correct room.

"Come in, Ambassador. Please sit."

"Thank you, Mr. Secretary. I know your time is valuable so I will make this brief. The Mossad has had a group of terrorists under surveillance for a time and has recorded a conversation that mentions a large-scale attack on the United States."

"Our intelligence services would like to examine this recording."

"I can assure you of its authenticity."

"Can I assume that you'd like something in return?" Hansen's eyes dug into Kishon's and pinned him.

"Mr. Secretary, no one wants another mass casualty event. Israel remains at war 70 years after its creation and our citizens face attacks every day."

The charade had gone on long enough. Either there was pertinent intelligence or not. Hansen knew the information would be his and that Kishon, at this point, could not but hand it over. If an attack occurred and the Israelis knew about it and hadn't shared the intel, it would not bode well for them. So the issue was, what did they want in return? Put it on the table and don't belabor it. He decided to forego the niceties.

"That your country is at war after so many efforts–including my own—is interpreted by many as lacking the desire for peace. Then there is, of course, the hypocrisy of enjoying nationhood but denying it to others. The advantages of constant warfare are not lost on me. Reprisals, incursions over national borders, and violating a host of international laws come to mind. Shall I continue?"

"Jews have been subjected to abhorrent treatment for thousands of years. If we are afforded additional leeway, it is deservedly so. Certainly that is not a position that can be defended publically or win you popularity. In fact, it will be seen as anti-Israeli."

You bastard, thought Hansen. *You assassinate anyone you wish, make the U.S. your whore, and you lecture me? You have no idea what I'm willing to risk.*

"Mr. Ambassador, popularity is overrated and has never appealed to me. And, as mine is an appointed position, I have leeway I did not have in earlier years. Now, if this is a credible threat, I am confident that the President and the American public will certainly show their gratitude to Israel."

"There are many in Israel that consider Prime Minister Neharin too close to the peace camp doves. If he is to survive no-confidence votes or hope to be reelected next year, he must appease the hardliners. An attack on Palestinians would serve this purpose but no one, here or in Israel, looks forward to another conflict. The Prime Minister can win the election if, say, he secures the release of Yonatan Meir. He and his advisors are confident the political windfall and publicity will return him to power where he can realize his political programs. We're talking about the Prime Minister's political survival."

There it was, thought Hansen. *The spy, Yonatan Meir. Again.*

Hansen decided to start softly and build from there; just like a rejection letter. Don't say no on the first line. Explain and justify first so rejection appears justified. He looked as if contemplating the offer and drew on the cigar.

Yes, he would remind the President of Israel's assistance in fighting terror, of humanitarian reasons for Meir's release, his deteriorating health, time served, similar precedents, and the "unfairness" of the sentence. He would recommend release and point to the benefits of Prime Minister Neharin's reelection. But, in the end, it was all he could do. It was still the President's decision and not a popular one.

He ended with, "You know the Meir case is very difficult. Bush Sr., Clinton, Bush Jr. and Obama had all supported clemency but had to backtrack in the end. Release is too unpopular. Meir's name is synonymous with Israeli anti-Americanism. The U.S. has been more than accommodating. All Israelis connected with Meir were given immunity. Meir was charged with only one count of espionage—he deserved treason for the thousands of documents he stole and years of treachery. And, I must point out, Israel denied the man was a spy and refused to cooperate for a decade. Even when Israel came to the table, you made our life miserable..."

"All unfortunate and in the past—and not this government's doing. Prime Minister Neharin pledges his full cooperation."

"The individuals have changed, but it remains to be seen if Israeli policy has changed."

"We are fighting for our survival as a country and as a people. The actions and policies we pursue are necessary—they may seem questionable to nations not similarly threatened. We must act in our self interest in matters of grave national security."

Hansen would end it now. The debate could go on forever like this.

"Perhaps this overture by Israel will be a harbinger of cooperation between our countries in their common struggle against terrorism. Possibly a precedent for mutually beneficial intelligence in the future."

Hansen got up.

"It is my fervent wish also, Mr. Secretary," Avner said and followed suit.

The two men approached each other and shook hands. Hansen took Avner's hand in both his palms and held it an extra second.

"I want to express my personal gratitude as well as that of the United States for alerting us to this terror threat. I will brief the President regarding Prime Minister Neharin's reelection efforts and consider how the U.S. can support him—through Meir's release or other means."

"Thank you. That is all we ask. Our services will relay an electronic copy of the terrorist conversation within the hour."

Kishon turned and left. Hansen sat in the leather sofa and looked at his cigar. It had gone out. He took hold of it. He relit it and savored a few solitary moments while he rehashed the conversation with Kishon.

"Let's hope it's nothing," he muttered.

45

Haboob

Sahel, Southwest Algeria

This particularly desolate stretch of the Sahara was in western Algeria but it could just as easily have been in Morocco. There was no border, no man made demarcation separating the Algerian province of Bechar from Morocco's Figuig; there was no need for borders in the middle of hundreds of kilometers of barrenness and sand.

This day the sun beat mercilessly from the moment it rose in the morning in a purple hue. The frigid night air passed the freezing mark, and then shot up another 74 degrees until it hit 122 degrees Fahrenheit. Such extreme ranges between highs and lows were normal here because of the lack of vegetation and the few natural features in the desert.

Nothing hindered the hot air from turning to a light breeze. It rose vertically above the desert and horizontally across it. Fine dust loosened and started a tiny dance. Then ever so slowly, lighter sand particles began to creep along the silicate surface. As the air strengthened, larger and larger granules lifted, became suspended in the air currents, and swirled this way and that with the breeze. Heavier grains rose and fell back to the ground. The process repeated billions of times, and more grains and more dust were dislodged from their resting place. Soon, the turmoil crossed a critical threshold and became a breeze. Then it further intensified and turned into a wind. Grains leapt over each other in a process known as saltation until square miles crept along.

Air rising from the earth's surface normally meets colder air in the atmosphere, which weakens it and stops its upward movement. Except, that is, during a temperature inversion when the rising hot air meets more hot air in the atmosphere. The inversion on this July day extended for several miles. What would have been a minor wind on most days now became a major sand storm.

In the Sahara, 70 to 80 such sand storms form every year. The larger storms come from central Sahara and head west into the Atlantic. They pass over the Canaries, cross the ocean and drop millions of pounds of sand in the Atlantic, the Caribbean, and Florida. Storms originating in Northern Sahara are channeled by the Atlas Mountains to the Mediterranean where, weakened by moist sea air, they collapse or make land in Europe's southern countries where they drop their sand.

In Algeria's Bechar, this storm found little vertical and horizontal resistance, and so gathered strength until its wall of dust and sand extended a full mile into the atmosphere. Strong air pressure gradients amplified the wind's speed until the haboob gorged and extended 50 square miles.

The small towns in the sparsely populated region came alive. Women pulled their clothes from wash lines outside single-level cement houses and called children in from their games. Shutters closed against the dust. Villagers knew the routine from infancy.

The nomads of Ouled Sidi Cheikh were not surprised by how quickly the desert turned into a simoon. Many traveled by truck now, but knew to stop and hunker down until the storm passed. Few knew the mechanics of the friction between ground and sand that created static electrical fields, which gave the ground positive charges and the moving particles negative. This electrical interplay on the atomic level lifted twice the volume of sand than physical forces alone. The Arabs and Berbers sealed every orifice until the danger passed.

The storm headed northwest at about 50 miles per hour. Once over the sea between Morocco and Spain, it would mix with moist air and weaken but it would make it across the Mediterranean. It would finally collapse and deposit thousands of pounds of sand over Spain's Granada Province.

The mile-high wall of turbulent sand approached Alhuceima and the terrorist boat. It blanketed the ground and darkened the atmosphere with an ominous dark fury.

46
Hertz

Airspace Over the Atlantic Coast of Spain

After his visit with the Intelligence brass, DARPA's Charlie Fui gathered his robotic engineers and gave them an abbreviated overview of the mission—just enough to get them salivating.

They were young and eager and they'd not pass up the chance to use the MAVs in a live operation. Going to the Mediterranean to use the equipment and technology in a live mission was an adventure. Jittery with excitement, they packed their PCs and experimental micro-air vehicles for the transatlantic flight.

They landed in Rota in southwestern Spain across the bay from Cadiz. The U.S. naval Station in Rota occupies 6,000 acres and consists of Air Force and NATO squadrons, cargo, fuel, and ammunition units. It has a 670-acre airfield, three piers, the Amphibious Readiness Group, and a staff of 3,000 men. But, Rota was 250 miles from the boat anchored in Morocco's Alhuceima Bay.

They had brought six D-flies, replacement parts, and several cases of interchangeable payload canisters of nerve agents, miniature explosives, experimental power packs, and miniature video cameras with IR, digital imaging, and live feed capabilities. Other cases contained the control center PCs, signal enhanced communication devices, and joystick units.

The first generation of Unmanned Aerial Vehicles were mostly normal aircraft modified to operate remotely. The next generation contained sophisticated technology tailored for missions like gathering intelligence, terrain mapping and supply drops into Afghanistan and Iraq. At the end of the Afghanistan War, they'd been used in targeted missions—a euphemism for remotely controlled assassinations from the air. The FAA had even given the larger and better-funded Global Hawk use of civilian air corridors and the ability to file its own flight path.

Micro-air vehicles were small, stealthy, and cost a lot less. On the down side, their range was limited and they were fragile. The MAV team would have to get very close to Alhuceima Bay and launch from the ground.

In a compromise, a SEAL team was accompanying the DARPA Forward Cell to perform clean up. Now they were all aboard a CH-47 Chinook heavy lift helicopter heading to Alhuceima Bay.

The MAVs would reconnoiter with the boat, surprise the terrorists and incapacitate them. The SEAL team would haul the prisoners back to the chopper. They'd take off and disappear into the night. Each team had 45 minutes for its part. MAV cameras would monitor from above. The SEALs would approach below water. MAV technology would minimize risk to personnel and render the terrorists immobile before they realized what was happening.

Charlie's insides shook and became one with the Chinook's vibrations. The chopper's metal framework, the engine's 3,700 horses, and he fused into one moving part. He no longer remembered what it felt like not to shake; all he knew was that he preferred it to this.

"Dr. Fui, ETA is 90 minutes," Flight Engineer Matt Herzenstahl came in over his helmet. Herzenstahl had introduced himself in Rota, and had added, "Call me, Hertz; everyone does." Hertz was the third member of the three-man crew that operated the Chinook; he was their liaison, he said.

Hertz was saying, "We're leaving Europe below. That's Africa over there. We'll follow the coast, and then head over the ocean in a more direct route to Alhuceima. That's Jebel Mousa—one of the Pillars of Hercules."

Erica was surprised at the arcane information that had just come from the mouth of maybe a 22-year-old. Hertz, on his first posting to Rota, had seen how eagerly the young Spanish officers coveted working with U.S. equipment. Following their lead, he'd learned that command of information made him valuable. He had earned his superiors' trust and was given more responsibility, which meant others deferred to him. Hertz was all about leeway.

Erica's look did not escape Hertz. He played along and responded with a mischievously coy look of his own, "Gibraltar is the other pillar—as in Prometheus, as in the Golden Apples," he added with a twinkle in his eye.

Before Erica could respond, Hertz didn't belabor the point, "I've been here a few times," he explained. "Exercises and all."

"How come we can't see Gibraltar?" Erica asked. "I thought we'd cross there."

"It's further east—our route is more direct," Hertz answered.

47
Plazas de Soberanías

Airspace Over Moroccan Coast, Mediterranean Sea

On leaving Rota, they had headed south. The Chinook stayed a few miles offshore to move down the Atlantic. Now over Gibraltar, cargo ships of all types and sizes could be seen waiting to cross to the Mediterranean or head out to the Atlantic.

Once in Africa, the helo picked up the coast and moved east to skirt the Spanish city of Ceuta. Spain had lived under threat of invasion from North Arica for 400 years and had fortified several islands off the coasts of Morocco and Algeria to keep Berbers and Arabs at bay. Several were still Spanish. The MAV and SEAL teams would launch their operation from one of these Spanish Sovereign Areas.

"Half an hour, Doc," the pilot interrupted. "Suggest final checks."

"We're ready," Charlie answered. "Communication over this noise might be an issue. We are not used it. We'll be launch-ready ten minutes after landing."

"We'll power down as soon as we land. You won't have any noise," Captain Brubaker said. His tone was, and had been from the start, one of military precision. He had not said one unnecessary word.

As soon as the Captain was off the commlink, Hertz came on, "Alright, let's go over landing one last time. Ready? Alhuceima will be on the right just past a rocky peninsula. The target boat is in the harbor—about a mile off shore. We'll get exact coordinates when we get there."

He paused for effect.

"We're going past the city and the bay to a group of three small islands. They're in Moroccan waters but the islands are Spanish. Our cover is good as long as we don't get too close to shore. Everyone follow so far?"

Hertz youth belied his professionalism. He had enlisted straight out of high school and was now in his fourth year. He looked at the SEAL commander, then at Charlie Fui who nodded, then glanced at Erica, Kyle, James and Taqo.

"There are three islands, 5.5 clicks past the bay. The most identifiable one is the one farthest away; it looks like a fortified building sitting atop the water about a half a mile from the beach. In fact, it's a manned garrison with 60 Spaniards, a couple of houses and a church— essentially a fort on top of a rock. That's for reference; we are not landing there. The other two, the Islote de Mar and Islote de Tierra, are closer to Alhuceima. All three are tiny, measured in square meters. We're landing on the flat barren one, the Islote de Mar. As soon as we touch down, you'll exit the chopper through the rear bay doors, find a suitable spot and set up. Use the chopper for cover. Commander Wartel and the SEALs will secure the area and get their gear in the water. The Islote de Mar is about a mile from the beach so visibility and appearances are important. As soon as the chopper is down, Captain Brubaker will power down the engines."

"How long for the power-down?" Kyle asked.

"Under a minute. We have a couple things going for us. The islands have been Spanish for centuries and the locals are used to seeing Spanish personnel. You may have noticed the chopper's colors are Spanish. The Islote de Tierra is in front of the Islote de Mar so we'll have some additional cover.

'Now, a chopper this large is going to get noticed, no matter what. It will be dusk, but still...We take off as soon as you're done.

Commander Wartel, that means you might be transporting your prisoners in the dark."

"Already taken into account—not a problem," replied Wartel, the SEAL commander.

Hertz continued, "We should be out in 90 minutes. You folks handle your end. Any questions?"

Before anyone had a chance to respond, the Captain came in over their helmets, "Twenty minutes to touchdown."

Hertz jumped in, "Conditions on location, sir?"

"Eighty-five degrees Fahrenheit with 5 to 10 knot winds."

"We'll take it," said Erica. "At least the weather is on our side."

"Now we're talking," Taqo smiled eagerly. "Might have time for a dip after all."

Everyone's stares pinned Taqo.

"Are you *kidding* me?" Wartel asked incredulously.

"What?" Taqo said, feigning a hurt look as if taking a dip was the most natural thing in the world. "It's July, the Mediterranean. Eighty-five degrees."

Erica shook her head as if she couldn't believe the gall of some people. Micro-vehicles and a swim shared the same space in Taqo's mind.

"We're about to kidnap some nasties and you're talking about swimming. You might want to take things a bit more seriously," Erika complained.

"Have I ever let you down? The SEALs will take care of the nasties. Yesterday, Ohio; today, the Mediterranean. Maybe you'll change your mind when you have a half hour dead time," he winked, his spirit and optimism intact.

"Yeah, well, while you're thinking of yourself, *I*," Erica said emphasizing the 'I' and pausing for effect, "am concerned about the distance to the boat," she said soberly as if Taqo's flippancy reminded her of everything that could go wrong.

"We'll be fine," James reassured her. "Taqo is just being Taqo. Conditions are excellent…not an issue. The energy cells will hold up. You'll see."

"And we can always ditch if we have to. Won't happen, though, not with me at the controls," Taqo added needling her some more.

Hertz followed the back and forth banter for a moment then his focus drifted off as if listening. He raised his hand, "Hold on," he asked for quiet. "Something's coming in."

"Confirm current speed and ETA our location," he said into his helmet.

Thirty seconds later Brubaker, the pilot, broke in. Everyone heard the urgency in his voice, "Folks, Dr. Fui, Rota just reported a large dust storm is headed our way. Approaching at a nice clip."

"So much for my swim," Taqo said dejected. "You had to jinx it."

48

Jitters

Airspace Over Alhuceima, Morocco

"The sand storm is heading straight for us," Brubaker, the Chinook pilot, said in their helmets.

"What does that mean, Captain? How much time does that leave us?" asked Charlie Fui.

"Moving at 35 to 50 knots. Maybe three hours."

"Does that give us enough time?" "Aw, shit." "Are we still a go?" "We're not aborting, are we?" Groans rose from Erica, Taqo, Kyle, and James.

"Rota says it stretches for 50 square miles; high winds, tons of sand. I can outrun it but can't fly through it. Pretty common around here given how close the Sahara is. Rota says if you think you've got time, go ahead, if not, we're heading back."

"Give me five minutes," Charlie said his lips tight with tension.

They would use gas canisters in the D-flies to knock the men out. The four-man SEAL team would recover the bodies and haul them to the chopper. But, that was before the storm. They had less than three hours.

"O.K. gentlemen," Charlie said, "listen up. The original timetable is out. We've got two hours and one for safety. That leaves one hour for our end and one for the SEALs. Is this do-able or do we abort?" He paused, locked eyes with the group, "Now's the time to speak up, people."

"We'll *never* get a chance like this again, or data as authentic," Erica said. "If we succeed here we'll never have to beg for research money again."

"A lot's at stake, no doubt. If there's a chance we can pull it off, we do it," James, the MAV pilot, concurred.

"I'll hate myself if we don't get the D-flies in the air after coming all this way," Taqo added.

A somber mood settled over the group. No one spoke for a few seconds while considering possible scenarios.

"Maybe we can get the chopper closer to the target and launch from there. Minimize D-fly travel time," James said.

"Maybe we can land on the beach in Morocco," Taqo added.

"That will cut recon time down to 10-15 minutes," Kyle said slowly. "Take a quick look and engage."

Erica turned to face him, "Lots of unknowns. We have no idea how long it will take to get close. If we're spotted, it's over."

"True, so let's get there and find out what we're dealing with," Taqo insisted.

"Can't know ahead of time how long recon will take," Erica insisted.

"Lots can screw this up. We set aside 15 minutes for the boat. I don't see any way of speeding that up," Charlie summed up.

"Bypass the diagnostics…that'll help. Inspection back at Wright-Pat is good enough. I know it's against protocol."

"That gets us another 10 minutes."

"Commander," Charlie asked Wartel, "what do you think?"

Wartel, the SEAL commander, sucked in some air, controlled his breathing and shifted his weight. Techies had no idea of the variables that went into live operations—which was strange since they knew that the simplest task was highly complex from a technical point of view. He forced his mind to think logically and control the adrenaline pumping through him. He was not in command here, he reminded himself for the umpteenth time. But, he'd be damned if he didn't say his piece. He'd not let these R and D types bungle the mission. It wouldn't do anyone any good. They'd taken an easy mission and complicated it by not giving him full control.

"Changing launch sites is not a good idea," he said matter-of-factly.

"Why?" Charlie said patiently.

Wartel shifted his weight to his other leg.

"If we land on the beach, the whole city will have a front row seat. Do we want to deal with sovereign air space violations? Accusations of kidnapping? Changing anything this close to zero hour will only make things more difficult."

"Circumstances have changed," Taqo blurted out. "We've got a dust storm on the way and we're not in Kansas anymore. We adapt," he added seriously. "Let's take these guys down quick."

"Yeah, well, landing on a beach in full view of thousands of Moroccans is not the way to do it. Look, two teams with two agendas only increases uncertainty. I'm not comfortable with it—that's not how SEALs operate. The simpler things are, the less chance of a screw up. I say scrap your end of the mission completely."

Then staring at Taqo, "I *am* adapting to the situation. My team runs the whole operation out of the inflatable. The DPD will get us under the boat. The hostiles will never know what hit them."

Everyone stared stunned. Then Erica ventured, "And the DPD is?"

"Diver Propulsion Device. It'll get us under the boat in less than 10 minutes. We take the men out and bring them back. It's not that complicated."

"Commander, our orders are to use the MAVs to ensure the hostiles are taken alive for interrogation. I can't believe you want to eliminate the drones minutes from launch. You said it yourself…simpler is better and the simplest is to stick to the plan we've prepared for. We're using both teams."

Hertz intervened, "But, sir, we can't land on Moroccan territory. There are eyes in the sky, radar, and spy sats. Whatever we do is going to be recorded. The Air Force will find out—maybe not in real time but soon enough. We can't justify landing in Morocco. There's going to be hell to pay. We need permission."

"So there is a down side to technology…," Taqo said slowly as if revealing a truth that had escaped the rest.

All eyes turned towards him ready to pounce on him for another flippant remark. Met with a grim and steady gaze, no one complained.

"Ten minutes to touchdown folks. I need a decision," the pilot asked over the din of the chopper.

"We have a go, Captain," Charlie said.

Charlie looked up, "O.K. We stick to the original plan," he said with conviction. "We launch the drones. Commander Wartel, get your men under that boat as soon as you can and hold position. Once we have a visual, we decide if we're using gas or your men for the take down."

"Yes, sir," Wartel said. He may have had misgivings, but he'd gotten his orders and he'd make things work. He turned and went to his men.

Charlie now faced his team, "Unpack our equipment. Take only what's absolutely necessary—no cases, no spare cameras, install the nerve agents. Power up control stations, now, before we land. Assemble the control units and load the energy cells. We'll take everything off the chopper juiced up. I want to be launch-ready five minutes after touchdown. That will give us another 10-15 minutes on top of what we manage to save on the boat. Go."

They scrambled to follow Charlie's orders. Erica grabbed her monitoring equipment and the two pilots readied their sets and hookups. Kyle moved storage cases to the front of the chopper while Taqo and James collected equipment by the rear bay door. Wartel and his men hoisted their packs. They freed the long metallic DPD from its straps and one SEAL carried the large pack that would become the inflatable boat.

"One minute to touchdown," the pilot, Brubaker, announced.

49
Native Son

Café Solipsista, Los Llanos de Aridane, La Palma

"Were you keeping it from me? Did you think I wouldn't find out? *È un segreto?*"

"No, of course not. I didn't hide it."

"We've been colleagues for months, *e ho scoperto adesso?*"

He looked at her blankly.

Isabella explained the Italian, "I find out now? We talk about everything, the programs, the research, the morphology, *i ristoranti che preferiamo*—and you never tell me you are born here?"

"It was not related to what we were talking about."

"Nothing to do with Cumbre Vieja, Taburiente, the *galerias? Tutto deve essere noto a tutti.* I explain everything and you never say you know *queste cose. Sono andato avanti e avanti pensando che sto dicendo informazioni che non hanno e non dite niente?* This is a *commedia* to you?"

"English please. I don't understand everything you're saying. No, I never hide where I was born. I just didn't advertise it. You were explaining the seismology, the growth stages, the collapses, the tremors, the scarps, the *dorsales*…well, I knew about the *dorsales*…but you made connections for me… really…I listened to everything you said…"

"But you're the geologist! I...I should ask you questions."

"I don't' know much about La Palma's geologic formation, and..."

He stopped.

"Say it."

"It was refreshing to hear talk about the island's creation and...you were so... passionate..."

She was staring at him, but he saw her waver. Her eyes were no longer angry but she seemed unsure of his sincerity and motives.

"*Grazie*...I guess," she finally broke the silence.

"I've been to some locations—well to most—but there are many I don't know," Enrique now explained himself. "Besides I was young when I left. That was eight years ago. I know La Palma surficially, but the geology...not so much. Things are different than I remember. You explained so much and the research..."

"You are familiar with the *Calle de la Montana* and the *Observatorios!*" she announced as if it was a new revelation. "I talked and talked...and I described the clouds cascading down the mountains...I was foolish!"

Now Enrique smiled good-naturedly. Then he mimicked her accent, "'*Gli osservatori guardano in cielo, ma i vulcani ci ricordano l'inferno sotto di.*' My Italian is not good, but I think you said, 'The obsevatories look into heaven, but the volcanoes are a reminder of the hell below.'"

"Now you make fun..."

"No. It's a compliment." He stopped and looked embarrassed not knowing how to finish, unsure if he'd gone too far.

She took in what he said but said nothing in return. If he had expected her to verbally joust with him, she didn't. She looked off into the distance but did not really see the mountains towering in front. She became oblivious to his presence and their surroundings.

He let her be.

She was atop the Roque de los Muchachos ridge, 2426 meters high, looking at Enrique and her own back from behind. The Dutch Open Telescope was at one side and a dozen other observatories dotted other parts of the ridge. Taburiente, the largest erosion crater on the planet, stretched below them. In her mind, she saw the vegetation and Canary Palms among the volcanic landscape and in the ravines and collapses that stretched to the ocean. Instead, she was staring at the top of an immense cotton cloud that was cascading over Cumbre Nueva and dropping hundreds of meters into the caldera blanketing everything below. Only the peaks of de la Cruz, de la Nieve, and Colorado broke through the pillowy layer and interrupted the whiteness that extended for several kilometers. The atmosphere in the shape of an immense dome, blue and limitless, stretched everywhere above; beyond, she imagined dark space extending forever into the galaxy. Next, she saw an image of the two of them standing like obelisks atop the pristine landscape and framed against the horizon. She became unsettled. Maybe it was the clouds hiding everything below and hiding the volcanic terrain, which continued for six kilometers to the volcano's base at the bottom of the Atlantic Ocean. All of a sudden, she was in awe of the immensity of some things and the insignificance of others.

Enrique was in agony. His mind struggled to bridge the void that had opened between them. He was teetering on the edge of a scarp, and the next few minutes would determine a big part of his future. Was there a future with this woman? Did he dare imagine one? He turned and focused in the distance where the sea met the sky and the two blended into a single indistinguishable boundary. He remembered staring at the line in the horizon as a boy and wondering what lay beyond. His earliest memory was swaddling around the house's veranda and feeling tiny between the immense mountain walls to the east and the ocean and sky that culminated at the horizon to the west. His head was inside the balcony's wrought iron rails that encircled the balcony on the second floor of the house and staring. Then, he was in the present of a few months ago when he'd returned and seen his ancestral home again. Patches of grey moss covered roof tiles that had once been an earthen bright red and he was shocked at how small and low everything really was. School in Oregon must have something to do with that, he guessed. He'd first ventured into the world by crawling on all fours around this balcony. The limitless sky, the impenetrable ocean, and the island had been his world for 18 years. Now he understood the lesson they'd been trying to teach — that life and space were limitless and rare things.

His identity had been shaped and was now framed by this land, this ocean, and this sky. They had beckoned and had created his wonder and fueled his desires. Now he knew that heeding their call and discovering what they held in trust for him was his life's calling. He'd discover and understand. They'd always define who he was.

"If you're going to explain, now is the time," Isabella broke into his reverie.

50
Tremors

Café Solipsista, Los Llanos de Aridane, La Palma

Isabella's voice was calm but contained a hint of curiosity as if the scientist in her had concluded that Enrique was harmless. He was nothing like the scientists that passed through the observatories and the Instituto on the obligatory tour. They never saw her an equal; they were interested in Isabella the attractive younger woman. She had guarded against their ilk since her first year at university. They might be experts in their field but utterly presumptuous when it came to male-female relationships. She was an oddity in the male dominated earth-sciences field. She had forged ahead and let the privileged but crass idiots gaze after her. Soon she got into the habit of thinking them delusional—that they thought themselves superior to defend against their shortcomings. Didn't they understand that women selected their mates? That they had criteria? Maybe cavemen took their females by force, but today even patriarchal fathers had little say on their daughters' choices of males. A man often found himself alongside a woman having little idea how he'd gotten there.

Isabella's Italian-Swiss upbringing had given her a light complexion and faint brown freckles. That, and her wildly unkempt sandy hair flowing in wavy streams made her relationships with men, in their minds, physical first and maybe later, with effort on her part, professional.

"Maybe I could have mentioned it sooner…but you didn't make it easy. You were on a roll…"

"What does that mean?"

"It's an American expression—it means I couldn't stop you. I learned how remote La Palma was when I went to university. It made me insecure, while you grew up in Milano; you have confidence and you knew everyone at the Instituto. You were intimidating…"

He paused, and then blurted out, "I was in awe…"

"And you couldn't stop me?"

"No. You were so passionate about the morphology…I saw places the way you described them, not the way I remembered them…I could not tell you I'd been to some of the places. I mean…I hadn't seen them the way you did. I'm trying to explain. I had good reasons for not telling you. I mean—it wasn't right not to tell you but I didn't trick you or lie to you. Now, I'm not sure what I'm saying, or how to say it."

She looked into his eyes and saw his earnestness. She held his eyes for what seemed many seconds. She looked and looked without blinking as if following the darkness in his eyes back to their innermost core.

"Say something," he finally said, self-conscious, his voice pleading.

"I'm trying to decide," she replied. "You compliment me, but I think I should be angry."

She wasn't however. Her face had softened and her defenses had dropped. She was teasing him.

"Now wait," he responded having gotten his wind back. "That's not fair. I was born here and I wanted to be stationed here. But, La Palma is not how I left it—I mean the land is the same but…things are different. I grew up with the sea and the mountains, but coming back from the university, everything is different. I never thought I'd have this dilemma. It's not been easy. I've changed, but nobody else has—not my family and not my friends. You helped me make sense of things I've been trying to understand for a long time. The caverns and the tremors we felt on Tuesday…" he stopped.

"Something is troubling you? Before you found *mi prospettiva* fascinating, now it's the geology?"

She lowered her eyes and took hold of the cappuccino in front of her. The white ceramic cup with the green and red stripes approached her mouth and her lips parted ever so slightly. She touched the cup as if planting a delicate kiss on the cheek of a three-month old baby. Her lips took on a shade of cinnamon moistness. She savored the coffee rather than actually drank it. Then, instead of setting the cup down, she held it with both hands halfway between the metal table and her glistening lips. She stared off into the distance where a forest of laurel trees formed a band of subtropical hardwoods part way up the otherwise grassy sides of the Cumbre Nueva.

"I remember my grandfather telling me about the tremors and the eruptions he lived through. I've gone about 800 meters inside Cumbre Vieja…and taken some worrisome measurements. I think it's going to erupt."

Isabella was shocked. "You've gone 800 meters in? How is that even possible?" she managed to ask.

51
Note to Self

Islote de Mar, Moroccan Coast

The five members of the micro-drone team stood by the chopper's bay doors holding their equipment and waiting to disembark. Every face was tense. They were, after all, a research and development team. Prior to this, they'd only been on controlled field tests in secure environments. Now a real-world mission was seconds away and the stakes were huge. They'd rushed the D-flies into service and weren't in the laboratory where conditions were monitored and adjustable.

The whop-whop coming from the Chinook's rotors was deafening because the side door was open. The rumble of the two power plants sounded mechanical and menacing signaling they were unforgiving and that life and death were near each other.

The stakes were high. Erica's mind flooded with worry. She felt out of sorts the way one's conscience is nags when an item is misplaced and can't be located. It was all she could think of. She was anxious to get started, but the chopper had to land first. They stared at the Moroccan coast and the tiny rocky islet below them in the sea. The few shrubs amongst the rocks were really no cover. They'd be visible from Morocco.

Wartel and his men would perform a quick recon of the Islote de Mar and give the all clear. Erica and the others would rush and set up the control stations.

The tiny island had no noteworthy geographic features and a few low and spiny acanthoclada type shrubs hardy enough to withstand the salt. The Islote de Mar was nothing more than an elongated flat rock 850 feet long by 215 feet wide and barely rose 15 feet above water. It was partially hidden from the coast by its sister rocky ledge the Islote de Tierra. Only 200 meters separated the two.

Hertz opened the side door and leaned out of the Chinook. Wartel moved to the center of the opening and scanned the terrain below. The others stirred and held their equipment ready to exit from the Chinook's large bay door. As soon as the helicopter touched down, its rear wall would open like a drawbridge and become a ramp.

The first order of business was to pick a spot near the Chinook for the control stations. It had to be fairly flat, but given the low speed of the micro-air vehicles and their tiny size, any flat 15 feet would do. Then the D-fly team was on its own. Wartel and his men would get the inflatable boat and the DPD into the water and launch. The D-flies should be in the air heading for the boat in less than ten minutes.

Wartel, in helmet, glasses, and pack, jumped off when the chopper was about four feet above the rock. His main weapon was on his back and a sidearm was strapped to his thigh. His bent knees and torso absorbed the weight of his body and his pack. Charlie Fui stood behind Wartel holding a black plastic case.

The chopper jerked as it touched down. Hertz began working the bay door and the inside of the chopper lit up as natural light seeped in. The intense white-yellows of day were waning but the sun wouldn't go down for another three hours over the flat Mediterranean Sea. A SEAL scrambled out, took point position and then made eye contact with Wartel while his mouth spoke unheard words into his helmet. They waited for the SEALs to give the "All Clear" and Charlie's team rushed out. The SEAL indicated the large arc behind the chopper from which they were to choose a location for a base.

The Chinook's engines powered down. Charlie chose the spot he wanted. James and Taqo dropped to their knees, unfolded tables, and then placed the control stations on top. In two minutes, they were in their seats calibrating controls and syncing communications.

"Ready? Like we planned. I'll hover at 200 feet while you make the first pass at 700. Let's see what's doing on that boat."

"Ready when you are. Here we go. Lifting off."

Both men held their joysticks and became oblivious to the water lapping across the rocks feet from their workstations. Taqo's MAV would conduct initial surveillance as its camera had higher resolution and infrared sensors that could identify heat signatures on the boat. First, they'd locate the occupants and get an idea of the boat's interior layout. Then, they'd decide on the next step.

On the screens, the target vessel was in the foreground. The boat was separated from other vessels hundreds of meters. To the right was the rocky quay that protected the harbor and gave it a boundary. In the background, the city of Alhuceima was nestled under a large hill. The terrorists had unloaded their cargo of men and detonators on a deserted beach several miles away and then anchored closer to Alhuceima.

"Approaching position now," Taqo declared, looking intently into his monitor. "The glare is brutal on these screens," he added. He grabbed the edge of the screen and moved it to the left. Then after a momentary pause added, "Note to self: 'Recommend equipping monitors with visors. Possibly a tarp for sunny conditions. Would be nice to jury-rig a shade for now.'"

"I'll make a note of it," Erica said condescendingly.

"I'm serious," Taqo said looking up. "The picture would be so much better if we reduced this glare." He flashed the Taqo smile that was his passport to things denied everyone else. He became serious and turned to his monitor with renewed concentration.

"Bogey next to our target," he announced a moment later. Then, "It's a small skiff."

"Now what?" an annoyed Charlie responded. "Don't forget the storm." He bent next to Taqo's cheek to peer into the monitor.

"Beginning initial survey now. First pass at 700 feet. Let me zoom in…make that a motorboat. A single individual is handing off items to two men in the larger boat. Maybe provisions? Should I descend for a closer look?"

"Go to max resolution. Check for suicide belts—that's priority one. Then we can worry about what they're doing."

They watched the ocean move closer as the MAV camera zoomed following the motion of Taqo's hand. The image stopped and came into focus. The skiff filled the screen. A weather-beaten man was standing in the center of the smaller craft with legs apart. Around him were several white square containers. He grabbed one and, with some difficulty, hoisted it up to waiting hands on the larger boat.

"They look plastic," Taqo said. "Diesel? Water?"

James answered, "There's no color—probably water. I can't tell if they're wearing vests or belts."

"This is going to delay us," Charlie added in a deflated tone. "How are we doing on time?" he asked.

"We've given 15-20 minutes to this phase. Still within parameters," Erica, who was in charge of logistics, answered him.

"What's with the containers?"

"If it's water, they're planning a long trip."

"Maybe heading back to Cyprus."

"Maybe."

"I don't think so. They've been here since Sunday. If they were going back, they would've left before this," Taqo responded.

"This is not good. If they're preparing to leave, we'd better move now or risk losing them. Can't keep the D-flies over the boat too long either; they'll be spotted and we'll lose surprise."

"Note to self," Taqo said. "Recommend camouflaged MAVs for future operations—suggest variations on blue sky patterns."

Charlie didn't even glance at Taqo, "How long before they're done, you think?"

"A minute or two. We can wait them out," Erica responded.

"O.K. Pilots move back out of sight and monitor. As soon as the skiff leaves, move back in. I'd better give Wartel the news."

"He'll be thrilled, I'm sure," Taqo snickered.

Ten minutes later the tension in the group had increased. To everyone's surprise the Moroccan had been hoisted up leaving his supply skiff tied to the larger boat. James guessed the deliveryman had boarded to be paid and would leave any minute. However, the man remained on deck and chatted with the other two as if they were old acquaintances. One man went below and returned moments later carrying a tray and a pot and what turned out to be snacks. He placed the tray on a makeshift table and poured a darkish drink. All three drank, snacked and chatted.

"You gotta be kidding me!" Kyle said exasperated. "We're sitting here pissing away our future and these guys are having tea?"

52
Zero Hour

Islote de Mar, Moroccan Coast

"Now we're screwed," added James dejectedly.

"Yeah, well, our time crunch doesn't make it an emergency on their part, now does it? Damn this storm," Taqo said cynically.

Charlie looked defeated. His face showed wrinkles that had gone unnoticed until now. His body was zapped of energy and he had aged before their eyes.

"Not much we can do," he said to no one in particular in a subdued tone. "I'd better hand it over to the SEALs."

Wartel suggested the micros create a diversion above the boat giving the SEALs time to board. One D-fly would be their eye in the sky and provide video while the other buzzed and created the diversion. With the terrorists preoccupied, the SEALs would board and overpower the three men.

"How soon till you're in position?" Charlie asked Wartel.

"DPV is about 200 meters out. Seven minutes. I'll let you know."

Exactly six minutes and 45 seconds later, Wartel confirmed his men's readiness.

"No change. They're still on deck talking," Charlie told him.

Suddenly James interrupted, "We've got movement."

The drone team stared at the screen. The men had risen and were embracing in an elaborate farewell ritual.

Charlie grabbed the microphone, "Wartel, hold your position! Hold your position! Stop the SEALs! The guy's leaving."

Wartel practically screamed, "Alpha, hold your cover! I repeat, hold your cover!" Then, "They're about to break the surface, dammit."

Everyone watched intently to see where the SEALs would surface.

"There they are," yelled James, the excitement in his voice bursting through.

"Wartel, we got a visual on the SEAL's," Charlie relayed. "They broke the surface.

A black arm had risen from the waterline next to the boat. Against the boat's white, the SEAL waved an arm to make visual contact with the MAV monitoring team. He was on the starboard side. On the port side, the deliveryman was descending to the skiff. Above him, the two on the boat were seeing him off.

"There is a God," Taqo said, and crossed himself.

"Wartel, hold position. The local is leaving. Wait for my signal."

Seconds later the SEAL by the boat indicated with another hand signal that he understood. They watched as the lone terrorist descended to his skiff and left for shore.

"That was close," Erica said, the relief evident on her face.

Charlie Fui, meanwhile, sent a quick message to Col. Randall alerting him that the deliveryman had left and that the mission was on.

"I'll see if we can put a tail on him," was the response.

Taqo kept his camera on the skiff heading to shore. The man tied his boat and entered a side street leading away from the harbor. He disappeared from view.

Hertz, the chopper's flight engineer, appeared behind Charlie and the workstations.

"Dr. Fui, the Captain says you have 20 minutes. The storm's almost here."

The group looked up at the hills over the African mainland. Off in the distance a brown cloud a kilometer high had appeared. The whole mass looked stationary, but a moment's gaze revealed tumbling shadows and altering shapes. Dirty clouds moved forward and were overtaken, in turn, by other masses as the moving wall rolled over itself.

Taqo broke in, "Ready with diversion, Sir."

"All right. SEALs get ready to board. Let's put on a show—dive, loop, anything to distract them," Charlie said.

They watched in real time as Taqo held position to provide video. James's drone dove from its hover position towards the boat below. The angular faced man looked up puzzled trying to make out the source of the buzzing.

"Now, Wartel! Now!" Charlie yelled into his mike.

On the boat's starboard side, two SEALS bobbed above the water's surface and threw grapple hooks on the railing. They pulled themselves aboard. The DPD with the third man broke to the surface to provide support.

"Damn it," Taqo said, breaking everyone's frozen look. On the screen, the two SEALs were facing off with the terrorists.

One man had his sleeveless vest open. His mouth moved saying something that no one heard because the screen went cloudy and bright. Above their screens, an inferno of dark smoke rose. A second later, they heard the noise of the explosion.

Then another more massive explosion—maybe the boat's fuel tank —engulfed the area. Billowing smoke shot out like a pyroclastic flow from a volcano. A third smaller explosion, possibly a propane tank, followed.

Everyone was glued to the screen. The only sounds were breaths being sucked in and Erica's "Oh, my God." The images relayed by the D-fly shook as the force wave reached it and it lost its focus on the boat. Smoke plumes whirled and shot up into the sky.

Taqo readjusted the MAV's camera and moved the control towards the left where the smoke was heaviest and rising in streams. He tried to locate the boat but the smoke was dark and still convulsing.

"Damn, damn, damn," he repeated in disgust.

"Quick, get some altitude and zoom out," Charlie yelled.

Taqo pulled the camera closer and the image raced back. Then he panned downwards. Weaving and twisting smoke was spreading and covering a wide section of sky. Taqo locked on and then followed the funnel shaped darkness down to the water. White pieces of jagged fiberglass appeared and disappeared in the froth of the now churning sea. Bits of debris fanned out in the water and formed a rough circle testifying to the violence in the center. There was no boat.

53

Abdellatif Ferroukhi

Rif Mountains, Morocco

A thin layer of dust covered the van's exterior giving the blue metal a fuzzy sand-colored hue. The paint was bleached from the heat of the Moroccan desert and from the dust-laden wind that strafed the countryside. The van's travails included climbing the Rif Mountains five or six times a year for fifteen years now. Age and the thousands of miles had taken their toll on the engine so that every spin of the wheels and every turn of the crankshaft was now a struggle for one more meter of territory.

The metal hull rose and fell like a boat lumbering in water; when the wheels encountered cracks and dips or searched for traction, creaks and springy sounds came from its worn shocks. Occasionally sand and wind drifted over the decades old pavement and, for a moment, muffled the clanging.

An annoyed horn blared as a car sped past the van; the van's driver paid no attention as if the other vehicle did not exist. When the car's rear became small and blurred in the day's heat in the distance, the driver's gaze landed on the old Renault, but only because the vehicle had entered his field of vision. It was a momentary diversion—it may as well have been a fakir trying to separate a few santim from a lifelong street savvy native.

Wadis and sparsely vegetated hillsides came and went. When faster vehicles approached from the rear, the driver paid no heed, nor did he, as was the custom, wave 'clear to pass' to the drivers. Abdellatif Ferroukhi, the driver of the van, did not care. He'd driven too much over the years and seen too much. A minute more or less meant nothing.

In the early days, he'd kept a tight schedule and rushed from market to market and town to town. The novelty of the villages and the thrill of hard cash energized him. But after several tours, trip blended into trip, one banal town was like another, and his earnings changed little from season to season. He saw what the rest of his life would be like. He settled into a routine and a familiar route around the Rif earning just enough to survive.

But on the road, he learned how little he actually needed. He started transporting a bit of kif to Alhuceima and delivered it to a trusted relative. He got a reputation for reliability but also for never accepting more than a half-kilo. His preparations were meticulous and he delivered as promised. He preferred the regular and steady income of small discreet quantities and avoided the risks and ruthless characters that trafficked larger quantities. Just a bit of extra income.

He used networks already in place since roles and terrain were already allocated and every sliver of turf passed from father to son for generations. Tribal relationships were intricate and going at it alone was foolish and risky. Every link in the network was a patrimony that was defended zealously.

Abdellatif reached a point of equanimity (or perhaps composure) which meant being responsible for his own virtues and shortcomings. The same logic dictated that Allah provided for the faithful. Those that managed to eke out an existence must be satisfied with the bounty that Allah deemed appropriate. Money or consumer luxuries didn't matter. He loathed the illiterate and brusque mountain women that crowded his van at the little out of the way towns dotting his territory. They were taken in by trivial glittering trinkets and lusted after any newfangled consumer gadget.

He smiled in triumph. Today, no one would surround his van because he would not be stopping.

He stayed in third gear as much as possible except on steep hills when he had to go to second. The deep resonant chugging of third had ingrained itself into his body long ago so that its droning was a reassuring companion. The deep bass of second gear was gruff and impinged on the tone that had soothed him over the years. He didn't care much for fourth gear either—too fast and light; the hulking van careened over the road barely under control. No. Third gear fit the road, hills, and wadis and he could actually gander at the landscape as it went by.

Abdellatif could distinguish the slightest variation in the engine. At cities along the coast, he bought knick-knacks and household goods to sell to the Rif villagers. Even today, assorted bundles and plastic goods crammed his roof rack from end to end. A tarp covered half and a net the other half. Basins and watering cans, both plastic and galvanized, were secured from the railing and dangled off the sides. Today they'd not be sold; they hung there out of habit. A bare van would not do.

As always, the Berbers would assume the van was loaded down with cartons of foodstuffs, kitchenware, and dish detergents. Today it was loaded with detonators, fuses, and charges.

No, day-to-day trifles were not important. Finally after many years, Abdellatif was finished with them.

54
eLRAD

Moroccan Airspace

"You heard about the boat?" Colonel Randall asked.

"Just got off the phone with Collins. Doesn't leave me much. Can't catch a break on this one," Ben answered.

"Doesn't seem like it. Things will take a while to sort through here."

"Anything I can do on my end?"

"You still on the job, then? They're not calling you off?"

"I've got a terror response team with me. Rapid Reaction Force the British call it. Makes me valuable."

"Like old times in Afghanistan, eh?"

"Collins is hedging his bets—probably buying some time."

"Glad someone's thinking. You know we lost three SEALs in Alhuceima?"

"My condolences, Hank. That sandstorm didn't help."

"Mucked everything up. Not an easy mission to begin with—don't have to tell you about those. Maybe the drone techs screwed up, maybe the SEALs—I won't know for a while. The shit's about to hit the fan with damage assessment, committees, and the investigation. They'll want my ass on a platter."

"Not much changes. What's the short version?"

"Predator scenario all over again. UAV's are Air Force Research, but once deployed, they're under Army control. Same for the micros. The drones in Alhuceima were a DARPA Forward Cell and still in R and D—blame is going back and forth between Army and Air Force. The Army wasn't even in on this one. Bottom line, I'm gonna be busy."

"I feel for you."

"Listen, I may have something. Same day as the Casablanca bombings, two research ships off the coast of Mauritania and Morocco were attacked. First thought was piracy but pirates have never operated this far north and by the time the CIA figures it out and decides who to brief, it may be too late. Anyway, one ship fights them off with water cannons but the other, the *Pytheas,* is boarded."

"What happened?"

"They took no hostages—only a sonic device used for oil exploration which can penetrate a mile and a half into the ocean floor."

"They installed those tankers and cruise ships after the *Cole* to ward off pirates, didn't they?" Ben asked. "What's all this have to do with Alhuceima?"

"This eLRAD device has lethal applications."

"Doesn't sound like a warlord looking for cash or to make a name for himself."

"We've identified the leader from the Captain's description as Rafiq Al Jabiri. This is where it gets scary. He's a known militant with a price on his head. Every time he's sighted, the location goes hot with suicide bombings, roadside explosives, assassinations—you name it. No connections to Al Qaeda or ISIS. In fact, if not for them, he'd be at the top of the terror watch list. He's an original going back to the 1970's—Fatah, Black September, Abu Nidal, Egyptian Islamic Jihad. Never been caught. Even made it out of Sabra and Shatila alive. He's still alive because he trusts no one."

"A lone wolf."

"The Captain said Al Jabiri was smooth and in control. Even quoted the Koran, '*On the day of resurrection, Allah will grasp the whole earth in His palm; glory be to Him, and may He be exalted.*' Sound familiar?"

"My hostiles said something similar."

"That's what I thought."

"We heard 'palm' and thought Dubai. But 'Palm of God' can refer to a number of things. I see a pattern here—the Casablanca bombing, the Alhuceima boat explosion, the eLRAD heist…"

"Oh, by the way, Al Jabiri? Took the eLRAD and headed north. Can't all be coincidence. I'll be out of commission for a while with the Alhuceima inquiry, but you, see what you can do."

"Thanks, Colonel."

"Huntley…"

"Yeah?"

"Good luck and bring'em home."

55
On the Trail

In Globemaster, Over Morocco

The voice on the other end of the line was saying, "He's been heading south into the Rif in a vendor's van for about 90 minutes now. Doesn't seem in any hurry."

"And the Rif is?" Artemis asked.

"Mountainous region of Morocco. Supplies a large chunk of the world's hashish."

"Any idea why he'd be going there?"

"Maybe his job is done and he's gone back to his regular life—making his rounds."

"Or is moving on to the next phase. Have you been able to find out what the boat's been doing since it got to Morocco?"

"Analysis still in progress."

"So, we don't know where its cargo's gone. The vendor is our only lead. Has he stopped to sell anything?"

"I don't know about that. Our tail's been on him since Alhuceima. We had no one, so the Spanish lent us an agent. I'll ask."

"Can we talk to this Spaniard? Does he have a cell phone? Let's try that, shall we?"

"That has to go through channels. It could take a while."

"Really? Are you listening to yourself? We may not have hours. Look, just get me the guy's cellphone, O.K.? That's not too much to ask."

"Let me see what I can do."

"The sooner the better," Artemis raised her voice in frustration. "Listen in, if you want."

"I'll let you know."

A short time later Artemis was filling Ben in on her conversations with Washington.

"The Spanish tail says the van has gone through several towns and not stopped."

"What do we know about terrorist organizations in Morocco?" Ben asked.

"That's me," Potsbury answered. "The one on the terror list is the Moroccan Islamic Combatant Group. It's a Taliban offshoot comprised of disaffected students, the unemployed and aimless. Recruits come from the shantytowns around major cities. Intelligence thinks it gets its money from hashish courtesy of the Rif."

Ben nodded, "Classic Taliban—preach religion with one hand and sell drugs to finance violence with the other."

"Kif has never been connected to the ICG but it sounds reasonable," Potsbury retorted.

"And Kif is?" asked Artemis.

"A blend of hashish and tobacco—half of Morocco is keen on the stuff. The government cites it as a major health concern but tolerates production since a large portion of the area's economy depends on it. Economic gain trumps health mentality."

"Like opium poppies in Afghanistan and blood diamonds in central Africa," Artemis contributed.

"Terror groups may share methods," Potsbury interjected, "but local conditions always dictate goals."

"Islam is not monolithic," Ben responded. "Centuries of religious and tribal allegiances shaped the Middle East just as Christian rivalries shaped Europe. Christ and Mohammed are one more reason for people to kill each other."

"Yeah, well, Muslims seem to take the Koran more literally than Christians the Bible, don't they?" Artemis added.

It was the first condemnation that Ben had heard from Artemis. It sounded bitter and harsh. Maybe the frustration or the lack of progress was getting to her. Maybe the whirlwind of the past few days was catching up.

"*'Love thy neighbor'* didn't stop Christian Serbs from massacring 8,000 Muslims in Srebrenica—and that was as recent as 30 years ago," Barnes added.

"Yes but Western Europe is ruled by law while the Middle East is run by sheiks, dictators, and theocrats that twist the Koran for their own purposes," Artemis challenged him.

"The West is responsible for good chunk of that," Barnes replied.

"And others say that the West is run by money and corporations not religion and law," Ben said. Maybe she wasn't tired, he thought. Frustrated, yes. "Lots of differences, rivalries and cultures in the Middle East. It's never 'us and them' the way Langley and Washington think it is. Pet peeve of mine."

"Ahm…the Spanish Agent," Potsbury announced. "He's worried he'll be compromised. Says he and the van are the only two vehicles on large stretches of very sparse territory. Says he may have been noticed."

"Get someone to alternate surveillance with him," Ben suggested. "As soon as we can," then he thought better of it. "That's not likely to happen. Tell him, to hire a taxi and follow in that. He can't lose the van—it's our only lead. Meanwhile, can we get satellite surveillance on him?"

Ben turned to Barnes, the British ranking officer on board and the man who would have to relay the orders to the British Rapid Reaction Force, "Let's prepare a rendezvous. Do we have a landing site?"

"We do…a decommissioned base called, Ben Guerir. It's farther south and can handle the C-17."

"Let's bring the bastard in before we lose him."

56
Drones

The Waters Around La Palma, Canary Islands

Rafiq Al Jabiri communicated to everyone that he was a man apart—someone they would never be. Perhaps it was his lack of hesitation when giving orders or the determination in his body when he walked. The message was clear—he was in charge. He was lean and wiry but not due to exercise or any other conscious attempt—it never occurred to him to set time aside for exercise or that he had such a choice. He did not.

He only knew there was work that needed doing and that those that did nothing should be condemned. To be wrapped up in oneself and to dedicate precious hours to the embellishment of his body was anathema. He was a man of work and of action—the two were the same and consumed him. If fat had ever been on his body, his mind had stripped away every ounce until his body served his mind. There was much to be done and few able or willing to do it, so he took it on himself. His body would do his mind's bidding, which was to right the wrongs. The body was an agent—an instrument of the mind.

A lifetime of scuttling back and forth to sustain operations and contacts had created nerves of steel. He had no use for muscle. Nerves were sinews and inner strength and got results. Nerves were tempered by confronting the chasm between what could be and what was. He believed the two could—and should—be the same. Muscle could never compete. A muscular body was a trained body but it did not have the commitment of nerves. It did not comprehend loss, family, country, and ideals—everything that transcended a person's trivial life. Muscle was shortsighted and concerned with the here and now. It had no access to, probably not even an awareness of the universal. Muscle was nothing in the presence of nerve.

He looked to be in his '50's but was actually 63. He monitored his own progress, others' efforts and failures, and the state of Islamic society compared to Western and Oriental. His reputation drew people to him, but his personality kept them at a distance. The few that got close were quickly left behind for Rafiq was a loner and uncomfortable with crowds. He was not a populist—populism wasted time on politics and negotiation and left too little time for action.

His education was having done much. He looked for undercurrents below the machinations of nations and popular movements. He was streetwise and seemed to know what others didn't. He was impatient with those that couldn't see what should be obvious. Most thought his demeanor as superiority, but it was only that his mind was preoccupied. He appeared standoffish because so many inadequacies surrounded him. Too many had failed him, and too few measured up to his capacity and determination for work.

Ahmed had seen it firsthand at a small city of 10,000. They'd come up to a disconcerting sight at the main square. Ahmed was out of breath keeping up with the older man as they moved from shop to shop and entered basements to meet contacts. Then they came to tens of old men sitting in chairs, all facing one direction, all looking similar. They appeared old to Ahmed, but Rafiq could have easily fit in with them.

It was ten o'clock in the morning. Row upon row of men, perhaps a hundred, in dark jackets and white tieless shirts in front of several side-by-side cafes. They sat, chatted and drank tea in what was clearly a daily ritual. Rafiq's eyes blazed and his teeth clenched. Sinews tightened on his face and fists clenched, and a torrent of curses spit from under his breath, "Leeches, bums. Work you excuses for men. Sit and suck others dry."

Then, looking off into the distance and as if commenting to the world but with only Ahmed near enough to hear, "So much to do and they sit. Drones, drones," he used the word as if it were a filthy curse.

Ahmed stared from Rafiq to the men and back again not sure what Rafiq was talking about. His uncle's bees in Ateret came to mind. Images of the commonly thought of as lazy drone bees superimposed themselves on the rows of men uniformly facing the open square twirling beads, smoking, all energy sucked out of them. Like drones who sat and guarded the queen, the men sat and did nothing. Drones. Obviously, there weren't many concepts or insults as offensive or demeaning to Rafiq. In his mind, if a man exerted too little effort, in one day or a lifetime, he was a sorry excuse for a man.

Ahmed thought of his family. They were on the road by sunrise and returned at sunset. The work moved indoors while the women prepared the meal. One season became another, and only the type of work changed. They picked olives in winter, tilled the fields to plant wheat in the spring and moved to the irrigable vegetable fields in early summer. Talk over dinner consisted of who did what, how much they planted, when the Cypress field would be finished, how many orange trees were left to prune, who would re-hang the tomato plants, who'd go to Saturday market, and how every other job would get done.

Ahmed stood at the edge of the mass of men as Rafiq charged into them shouting and gesturing, "Talk. Talk is cheap. Who's going to feed your children, who will give them a homeland? Is this how you'll do it? Why should they work, if you don't? Will you leave them better off than you? Women work harder than you," he spat. "And, you sit and blame others for your failures. Will *kafirs* solve your troubles for you? *Sharmutas.* You think the Jews and the Americans will drop riches from the sky? Sit and let them violate you and take from you—as if they haven't taken enough. You *let* them take it! They do what benefits them, as you would do, if you were men. Worthless *kalbas.* Your children have been maimed and laid in graves. *'The eyes shed tears and the heart is grieved,'* and you do nothing? Is this how you submit to the truth of the

Prophet? *Munafiqun!* Will your fathers be proud? Did you have fathers? Fatherless drones. This is your contribution?"

He stopped. Then, facing the frozen faces, he got a hold of his anger. Understanding, perhaps remembrance of the ways of the world came back to him. With a resigned voice, he said, "Yes, let others do the work, for you are worthless."

His face was pained. He was above the world and saw forces, concepts, relationships and the role of the select few who dared correct wrongs while others cowed helplessly.

He accepted the burden. It was his duty and he'd be worthy. He turned and walked away. Ahmed followed. Rafiq's face winced with pain and Ahmed's soul felt it.

"They'll never know," he said, "what they can accomplish because they don't do the work. They only wish to survive, not to thrive. You think they know the difference? A man is not a man unless he works and prepares—unless he can say, '*I leave things better than I found them. I took my family's accomplishments and I added mine. I contributed.*' It's every man's duty to labor until the last day of his life. Only then can he expect Allah to greet him with open arms."

Ahmed heard truth; it resonated as the inviolate law of God. Rafiq's words matched the life Ahmed had been born into. It was all he knew and so thought the way life should be lived. Rafiq had put it into words. It was the truth and the essence of life—the purity of a Muslim. Ahmed had been shocked by Rafiq's fervor and his courage to shout his beliefs. It was bold and liberating. He deserved Ahmed's devotion. Rafiq set high standards and, from what Ahmed had seen over the past two years, Rafiq was equal to them.

For the next ten minutes, Ahmed was immobilized by his awe of the older man. He remained quiet and deferential. He was in the presence of a true *amir* worthy of leading *jihad.*

On the drive back, Rafiq surprised Ahmed a second time.

"I have disappointed you, I know. I would be in your debt if you did not mention my tirade to the others," Rafiq said in a tone that indicated shame.

Ahmed fumbled to protest. That's not how he had seen the events at the square. He was awed by Rafiq's courage. It was one thing to profess to be a Muslim and another to be one. There were so many *kafirs*. Those that had strayed from the true path were to be distinguished from true believers. It was up to men like Ahmed and Rafiq to bring them back. Rafiq's insights were just beyond Ahmed's reach but everything seemed possible through Rafiq.

"Does not the Prophet, peace be upon him, say to speak good words? And, that *'A bad word is like a bad tree cut at ground level that has no roots to keep it standing?'* Rafiq quoted. "What I did was blasphemy and not to be emulated. What did I achieve? Allah knows who rejects truth and who is misguided. He commands a believer's best effort and expects him to teach others, to witness, not to insult and blaspheme."

"But those men are failures!" Ahmed burst out.

"You think anyone was convinced? I was the voice of the donkey. *'Do not treat people with arrogance, nor roam the earth proudly. God does not favor arrogant showoffs. Walk humbly and lower your voice.'* I have no right to speak for others. Allah will decide their worthiness, not you or I."

Ahmed fell silent. This was new perspective. He receded into himself to wrestle with the intricacies and implications of this wisdom.

Even now, after two years of assisting and living in mentor's shadow, he struggled with the explanation Rafiq had given that day. But, he clung to it as an insight and access way into a life beyond the mundane one of this world. It didn't satiate him nor did he understand it, but he took it on faith as coming from someone who knew God better than he.

57
Into the Belly of the Beast

Atlántida Cave, La Palma

Rafiq's boat slowly waded deeper and deeper into the cave. The water was smooth and still and the smallest sound reverberated among the stone and immense space.

They'd hid inside the mouth of the cave for two days waiting for communications from the surface team and the other boat. The surface team signaled they were ready; nothing was heard from second boat. They would wait no longer.

Faruq had been with the device since it had been brought aboard. He had brought the reserve generator on-line and had spent every moment with his new toy. He made the modifications that would produce the anti-material frequencies that would disrupt the terrain and jar the mountain loose. He asked to coordinate with the second eLRAD with increasing frustration but Rafiq had stared him down. Fervor took over the normally neat and intellectual looking Faruq. He blurted out, "We need both machines to shake the earth and begin the slide! If we don't use enough power, nothing may happen!" He was clearly fatigued, his eyes were bleary, his hair unkempt and his face dark with stubble.

He took a deep breath. He needed to make them see the significance of coordinating. "Think of ocean waves," he said. "Usually they are navigable even during storms but sometimes they join and add to each other and grow to be 35 meters high and destroy everything in their path. The same will happen here. With two machines, the frequencies will overlap and increase exponentially in size and power. These are the vibrations needed to dislodge the mountain, and, if Allah wills it, slide it into the ocean."

"The other ship may come or it may not," Rafiq responded. "If it does not, we proceed alone. *'Those that heed their duty to their Lord shall be conveyed to the garden; its doors shall be opened, and its keepers shall say to them: Peace be on you, you shall be happy; therefore enter it to abide.'* Our commitment to *jihad* is our test, not whether the other boat arrives, or if there are two machines. Prepare your part." Rafiq's admonition sent Faruq back to the eLRAD.

On deck, spotlights lit the boat's way through the canal-like waterway. One beam pointed forward and two others pointed off the sides to illuminate the walls. Shadows skirted the walls and colors reflected from the oil-smooth water. Shadowy forms and movement continued below water adding depth and otherworldliness to the cavern. Men kept watch and warned when the boat got to close to limestone outcroppings that threatened to tear gashes in the boat's sides. So far, they'd had no problems. Except for some erosion that had created piles below the surface, the lava tube was a smooth cavern of rock.

The men had not believed that they'd actually enter the cave because it had sounded too farfetched. But, Rafiq had explained (Ahmed thought he did not have to) how it was possible: the cave was at sea level, on the coast. It was smooth and navigable for almost a kilometer inland. It was a blessing and Allah was smiling on them. Ahmed and the others would follow Rafiq regardless, but to be willing warriors led by a crusader like Rafiq, to be believers added another dimension. They would stand before Allah worthy protectors of the faith. Imbued with Rafiq's guidance, they would do willingly what each would never be able to do on his own. They would succeed and accomplish more for Islam than anyone else in its history. The prophet, peace be upon Him, said that the deeds of martyrs in Allah's cause will bring them to paradise.

The deep idle of the diesel motor came back as a throbbing echo from the rocky sides. Bands of reddish rock covered the ceiling and moved off in angular shafts. Known as layered scoria, they were remnants of the original rock lining and had eroded leaving behind the empty space that now made up the cavern. The cave was too young for stalagmites and stalactites but hair-thin strands were beginning to dot the ceiling.

This far from the ocean, the water was still. As the boat glided forward in a slow idle, faint ripples left its hull and went to find the walls. The spotlights shone and revealed blue-green algae and multi-colored rocks lining the edges and extending under water. On the bridge, the Captain and Rafiq kept an eye on the bottom via echo-sounding sonar.

The boat stopped. Rafiq descended the stairs, went over to Faruq and told him he could consider this their final destination. He was to locate the fault line and the volcanic vents overhead.

"I have been sounding the mountain and have an approximate location for the tunnel," Faruq responded.

"Find the rift and target it," Rafiq said.

"The volcanic throats are aligned north to south. The fault extends two meters on the surface, but is close to the caverns. I need to pinpoint it in relation to our position and send a few test emissions. With the other eLRAD, we could triangulate and bombard the fault line at two different points targeting a whole section. The explosion and our waves should start a landslide and open at least one vent. But with only one eLRAD, nothing may happen."

Faruq was unsure how much of the science Rafiq and the others understood. Rafiq had a determined but not very revealing look on his face.

"We have the tunnel, the fault line, and the volcanoes. Target the weakest point," he responded tersely. "Everything else is in God's hand."

Before Faruq could respond, Rafiq turned his back. With a spring and lightness to his stride, he walked away leaving Ahmed and Faruq to stare after him.

58
Cumbre Vieja

Café Solipsista, Los Llanos de Aridane, La Palma

"First tell me about the island's growth stages and the landslides…" Enrique prompted Isabella.

"La Palma is actually a volcano that grew in the Atlantic; there are places where pillow lavas, breccias and hyaloclastites are visible. In the first cycle, Garafia, ash and rock deposits accumulated quickly and created steep inclines; gravitational slides and cycles of stability and erosion followed and created the northern shield. Then 500,000 years ago, the second phase, Taburiente, grew atop Garafia's discordance."

"Which also grew rapidly and also collapsed from extreme height."

"Which you already know," Isabella said with a hint of her former annoyance. "The volcanoes of *Las Canarias* are characterized by extreme elevations and frequent landslides. The *edifici* from the ocean bottom to the top, at Los Muchachos, is 6500 meters. The Taburiente and Cumbre Vieja avalanche fields fan out 20 kilometers under the ocean—*en un classic esempio* of the Sisyphus Effect."

"Which explain the presence of rifts and erosion deposits."

"Taburiente basalts migrated south and formed the Cumbre Nueva north-south dorsal ridge. When it grew too high, it also subsided and resulted in the Valle de Aridane. The next cycle created the Bejenado stratovolcano."

"And Cumbre Vieja?"

"Cumbre Vieja is new—only about 150,000 years old."

"And the rift?"

"What about it?"

"It was in the news when I was in school—that it was evidence of an impending collapse."

"And you believe it? It's hype—rumor. "

"You just said there have been several growth and collapse cycles."

"You can't believe it!" she said, exasperated and confronting him. Her eyes were large and round and her mouth open in a disbelieving look. Her reaction distracted him and his gaze moved to her unkempt swaths of blond hair. She slowed her breathing and exhaled.

"I was at school in Oregon," Enrique explained, "homesick and heard talk of a collapse."

"*Pensi che sia possibile, posso dire!*" she blurted.

"You don't believe it?"

"It's about geology, not belief."

"That sounds like Professor Araujo."

"Ramon? He takes the research of others and polishes it for the Ministry. Dr. Mendoza puts up with him—something about Ramon's connections in Madrid. They sent him here so he wouldn't do any damage."

"Is he right? Are the faults surficial?"

"He supported the landslide theory when it was popular. Now that it's no longer *nella moda*, he's against it. Volcanic activity is moving south. The northern shield is extinct. The *triangolo effettivamente* makes the rift more secure."

"So we're not at the beginning of an erosion cycle? A landslide is not likely?"

She looked as if she was surprised by the sudden cross-examination. She answered, "Some of the triple-pronged rifts do show some evidence of settling."

"So a collapse is possible?" Enrique pressed the point. Isabella moved her hair out of the way and stared him down.

"Yes, but thousands of years from now!"

"It's been thousands of years since the last one. What about the eruptions of 1949 and 1971? An eruption cycle is past due," Enrique persisted.

"Cycles do not predict eruptions."

"But they are one variable. What about the seismic swarm in El Hierro last month? There's been activity at the other end of the African Plate too.

"The fault in the west is only a meter or two deep. Rift zones and material slippage are common in active zones. It's not easy to predict. Some see it as evidence of increasing stability and others think it's a sign of decreasing stability."

"How both?"

"Because La Palma's volcanoes are moving south into the ocean so there's less activity in the north which means stability has increased. But, landslides occur due to height, steepness, tremors, and lack of structural support—which are still in place and so some believe instability has increased. But, it doesn't mean a *collasso catastrophico*. Most collapses occur gradually from erosion. I am not an expert on landslides."

"And if the fault is deeper? If it's not surficial?" Enrique continued.

She stared at him. Her frustration was palpable now.

"There's no evidence—the 1971 eruption produced minor seismic activity and no rift movement."

"You mean surface telemetry. Anyone use ground-penetrating radar or echolocation? Anyone check temperatures inside Cumbre Vieja?"

Her mouth stuck open for a second. Then a wrinkle appeared in her brow as if a flaw had appeared in her armor.

"That's what this is about! What did you find out?" she looked at him suspiciously.

"My grandfather told me that during the 1949 eruption the ground sank the height of a palm tree."

"O.K. that's more than two meters."

"That's not what worries me."

"What then?"

"He saw it in a cave inside Cumbre Vieja…500 meters below the surface fault. I've been there. I've seen it."

"Are you saying you have evidence the fault everyone thinks is two *metros* deep is actually 500?!"

They squared off letting the implications of such a possibility seep in.

In a matter of fact voice Enrique said, "We'd better find out, hadn't we?"

They got up but their movements seemed peculiarly numb. Enrique left money on the café table for the coffees. Lost in thought and each now oblivious of the other, they headed for the car.

59
Connections

Ben Guerir, Former NATO Air Base, Morocco

The C-17 taxied to a weather-beaten hangar at a decommissioned NATO base in central Morocco. Morocco's military was mostly concentrated in the south where it controlled the disputed Western Sahara territory and in the north where it protected Morocco's fishing fleets in the Mediterranean and Atlantic. However, Ben Guerir's runways were still serviced and permission to land had not been difficult to obtain.

The C-17 had the capability of operating as a mobile field base and its communications equipment linked with U. S. and NATO command. Artemis, Ben, and Potsbury spent the flight speaking to superiors, analysts, and various government agencies in America and Britain.

Now they gathered the men.

"Some developments you should know about," Ben started.

The members of the British Rapid Response Force and their commander, Rick Barnes, massed around Ben. What Huntley said now would decide their next step if there was one. They might be going home with only a flight from Cyprus to Morocco via Saudi Arabia to show for their efforts.

"Word just came in that the effort to take the boat and its occupants failed. A team of SEALs and drone operators launched at 1700 hours but the sandstorm we dealt with yesterday played havoc. End result, two hostiles blew themselves up and killed three SEALs in the process."

Groans rose from the men. Faces quickly became rigid and filled with determination. They took in the adversity and steeled themselves for the response.

"Where does that leave us, Colonel?" Barnes, the head of the British contingent, asked the question on everyone's mind.

"On our side, we have Colonel Johnston, three SEALs and 44 civilians dead in Casablanca. On the militant side, two dead bombers in Casablanca, two dead in Alhuceima and at least one active terror cell somewhere in Morocco en route to target. It is clear that this is a devoted and well-organized group who won't hesitate to kill."

"Are you connecting the Casablanca bombings with our boat?" Barnes asked. "Do we have confirmation?"

"No, but it's a safe bet. Two deadly events, within days of each other right where we just happen to be—it's a stretch for coincidence. So until we hear otherwise, we assume there's a connection that we just haven't found yet. Washington and Vauxhall don't have much to add, so they're keeping us in the field because, basically, we're boots on the ground. "

That last bit of information sent a wave of enthusiasm throughout the group.

Artemis added, "More to the point, we have to assume that the terrorist attack has not been compromised and is about to be launched as we speak."

"We've yet to identify a target, an agenda, or the group responsible. We have nothing to go on," Barnes said.

"Now, that's not quite true," Ben said with a faint smile. "We have a couple of items we didn't have before. One: bodies are piling up on both sides which tells us the stakes are high and they have no qualms about blowing themselves up to protect the operation," Ben added.

"Which was what happened in Casablanca and Alhuceima," Barnes said.

"Sir, if I may," Potsbury spoke up.

"Go ahead," Ben said.

"Beg your pardon, sir, but the Casablanca terrorists detonated their devices only after an unplanned confrontation with the owner—they had no other option. Same goes for Alhuceima; the hostiles detonated rather than be taken captive. Both events are best characterized as unintended mishaps. What they do share in common is a distinct lack of planning. They were blunders and the suicides nothing more than an attempt at damage control."

"Actually, Sergeant, the crucial element here is that the secrecy and integrity of their plan remains intact. We're facing disciplined and highly committed men with an agenda—*that's* what makes them dangerous, not that the detonations were mishaps. Clearly, we must assume more hostilities are on the way."

"It's a near certainty," Artemis said. "We are facing a conspiracy, which means that by definition, the threat is larger and extends beyond the individuals we've encountered so far. Our assailants have earned the 'most dangerous' designation as they're actively engaged in some sort of attack."

"Colonel Huntley, you said we have two items we didn't have before," a member of the British force commented.

"During the SEAL operation, a militant from the boat went ashore and we managed to get a tail on him. Thanks to NSA imaging, we know where he's going, and, we're going to intercept."

60
Death in Morocco

Moroccan Countryside

Live communications with the Spaniard didn't last long. He had been on the road for four hours with no end in sight. At Fes, he nearly lost the man at the walls of the medina. The city's modern outskirts surrounded one of the world's largest old cities. Since vehicles were not allowed inside the densely built old section, he parked and walked in through the intricately carved gate. Colorfully dressed locals walked about or sat at cafes and tearooms while shops teemed with dry goods and assorted wares. Donkeys loaded with bundles hurried along delivering goods. He figured, rightly, that he'd lose the Arab as soon as he followed him in. At a loss what to do and facing labyrinthine tiny streets, the Spanish agent decided to exit the medina and instead watch the blue van.

He bought a disposable phone from a street vendor and waited for the driver to reappear. He was hungry, in a foul mood and a foreigner in a city he knew nothing about. With evening approaching, he was annoyed and ready to quit. Washington initiated procedures to track his new cell phone signal. Meanwhile Diplomatic Security and the CIA scoured their databases and contacts in Fes for personnel to assist with tailing the van. They finally enlisted a former state department employee turned director of the local American Language Center, a woman in her late 50's. She was a reluctant participant at this stage of her life but agreed to help when permitted to use a 25-year-old second language teacher as her driver. With the promise that this new team would take over surveillance, the Spaniard agreed to tail the van until the American team from the school showed up.

Before the spinster could rendezvous with the Spaniard at the gate of the medina, the Arab reappeared, got in the van, and started off. The Spanish agent had no choice but to follow. He did not know that now he was being tailed and was a marked man.

Sometime during the long and solitary trip that began in Alhuceima, the Arab realized he was being followed. He did not dare confront his pursuer due to the cargo he carried. But once inside the Fes Bali, he alerted his associates.

Three vehicles now headed out of Fes—the van in front, the Spaniard behind and, at a discreet distance, a white Citroen with three men. Once outside Fes, the Spaniard radioed that the van was entering the N8 highway towards Marrakesh.

#############################

Ben traced a finger over a map.

"Fes is there," he said. "We're here at Ben Guerir. Marrakesh is 30 miles to our southeast."

"We wait for him on the approach to Marrakesh," added Artemis. "If he gets to another population center, we'll never get him."

"We set up a welcoming party. Scout the area and decide on a spot to take him alive. It's time we had some luck."

Potsbury broke in, "Sir, Washington has lost contact with the Spaniard."

"What happened?"

"The team from the school says a car side-swiped him and pushed him down a ravine—no way he survived. They're refusing to follow."

"Then it's up to us," Barnes said.

"It's not going to be easy to find him. The whole territory is mountains and deserts," added Artemis.

"He's not hiding," responded Ben. "He's delivering materiel—probably to Marrakesh."

Barnes now perused the map. "At his speed, he'll be 20 to 40 miles outside Marrakesh…" He did some mental calculations and then said, "… at 6:00 a.m."

"Plus he has an escort—the Citroen," Artemis added. "That means he's worth protecting. He's heading for a rendezvous."

"So let's settle on a location and lie in wait…" Ben said.

He did not say he had no intention of losing any more men or suffer a setback like Alhuceima.

61
Call to *Jihad*

Atlántida Cave, La Palma, Canary Islands

"Faruq will explain," Rafiq Al Jabiri said to the gathered men.

"We will attack with our machine. Our brothers are using different timer fuses so several explosions occur. The sound waves will join with the ANFO detonations in the tunnels and shake the mountain until it collapses. It is inevitable. If it is the will of Allah, it will fall into the ocean and create the largest wave in history to destroy America."

"*Al-ḥamdu lillāh,*" a few in the crowd intoned.

"This is *al-Yd al-Ah*. We are the fortunate. The island is volcanic and porous like a sponge."

"And this will work in our favor?" Rafiq prompted.

"Oh, yes, certainly. The detonation will grow at 6,000 meters per second and create millions of kilograms of pressure. Gasses and steam will build in the tunnels and caverns and further magnify the explosion ensuring a very large collapse.

'The sonic device will shake the faults and caverns in the volcano. Here, too, Allah has been generous with his favors."

His face was one large smile and his eyes sparkled. It was evident that he was fascinated with the geology and the volcanic features of the island.

"We placed the explosives at the island's weakest point next to several volcanoes. If Allah blesses our sacrifice, we may open a volcanic vent and begin an eruption; that would be glorious!

'Two hundred to 500 million cubic meters of earth to break off and roll down the mountain into the ocean. It will be magnificent!"

He stopped and looked at Rafiq.

Rafiq was euphoric. He raised and indicated with his hands at the men around him.

"Allah's *mujahedin* will destroy the Great Satan! The greatest age of Islam begins with us!"

Cheers rose from the crowd.

"La ilaha illallah, Muhammadun Rasulullah. Brothers and *mujahidin,* our time has come. This is the moment. Many of you doubted this day would ever come. Look where you are and consider what you are about to achieve in the name of Allah. Be convinced that all things are possible if it is His will. He has shown us the one righteous path.

'Since the time of the Prophet, the unbelievers have enslaved our fathers, defiled our lands and taken our wealth. The infidels and their children have prospered at our expense. They have gorged and enriched themselves and have not been satiated; they will continue to take from us unless we stop them. We have survived on the scraps they throw us. We have lived according to their will and our lives are decided by their whims. No longer!

'For centuries, they have set one tribe of believers against the other. They have ensured our subservience and their apostate ways. They fill our children with indecent images and corruption. They do not ask us; they tell us. They do not purchase; they take. The *sharia* is anathema to them. They do not serve the one true and merciful God. They live in wealth while we starve. The faithful have suffered and been killed since the time of the Prophet. Who among us is not humbled at the sacrifice of our brothers? Who among us has not lost family in the struggle to right the injustices done to us? We all have!

'Today, *we* right the wrongs! Today *we* avenge the martyrs! *We* are their hand! May Allah find us worthy.

'The devotion we have shown these many years to reach this moment is proof of the righteousness of our cause. *We* are the fortunate, the chosen, the ones who will punish the unbelievers. Rejoice in this, but do not take it lightly. What we do, we do for the faithful. We are Allah's Hand. Truly, we will be blessed and enter Paradise. This I humbly believe.

'We are Allah's mujahidin and we sacrifice ourselves willingly. Our legacy will be the humility with which we accept *jihad*. Our reward is near, be assured. *Do you think you can enter paradise unless God knows that you have worked in His cause, and that you have been patient in adversity? Everyone will taste death, but only on the Day of Resurrection will you be rewarded for what you have done—he that is drawn away from the fire and brought into paradise will indeed have gained a triumph: for the life of this world is nothing but an enjoyment of self-delusion.*

'You are believers and are here. Then believe what I tell you now: this is the moment of victory. By our act, we are worthy to be in Allah's presence. We will enjoy the fruits we are due. *Allahu Akbar!"*

Shouts of '*Allahu Akbar! Allahu Akbar!*' and '*La ilaha illallah*' rose from the men and looks of euphoria filled their faces. If being in a boat in a cave under a mountain had raised doubts among the men, Rafiq had refocused them on the task at hand.

62
Al-yd al-Lh

Marrakesh Countryside, Morocco

The blue van finally came into view. It had been spotted travelling a line in the hillside that was the road. It looked like the body of a once bright-shelled scarab slowly ambling through the sparse dry landscape and low-lying hills. The road was the N8 going from Fes to Marrakesh and it would eventually lead to the men lying in wait.

Barnes and his team leader, a hard looking man named Smythe, chose an isolated section about 25 miles outside of Marrakesh. They had a good vantage point of the road and the approach. The intercept would take place on the inside of a hill. They formed two groups—one would go for the van and the other for the Citroen. They'd separate the van from the car as the road wound into the hillside. They'd surprise the terrorists so they'd not have time to react and take them alive. Surprise was critical—it would increase the chance for success and minimize confrontation. If all went as planned, they'd not even fire their weapons. The faster and quieter the intercept, the greater the chance that travelers, sheepherders and farmers in the area would not notice. Conducting a clandestine military operation without the explicit permission of the

Moroccans was a major upping of the ante—one that could make or break the careers of those present.

Back at the base, Ben and Barnes had debated informing the Moroccans and asking for clearance. They decided against it fearing they'd be thrown into bureaucratic limbo while the Moroccans pushed pencils back and forth, or worse, were shut down while the Moroccans took over. They also risked losing the opportunity to question the terrorists, which was the whole point of the intercept. Best leave the Rapid Reaction Force do what it was good at and leave diplomacy to others.

"I don't see the car," Ben said as the blue van came into view.

"The van's alone," responded Barnes. "It's not here."

"And left the van exposed?"

"One way to find out," Smythe contributed, and motioned to his men to get ready for action.

Before the man in the van had an inkling of what was happening, the British commandos were on him. The van's door was open and its slow speed made capture easy. In fact, too easy.

The man spoke no English. Ben had a smattering of Arabic at his disposal but he and the Arab hardly understood each other. It was soon apparent that he was a Moroccan Berber and his dialect was worlds away from Ben's basic Arabic. Worse, a search of the van turned up nothing illicit—no contraband, no weapons, no explosives.

He knew something though. After his initial surprise at finding himself in the midst of combat troops and immobilized, his demeanor changed. Perhaps he understood Ben's Arabic better than he let on, perhaps the sight of foreign soldiers awoke his convictions. Maybe he expected to be caught and only the moment had been a surprise.

Smythe whispered something to Barnes who then approached Huntley.

"Smythe wants to have a go at the Berber—says he'll have the man talking in a couple of minutes. What do you think?"

"I don't like hurting people but we need to find out what he knows. Go ahead."

Smythe spoke to his men. A commando took the Berber to the British Panther Command and Liaison Vehicle. The man's hands were tied behind his back with plastic restraints. The commando secured him to the CLV and stayed to guard him.

Smythe and three others fanned out. They looked at the ground, approached rocks and small boulders, which they turned over carefully. A few minutes later, one of the men shouted for the others. They bent over a rock and one took off his helmet and brought it to the ground. They returned with Smythe holding the upside down helmet in one hand and a survival knife in the other. Peering inside, Ben saw a black scorpion with the largest and thickest tail he'd ever seen.

"Androctonus Mauretanicus," Smythe said matter-of-factly. "Mauritanian man-killer. I got a crash course on Morocco on the way from Saudi Arabia," he added. "Can never know enough, I say."

He raised the military knife and pushed the scorpion back into the helmet. "One of the deadliest on the planet," he said, "I'm sure our man will recognize it."

The Berber must have known all about the scorpion because his eyes went wide as soon as the helmet was brought near him. Smythe grabbed him and cut the plastic tie holding his hands. Then while a commando held one elbow behind the man's back, Smythe forced the man's free hand to the helmet making sure he understood they planned on inserting it. The man started jabbering in panic.

"The Citroen," Smythe demanded. "The white car, where is it?"

The man looked to the northwest and jutted his chin out. He then swept his whole head from the northwest to the southwest indicating a route parallel to the one he had travelled.

Ben caught on, "He was a decoy," he said. "The car must have taken another route and bypassed us."

"Marrakesh?" Smythe asked of the man and again moved the hand closer to the helmet with the scorpion.

"Agadir, Laayoune, *Al-yd al-Lh,*" he responded. *"Al-yd al-Lh,"* he repeated.

Apparently, the man was finished because all tension left his face. His body let go and a look of contentment came over him. For the first time since his capture, he smiled with satisfaction.

"What's he saying?" Barnes asked.

"Agadir and Laayoune are cities in the south on the coast," Smythe answered. "The rest I don't know."

"'*Al-yd al-Lh*,' I think means 'Hand of God,'" Ben said, glumly.

Smythe, Barnes, and Ben exchanged quick glances and a silent understanding passed between them.

"Let him go," Barnes said to Smythe.

Ben moved a bit closer and lifting his hand pointed at his open palm, "*Al-yd al-Lh?*" he questioned with hate in his eyes.

"*Yd al-Lh Sydmr al-Kfār Mn La Palma,*" the man responded defiantly. He lifted one open-palmed hand and brought it down on the other with a resounding slap.

Ben made a sudden move and the gathered men followed the Arab's head lead the rest of him into an unnaturally violent and angled drop to the ground. He lay there. Ben stood over him in a street brawler's stance with legs apart and hands tensed ready to hit him a second time. There was no need. The man was sprawled out and limp. Neither he nor anyone else had seen or expected Ben's punch.

Ben turned and headed for the CLV.

"Let's go," he said. It was not a request.

Barnes motioned to his men. One commando took hold of the man under the arms while two others grabbed a leg each. They brought the senseless man to the van, put him in and got in. Smythe got into the driver's seat and started it. Barnes and Ben got into the CLV and left. No one said a word.

63
Nothing Death Can't Fix

Ben Guerir, Air Base, Morocco

"What the hell were you thinking?" Artemis demanded.

Ben whipped around surprised at the anger in her voice. She stared at him and did not back down.

"What do you mean?" he finally asked. He'd have to tread lightly here.

"Barnes says you almost killed our only lead," she replied. Her tone said she did not approve.

"Not one of my best moments," he replied his face grimacing. Again his voice sounded subdued, almost defeated. He didn't want to feed her challenge, but to draw her into talking; she would make her accusations, and in the venting, get her emotions out of her system. She'd vent and then calm down.

If he went head to head with her, the confrontation could lodge a wedge between the two. The last thing they needed at this point was to complicate things even further.

Ben had left the scene of the interrogation in the British armored vehicle with Barnes. Smythe and his men were driving back with the prisoner in the slower van. He had sat and stared sullenly off into the Moroccan countryside. Olive trees whizzed by and alternated with cultivated green plots and sparse ground covered with dry brush. Figuring that Ben would speak when he was ready, Barnes let him be.

When they got to Ben Guerir, Ben trudged to the Globemaster. Barnes filled Artemis in on the details of the intercept on the highway. Artemis then charged into the aircraft to confront Ben.

"You risked our whole reason for being here. There's no excuse for a move like that.

"I know," Ben said quietly.

"You could have wrecked everything!"

"I know!"

"He'll probably clam up now," Artemis said, not letting up. "We'll never get him talking." She took on a sullen look and Ben could've sworn tears were close by.

"I was wrong, O.K.? There's not much more I can say. It's done. Let's move on."

Silence. They faced each other, one probing the other without words. Finally, Artemis looked away. Then she spoke in a quieter tone.

"My sister called a while ago," she ventured. Anger and accusation were no longer in her voice. "Mom's not doing well. Aphrodite has her hands full with the kids and her jerk of a husband, and I'm here waltzing around Morocco. She's so good…when she was younger, people got one look at her and were captivated…but to me she was always my sister to me—the kindest person I've ever known. Whatever she did for others…we're twins, you know."

"Oh, wow. How's your mom? Will she be alright?"

"No, she won't. Heart, Alzheimer's, my dad's death—the list is too long. Old age is just grand—nothing death can't fix. She won't last long. And I'm jetting around the world."

"Do you want to go back? It's all right. I'll arrange it and cover for you."

"No…Thanks. She's stable for now. Aphrodite will call if things change. Been a long time coming. I knew exactly what I signing up for.

I'm not worried about mom but Aphrodite. I worry about her more than she does."

"Well, do what you have to do. Don't feel you have to stay."

"We have a job to finish and, from what I've seen, this thing's bigger and more important than what I can do for mom or Aph. Getting these guys is super important to me right now—if you can understand that. I just had a moment…So what did he say?"

"Who?"

"The Arab you knocked out. What did he say that you had to hit him?"

"*'From La Palma the Hand of God will destroy the unbelievers.'*"

"There's the 'Hand of God' again. Will he be all right? Can we question him some more?"

"He's the only lead we have. For all we know, he cut Sam's throat himself. He'll be fine."

"I had no right to blame you. Aphrodite's call upset me. All you did is hit a bad guy. I was out of line."

She was contrite and her remorse was genuine. He saw honesty and acceptance in her eyes. Criticism was no longer there. The emotional toll of trying to balance her personal baggage with the current pressures gave her a pained look and her eyes a deep shine.

At that moment, he hated himself. Whatever he took on, he worked hard to control his actions and consider repercussions. And yet at a critical moment, like finally having a live prisoner, his discipline failed him. Instead of engaging the man and trying to draw him out, he may have shut him up for good. Artemis's outburst wasn't even entirely due to his screw up; she was angry and felt guilty for abandoning a family that needed her.

She wasn't wrong, though. If the guy felt insulted he might not talk. How would he have reacted if the situation was reversed and Artemis had fumbled? Or, if Smythe or Barnes had screwed up?

"Thanks," Ben said softly.

"For what?"

"For staying, for wanting to solve this, for being a good partner."

"I haven't been much help."

"You have, and it means a lot." Then, "You have a lot more to give, dammit, and I expect you to give it," he chided her.

"I'll do my best," she said contritely. She noticed his light manner but chose to focus on the thought beneath it—that she was valued and needed. She felt the energy seep back into her and felt better. Working with others and having a common goal was affirmation. They were facing a conspiracy to hurt America and kill thousands. Home was a nice place and she didn't want her nieces and sister hurt.

"We'll talk to him when Smythe gets back."

She looked at her watch, a thin gold piece with a black face around her wrist, and said, "Barnes said Smythe was quite persuasive."

"The Berber and the van were decoys," Ben started. "The main group must be heading to Marrakesh—might even be past it by now. The Berber said they're heading south—obviously with the detonators and explosives. Our guy must be a low man but I bet the leaders are with this cell."

Outside, Ben and Artemis met with Barnes and the C-17's pilot.

"They have to pass through Agadir and Laayoune," Ben was saying. "There's only one road south. Probably moved up their timetable. At least we know La Palma is the end of the line. Best place to intercept them is out in the open."

"We could leapfrog Agadir and meet them on the way to Laayoune," Potsbury contributed.

"That's going to difficult," Barnes said. Ben stared at him as if he'd been stabbed. "We're still waiting for fuel for the C-17," Barnes said, indicating the pilot who nodded.

"Laayoune is about 400 miles southwest. The tanker won't be here for another five-six hours. But we have HAR2 on board," Ramsey, the Globemaster's pilot, added.

"That's it!" Barnes said euphorically. "We take the chopper," he explained.

"Does it have the range? What about passengers? How soon can it be ready?" asked Ben.

Barnes looked at his watch. "Less than an hour; that will put us outside of Laayoune in three hours. We hoist the CLV and take it with us. That will give us transportation and flexibility."

"The chopper can do that?" asked Artemis.

"It's got two Pratt and Whitney turboshafts…" he stopped. "Yes, it can," he finished. "And eight passengers."

"That's it, then." Ben said. He looked around. "Anything else?" he asked.

"Just to be clear—three hours as the crow flies; there won't be any fuel to search for the hostiles," Barnes added.

"The Globemaster will follow after refueling," Ben stated.

"Rendezvous sometime after 20:00 hours," Ramsey responded.

Ben to Artemis, "Inform the intelligence services. Maybe Geospatial or National Reconnaissance can get a visual on these guys. God knows they've not given us much so far. We're looking for a convoy of several vehicles—one a white Citroen."

During the tail end of the discussion, the blue van with Smythe, the commandos, and the Berber arrived. The prisoner did not look so good. Further interrogation had obviously taken place.

"Let's see if Smythe learned anything," Ben said.

64

St. Andrew in the Desert

Moroccan Controlled Western Sahara

From a distance and against the backdrop of the undulating desert, the British Search and Rescue chopper known as the HAR2 resembled a dragonfly single-mindedly scurrying away with a prize dangling underneath. The "prize" was the Command Liaison Vehicle, the British counterpart to the American Humvee. It was tethered by steel cable and hung at an angle due to the chopper's pull. Below desert stretched in all directions as far as the eye could see. Occasionally thin dark patches of terrain that resembled varicose veins broke the monotony of the creamy expanse. These were eroded sections that had turned into wadis where grasses and vegetation had taken hold to create a bit of shade. Off to the right was the N1 coastal road, which the HAR pilots used as a guide. The ocean came in and out of view.

Smythe pointed at the desert. "Not many places as barren as that, I'll wager," he said to no one in particular.

"Another tidbit from your knowledge of the lay of the land?" Ben asked remembering Smythe's resourcefulness with the black scorpion that had been so effective on the Berber.

"Of interest to those less travelled may be the conveyor we'll be meeting further on. Right in our way, it is."

Over the din of the chopper and the muffle of the helmets, no one was sure if he or she heard right. Heads turned towards Smythe looking for clues and an explanation.

"Say again," one of the commandos asked.

"What is it?" Artemis said simultaneously.

"A conveyor in the desert should be just ahead."

"Like at an airport?" Artemis asked.

"Same concept," Smythe smiled, "but industrial. Longest in the world, in fact."

"In the middle of the desert?" Ben asked. "Why?"

"Simple really—serves a mine transporting phosphate ore 60 miles to the nearest port. Eliminates artic lorries and the human factor rather nicely."

"Should decide on a landing site soon," Barnes's voice broke into the headphones interrupting them. "Fifteen minutes of fuel left."

"Let's find a spot then."

"We want to remain hidden from the road, correct?"

"How about that hill over there?" Ben indicated a hill, which was basically a pile of sand but higher than other dunes. "We'll be out of sight. Two-three miles from the road?" Ben continued.

"Sounds about right."

"That's good. Head there."

The HAR2 with Barnes and Smythe at the controls made for the dune. In the distance, the narrow line of the road snaked across the landscape but empty of traffic. Sections disappeared behind dunes and reappeared further on.

The first task was to set the armored CLV onto the ground. Then the chopper would land and they'd get to the highway and lie in wait for the militants. Barnes circled behind the hill. Desert stretched on four sides. In the west, the ocean was 20 miles away where the N1 stayed inland for a more direct route to Laayoune.

Barnes lowered the chopper behind the hill. He hovered and some sand lifted and formed a light dust cloud. The hill's incline forced the sand up the bank where the rotor's downforce sucked it in and turned it into a whirlwind that hit the hillside and lifted more sand. The longer the chopper hovered the more the volume of sand increased and visibility decreased. Barnes concentrated on lowering the CLV and waited for the tug of the vehicle to signal it contacted with the sand. The ground was no longer visible beneath the whirlwind. Dust churned around the chopper.

"Captain, you may want to move off a bit," Smythe warned.

The HAR banked to the left as Barnes tried to get some visibility and distance from the dune. Even with the move, the dust and turmoil increased. Fed by the whirling blades, the desert sand moved up the hillside where it rolled, turned, and came at the chopper in a churning sand cloud. In seconds, the desert engulfed the chopper and erased any semblance of direction, location, and visibility.

"It's not lifting!" Barnes suddenly screamed in panic. Beeps and flashing lights came from his instruments. "It should be lifting! What the hell is going on?" He was staring at his gauges and pulling at his sticks in panic.

Inside the chopper, bodies were being tossed about. Outside, the maelstrom of twisting brown dust whipped violently. The whopping sounds of the twin turbo shafts went from a smooth whine to a grinding cacophony of metallic sounds that tore at everyone's mind and gut. They held on to seats to keep from slamming into each other or the chopper's sides. Billows of black mechanical smoke now streaked past the windows. In seconds, the chopper had gone from a controlled hover over the quiet sands to being engulfed in smoke and dust, to complete blindness, to fighting for its life.

No one had felt it, but the armored vehicle had contacted the hillside. As Barnes tried to lift, he dragged the CLV, which acted like an anchor. His efforts to gain altitude had forced the chopper uphill where more sand had been sucked into the chopper. The dust entered the engines and ground into every moving mechanical part pitching the HAR further out of control. Alarms blared and then a massive jolt came as the rotors tore into the hill. The blades sheared off and the chopper pivoted and rotated more than 120 degrees in response to the resistance. The metal body slammed into the hillside and stood still for a split second as if jammed into the sand. Then it toppled, hit the ground and started a slow roll downwards. After two jerking rolls, the tail section broke off strewing bits of metal into the sand and air and then continued rolling leaving a trail of debris and gouged sand behind.

After about three and a half rolls in what seemed slow motion time, the hulk jarred to a stop. The dust that trailed the chopper's descent rose from this new resting place. The armored vehicle that had doomed the chopper had continued behaving as an anchor and had slowed the wreck's downhill acceleration. It saved the chopper from greater damage and more rolls. Farther up the hill, two rotors were left jutting from the sand in a giant St. Andrew's cross—a stark marker at the site of the disaster.

Several miles off to the right on the N1 road, a convoy of several vehicles, including a white Citroen and several flatbed trucks, drove past heading south. At their back, too far away and obscured behind dunes to be noticed, dust and smoke rose at the scene the disaster on the hillside.

65
Setback

Muffled groans came from the chopper cabin. Ben was back in Afghanistan in his nightly nightmare. His Chinook was hit and banking sharply and Ortega and Saddle were falling out the door and they had five minutes to live before they'd die at the terrorists' hands. Everybody that had given the all clear had fucked up and not noticed that the entire hilltop was riddled with al-Qaeda bunkers. By the time the flyboys got the coordinates and provided cover, he had two dead, and Ramirez hurt so badly in the crash that he'd be gone in an hour. Then Parnell and Parente were gunned down defending their position. Huntley lost the chopper and he and his remaining men were pinned down for 27 hours—plenty of time for another four Marines to be picked off. He hated the screw-ups responsible for the fiasco and the S.O.B. pencil-pusher officers who kowtowed to politicians and cost fighting men on the ground their lives.

In typical military-think, the rules of engagement denied air cover to men on the ground when aircraft had been lost no matter how dire their circumstances. That meant Ben's men were picked off one by one.

He re-lived his helplessness every night. One minute they were joking, the next their chopper was spiraling out of control and men were falling out because they'd been hit by an RPG in what had been designated a safe landing zone. Ortega and Saddle were shot in the chopper's open door during the approach. Ben wound his body so tight to prepare for what was coming, that he woke and stared at the wall but did not see it. Sometimes he bawled like a three-year old. Commanders, politicians, army intelligence—they failed his men and they failed him and he had failed everybody by surviving. He screamed with hate at the snafu that had never given him and his men a chance and then he was suffocating and being crushed by a mortar falling from above and he flailed his arms but couldn't move.

"Colonel, you're all right! Colonel, you're all right," a voice finally made it into his head. He tried to open his eyes but they did not respond and he searched to locate the right muscles and get them to obey. Then he connected the voice to Smythe and felt his arms being shaken and he found his neck muscles and lifted his head and knew exactly where he was and what had happened.

It can't be as bad as Afghanistan, he thought. *It just can't.* "Everybody report in," he managed to say. He heaved and groaned and then remembered to check his own body.

Incoherent noises and moans answered him.

"Watkins…here…pretty sure I've got a…broken leg, sir," one of the commandos breathed heavily and umpphhed his answer.

"Potsbury here…only bruised…I believe," Potsbury answered from the second row next to Watkins. "Watkins, let me take a look," Potsbury turned to the hurt Watkins.

Smythe had moved on and could be heard talking and checking the rest of his team. "Smythe, O.K.," he responded.

"Boyce, here, just banged up."

Smythe spoke again. "St. Clair's…missing."

They waited for Artemis and Barnes to report in but no sound came from them.

Ben turned to look behind him where Artemis had been sitting. She was slumped over. He checked her and saw that she'd been knocked out. Gently, he went about reviving her.

Barnes's head was bent at an abnormal angle in the pilot's seat.

Ben started shouting, "Everybody out! Everybody out, now!"

The chopper had come to rest on its side. Besides the large windshield and the large rectangular window on the pilot's door in front, the HAR had two even larger square windows further back on either side. Bothe had shattered and the one on top faced the sky with a large opening. The occupants scrambled up and over to evacuate the chopper. It took a bit of doing to get Watkins with his broken leg out but between Potsbury, Boyce, and Smythe they managed it. Barnes remained motionless. Smythe checked him and shook his head to indicate Barnes would not be reviving.

"Possible aneurism or massive trauma. I'm not sure," Smythe had explained. They left Barnes in his seat.

They scampered from the chopper to a spot a 100 yards away and waited for the explosion that Ben feared. None came.

"The tank must have held. Barnes said we were low on fuel," Potsbury said.

Ben and Potsbury bent over Watkins and checked Artemis whose color had not yet returned. Smythe took Boyce and the two trudged up the hill in the direction of the armored vehicle. Further up, the massive St. Andrews cross, embedded into the hillside and still upright, was reminiscent of a scene from a Hollywood Golgotha. On the way they came across the other commando, St. Clair; his body lay in an odd angle obviously crushed and lifeless. He had been thrown from the smashed windows and then the chopper superstructure must have passed over him.

"The bugger mustn't have had his harness on," Smythe commented. On seeing St. Clair, Boyce was clearly affected. He moved off and vomited. Smythe went to him and both went up the hill to investigate.

Fifteen minutes later Smythe and Boyce returned. To Ben's questioning look, Smythe said, "St. Clair is dead. The CLV is mangled. Bent axle and fluids everywhere."

Ben looked around, "We need to get out of the sun," he said to no one in particular. He faced Smythe. "You think it's safe to go back to the chopper?" he asked.

"I think so. We can set up shade using the tarp and rescue blankets. We'll form a lean-to, regroup and assess options," he stopped. "See about first aid for Watkins here. Colonel, you have some gashes yourself that need tending."

"What do we do about Barnes?" Potsbury asked.

"What we did for St. Clair," Smythe answered. "We put him in the ground. Let's set up that shade."

"We should check communications first," Artemis said. She was sitting in the sand looking pale and sweating. She held her palm over her forehead for shade to look at them.

"Right. Let's do that now," Ben responded.

"I have no signal," Potsbury said.

No one had reception. They had passed over one or two tiny seaside villages some miles back but then had headed inland to follow the main road. They were tens of miles from civilization.

"How far to Laayoune?" Ben asked of no one in particular.

"Approximately 20-25 clicks that way," Smythe answered pointing to the southwest. "Likely our best choice under the circumstances."

"What about the chopper's communication system?" Ben asked.

"I'll check," Smythe said. "Boyce, lay a hand on Watkins here."

Watkins was in shock and his pants were dark red with blood. A few flies had discovered it and trailed after him as Boyce and Smythe lifted him. Ben and Potsbury lifted Artemis and steadied her as they limped towards the chopper.

"We could use some water," Ben said, feeling what must be caked blood tugging on his skin inside his shirt.

Fifteen minutes later a tarp had been tied to the chopper's side for shade and they'd all had a few gulps of water in them. Ben looked from person to person and got up. He took a stance as if standing on a line in the sand from which he would not retreat. With a firm voice, he took command.

"Let me say this to all of you," he said. His determination was palpable. "No matter what's happened here, this is not over. I'm not giving up—I intend to stop the terrorists. Barnes, St. Clair, the SEALs, and Sam Johnston did not die in vain. I will not just accept their deaths and do nothing in return. Their mission is unfinished; they did not see the results of their efforts—so it's up to us to ensure they died for a reason. No one knows when his time will come but we have more time than they had and the duty to finish what they started. That's where I stand, and I think that's where you stand. No matter what's happened here, we're not done by a long shot.

'Potsbury, you're with Watkins. The N1 road to Laayoune is two-three miles west, you remember. Get there and wait for a car—one's bound to show up sometime today or tomorrow. Rendezvous with Ramsay and the C-17 and wait for us."

He paused and before anyone could respond, he smiled full of anticipation and energy, and said, "I intend to get to La Palma and end this thing once and for all. And thanks to Smythe, here, I know just the way to do it."

66
The Line in the Jungle

Moroccan Controlled Western Sahara

"We must be close," Smythe said.

"I don't think I can take this heat much longer," Artemis replied.

"How can you tell, Sir?" Boyce asked Smythe.

Another time Smythe would have taken the opportunity to make this a teaching moment and lead Boyce to figuring it out for himself. He was analytical to a fault and averse to reflexive rejoinders that put the burden back on the speaker while the listener did no thinking. He expected his men to make connections and follow logical progressions to arrive at reasonable conclusions. Dead weight did nothing to make a team versatile and effective. Fools missed things and were surprised by results; they didn't learn from experience and continued filling the air with thoughtless drivel.

Today was not a day to be hard on Boyce. They had buried Ronnie St. Clair and Smythe thought about St. Clair's impish pregnant wife and child that Ronnie would never see. St. Clair was a good lad and had been about to thin out for the kid's birth. They'd placed odds on whether it'd be a boy or a girl. Smythe still held the pot; Ronnie had gone for a boy.

So Smythe simply answered with, "You want to look at the terrain, laddie, see the color of the sand you're stepping on. I've a mind to doubt you're a squaddie. Too many city blokes today—raised on chips and telly is all. Time on the land would be part of basic if I had a thing to say about it. Last week I asks me 4-year old niece, *'Where's that milk you're drinking come from, Bean?'* She looks at me like I'm bollocks. Know what she says? *'The grocer's, course.'* You hear that? The bloody grocer's. I don't know to laugh or go melancholy."

He shrugged and continued matter-of-factly.

'Ways back, the Sahara was both ocean bottom and jungle. You're walking on silica and vegetable remains. The color's changed in the last half-hour—I'm guessing on account of the phosphate particulates blanching the sand. That, and we've been bloody walking for three hours," he smirked.

"So it's close," Ben said in anticipation. "We have a chance," he added.

"Have a chance?" Artemis snapped. "Did you say have a chance?!" The cloth wrapped around her head and face against the sun came loose. Her eyes became larger and, as if having a revelation, she said, "You never thought we'd get there! You had doubts!" She was incredulous.

Ben returned her look with an innocent grin that if put to words would have been, "Who me?"

"Of course, I had doubts. We've had no luck since Cyprus and, as far as I can tell, we're a long way from where we need to be. We've no idea what we'll find at the conveyor, or if we'll make it to La Palma on time. Yes, I have doubts. I'm full of doubts."

"So this is not a good time to talk about spending the night in the desert?" Smythe asked tentatively.

Artemis spun around and glared at Smythe. "What now?" she asked, "Animals?"

"No," he answered. "Hypothermia. That's loss of body heat," he explained. "It can kill ya."

"I know what it is," she snapped back. "I thought you said the conveyor was a couple of hours from the crash site?"

"An educated guess, you might say. Could be three, could be twelve," he feigned a smile.

Artemis opened her mouth to say something, held it open for a second, thought better of it, and closed it again.

"Don't really know if it's working or on the blink either," Smythe said adding more fuel to the fire.

"You agreed to this?" she stared Ben down but indicated Smythe with her arm. "You knew it and agreed to it?" she added.

"Seemed like a good idea at the time. We'll find out soon enough."

Artemis turned and stomped off in the direction they were heading.

Smythe smiled lightheartedly as he looked after her. Ben looked, too, but his face was worried. He wasn't thinking about the desert night but about what lay ahead. They had to reach Laayoune and then get to La Palma. Just waltzing into Laayoune and asking for help would mean dealing with local officials, which in this part of the world could turn into days of waiting for their requests to navigate labyrinthine bureaucracies. On the other hand, no one knew what had happened to them—only that the chopper was MIA.

So, they had to do something, or else Laayoune might be the end of the chase. And the terrorists? More than likely, they'd get the time to launch their attack. *What the hell were they up to?* No. They had to keep up the pressure and make the rendezvous at Laayoune Airport. Ramsey and the C-17 should be waiting. They'd head to La Palma and might even get there before the terrorists.

They were 10-20 miles from Laayoune; no communications; no idea if the conveyor could get them there. Meanwhile they still didn't know the connection to the U.S., and La Palma's role. *A huge piece of the puzzle is missing,* Ben thought. *Something's going to happen on La Palma. Let's see: Detonators and wiring are stolen on Cyprus; Sam makes a beeline for the secret British base on Olympus. Somebody makes sure he doesn't get there to protect some plot—*

"There it is!" Boyce's voice reached them. "I see it." Boyce had gone alone ahead. Now he was calling back and waving. Artemis who had stomped off angry and was 50 meters ahead, stopped, dug into the sand with her feet until they felt cool, and sat to wait for Ben and Smythe.

A moment later Smythe smiled at her.

"Has your faith been restored?" he asked.

They looked towards the horizon. An unnatural line lay across the flat terrain. Boyce was jogging towards the bleached metal skeleton of the conveyor belt.

67
Leap of Faith

Moroccan Controlled Western Sahara

Boyce was a small figure in the distance and seemed to be walking right into the dark line in the desert. The belt was reminiscent of the understructure of an elevated monorail. A low mechanical rumble could be heard in the background. Five minutes later, the grating and whirring of metal on metal was loud enough to shut out a conversation.

It was an odd scene. The desert terrain had turned hard and rocky. Here it had been and had been leveled by thousands of years of abrasion. The horizon's low wavy ridgeline was 15-20 miles away. A hazy and dusty blue domed sky dominated the other 180 degrees. A cacophony of metallic whirs and rumblings overwhelmed the wide expanse and felt like an invader who had no concern the serene landscape he was disturbing.

The understructure of the conveyor consisted of blanched I-beams welded in the shape of X's for strength against the sand, wind and heavy ore that moved over it. A belt of canisters flew steadily across the top track anywhere from five to twelve feet off the desert floor. The conveyor originated in the giant Bu Craa mine in the east and ended at the ocean some 60 miles in the west; it stretched as far as the eye could see in both directions. The apparatus reminded Ben of the oil pipelines he'd seen in Saudi Arabia except here the racket was overwhelming. The pulleys, belt and metal cubicles all operated as an amorphous droning noise. Above the scraping of metal, the sound of thousands of spinning ball bearings could be heard as a high-pitched rhythmic whine. Ben wondered how much wear and tear the desert inflicted and how often the pulleys and bearings were replaced.

Boyce came back to meet Smythe, Artemis, and Ben so they'd be able to hear each other.

"How do we get on?" Artemis asked. "It's moving awfully fast."

"We jump on," Boyce answered.

"Boyce, do you see any elevation where we might try that feat?" Smythe almost pounced on Boyce.

"Maybe further on," Boyce replied quickly. "Possibly latch onto the containers and pull ourselves up," he added trying to salvage his pride.

Smythe stared at Boyce. "What about the metal footings?"

"Might make travel a bit exciting, that," Boyce added. "It's a risk—but I could make it," he added.

"I can mount a running horse, but I don't think I can get atop this thing," Artemis said. The sparkle in her eyes was no longer there. She was tired and near her limit. "Someone will get hurt."

"Which will slow everyone down," Ben said. "The posts are too close together."

"We've an hour or two till dusk," Smythe said. "Let's rest, and find a safe way on, shall we? Otherwise, we're walking two days."

Ben looked at his watch, "No one's walking two days; 17:30 hours. We don't have the time. Let's get on before it gets dark."

"While you boys figure it out, I'm going to get a hold of that grating before it drives me nuts," Artemis said.

"You can do that?" Boyce asked.

"Sure."

"How?"

"It's a matter of getting my bearings and setting priorities. The idea is to move sounds and irritants to the background. If left on its own, the brain will suffer and may never adjust to the clatter. I give it alternatives and try to refocus it. Works to an extent."

"Like using white noise to?"

"Exactly. I use meditation and create an internal alternative."

"You realize we'll be on that thing for hours?" Ben said.

"Exactly my point. Certain frequencies brutalize bones in the brain and organs in the body. The faster I come to terms with the sounds, the less risk of a migraine or vomiting those tasty MRE's we had on the way here. I'm not kidding. There are several lethal weapons systems based on sound. And, not much that can be done against them."

"You go ahead," Ben said.

Ben went and sat with Smythe and Boyce.

"…we find a spot where we can leap on," Smythe was saying. "We work together to reduce the risk."

"You think you can get on?" Ben asked. "Honest now."

They answered immediately, "No trouble," and "Yeah, sure."

"Major," Boyce brightened, "you and I go back a ways and get on. The Yanks wait for us at a low section and we yank them up." He smiled at his quip.

Smythe thought to himself. Then to Ben, "You'll need to run as fast as you can and get your bodies up to speed. It'll be a violent pull." He looked up. "It'll do," he smiled.

"What about the posts?" Ben asked.

"Boyce, two-step process: we grab and lift, then swing them on. You understand?" he looked at Boyce and Ben.

"Like parents lifting a child between them," Ben imagined the scene. "It could work," he added energized. "The physics are sound. Just watch the I-beams…"

"I think we can do it, Colonel," Smythe answered gravely.

Ten minutes later, after Artemis was mobile again, Ben explained the plan and ended with, "It's dangerous. You up to it?"

"Staying here is no solution."

The two of them returned to Smythe's position.

"It's settled," Ben told him.

"You too, Colonel?" Smythe asked Ben.

"Sure. Pull me up. I'm not 24 anymore."

"Boyce and I will be moving at a nice clip. As we approach, run as fast as you can as close as you can next to the conveyor. The faster you run, the easier we'll get you on. When we grab you, cross your legs and pull up with your arms. You understand—the more compact you are the easier it'll be to get you on."

Artemis and Ben looked at the I-beams visualizing the operation. Every few yards, the metal posts stood like sentinels securing their prize and stretching off in a long arc into the western horizon.

"We've come too far to fail now," Ben said in a voice that seemed a trifle in the face of the machine in the desert.

Ben was the slowest runner. Smythe insisted that Artemis and Ben run next to the conveyor for practice. He wanted the two of them to become familiar with the maneuver so it'd routine when the moment came. They got winded in the process before Smythe was satisfied.

Boyce and Smythe would follow the conveyor towards the west for about a mile and half where they'd get on. If either failed, the other would jump off and they'd try again. They had time for at least two or three attempts before they reached Artemis—that is barring a mash up on the menacing I-beams. Once on, they'd position themselves about a foot apart and work as a crane of sorts. Their combined strength would lift Artemis and Ben. They would each grab a hand and use the forward momentum of the runner and the inertia of the conveyor to advantage. It was the only way to achieve enough lift to swing Artemis and Ben onto the conveyor and avoid the I-beams.

Ben and Artemis would head to the west. Artemis would wait about a mile from their current position while Ben would wait at the mile and a half mark. They were giving themselves plenty of space, time and leeway. They'd pull Artemis aboard first since she was lighter. She was a trial run for lifting Ben who was heavier. Bringing his 185 pounds successfully atop the belt would not be easy.

68
Mounting the Monster

Moroccan Controlled Western Sahara

An hour later, and with the sun turning a dark stained orange and approaching the horizon, Smythe and Boyce were riding atop the conveyor, legs spread out for balance, and approaching rapidly. Artemis thought about doing another trial sprint but decided against it for her heart was beating rapidly enough from nervousness. She got into a runner's stance and kept watch over her shoulder. Smythe was signaling telling her to wait, then, that she move closer to the conveyor. Two hundred yards out, his animated signal told her to start running. She took off in panic, passed two I-beams, and then swung in close to the conveyor until she felt the metal brush past her, then threw her hands up and she was flying, legs pumping air because the ground was no longer there. They had her!

"Legs!" she heard a shout and she wound herself into a ball and she was four years old holding Aphrodite's hand as the two of them took off into the sky between mom and dad. She landed cleanly on the belt but her butt slammed into the rough mineral ore. She brought her head forward so she'd not fall back from inertia. The maneuver was quick;

she opened her eyes and Boyce was bent over her and had his hand on her shoulder to steady and reassure her.

"You're on! You're safe! Stay here," he said and walked over her to catch up to Smythe who was already moving ahead. She focused on their backs and saw them talk to each other. Boyce took a firm bent stance with legs apart while Smythe stood upright.

Artemis strained from her sitting position and a hope stirred up in her. She wanted this to work, with no complications, no delays. Let him be safe. He was a pillar—stoic, solid, honest and simple. He was the critical cog in the whole affair. Things had gone to hell, and he'd rallied all of them. He had cut through crap and got to the core of things. He had to make it.

Her hands tightened on the metal until her fingers hurt. The she saw Ben running, and Boyce and Smythe crouching and reaching over and lifting, and then she saw a foot lash out and they were swinging him to the left, and dumping him on the conveyor. Then, a pile of bodies atop the snaking metal and she was up trying to reach them but had to navigate atop the uneven ore.

Smythe was ripping Ben's trouser leg. Artemis felt sick to her stomach.

"Is it bad?" she managed to yell.

Boyce looked up distraught.

"I don't know," he answered. "His leg hit the post and then we fell over."

"I don't see anything," Smythe answered. "I'm going to pull the shoe off, Colonel. I'm going to check the bone. Ready?"

Ben nodded, wincing and oblivious. "I nicked it, I think."

Smythe carefully checked the leg feeling all around.

"Nothing hurts?" he asked.

"It's numb," Ben answered.

"Nothing's broken," Smythe said looking up and smiling. "There is a god," he added.

Boyce skipped around energized and thrilled at their success. Then he moved a few feet in front, pulled his body to its height and stood erect with legs apart facing forward. He lifted his head and spread his arms to their widest with palms open letting the air wash through him.

The conveyor moved in front of the dirty orange orb of the sun, mere inches off the desert horizon.

Boyce became a dark featureless silhouette. A long sustained victory yell rose over the clangor, moved over them and then eerily distorted and faded as they passed through it and left it behind.

69

Into the Cumbre Vieja

El Paseo Tunnel, La Palma

"I've passed this gate so often," Isabella said, "thinking it was only a water infiltration gash."

"And I never imagined it connected to my grandfather's cave," said Enrique.

"I could have had so much better data."

"Where someone sees a burr, someone else sees Velcro."

"*Che cosa?* What does this mean?"

"Burrs are plant seeds shaped like hooks—people think of them as annoyances but that's how the plant spreads its seeds. Burrs gave someone the idea for Velcro."

They were in the Paseo. They'd set up warning triangles in front and behind the Instituto's small utility truck. Enrique unlocked the gate at the tunnel wall.

They had packed their provisions into two sacks—Isabella's had a reserve headlamp, first aid kit, cow's tails and Petzl ascenders and descenders, a tremor seismometer, geophones, and a data recording unit. Enrique carried a digital station with a gas analysis chamber, a new

FBA-23 Force Balance Accelerometer known as the Episensor, and a K2 Strong Motion Accelerograph that came with its own four-legged base. They carried no water, which saved some weight—there was plenty of runoff and rivulets to drink from. Enrique put on his belt and an old dented aluminum cup hung from it. Isabella looked on inquisitively.

"My grandfather's; had it with him when he fought Franco with the 26th Infantry and later with French Resistance." He shrugged, "Still holds water."

"*Credo che sia così nobile,*" Isabella said. "I like it. So you are not shallow *e interessati nel mio corpo solo.*"

He squirmed uncomfortably. He changed the subject.

"Elbow and kneepads—a fall inside and we're in trouble."

He handed her a thin cotton cap.

"It's an old trick," he said. "Protects the scalp from the helmet."

She put it on and tried the helmet. Enrique adjusted her headlamp.

"Ready?" he asked.

"Lead the way."

"Lean forward if you think you'll lose your balance. We'll stop and rest—and we can look around. There's lots of erosion so weathered basalts, sharp scoria everywhere…wear the gloves. Some nice examples of vesicular olivines also."

"I want to see the lava tube. How big is it?"

"Not sure exactly—maybe 400 meters, four to six meters high—circular, smooth, in pristine condition—a surprise considering the water in the Cumbre Vieja. Haven't gotten a good look at it. I was more interested in setting up the recorders."

"We'll download the data and get the new ones on line. We come back in a few days and get a comparison stream. On the surface, I've been using Electronic Distance Measurement *concentrandosi sui cambiamenti* on faulting and geometry. But the deformation network is not calibrated with GPS."

"The lava tube is long enough—we can get laser ranging of leveling and triangulation."

"…now that will reduce *mia frustrazione.* Maybe we can confirm the displacement of the 1949 fault system using the Hawaii and Canary models—check if the shift is inside *i margini di errore.* I can't wait."

"Any recent fumarolic activity?"

"Only a few vents are monitored. There have been some spikes but nothing that stands out. Just some increased gaseous content in the hydrology—we should get pressure readings while we're here…"

"Ahhh…I just scraped my leg. How are you doing back there?"

"Right behind you."

"Let me know your status as we move on, O.K.? A stream coming up—we're crossing over. It's slippery. Commit your weight only when sure."

"Non ti preoccupare che posso fare."

"What does that mean?"

"I am fine. You'll be the first to know if I have trouble."

"That may be too late."

"You are worried?"

"Communication is essential in caves…yes, I'm worried."

"You lead, and I follow, O.K.?"

"Another descent here. To the right and step down. Watch for gravel piles. The cavern opens up a bit further on."

70
Grotta di Abuelo Theo

Inside Cumbre Vieja, La Palma

Forty-five minutes later, Isabella and Enrique were in a large domed cavern. Dark crevices that had been filled with volcanic soil once but were now eroded absorbed the light and cast dark shadows. Inverted strangely shaped cones in various sizes littered the area. One massive structure intruded and obscured a large section of the space. Enrique cast his light up at a twenty-degree angle. A hole in the wall absorbed the light.

"There it is," he said.

He lowered the light below the lip of the opening. A large mound of earth started at the opening, formed an incline, and ended at their feet.

"We climb," he said. "Step in the indentations, there."

Then he thought better of it.

"Actually, stay here. I'll go up and pull up the packs. No sense in risking a fall and damaging the sensors."

A few minutes later, they were both inside the lava tube. As soon as Isabella got over the lip, she stopped, stood up and took it all in.

"Wow," said. "Is like the Milan Metro."

"Can you believe those walls?" Enrique responded.

"I want to see," Isabella said excitedly. She took off her helmet and the cotton cap and tossed her head to loosen her hair. In the light, it took on a golden glow. She turned and walked away. Whatever fatigue she felt from the trek into the mountain was gone. She was excited and absorbed by the promise of a never before examined pristine place that was about to reveal its secrets.

"What about the instruments?" Enrique called out.

"Later," she said and her voice went forward and came back as a reverberation. "I want to see first."

He went after her.

"I can't believe how smooth the floor is," she said. "No erosion—no ceiling collapse. Wow! Is your grandfather's cave this way?"

"No, no. This is a dead end. The cavern ceiling back there collapsed and revealed the lava tube."

She stopped. They faced each other. Her eyes were wide and she was excited. A streak of dirt stained her forehead.

"This is beautiful," she said softly.

"What? The scientist left the building?" Enrique prodded.

"Per il momento."

He took off his glove. "You look so happy…and this andisol makes you look good." He pushed her hair back to reveal an ash stain stretching from forehead to cheek. "I like it when you're happy."

She took his hand and pulled him forward towards the unexplored part of the lava tube. When they got to the end, she stopped and turned.

She moved closer and her face and hair glowed. Every nuance of eyes and mouth magnified the delicate and significant moment. She leaned until her back was against the wall. She pulled him until their breaths met, earth and human scents blended, and pheromones lifted emotions and hopes. With open eyes, lips moved near to test and explore. The energy was palpable for they were centimeters from each other and felt the other's warmth but had not yet touched. When they did touch, it was delicate as if testing the union and savoring the contact. Every lip crevice tingled with electrified energy. Dams that had held back inhibitions and yearnings felt full and overflowing as if having found their complement. Each touch and each movement answered a question and each angle set off rare emotions and new cascades of sensation.

Isabella pulled back a bit. "You know what? You have to name the tube…you found it."

"I've not thought about it. You do it."

"What was your grandfather's name?"

"Theophilo. Abuelo Theo."

"That's it. *Grotta di Abuelo Theo.*"

"He would have liked that."

"Does it feel warm to you?" Isabella asked. "Here. Feel the wall. It's warm!"

"And I thought it was us."

"I'm serious. Maybe a throat is nearby."

"Maybe. How about we check the data and get that station up?"

They walked to the recorders that Enrique had placed weeks back.

"My initial reading was 21 degrees. Let's see where it is now."

He peered at his machines. "I can scroll to one reading per day—we'll get the full printout at the lab. Let's see. Started out at 21…21.3…21.7…definitely an increase. Last week, Monday, 22.2; Tuesday 22.3; Wednesday, 22.5; 22.7, 22.9, 23.1… today…23.2."

"It could be a cyclical increase."

"No. Those are big jumps. Let's set up. I still have to show you the fault line and the drop in the terrain. Then we need to get back and look at this data."

71
Ever Forward

Moroccan Controlled Western Sahara

"How's the leg?"

"Smacked it against the piling—but I think it hit the leather. Another inch and my ankle would've shattered. I'd be in serious trouble."

"*We'd* be in serious trouble," Artemis corrected. She brightened, became cheerful. Then, "We'd be lost without our fearless leader." Her eyes danced and she felt euphoric.

Sure, she was relieved, but was it more than just concern for a member of the team? Could she be happy for him personally? Did he dare think that?

He said, "The three of you would be scraping me off the desert floor. Thanks for asking."

Perhaps this was the calm that follows a storm—the release of built up tension, the pause that gets things back on track. After the crash and the trek across the desert, they had waited for dusk and allowed themselves a much deserved two-hour rest. Artemis got her wits, and after more days than she knew, had meditated and regained a semblance of perspective and peace. They'd made it atop the conveyor and were on their way to Laayoune. They'd meet up with Potsbury…if he'd made it to Laayoune and if the C-17 had arrived with the rest of the Rapid Reaction Force.

She moved closer, kissed him lightly on the cheek, and then hugged him. "I am happy you're O.K.," she said. "Really."

"It's been a hell of a day," he said. It was like day's end in Afghanistan. He felt comforted as if he'd been patted on the back for a job well done, as if someone was waiting for him, welcoming him, accepting him—someone who knew what he'd been through because he'd been at his side and experienced it also. *She* not *he*, he corrected himself. She'd held up well. She had toughed it out, pulled herself up, didn't complain and did what had to be done. There was value and goodness in doing one's duty and seeing the task through for no other reason than having committed to it.

The rattle and noise of the conveyor was a force to be reckoned with. The metal was solid and heavy since it carted phosphate ore to the coast. Now with the vibrations jostling her, Artemis felt the bones in her body, even the cartilage that held them together, buzzing with motion. She and Ben were seated on the ore and the shaking entered her butt and legs and spread in thousands of tiny waves to every appendage, every bone, every muscle, and every cell.

Ben was safe. They were on their way to civilization. All she needed was a bathtub to soak in, to rid the grit and feel like she weighed a fraction of what she felt she weighed now. She imagined falling asleep and floating in the warm sudsy water for hours. Then she remembered her mom's fascination with sateen. *If you want your man happy,* she had said, *give him a good bed and a bit of attention. For the bed, use sateen…not silk; silk's too cold…if you want silk, wear it to a formal affair. For the bedroom, choose a nice cotton sateen, and replace it every few months. There's nothing like it and, he'll notice it.*

What about happiness? Artemis had asked.

That I can't help you with, mom responded. *If your father and I raised you right, you'll find it…happiness show up on its own. You make happiness.*

Artemis had learned. *Don't think only of yourself, but of whom and what you'll impact, and whom you're bringing into the world—equal parts ego, altruism, and love.*

"Do you mind if I rest my head?" she asked.

"No," Ben replied after some hesitation. The signs were good.

They did not really fit side by side so Artemis stretched as best she could and lay her head in Ben's lap.

For a moment, he didn't know what to do with his hands. Then, slowly, he reached over and with a bent finger moved a bang of hair out of her face. She smiled up at him her eyes signaling the caress was welcome. Her whole body let go.

They traveled this way for some time. The noise was loud and regular and soon the droning lulled their senses and turned their bodies to jelly. The temperature dropped and the chill in the air bit into fingers, ears, and other appendages. Exposed skin lost feeling and the two of them moved closer huddling as best they could to preserve body heat.

After about 45 minutes, the vibrations, noise and conveyor stopped abruptly. They got up and looked back and forth over the endless snaking line but saw nothing except for Smythe and Boyce coming towards them with the same confused look on their faces.

72
Limbo

Moroccan Controlled Western Sahara

"Now what?" Ben asked.

"Maybe it shuts down at night," Artemis said hopefully.

"This can't be routine," Boyce answered first.

"Anyone hear anything unusual? A malfunction?" Ben asked.

"Over the rattle of this contraption?" Boyce sneered.

"As long as it's not Polisario saboteurs," Smythe volunteered. Boyce's hand went to his sidearm ready to pull it out.

Artemis went on edge, "And who might they be?"

"Sahrawi Rebels. Morocco controls the phosphate mines and the territory, but the locals have been fighting for independence for decades. They occasionally sabotage the conveyor to make a point," Smythe said smartly.

"And…you didn't think to mention this before we waltzed all over their territory?" Artemis's wide blaming eyes drilled into Smythe.

"Now that might be an un-needed worry, mightn't it?" Smythe smiled back. "There's been no violence for years. But negotiations did break down a few months back…" He smiled mischievously, then seriously, "Really, no cause for alarm. It's likely a mechanical concern."

"Let's keep our wits, shall we? No reason to panic. We'll set up a watch and wait," Ben suggested.

"We could be stuck here for a while, is that it?" Artemis persisted.

"We can always walk. But if the conveyor restarts, there's no way of getting on again in the dark. I say give it until 0400. If it doesn't start up by then, we walk," Ben suggested. He was looking at Artemis and was obviously trying to calm her. He pointed towards the horizon where an arc glowed over the desert near the horizon. "That's Laayoune. Can't be more than 10-15 miles away. We should get there by 0600."

"Agreed," Smythe sealed the plan.

The conveyor was silent but residual ringing from the clatter continued in everyone's ears. They sat on the ore resigned to wait except for Boyce who paced nervously and glanced every which way over the desert. The moon was out. With no trees and only low-lying sand dunes and shrubs about, the landscape was visible to the horizon. Dunes, rocks, and shrubs all cast amorphous dark shadows; the sand was a muddy gold and the sky a dark purple. The pale yellow of the moon showered everything. A breeze wound its way around the dunes and created a low rumble whose volume increased and lowered. Gusts passed through the conveyor assembly creating a low strained whistle pitch. Compared to the clanging and whirring they'd endured for the past hour, the desert was now disconcertingly quiet.

"Boyce, you're likely to give us away," Smythe said to Boyce who was pacing from along the belt. "You'll arse over kettle. Let's not attract any attention. What d'you say, lad?"

Ben looked out at the long serpentine conveyor that stretched for miles in either direction. On top of the otherwise identical and symmetrically precise containers, the bulges that their bodies made would be spotted easily from a distance.

"We're sitting ducks up here, aren't we?" Artemis asked.

"No one's looking for us," Ben said in a voice that was surprisingly unconcerned and nonchalant. "We'll be fine."

Artemis examined his face trying to gauge how much he believed and how much was bravado.

"Let's just wait and try to keep warm," Ben said.

Ben motioned to Artemis. They sat apart from the others and again huddled close together.

"Sorry to be so close," she smiled.

"Not at all. You're welcome," Ben smiled back. "It's cold."

Silence for a while. They looked out at the desert, the clear night, the universe above.

"Can I ask you something?" Ben asked.

"Sure."

"Are you ready to die?"

She stared not comprehending.

"What kind of question is that? I thought you said we had nothing to worry about," she said with a frown.

"Oh, here? We'll be all right, here. Compared to the chopper crash this morning, this is nothing. That's not what I mean." He stopped and she saw he was grappling for words.

He looked past her with an unfocused look. Before the conveyor had stopped, his caresses and warmth had lulled her into feeling safe and had soothed her physical and psychic angst. His touch had tingled like a salve, invigorated her skin, and rejuvenated the rest of her. Now she wanted more of the same. The absence of companionship, of a kindred spirit hit her. It felt like a heaviness hanging over her. Suddenly she was aware of the gaps and disappointments in her life. Unfulfilled promises hung in some limbo just out of reach. It was time she reached some of what she wanted.

She was in the auditorium in her Art History class in college and on the huge screen was the universe depicted as a round and small finite place. It consisted of the earth encircled by several spheres—places for angels, holy men, Heaven and Limbo. Below earth were several layers of Hell. But in her mind, Limbo was the saddest of all. It was nothing but a holding pen filled with wretched souls. Neither here nor there. Just waiting—a type of hell. Maybe even worse. Waiting for? Meaning, salvation, mercy, love, oblivion, damnation?

She looked at the stars twinkling in the dark blue sky and was surprised by how clear the milky streak of the galaxy was. Today, many more layers separated heaven from earth—now they had different names: dimensions, possible realities but, as far as she was concerned, they were still unfulfilled promises.

"We're in no danger but you want to know if I'm ready to die? Is that it?"

"I don't mean now—I guess in theory, we could die at any moment—I mean no one should die until he's accomplished whatever he set out to do and has something to show for his time on earth."

"I don't know anyone that's done that. It'd be nice to find Sam's killers and catch the terrorists, if that's what you mean." She stopped and checked to see if they were on the same wavelength. "Our jobs are risky. Not much separates life from death," she added.

"True. I thought I'd accomplished a few things—for the U. S., for Afghanistan, for Cyprus, even against human trafficking. Right now, I feel like I've done nothing. The Middle East is a mess and human trafficking is still thriving."

"Did you mean to fix it all by yourself? As long as there are poor, they'll be bought and sold. Especially during war. Nothing to do with you."

"Lots of lowlifes out there," he said.

"Always has been, always will be."

"Maybe the deaths and the past few days are getting to me—the chopper crash and that close call on the conveyor."

"You're not ready for a tally. I get it," Artemis finished his thoughts.

"In Cyprus, I fell into a rut. Became a bureaucrat. I hate bureaucrats. They got my men killed in Afghanistan."

"Not much separates justice from injustice. I've got news for you. You've passed the test—you still care."

He was quiet.

"I'd have left you back in Cyprus if you hadn't," she continued. "You can't think that way. Only leads to despair. Don't you dare think that way. Leave it to the 20-year-olds coming back from Syria, Iraq and Afghanistan in pieces. Don't need any more downers. We need more good guys fighting the good fight. The bad guys can't win."

"That's what I'm getting at...I still have too much I haven't done. We've not found Sam's killers, and we may not be able to stop thousands from getting killed…I'm not ready for my reckoning with the guy upstairs."

She was about to say something but the conveyor creaked, strained, and moved. Artemis and Ben held their breath to help it along. It kept moving and the noise was louder than she remembered but a minute later felt strangely normal. Finally, secure in knowing they were on their way, they glanced at each other.

"Halleluiah," Artemis said. Then looking really happy, she kissed him. Ben, taken aback, welcomed the respite and gave himself up to the passion of the moment and, elated, enjoyed her affection.

Her upper lip touching his, she said, "See? It's not over. We'll be all right. Let's go get them."

73
Convergence

Outskirts of Santa Cruz de La Palma

The eighteen-wheel diesel truck pulled out of a fuel storage depot just south of La Palma's capital, Santa Cruz and headed north. After a few hundred meters, it drove the perimeter of a roundabout and turned south. Two hundred meters later, it rounded a switchback that turned it back north. The grade immediately became steeper and the driver engaged a lower gear. A car engine revved on the left and darted forward passing the lumbering and obviously full tanker.

The mountain that was the island of La Palma began immediately at water's edge. Five hundred meters from the water were the remnants of a kilometer-wide volcanic crater. One-third of its rim had collapsed and its interior was now exposed to the ocean. Between the crater and the ocean lay the coastal road, a warehouse, and further north, a number of large round white fuel storage tanks. The port came next and beyond that the streets of the capital, Santa Cruz de La Palma.

The arc of the intact two-thirds of the volcano rose for half a kilometer in a typical cone shape and towered over the city and the port at its feet. Behind the city and the crater, the interior mountains rose more than two kilometers in an incredibly steep incline. The truck lumbered slowly across the front of the crater. The driver looked to his left and shook his head. A residential development with hundreds of apartments complete with tennis courts in front took up most of the crater's interior. The truck slowed further as the grade increased and the driver shifted to an even lower gear to climb up La Palma's mountains.

A few minutes later, the driver was above and behind the crater and entered the small town of Cuesta. There he picked up the LP-2 road and started the ascent and the switchbacks that led to the tunnel that crossed to the west. After his reconnaissance run, he had decided on an average speed of 15 kph and had counted 23 switchbacks in the road. From a distance and looking up the mountainside, the road's switchbacks resembled a taut spring laid atop green vegetation. The driver had also taken note of dips and sharp ascents as the two-lane road crossed the 11 ravines where the volcanic earth had eroded or settled.

He had given himself 50 minutes to reach the tunnel. Forty-five minutes after that, he'd be at the banana plantation.

#########################

On the other side of La Palma, a man came out of a hostel, stopped and looked out over the housetops at the ocean in the distance. He lit a cigarette. Below him, the town's small Spanish style houses appeared stacked atop each other and covered a section of the mountainside. Erosion ravines and a few small volcanic cones were strewn about below. Closer to the ocean and stretching along the coast, banana plantations took up most of the landscape and ended at the sheer eroded cliffs at ocean's edge. From this elevation, the ocean was a deep blue that extended to the horizon. The man looked off to his right and across the ten-kilometer expanse of the Caldera de Taburiente.

If the landslide we create leaves a ravine of this size, Allah will truly smile on us, Selim had said. He and the other men had stared at the huge erosion crater trying to visualize a quarter of the island sliding into the ocean, the turmoil that would result, and the wave racing and smashing into America. *The wave may be small, Selim had said, but do not be deceived. It will be large under the surface—so large that its power will change history. You don't believe me? Imagine a wave the size of this mountain behind me striking 2,000 kilometers of coastline several times. Now understand the favor that Allah grants us. Celebrate your good fortune for we will be Allah's Hand and destroy America!*

As if to comprehend and fit the idea into his imagination, the man looked up at the summit two kilometers above him. Finally, he flicked his cigarette from between his index and thumb. He watched it arc to the ground and land about five meters away. Then, with little concern, he walked over and stepped on the butt. He stood for a moment, looked down and smiled. He was an 18-year-old nervous conscript facing 45-year-old Captain Suleiman who was shouting orders. He and the other recruits stood at attention, confused by the order until Captain Suleiman barked it again slowly and more deliberately. Not understanding, they simply did what the directions told them. They stood on the gravel and faced the camp's yellow grass. Captain Suleiman paced and then held his hands behind him as he ordered everyone—smokers or not—to light a cigarette. After taking a few drags, he barked another order—to toss the lit cigarettes on the dry grass. The final command of the lesson, for it was a lesson, was for each recruit to pick up the butt, spit on it to extinguish it and stamp out any flames that had flared. "For the rest of your 24 months with me, this is the way you will put out your cigarettes. If you do not do as I have just instructed, you will be charged with malicious insubordination and answer not only to me but also to my superiors. Is that understood?" Then, "The land of our fathers is to be respected. Is that clear?"

May Allah grant you peace, Captain Suleiman, wherever you are, the man thought. *I don't need to put my cigarettes out any more, but it does satisfy to do so."* His mind stopped for a moment as a truth dawned on him. *We cannot escape what others have made us. We continue what they started and it is appropriate and fitting. 'In our daily rites, we are mindful of the eternal.'* This time the words of the Doctor had come to him.

He looked at his watch. He walked over to the flatbed truck stacked with plastic fertilizer bags and entered the cab. The engine snorted an angry cloud of diesel that rose and wafted over the tops of the houses of the town of Los Llanos de Aridane.

There was plenty of time.

In the distance to his left, terraces lined the hillside. Banana trees were everywhere below and thin access roads were superimposed like a grid onto the green plantations that covered the fertile landscape. Acres of plastic sheeting fluttered over many groves protecting them from the wind. The flatbed loaded with sacks of fertilizer would be a normal sight when it drove past banana groves and irrigation cisterns filled with water. It would enter under the plastic sheeting of the warehouse to deliver its load.

74
Laayoune

Laayoune, Morocco

A dirty orange dawn rose over the flat rooftops of the low square buildings on the outskirts of the city of Laayoune. This early, the lack of color shrouded the places where people lived, worked, struggled, and died. They toiled in the same neighborhoods they were born, and their streets and homes changed little over a lifetime. In an hour, when the sun rose and the blacks and whites of night became the dull yellows and sandy browns of day, these same buildings would look drabber and grittier still.

A few residents moved timidly towards the first chores of the day. It was pleasant and cool and the air was clear for the haze of midday was several hours away. Dark was slowly ebbing to hints of oranges, violets and dark blues indicating that dawn was close. The beauty wrought by earth and atmosphere would hold for a few euphoric moments until it would be overwhelmed by the sand and hot sun of day. The light would complete the desolation and reveal men's garish attempts to alter the desert and make a small piece of it habitable.

The four pedestrians entered the outlying streets and one limped visibly. The streets were unpaved, or if they were, it was hard to tell where sand ended and pavement began. Trash and debris were next to buildings and yards fenced with sticks and wire held goats and chickens. A rooster crowed and another answered nearby and then another further away. A dog barked from a half a block away but it was a warning only and not the constant gnarling that would have warned of the violation of the animal's invisible boundary. The four pedestrians zigzagged around two corners and headed northwest towards the center of the city.

A soft wail rose from the distance and broke the silence. They stopped and looked up. The voice's volume rose and undulated, and they recognized the chant of the muezzin calling dawn prayer. Ben pointed towards the sound. They adjusted their heading and walked straight towards the chant.

Soon they saw the minaret where the chanting emanated and knew the direction of the central square. A few short minutes later, as the muezzin finished fajr, Ben, Artemis, Smythe, and Boyce squeezed into a small taxi and headed out of town towards Laayoune's airport.

Half an hour before while still riding the conveyor, they had approached the glow of the city. They finally got a cell signal and contacted Potsbury who was delirious on hearing from them. They'd been out of contact since the previous day when they'd gone their separate ways. The Globemaster and the rest of Rapid Reaction Force were at the tarmac at the airport on Laayoune's north. The mining conveyor stayed outside the city to the south and ended at the port where it was loaded onto ships. They jumped off and briskly walked the few miles from conveyor to city.

"Simplest is usually fastest," Ben said.

Smythe looked at Ben and read his face. "How about a taxi?" he inquired.

"Why not?" Ben raised his index finger and dropped it to confirm.

Laayoune city center consisted of a large piazza surrounded by four minarets and was large enough for thousands to gather for prayers. Geometric gardens and greenery were off on one side. Four wide streets served as the perimeter of the square. In one corner, four taxis were lined up waiting for customers. One was stowing his prayer rug in the trunk. Ben headed for the lead driver. He was smoking and leaning on his car and Ben hoped that meant he was less orthodox than the others and, therefore would not ask questions. A minute later, they were speeding for the airport.

From the back seat, Boyce indicated the huge and hard to miss C-17 off to one side. The airport was quiet and open to the desert. Ben motioned to the driver who turned onto the runway.

Potsbury and several members of the Rapid Reaction Force were waiting on the tarmac. As soon as Potsbury noticed the taxi, he jogged towards them. They exchanged embraces, handshakes and smiles as the excited Potsbury made the rounds and greeted everyone.

"Water for everyone—and your report, please," Smythe spoke to Potsbury bringing him back to the practicalities at hand.

"Yes, sir. This way," Potsbury indicated the Globemaster. They boarded the plane.

"First, Colonel Huntley, a Colonel Randall left a message for you. I am to tell you—to quote word for word." Potsbury took a piece of paper from his vest pocket and read, "Quote, *'Pirates confirmed in possession of eLRAD from Pytheas and headed north—not for the African coast. I am in the process of locating said vessel.'* End quote. He said you would know what he meant."

Ben winced at this bit of news while everyone else looked at him inquiringly.

"Any news on the vehicles and men we're after?" Ben asked.

"No, sir." He looked at his watch. "We can presume they've amassed approximately 18 hours to their advantage. We've alerted the Ministry of Defence regarding the loss of Flight Lieutenant and Corporal St. Clair as well as the HAR." Potsbury turned to Smythe, "They wish to speak to you, sir, as soon as you arrive."

"What's the news on Watkins?" Smythe asked.

"Broken leg, I'm afraid. He's at the local hospital since arrival last night. Donohoe is with him. Sirs, there's something else."

"What?"

"We've had another go at the prisoner. His name is Khalid Mohamed and we've confirmed he was on Cyprus."

"He cooperated?" Ben asked. "Or, don't I want to know?"

"Actually, as soon as we accused him of Colonel Johnston's murder, he spoke freely. It took 15 minutes to explain it to him. He's laid out his movements on Cyprus but denied involvement in Johnston's death. He says thousands of Americans will *be smitten by the Hand of God,*' but he didn't kill anyone on Cyprus. He rejoices at the death of any American but will not take responsibility for what he didn't do. He says he and few others, including someone he calls 'The Doctor,' were on Cyprus gathering detonators. He's accounted for their whereabouts in detail. Sir, I believe him."

"Sergeant, if this Khalid and his accomplices did not murder Colonel Johnston? Then who did?"

"That I don't know. Khalid says all they did on Cyprus was break into the mine to procure the detonators."

"And Sam discovered their plan and was killed for it."

"We made that connection," Artemis said emphasizing the 'we.' She looked at Ben and added, "Speculation, on our part. We assumed the theft and the murder were connected because they happened near each other and at about the same time. Doesn't mean one led to the other. The operation name and intel came from the Israelis, which they got from the terrorists. Kahlid has now confirmed it. "

"The threat against America takes precedence over the investigation into Sam's death. Our focus needs to be on preventing this *'Hand of God'* event," Ben said.

"Sergeant, you're just taking the man's word," Smythe said sternly. "There are likely loads of hours unaccounted for in his time on Cyprus."

"We never told Khalid when or where Colonel Johnston was killed. He documented every hour of his time on Cyprus. Turns out he and this "Doctor" were at sea when Colonel Johnston was killed."

"But you can't verify that. You're trusting a prisoner," Smythe said.

"Sir, the man's a religious fanatic. He says he does not lie…some honor code about getting into paradise. I stand by my analysis." Potsbury turned to Ben. "I know it's not what you want to hear."

"I only want the truth, Sergeant. I want to get the scum that kill and destroy because they're taking the easy way and are too lazy to do the hard work of building. Never apologize for the truth, Sergeant.

Charlatans spin the truth. The world can always use a bit more objectivity."

"One more thing, Sir—a bit of a puzzler—Khalid demanded he be allowed to pray at 1:00 and 4:30. Don't Muslims pray five times a day?"

"He doesn't care what happens after 4:30!" Artemis almost shouted. "The attack has to be today—at 4:30!"

They all stared at her.

Ben turned to Smythe, "How about it, Captain. How soon can you can get us to La Palma?"

"We leave immediately. Defence is sending a team to La Palma to join us but we'll get there first," Smythe answered.

75

The Glory of the Faithful

La Palma

In Santa Cruz de La Palma, a large flatbed truck loaded with non-descript plastic bags pulled out of a storage facility. It was followed closely behind by an old battered public works truck. For all anyone knew, the flatbed was making a delivery to the western side of the island and the public works truck was off to make road repairs.

At the same time on the other side of La Palma, another flatbed emerged from under plastic sheeting and slowly navigated the narrow agricultural access roads that serviced the banana plantations. A few minutes after that, an Iveco public works truck pulled out from under the plastic. White powder littered its sides and it was obvious it was heavily burdened. The load was not visible because of the truck's sides and the tarp that covered its contents. The trucks moved slowly and changed gears frequently.

A few miles to the north, the trucks would pass the small town of Puerto Naos and then climb to El Pedregal where they'd pick up the main highway that led directly to the mountain pass. There was little to worry about. La Palma was an agricultural island with little traffic. The drivers had only to concentrate on the steep uphill grade and the ominously overhanging mountain that kept the western side of the island shaded until midday.

The ten-kilometer journey entailed climbing 1600 meters to reach the tunnel that crossed the island. Terraced banana plantations became smaller until the incline and elevation made them impracticable. The higher up the island, the more volcanic soil was exposed. The vegetation grew sparser and the tree leaves thinner and longer. In places, several types of cactus and endemic spurges grew to almost nine feet. Past the 300-meter elevation mark, these gave way to juniper, dragon, and Canary Palms. Finally, as the road passed 700 meters in elevation and approached the mountain pass, the climate became mountainous and the trade winds stronger and constant. Heather, Azores Laurel, and Canary Pine evergreens dotted the ravines and mountainsides.

Higher still, the mountaintops were mostly bare. Here the conditions were harsh and there was little water. At 2000 to 2400 meters above sea level, the mountaintops were above the rain clouds and the vegetation consisted of only a few most resilient and resourceful plants.

The mountaintop will slam into the ocean like a palm slaps a housefly, thought the driver, Abdul-Qawi, pushing the gas pedal until the truck groaned in protest. He put his hand out the window and urged on Mu'adh in the large flatbed ahead.

He smiled. Seeing the rear of the eighteen-wheel flatbed, he felt elated. He looked behind for anything out of the ordinary. He shifted his weight in anticipation and again waived the large truck forcefully forward. They were on their way. The day of reckoning was here.

The flatbeds would take position in the center of each tunnel. Once the Ivecos pulled alongside the flatbeds, Mahmud and Selim, the explosives men, would transfer the charges to the flatbeds and arm the explosives train. The two men had stressed the importance of parking next to the cavern to maximize the explosion. Once the charges were transferred, Mahmud and Selim would connect and arm the charges. Meanwhile, the smaller Iveco trucks would stop and set up signs shutting down the tunnels for maintenance.

The tunnel entrances were perfect for making a last stand. If God's *mujahedin* had to, they could keep law enforcement out for hours. By the time the island authorities got wind of the unscheduled closure and came to investigate, preparations would be complete. At the last moment, the Ivecos would detonate their allotment of 500 kilos of ANFO each and seal the tunnel. *"Our last moments before we enter paradise should be glorious,"* he had said. *"We fight in Allah's cause and slay and die. In return, Allah has promised paradise. And, who could be more faithful to his covenant than God? Rejoice, then, in the bargain we have made with Him: for this, this is the supreme triumph!"*

Selim and Mahmud had explained detonators, 'explosive trains,' delay elements, primer and main charges but all were above Abdul's understanding. The only thing that stayed with him was the importance of detonating at precisely 4:30 to match the attacks from the boats below. On getting the signal from the flatbeds, the smaller trucks at the mouths of the tunnel would detonate and seal the entrance to the mountain passes. Then the main explosion would come seconds later when the 80,000 kilos of ANFO on the four flatbeds detonated in the two tunnels. The heat and gaseous pressures would equal a nuclear blast. The gasses from the west-east tunnel would rush into the cavern. The extra expansion allowed for by the cavern would magnify the explosion several times. Selim had said 200 cubic tons of material would slide. The number was meaningless to Abdul. He imagined half the island sliding and rolling to the bottom of the sea six kilometers down.

He thought of their brother martyrs under the mountain. The last communication with the boat with the sonic weapon had been the day before. The men had exchanged greetings, prayers and farewells. Finally, they made promises of reuniting in paradise. The boat entered the cave on its way to its position two kilometers inside the mountain. He and his brothers would do their part regardless of what happened to the others in the two tunnels in the mountain.

No word had come from the second boat and no one knew its fate. The Doctor had said the attack from below with sonic waves, and two massive explosions in the tunnels would loosen La Palma's mountains and send them into the ocean. It would be glorious.

76
Shearing a Mountain

Over the Atlantic

The C-17 was heading west over the Atlantic. The sunlight, the ocean, and the sky were pristine. Ben scanned the faces of the people he'd become so fond of in the last few days. They did not look beat. The Rapid Reaction Force was rested and appeared anxious; their pent up adrenaline and force of will was ready to be used. They had a score to settle and were tired of sitting around. La Palma was the end of the line, and finally, they'd engage in the fight denied them for so long. Artemis, Smythe, and Boyce sported reddish and roughened faces from their adventure in the desert. Rather than looking ragged, they appeared weathered and toughened.

Finally, Ben said, "Last stop, ladies and gentlemen. Let's get ourselves prepped. Sergeant, Artemis, the two of you, find out everything you can on La Palma. Why are the terrorists headed there? See if you can tie Rafiq Al Jabiri and the boat with the sonic weapon to this mess. Check number of Americans, tourist destinations, basically, determine the terror value of everything on the island. Smythe, concentrate on infrastructure. Get any locals and military that can help.

Bring La Palma's authorities up to speed. We need resources. I'll talk to D.C. Oh, and Smythe, get some transportation for us. Any questions? O.K. go. Report in half an hour."

They disbursed to the monitors and communications equipment near the cockpit of the Globemaster.

Half an hour later, they collected. Smythe went first.

"The only military contingent on the island is the Guardia Civil which consists of seven men and one armored vehicle. Local police have no combat or terror training and no assault weapons—useful only as support. Tenerife—that's a nearby island—has a military unit with drug interception and raid experience but they'll need orders from Spanish Command—at any rate, we'll likely be there before them. For the most part, we're on our own militarily. We can't be arsed."

"NATO? British, American forces?"

"Alerted, but equally distant. Rapid Reaction Force is on its way from Gibraltar, but won't get there for five to six hours."

"Sergeant?"

"Right. La Palma is the westernmost of the Canary Islands. It is of little renown and, like all the Canaries volcanic in origin. Tenerife and Gran Canaria are much more popular destinations and have well-developed infrastructures. Both are better targets—Tenerife with 900,000 residents compared to La Palma's 65,000. La Palma is remote. Main preoccupation is banana production and local cottage industries. No military importance or presence, no industry, no chemicals, nothing that makes it a target in the normal sense. It's only noteworthy for its geology and volcanoes, which may make it a target. Really a stretch though."

"How is that?"

"As I say, there's nothing else of significance. The island is known for its pristine atmosphere, which has led to the presence of a number of telescopes and observatories. However, these facilities are remotely situated and manned by a few scientists only. Not high value targets—cost versus gain. More foreigners can be killed almost anywhere else."

"The point, Sergeant," Smythe snapped impatiently. "Get to the point."

"Right," Potsbury refocused on Ben. "La Palma is often mentioned as the likely source of a landslide which will produce an ocean wave large enough to devastate the coastline of a number of countries bordering the Atlantic—a tsunami actually. La Palma's volcanoes are also very active—so much so that a volcanological station constantly monitors activity. Given that the threat is against Americans, that the number mentioned is in the thousands, it's the only thing that remotely makes sense as a terror attack."

A quiet fell on the group as this sank in.

"Is that even possible?" Ben asked. The creases on his forehead indicated he was trying to digest this possibility.

"It's a theory, as far as I can see in the little time I've had, that depends on the height, steepness and volcanism of La Palma."

"But what does this have to do with the terrorists?" Artemis asked.

"The controls and charges stolen from Cyprus were used in mining and specifically in separating sections of earth by detonating a mixture of amonium nitrate and fuel oil," Smythe answered.

"ANFO," Ben said in a deflated tone. "As in the Oklahoma City bombing. Remember Kahlid slapping one hand atop the other?—does that remind you of earth hitting the ocean?"

"Are you saying that these wackos plan to shear off a section of a mountain and have it hit the ocean to start a landslide?" Artemis asked.

Everyone looked uncomfortable and ended up facing Potsbury.

"It explains the connection between the detonators and La Palma. And considering the scale of the threats made in Cyprus and by Kahlid, it fits all the angles," Potsbury answered.

"Let's talk to someone who knows," Ben concluded, "someone at the volcanological station. Artemis, there's a resident on the island we should talk to. Highly recommended—his name is Kal Thornaksen."

77

A Brighter Candle

La Palma Airport

On touchdown at La Palma's airport, a group of fifteen individuals poured out of the Globemaster. A distinguished looking older man jogged towards the plane. He wore a khaki windbreaker, aviator sunglasses and a blue cap with a yellow and blue coat of arms with 'Barca' stitched below it.

"Kal, Kal Thornaksen," he introduced himself shouting over the engines of the Globemaster. "I'm a friend of Hank Randall's."

"Ben Huntley," Ben answered. The men shook hands warmly. As Ben introduced the others, Kal gazed deeply into each person's eyes without himself blinking as if that one look would tell him volumes about the newcomers.

From the two-story faded yellow terminal, a police vehicle approached and stopped nearby. A small suntanned man in uniform got out and hurried over. Kal moved towards the man, in effect intercepting him, before he made contact with the new arrivals. They shook hands and Kal spoke to the airport official for a moment. Moments later, Thornaksen turned, found Ben with his eyes, held up four fingers, and pointed to a helicopter about a quarter mile away. Ben nodded then conferred with Smythe who placed his hand on Ben's shoulder in a goodbye and the two men separated. Smythe turned over a non-descript bag filled with firearms to Potsbury who struggled with it. Ben reached over and grabbed one end. They joined Artemis and headed for the helicopter.

A minute later, the chopper lifted off. Thornaksen handed headsets around.

"Thanks for coming to meet us," Ben said.

"Hank called; it must be important."

"It is. Colonel Randall says you are a resourceful man, Mr. Thornax…sun," Ben struggled with the name. "Sorry," he added.

"Call me, Kal," Thornaksen responded with a hearty laugh. "First time on the island I take it?" Then with a twirl of his index finger, he indicated the chopper's cabin. "Hard to have a civil conversation in here," he said. "Enjoy the ride—we'll be home in 20 minutes."

Kal reached over and grabbed a windbreaker similar to the one he was wearing and handed it to Artemis who took it appreciatively. The chopper gained elevation and entered the wet mist that hung over the coast. The chopper used its wipers and quickly rose over the rugged landscape dotted with green shrubs and exposed dark soil. Crags and jagged volcanic deposits, made more ominous and otherworldly by the pounding of the ocean, gave the coast a dark foreboding look. They passed over simple homes topped with red ceramic tiles. Occasionally a larger red roof indicated a tourist complex. But, the island was mostly made up of blotches of burnt blacks and forest greens while a web-work of small two-lane roads looked like the frayed threads of a randomly thrown net.

They headed south and crossed over the southern ridge to the western side. The earth was exposed and darker here with even less vegetation. Smoke poured from circular and ominous cones of some smoldering volcanos. A large number of inactive and lighter colored craters, remnants of long solidified lava, were strewn about.

Off to the west, the Atlantic Ocean went on forever. To the east was the steep volcanic mountain ridge with fumaroles, eroded scarps, and piles of debris. Vegetation and sapling trees were attempting to take hold everywhere but so far, they were still overwhelmed by dark and bare volcanic terrain. The further north the chopper went, the greener the landscape became. Finally, the trees became taller and older and took on the dark hue of a forest. The helicopter passed over a ridge and plunged down towards a large villa surrounded by tall and dense evergreens.

After landing, the chopper's engines ground to a halt.

"Mr. Thornaksen, this is beautiful," Artemis said, as they walked over a large patio with rounded and weathered flagstones. Flowers and hardy plants of all types surrounded the patio on its border.

"Call me Kal, with a K," Thornaksen responded. "No need for formality or family names here. You know, names in the past identified one's allegiance and pedigree. It's a démodé concept today and few look to the past for inspiration or knowledge. One of my ambitions, for the time I have left, is to achieve as much as my ancestors or to at least be worthy of them."

"Very difficult that," blurted Potsbury, "seeing that they're dead." He caught himself and looked embarrassed unsure if he'd overstepped the propriety of the host-to-guest relationship.

Kal turned and faced him.

"Exactly right, young man. But, *I* will know," he emphasized the 'I' and said the phrase slowly. "That's the measure. After all, life is a contest with oneself. It's the only way to measure oneself. All other comparisons are unfair because no two men are identical—more ape or less ape, as it were. Nor is any contest as meaningful as the one with oneself."

"But thinking that way, you can never be happy or satisfied," Artemis retorted looking distraught. "You can never win."

"My dear, from the moment we're born, we've lost. No one wins. It's not a matter of winning. It's a matter of achieving—of what one can accomplish in the time he has on the planet. Life is a 'brief candle' Will Shakespeare said and I must say I'm at the age where I have to agree. My fervent desire is for the candle that is most people's meager existence to shine a bit more brightly. Indulge me for a moment. Thirty years ago who could have predicted that the internet and Facebook would launch revolutions and turn the Middle East upside down? No one. Facebook didn't even exist 30 years ago. Or, that cell phones would turn millions from Stone Age subsistence farmers to global citizens overnight? They have no water or electricity but they have access to information that was available to only one percent of the population a few years ago. Today, in one year the planet creates more information than in the past 5,000 years combined. I find that fascinating and empowering. It's Shakespeare's candle burning more brightly than ever before. But there are pitfalls and consequences: rampant consumerism, the resistance of the established order, deforestation, polar meltdown, species extinction, the Pacific Garbage Patch…never heard of it? Plastic trash the size of Texas floating in the Pacific. In the last 100 years, man has managed to kill off God; now he's in the process of killing off himself."

He paused. No one said a word. Kal took a breath and added, "What makes me happy is giving humanity hope, solving problems—at least I hope to solve some problems."

"That's why we're here; we need your help," Ben replied.

Kal had been caught up in the moment and was obviously passionate. Looking apologetic, he said, "I'm acutely aware of the stresses on the planet, of the human condition, and my own limitations. Yes. First, I insist, you take a few minutes to freshen up. Follow Manolo there."

A local man looking weather beaten and wearing a white shirt with sleeves rolled halfway to the elbows had been waiting at the entrance to the white stucco house.

"Kal, we're pressed for time."

"I know all about your little adventure in Cyprus. I am most curious about this pirated piece of sonic equipment Hank's worried about. I told him…pirates operate a thousand miles south of here."

"He said you'd line up some experts on the island," Ben said.

"Already here, inside," Kal said. "We'll talk over lunch."

Above his head, the volcanic ridgeline towered over the entire side of the island.

78
Il Grilletto

Thornaksen Estate, La Palma

"Isabella and I were inside the mountain yesterday. The danger is larger than we thought," Enrique started.

"You mean the island collapsing and creating a tsunami that strikes the east coast of the U.S.? It's pure speculation—media hype, right?" Ben asked.

"If a landslide occurred and it generated a tsunami big enough, it would not only affect the United States. It would impact all of North and South America from Canada to Brazil," Enrique said looking at Ben. "It would inundate all low lying areas with Florida and the Caribbean suffering the greatest damage."

"But that's not likely to happen, right?" Artemis asked.

"Of course, it is *speculazione*," Isabella added. "We don't know for sure what would happen because tsunamis are *raro* in the *Atlántico*—well, that is to say mega-tsunamis are *infrequente*, but they have happened. In 1755 an earthquake 200 *kilometros* in the *Atlántico generato* a tsunami that destroyed *Lisbona, Portugal*. Waves of ten meters reached the Caribbean." She was excited and spoke rapidly. She threw in Italian words and her accent was more pronounced than normal.

"And in 1929, an underwater landslide in Newfoundland created a seven meter tsunami…" Enrique started to say.

"So there is cause for alarm?" Potsbury said half-questioning and looking for clarification.

"It's very complicated," Enrique answered looking frustrated. "The coasts of America, Europe and Africa are heavily populated today. And a tsunami is not a normal wave—the 1929 tsunami was seven meters in the ocean, but grew to 27 meters when it entered coastal bays," he outstretched his hands parallel to each other and brought them together to simulate the water being squeezed. "And, tsunamis are not one wave; the waters recede and come in again and again—as happened in 2004 in the Indian Ocean and 2011 in Japan. The destruction possible is unimaginable."

"But," Isabella added, "there are many unknowns. The…*consenso* before is that a tsunami from La Palma will *dissipare mentre attraversa l'Atlantico—but no one is sure—la dimensione della frana è più importante…*"

"…the size of the landslide," Enrique translated.

"…it may be 3 meters or it may be 300 meters. And before, everyone is…*pensano*, is thinking that a landslide in La Palma is not happening soon. But now…" Isabella trailed off.

"Something that large will impact the whole planet," Thornaksen said in a low voice to no one in particular.

Everyone stared at him.

"How is that possible?" Artemis asked Thornaksen in shock.

"A mega-tsunami has not happened in recorded history," Enrique managed weakly. "It could be a thousand times larger than the Krakatoa tsunami…larger than the wave that destroyed Atlantis."

They all waited not really understanding.

Enrique continued, "Current thinking is that Atlantis was the island of Santorini which was destroyed by the eruption of its volcano. The volcano created a mega-tsunami which reached Crete and destroyed the Atlantean Civilization on Crete—what we call the Minoans."

"Derivative effects are always worse," Thornaksen said matter-of-factly. "The 2011 tsunami created the nuclear meltdowns in Japan."

Enrique shook his head looking worried. "A landslide here is very different. In the worst case, several square kilometers of mountain may break off and keep sliding for four kilometers to the bottom of the Atlantic displacing water all the way!"

"And that could destroy miles of coastline in America?" Ben asked.

"A landslide can do that?" Artemis said.

"Yes, the displaced water has to go somewhere. Landslides are impact events that create mega-tsunamis. In contrast, the 2004 Sumatra-Andaman tsunami was 10 meters; the Japanese tsunami 40 meters. Mega-tsunamis have long wavelengths and pass unnoticed underwater but when they reach land they grow…maybe to 100, 200, even 500 meters…"

"That will cause world-wide devastation. Nothing can survive something that large," Kal said. "The world is too interdependent. After the physical destruction, trauma, cholera, and any number of epidemics will kill millions more. Desperation will set in. Infrastructure, society, and the food distribution network will break down. Wars will follow. It's too chaotic to predict beyond that…but it won't be good."

The group had just been given a vision of an unimaginable future. Faces were grim.

"But it's hypothetical—it can't possibly happen," Artemis persisted.

"That's what I'm trying to tell you," Enrique said exasperated. He spoke with the slight whine in his voice of one who knows but is not being understood. "It's been discussed and dismissed by many, yes, based on the geologic evidence we had until now. Isabella and I—we have new evidence—we've not told our colleagues at the Instituto. It will take months to confirm, to compare surficial and underground temperatures, ground deformation, reference seismic records, inspect tilt-meters, document changes in the geomagnetic field…" he looked at Isabella, "…do we have a proton magnetometer anywhere?"

"Yes, we record *continuamente* using a fluxgate system at station HD08…" Isabella answered.

Enrique looked off and catalogued the tasks they'd have to perform, "We have to examine the chemical and isotopic signatures of the subsurface gasses and measure modulations in flux and barometric pressure," he stopped and looked at Isabella. "We have to go back to the lava tube…we need help…this is too important; it has to take precedence over everything else."

He looked up at Ben and the others, "Only after there's a consensus on the data will we make an announcement. Isabella and I have to work within the scientific community."

His face became pained and the stress of the last few days gushed onto his features making him look tired and old beyond his 28 years.

"This is the two of you speculating?" Ben asked.

"We haven't had time! We've been working nonstop since yesterday analyzing measurements, checking the geology and verifying the morphology. We could be wrong."

"But you don't think so."

"I'll show you," Enrique said.

The group got up and followed Enrique outside to Thornaksen's veranda. The ocean took up most of the arc of the atmosphere. The rest was open sky, which created the feeling of being up in the air. Below was the island. Enrique pointed between house and ocean at the mountain.

"There is a four-foot fault, a drop, in the Cumbre Vieja about there," he pointed. "You can't see it from here, but it's well-documented and runs about four kilometers. The debate has been if it's evidence of instability, and if it will separate and slide into the ocean. But now, we think there may be a larger fault—maybe 24 feet—inside the mountain." Enrique looked at Isabella with a look of communion.

"What's the significance of that?" Ben looked from one to the other.

"We're not sure," answered Isabella.

"Best guess, we're running out of time."

"Even if not related to the surface fault, it's a sign of instability and slippage not considered before. Several slides have occurred before on La Palma," Enrique said and swung his arm to indicate the whole west side of the island.

"These are the largest landslides in the world…This new fault forces a reassessment of the whole geologic system and a reexamination of the landslide hypothesis. In the worst case, the surface fault may extend into the mountain and join or be the same fault as in the cavern. If it is, the fault may extend *500 metros* into the mountain. That, I cannot think about."

Everyone was quiet.

Isabella added, "It's a different situation—before, we think the landslide can happen, in 10,000 years, but now…now is like a *pistola*—it needs only the *grilletto*—how can I say?" Isabella formed her hand in the shape of handgun while pulling the trigger with her middle finger. *"Potrebbe essere l'inizio di un grande catastrofe,"* she finished.

"The tsunami-landslide hypothesis," Enrique added, "was based on evidence—the fault, the height of the mountain, the incline, the existing debris fields. Most geologists, including our director Aurelio Coelo, think a tsunami is not an immediate threat."

"Aurelio non ha le palle to consider a landslide," Isabella added rolling her eyes obviously not having Aurelio in high regard. *"Ma pensa if a landslide happens, l'onda risultante sarà di piccole dimensioni o dissipare."*

"Most think a tsunami will dissipate as it travels across the ocean," explained Enrique. "But with this new evidence…" he shook his head and creases formed on his brow. "The condition of the mountain may be more fragile than we thought. The slightest rumble from the volcanoes…"

"So explosions and sonic waves may get this slide started?" Ben asked.

"What sonic waves?" Isabella asked.

"It's possible that terrorists are planning to detonate explosives and use a sonic device to create instability. That's why we're here. Would that be enough to start a slide?" Ben said facing off with Enrique.

Enrique's jaw dropped and for a moment could find nothing to say. Finally, "Anything is possible."

"No one is sure of the stability of the mountain. The *frequenza* is critical," Isabella added.

"It could start this planet-altering landslide everyone fears?" he demanded.

Enrique's eyes were large and unfocused. He looked off at the mountains—his mountains. Isabella's face was pale and her head moved slightly as if suffering from vertigo.

"Because, we may have only a couple hours before that trigger gets pulled. Now, where is the mountain most vulnerable? Where might a collapse start?"

79
Dead End

El Paseo, La Palma

One armored vehicle and several small police cars of the *Policia Local* raced up past small residential houses on the outskirts of Santa Cruz de la Palma. The road wind up the mountain gaining elevation by switching frequently above itself, circumnavigating the bulges of hills and then winding through the insides of ravines. The vegetation was lush and green, and the ride scenic and peaceful for La Palma was sparsely populated and there were few cars on the road. It would have been idyllic had circumstances been different and the danger not real. Captain Renato de la Pena had all seven of his *Guardia Civil* men with him, all three of the unit's green emblemed cars, and had reinforced his small unit with another dozen men from the *Policia Local*.

Smythe thought they had a chance at securing the tunnel until he realized that de la Pena was talking about two tunnels and splitting the force.

"Tunnels? There's more than one?" he had asked confused.

"There are two tunnels—one east-west and the other west-east, two lanes each...one above the other...maybe one *kilometro* apart."

"We don't know which tunnel they're targeting! So there's an exit and an entrance on both sides—two on the east and two on the west?"

"Sargente Betancur is securing the exit on this side; we will secure the entry. Alert your team; use the satellite phone. *Telephonos moviles* don't work so close to the mountains."

They passed a tourist vantage point on the side of the road that looked over Santa Cruz. Tropical greenery spread out below and beyond the ocean; in the distance a mountain tip was visible on another island that had to be Tenerife. They approached the entrance to the tunnel. Thick vegetation of chestnut, laurel, and tree-heather surrounded the tunnel, which looked insignificant next to the immense mountainside.

They had no way of knowing where the terrorists would enter, and which tunnel they would target. Ben and the *Policia Local* would secure the entrance and exit on the western side. Maybe 20 men total to guard four openings in a mountain that was under attack from the inside and below. The below they could do nothing about the below.

In the west, Thornaksen's fancy Mercedes SUV raced towards the tunnel. From Thornaksen's house, Ben, Artemis, Enrique, Isabella, and Potsbury had followed the road down the mountain, left the Caldera and the Valle de Aridane behind, and picked up the LP-3 main road on the outskirts of the town of El Paso. For a while, Smythe and Ben stayed in contact and coordinated their movements. Their only goal was to rush to secure the entrances and exits. They had no eyes on the pass itself for the road was all twists and the incline on both sides was abrupt granting only a couple hundred meters visibility at a time.

Ben answered his cell, and listened for a brief minute.

"Smythe says two public works trucks are at the entry coming west. *'What? See what you can find out,'*" Ben said aloud, then stopped and listened. Then Smythe must have come back on the line, "De la Pena says the whole tunnel never gets shut down—they only close one lane at a time for repairs; never the whole tunnel. It has to be the terrorists."

Then Ben was yelling into the phone, *"What's happening? Smythe! Report! Smythe! What?! They're under fire! You're hit?! Get out of there! Regroup! Smythe! Smythe...!"*

He looked at the phone. To the rest of the team who were hanging on his every word he said, "They're too late. Entry coming west is shut down." His face went grim and his jaw tightened. The others in the car looked solemn knowing Smythe was in danger but not knowing how seriously.

Thornaksen speeded up. "We should be there in a few minutes," he said.

"Stay out of site when we get there," Ben told him. "Let's see what we're up against."

Before a bend, Thornaksen slowed and stopped. "It's around the corner," he said.

They got out. Artemis and Thornaksen followed Ben and Potsbury to peek around the hill. The mountain and forest towered above in bends and ravines. The tunnel entrance looked like a tiny hole in the mountain with the narrow two-lane road framed by a stone façade. With the mountain immense and impregnable behind it, the tunnel was a disappointment at only a seven-meter opening. A single public works truck lay across the road barring the entrance. Several cars were lined up waiting to enter and passengers were milling about and shouting at the truck.

"They look angry," Ben said.

He turned and they huddled for a strategy session. Ben looked at his watch. "It's 15:00," he said. Then to Artemis, "Looks like you were right, 16:30 seems to be Hand of God time."

"How about a frontal assault? Use my car. We drive up like we're tourists and then surprise them. They'll never know what hit them," Thornaksen said. "Heck, I'll drive myself."

"That could work. The other side is sealed off and Smythe and De La Pena are pinned down," Ben said looking up the mountain just meters away, "We're on our own."

"We can go through the woods, scale above the entrance and surprise them from above," Potsbury suggested.

Enrique and Isabella spoke in low tones to themselves.

"We need to get inside," Ben said. "These guys are gatekeepers giving the ones in the tunnel time to detonate. We can't get bogged down here; we have to get past them. Stopping the detonation…"

"They're moving!" Potsbury interrupted. "Going into the tunnel!"

Ben and Potsbury ran towards the tunnel with weapons drawn. The truck was driving into the tunnel and the few passenger cars were preparing to follow them. As soon as the truck entered, a blast burst from the black hole throwing dirt, rocks, and cement everywhere.

Potsbury and Ben ducked and turned back. They'd not gotten close enough to get hurt. Now they joined the others who came out to greet them from behind the turn in the road.

Dust and black smoke lifted and obscured the tunnel entrance. Rocks had been were thrown about and had rolled onto the asphalt and down the embankments. Clouds of smoke were lifting past the trees above the tunnel.

"They've sealed themselves in!" Ben said. "It's a suicide mission."

"Dio mio, dio mio," Isabella cried out. She grabbed Enrique by the arm and hung on. *"Il grilletto, il grilletto,"* she kept repeating.

Enrique shushed everyone. "Listen for aftershocks," he said.

"They're making sure they have time to detonate the main charges," Ben volunteered.

"A frontal assault is no longer viable," Thornaksen spoke the obvious.

"There's another option," Enrique said. "Not sure how long it will take, though—the cave that Isabella and I were telling you about—it connects to this tunnel."

Ben stared at him trying to make sense of what he'd just heard.

"It will get us inside? From the outside?"

"My grandfather's cave. It's a distance. There." He pointed to the northeast. "I connected it a few months back and have been using it to gather data."

"Can we get there in an hour?"

"Maybe, maybe not. There's some tough terrain and some tight spaces."

"Let's go," said Ben. "There's no other option," Ben said nodding to Artemis.

"Go," said Kal. "I'll only slow you down. I'll wait for the *Policia*. Take the car. Wait…" Kal reached into the back of the SUV and came out with a military rifle.

"Here," he said.

"The new M4," Ben said in wonder.

"M4A1, actually. Soon to be standard issue for U. S. services. Gas operated, nine inch barrel, safe, semi, and fully automatic options."

Ben put the carbine to his shoulder and checked it. "Thanks," he said.

"Go," Thornaksen said and handed Ben a box of ammo. He patted Ben on the back in a goodbye.

Enrique ran to the driver's seat, Ben got in beside him, and Isabella, Artemis and Potsbury scrambled into the back seat. The SUV spun around and sped back down the mountain the way it had come.

Two kilometers below, they passed two police cars speeding towards the tunnel with sirens wailing.

"God help us," Ben said.

"That's a tall mountain," Potsbury added, looking up where the ridgeline of the Cumbre Vieja topped out one kilometer above them. Another kilometer or so below them, the ocean crashed into old pirates' coves. Sheer cliffs were visible by the water where the land had eroded and collapsed over the centuries. Further south, the land's edge was ringed by banana and tobacco plantations and small coastal towns.

The Mercedes navigated the switchbacks and descended about a kilometer. Enrique slowed by a memorial cross topped with wilted but still red flowers where an accident must have claimed a life. He turned off to the right and entered a dirt road.

The Mercedes careened up and down over the dirt road fully testing the car's 100,000-dollar performance package for the first time.

80
From Bomb-Maker to Martyr

Inside the El Paseo Tunnel, La Palma

A single row of fluorescent lights stretched from one end of the tunnel opening to the other but the light it provided was minimal. In the tunnel's center, two long flatbed trucks were parked next to Enrique's gate. White plastic bags stamped with various logos and 'Fertilizer' and 'Ammonium Nitrate' were piled to the height of the cabs. Two men were working as a team at one truck's side. They pulled a bag free, grabbed it by the ears at the four corners, swung it back and forth for momentum and flung it on top of the others. They worked this way going the length of the trailer until four crevices had been opened on each side of the flatbed. Two others, their heads inches from each other, worked silently to arrange wires and insert compact brown packs into the newly created spaces.

The explosion from one end of the tunnel caught the men by surprise and they ducked and looked around hunkering next to the truck bodies. Seconds later, another explosion came from the other end of the tunnel and they turned to face this new threat. Mahmud recognized the detonations were not the mishap he feared—the blasts had come from the tunnel openings and not from his immediate area.

Then, too, the detonations were small and he was still alive. The tunnel ends were a distance away. The men suffered no harm and no debris reached their position. He motioned to the others to get back to work.

"Continue," the Doctor said. "It is nothing. We have sealed the entrance. No need to worry about the infidels any longer."

The fluorescent lights on the tunnel ceiling flickered but continued providing their meager light. A dust cloud finally approached and mixed with the lit headlights but the explosions were too far away and the dust weak and transparent.

Quiet returned. Relieved, Selim turned back to the explosives train he was connecting. He looked at the bags of ANFO but his mind's eye filled with images of Bashir and Maryam and the others blown to pieces by his bombs. After Maryam, he avoided looking at the martyrs so he'd not remember their faces—he provided the vests but others prepared the teens. At first, as an instrument maker, he was curious to see his creations work. All he saw was violence and pieces of rubble and shredded bodies twitching and burning. The image of Maryam's angelic face turned to smoky burnt flesh never left his mind now. Then Nadia was left disfigured and brain-damaged. The lump returned to his throat and he felt the twinge in his eyes. He tried to swallow, to get rid of the gag, but felt the pain in his throat instead. He thought of her and saw her in his dreams always wanting something from him. Again now, he mourned her. Her young, sweet face had been idealistic and unsoiled by adult affairs, unencumbered by routine, toil, or disappointment. She said her family were refugees from northern Iran, that they considered themselves descendants of Alexander's Greeks. He had stared in wonder the words strange and with little significance. Her eyes were a mesmerizing blue-green set amongst light supple skin. Her hair was hidden under a *hijab* and he saw only her eyes and face, but that small circle had been enough. Was she really an Iranian refugee raised in Southern Lebanon who'd taken on the Palestinian cause? He couldn't ask her now. He would never know the length of her hair, or learn the events that had brought them together. He knew that he could have talked about everything with her but he hadn't dared. He'd been warned not to get close to the martyrs, but she'd been excited as if planning a vacation. He couldn't help it. The idealism he'd felt at elementary school was awakened, still pure, still smoldering. Maryam's devotion reminded him of the dreamer he had been once. He could have tried to convince her that she didn't have to die. That she was the rarest thing he'd ever seen, that the last thing someone so alive should be doing is killing herself. That she could help end violence. He wanted her to understand that no matter what they'd promised, it was a trick. She could do so much if she lived. She should inspire others. Her death was an insult. The Prophet, peace be upon Him, had spoken of the beauty in life but the faithful were destroying life. Amir, Selim and others like them had twisted things. Now he understood that there were other ways. The *mujahedin* were killing her and something was very wrong in that. Suicide should not have been the way for her. What a waste.

He had followed and seen. Tufts of hair, strips of flesh, blotches of blood turning black, and bits of her charcoal grey *jilaabah* mixed with shrapnel, cement, and dust. She, the pure, had killed and been soiled by the detritus of the world. She deserved better. They all deserved better. There in Tyre, facing her martyred remains, he had resolved to an audacious act worthy of her fervor. He would build his bombs and bide his time, but also find a way to make the world fit for the faithful, the righteous, the innocent. He would be worthy of Maryam.

His focus returned to the one-pound booster charges. Once inserted in the gaps under the bags, Selim and Mahmud connected the leads between them. They checked the ignition elements. In his mind's eye, Selim saw a diagram of the explosive train setting off the larger train, which would set off the main charges on the trucks. An ignition element, very sensitive to heat and shock known as the 'match head,' would ignite the delay element, which would set off the primer charge, which would detonate a portion of the main charge. A hundredth of a second later the process would repeat and a split-second after that repeat again until all the charges detonated. They were using the older manually connected systems from Cyprus rather than the newer and closely regulated pre-sealed systems. The two men needed only connect the pieces, check them, and check them again.

Selim knew improvised bombs and the carnage they inflicted on the human body's soft tissues. Mahmud explained that explosives that moved earth were different. Dirt and rock were not flesh. In mining, explosive charges simply broke the bonds of earth on earth. Delayed explosions with time lapses were the only way to move large earth masses. Detonating in series dislodged rock and earth and created space for gasses, which further fed the explosions. The final act had nothing to do with explosives. The most important and most powerful tool in mining was gravity, which turned instability into slippage. Massive sections of earth moved which dislodged other sections and all tumbled searching for new resting places.

In La Palma, the plan was to destabilize a large enough chunk of mountain, which would turn into a landslide and hopefully, find a new resting place at the bottom of the Atlantic.

Selim's imagination reached its limit in understanding how the ocean wave would be formed and the destruction it was to cause in America. The new age that would come after this unworthy one were a vision, a rapture, but also his passageway into paradise.

Timing was critical, Amir said over and over again so the men would realize its importance. He spoke of the truckloads of ANFO and of the two devices in the sea cave that would bombard the geologic faults with sound waves making the earth plastic and unstable. The eLRAD waves would produce tremors and nudge the mountain past its breaking point. The ANFO would detonate in a series and shear off sections of the mountain. Gravity would take over. The steepness of the mountain, and the stresses built up over thousands of years of geo-volcanic activity and erosion would start Cumbre Vieja sliding towards the ocean. Each item affected another and together they guaranteed success. The only unknowns, the ones that would determine if a true apocalypse occurred, were the size and speed of the landmasses that would separate and the size and speed of the tsunami they would create. Still it would be the greatest act against the infidels since the time of the Prophet.

"Just another mining job, eh, Mahmud," Selim called out.

Mahmud paid no heed to the lightness but said, "If only we knew that the other eLRAD was in place."

"The mountain is hollow," Amir responded, "and the earth will separate, you'll see. We have two tunnels and the device in the boat."

"We are the Hand of Allah."

"May He remember us."

"It is our turn now. The mountain does not need much to slip towards the ocean. It will be our best work," Mahmud indicated the two of them and snickered seeing the humor in his pronouncement.

81

In His Hand

Inside the El Paseo Tunnel, La Palma

The men in the tunnel gathered around the Doctor. He had been walking about checking progress and keeping time. With his back to the truck and the stacks of plastic bags, he looked into their faces.

"I speak to you for the last time," he began. "Then we say Asr."

He stopped, looked over them again, the resolve working and strengthening on his face.

"What I do," he began slowly, "I do calmly and with devotion. I am at the door of Paradise and I ask Allah to find me worthy. Injustice has been my companion as long as I can remember—from the time of my birth and that of my parents' birth. Foreigners have decided how I and all believers should live our lives. Is this justice? Who are they to decide? Do they ask us before they send their bombs from the sky? We are not cattle; we are men and *mujahidin*! We are His Hand, blessed be his name! The apostates and infidels have profited from our toil and our lands while we have grown poor. The only peace we've ever known was as babes in our mothers' arms. We have struggled to feed ourselves because of the infidels. Our fate is our own! Our life is our own! That is justice! Allah be praised!

'While believers everywhere gasp for breath and are killed, I am composed and resolved in my course; I see my surroundings and know what I leave behind. I do this for myself, for my home, for all believers. My desire is to improve the world for the faithful and be an example to all *mujahidin!* No one can deny the grandeur and the selflessness of what we do here. We are benefactors, philanthropes. We do not only wish justice, or talk about it; we make it happen. Allah holds us in His Palm, and, as His Hand, we will right the injustice. Paradise has been prepared for us. Death to our enemies! Life eternal to the faithful! Rejoice in our success! *Allahu Akbar! Allahu Akbar!*"

Shouts of, "*Allahu Akbar,*" answered him. Fervor and emotion were evident on the men's faces.

The Doctor looked at his assistant who indicated time.

"Let us kneel for prayer," he said in calm equanimity.

Reverently and quietly except for the shuffle of movement, the gathered men bent to the ground following the Doctor.

82
Grotta Di Abuelo Theo

Cumbre Vieja Volcano, West Side of La Palma

The Mercedes SUV raced on the dirt road and a cloud of black volcanic dust swirled wildly behind it. It was evident that the road was not used much except as an access way for farmers to reach their vineyards or almond trees. Fallow fields with shrubs scattered about mixed in with the occasional tuft of evergreen. The road gained elevation and entered forested terrain and the road turned into a mountain trail lined with needles of pine. A sign identified it as part of the island-wide hiking and bike trail.

Then the trees became charred stumps and remnants of their former glory. They'd been burned by fire but some still had their branches, which were leafless black etchings on the barren landscape. Charcoal splotches of ash marked the places where bushes had once stood. The dust cloud behind the speeding and jostling Mercedes turned an ominous black that looked as if it would swallow the car if it slowed down. Small tufts of green vegetation were trying to take hold on a landscape that alternated from charred dirt to grainy volcanic soil to lava streams to bizarre rock formations.

Enrique stopped the car. "Up there," he pointed and everyone got out. Ben held Thornaksen's M4. Potsbury pulled out the firearms bag and passed a gun to Artemis who checked it by cocking it and aiming it. He gave three flashlights around and a gun to Enrique who took it reluctantly unsure what to do with it. Isabella held out her hand to receive hers.

Potsbury hesitated and looked at Ben.

"*Per la protezione,*" Isabella shrugged her shoulders. She smiled and looked at Enrique reassuringly.

"You know how to use these?" Ben asked.

They looked at him blankly.

"Let us do the shooting. But if you have to—hold firmly with two hands and pull." He looked at his phone. "The British have an anti-terror detachment en route—ETA La Palma 2 hours. Won't do us much good. Hold on. I'll tell them the entrance is sealed and what we're up to."

He typed on the device then turned to Enrique, "Lead the way."

They scaled a short incline up the side of the mountain. Enrique took hold of a shrub and used it to pull himself up. Thereafter all took advantage of bushes and saplings to help them climb. After two long minutes, they reached a large eroded embankment where the soil was exposed. A series of gaping holes opened into the mountain under some rocky overhangs.

"That one," Enrique said and pointed to one of the smaller openings.

They moved toward it. A large monolithic boulder was near the entrance and as they approached saw a large spiral petroglyph about two feet in diameter carved on the side facing the caves. Smaller lines resembling misshapen d's, b's, and p's were carved around the edges. Enrique ran his hand quickly over the spiral and entered the cave.

"Luck," he said.

The central ceiling arch of the cave reached a height of ten feet. Close to the entrance where there was still outside light, a series of stonewalls no more than three feet high partially closed off recessions in the wall.

"What are those?" Artemis asked.

"Graves," Enrique answered. "This was a Guanche holdout against the Spanish. Now listen…it's going to be dark; step in each other's footsteps and hold onto the belts or clothing of the person in front of you. There's a cache of lanterns a kilometer in at the lava tube. Once we have those, we'll move faster. Colonel Huntley, you're behind me, then Ms. Nelson. Isabella next, Sergeant you're last."

Ben added, "Be careful; we need to move fast and we can't risk an injury."

He looked and waited for all to comprehend. Then he turned to Enrique, "How does the cavern connect to the tunnel?"

"From the caverns, we'll enter a parallel passageway about 100 meters long—it's used as a service tunnel. Entry to the road is through a locked gate. I have a key. It's over a kilometer from here. Lots of slippery areas—some rough places. I have ropes in place."

"Got to get there in under an hour," Ben said. "Let's go."

They fell into position and moved single file. They scaled rock outcroppings heading towards the ceiling in the back of the cave. Once over the mounds, outside light faded. Eroded debris had accumulated at the base of walls or had abraded and trickled off the rough ceilings with the action of water, pressure, or gravity.

They walked for about ten minutes climbing and descending with Enrique cautioning about scoria rocks and sharp protrusions. Then he called out,

"Careful here. Water. Wait until I cross over and I'll shine the light back. Stay close. It flows off to the left. It's slippery. Watch the ground. Goes like this for another 20 meters. Step on both sides and swing back and forth. Make sure you have solid footing before you trust your weight to a step."

Fifteen minutes later the group had scaled atop a ridge using Enrique's ropes from previous visits. Artemis's palms were practically raw from pulling or steadying herself on the abrasive volcanic rock. Arms and sides hurt from colliding with jagged edges and oddly shaped rocks. Enrique tried to warn of upcoming obstacles, changes in direction and the slippery rivulets of water underfoot.

Now he stopped. He moved his light beam around to show a large hall-like cavern; his light got lost in some places where the recesses continued into other parts of the cave system. Dark shadows signaled there were gaps and spaces behind boulders and outcroppings. Enrique focused on one area.

"The lava tube is up there," Enrique said.

Ben checked his watch.

"We climb this debris pile here but up there, it's smooth and easy to walk. The equipment is 25 meters in. You'll see the LED lights. I have a few granola bars. Does it feel warm to anybody?"

"It is warm," Artemis responded. "Isn't temperature steady and cool underground?" She looked quizzically at Enrique.

"Yes, mostly," Isabella answered. "Enrique and I are studying this. We have not time to explain it yet."

"Use the notches to climb up. I'm going to check the instruments," Enrique said. He climbed first leaving them to follow.

"The lava tube is *perfecto* for monitoring temperature because it is deep in the mountain. *È possibile la temperatura è aumentata* because perhaps is close to a magma chamber. Only since Enrique came to La Palma is this possible because nobody knows about the cavern and the lava tube. He has recorded temperature changes and elevated gas pressures but we don't know the significance. We also must measure terrain movement but we need reference points *e confrontarle con punti* on the surface and from bore holes."

"Why does all that sound like pre-eruption activity?" Ben said.

"*È possibile.* We need more time to know these things *di sicuro.*"

After climbing and reaching the lava tube, they saw Enrique's light unmoving farther on. His outline could be seen bending over the instruments.

"Enrique, we're pressed for time," Ben said.

"Yes, yes. I need to check something. Get the helmets with the lanterns and put them on."

Isabella fiddled with the satchel and gave a Petzl headlamp to Artemis and one to Ben.

"Temperature is up two degrees," Enrique said. The tone of his announcement was not a happy one. "This is not good. Carbon dioxide, hydrogen sulphide, methane—pressures too."

"These are significant changes," Isabella said and bent over the instruments."

"This is strange. Look how regular it is. It's not possible…started 14 minutes ago…repeating at regular intervals…every ninety seconds."

"What is it?" Ben asked.

"A low frequency wave—very regular."

"Man made?" Ben asked.

Enrique opened his mouth but it froze in place and nothing came out. The significance of what the instruments were recording came to him all at once and his eyes opened wide.

"It has to be the sonic device," he said.

"…targeting this area…"

"Temperature has spiked, reached 23.7. Magma activity must be up. We've established inflection points and have been trying to measure rates of change based on Cumbre Vieja's past behavior. Pressure and temperature changes like these…" he looked at Isabella.

"…are signs of an eruption," she finished his sentence.

"So not a good time for a major detonation, low sonic waves or a landslide?"

"No!" Enrique blurted out. "A slide may breach a magma chamber or volcanic throat. You're talking eruption, lava, possibly a cataclysmic flow!"

83
Showdown

Cumbre Vieja Volcano, La Palma

"Did you feel that?"

"Was that a tremor?"

"The ground shifted! It's started!"

"The sonic waves must be loosening the ground. Perhaps started some settling!"

"We need get to that tunnel," Ben yelled. "We're running out of time. They can't detonate!"

They scrambled back towards the cavern. Ben and Potsbury jumped from the lava tube edge onto the debris pile and slid down as if on a water slide.

"This way!" Enrique called.

"Hurry!" Ben added.

Potsbury and Enrique turned to help Isabella but she'd interlocked elbows with Artemis and the two slid down together. They crashed into the two men, but their fall was broken.

The group fell into a single file behind Enrique. The extra lamps from the lava tube allowed them a faster pace and a new urgency.

Minor tremors came, and, at each hint, the group tensed, braced and held onto the cavern walls. The mountain had come alive and was in the throes of unfathomable strain.

"How much further? Will we make it?" Artemis asked while latching to a volcanic outcropping to steady herself.

"It depends what happens—how long the cave stays intact," Enrique's panting voice came back.

"That 4:30 deadline is only a guess," Artemis added. However, with a sinking feeling, she realized that the tremors proved the attack had started and that she'd been right—the earth was being made pliable and the detonation, which could come at any time, would force strata beyond their tensile hold and they'd snap and grind past each other in a violent and catastrophic release.

"And they only have one eLRAD," Ben added. "There is hope."

"There," Enrique said. "Behind the lights."

In the distance, they saw the purplish aura of fluorescent bulbs that lit the service tunnel.

Enrique led the ascent up and around crags and they entered the lighted service passageway. Ben signaled they were to move quietly and, in a whisper, asked Enrique the direction of the entry gate.

"About 50-60 meters that way," he whispered back.

Ben readied Thornaksen's M4 and nodded to Artemis and Potsbury to follow him. Suddenly a roar of shouts exulting *'Allahu Akbar!'* reached them from very close on the other side of the tunnel wall! Ben carefully approached the gate and looked through the wire fencing. He couldn't see much down into the tunnel but heard the murmur of voices off to his right.

A tremor shook the ground and the hum of the terrorists stopped for an instant and then started again with renewed energy.

Ben looked at his watch. It said 4:12 and now he too felt the urgency. He motioned for Enrique to unlock the fence door and he slowly pushed it into the tunnel and peeked around. The door was flush with the tunnel wall and the engine of a flatbed 18-wheeler was ten meters away. Another flatbed was parked behind the first and past that a two axle public utilities truck. Maybe eight to ten men were in the middle of the tunnel some rolling prayer kilims and others putting on shoes and talking fervently.

Ben turned to communicate to Artemis and Potsbury how they'd proceed but a yell of discovery forced him to pull his head back into the service tunnel.

"I think they saw me. Stay here," he said to Enrique and Artemis. Then to Artemis and Potsbury, "We have to engage them and we can't get pinned down in here. There's a truck 20 feet to the right. Let's get there quick. On three. One, two, three." He was out, and they were behind and all three were running for the truck. Ben fired at some men coming towards them.

A terrorist had seen the smooth wall of the cavern broken by the opening of the door and sounded the alarm. He had surprised his own comrades giving Ben, Artemis and Potsbury precious few seconds to start shooting and pick off a few terrorists. Some militants were cowering; others were grabbing weapons or scrambling for cover behind the trucks. Shots rang out from the fence door and Ben saw Enrique crouching and shooting and Isabella above him, her torso inside the doorway, but her left hand extended along the tunnel wall and shooting. Ben nodded to Potsbury and the two of them ran beside the truck down the center of road, shooting to cover their advance. A group of four-five terrorists fell dead.

A burst from a machine gun to the right froze them in their tracks but no bullets hit them and they realized they weren't being fired on. Instead, prill, dust, and bits of white plastic showered them from above. They reached the end of the flatbed and saw a man standing in the space between the two trucks firing wildly at the ANFO bags.

The earth shook violently and they and the shooter teetered to keep their balance.

"Illah rrahim tazhar alan li yadak," the man shouted and again sent a burst at the white ANFO bags atop the truck.

Potsbury fired at the man but Ben was drawn to a figure running towards the back of the second truck. His worst fear was that someone would detonate the ANFO. He sprinted after him and two seconds later peeked along the truck's long side and saw two men with hands inside the stack of white bags working feverishly. He fired at his quarry, but before he could shoot the second man, a shot rang out and the man buckled.

Artemis had followed the tunnel wall and had come on the men just in time to see Ben. She gave Ben a reassuring smile. He smiled back as Isabella and Enrique came up behind her.

"We got two," Enrique said.

A couple of lone holdouts shot from behind the second truck and the Iveco public works truck. Artemis and Ben ran to assist Potsbury. When the shooting stopped, they counted ten dead militants.

84
Earth, Wind, and Sky

El Paseo, La Palma

With the shouting and shooting over, the noises of the mountain returned. Tremors and deep tortuous groans came from below and above. The ground shook and cracks appeared in the tunnel ceiling where the cement was falling apart. Bits hit the asphalt, and the contact sounded dull and deep making it clear that the chunks had weight to them. The sounds of rock groaning against rock seemed to come from the very center of the universe and generated intense fear.

"Any ideas?" asked Ben.

"Back to the caverns?" Potsbury asked.

"It's 4:22," Artemis said.

"Not enough time," Enrique said.

"But a collapse may not happen," Isabella said

"The tunnel exit!" Ben said.

"It's sealed; there's no way out," Artemis said puzzlement on her face.

Ben looked at her and in a grave tone gave her the news, "I don't think we're getting out alive. It's our least worst option. Come on," and he ran towards the public works truck. The keys were in the slot. Artemis and Isabella got in next to him while Potsbury and Enrique climbed in the back.

The truck started and Ben drove trying to avoid the debris on the road. Another torrent of ceiling chunks rained down from what must have been a larger tremor. The truck veered sharply but its movement must have dampened the effect of this new tremor. The ride roughened into an obstacle course as the truck went over debris, but Ben navigated with quick sharp turns of the steering wheel.

They reached the tunnel end and got out of the truck but another shock knocked them off their feet. Then several deep thuds came in a row. Yells of surprise and pain burst from throats responding to the discombobulating loss of bearings and confusion in the trembling road surface. The tunnel was blocked with rocks and celling cements—they'd reached a dead end.

Earthquakes were one of the most terrifying forces for man because they clearly signaled he had little control over his own body and fate. It was a realization that he was at the mercy of forces beyond his understanding. No one ever imagined the solidity below his feet could not be depended on until it was literally no longer there. Once the grip of earth on earth let go, consequences were grim.

Balance, surroundings, footing, personal space—everything one needed to make sense of his world could not be trusted. Instincts and reference points got yanked away and primal fears awoke. Forces, which had no care for 180 pounds of flesh, wrenched man from the comfort and stability if his cosmic station. The world could tear itself apart and man couldn't do anything about it. People were insignificant compared to eternals like mountains, volcanoes, and gravity.

They got on their feet but another rumble froze them in place. Ben struggled and managed to get back into the truck. He raised the dump bed until the protective cover of the cab dug into the tunnel ceiling. He moved forward and jammed the flap farther into the ceiling until the truck came to a grinding stop. He revved the engine angrily and the metal scraped on the cement; the hydraulic metals ripped and spouted liquid, but the truck inched forward and the dump bed tore and fell backwards onto the road. Ben humped out ordering, "Get underneath!"

Then the greatest shudder of all. It was deep and felt first and only after the longest time did the blast reach the tunnel. The mountain rumbled as never before in a continuous shudder.

"That's the most powerful one yet," Enrique said.

"They detonated the other tunnel," Ben volunteered.

"Maybe a throat breached," Isabella said.

"Things will only get worse now," Enrique added.

"Now we see what the mountain will do," Isabella said matter-of-factly.

The tunnel reverberated and the rocks hitting the truck-bed made a horrible racket. The island was tearing itself apart in wrenching groans.

"*Merda!*"

"The ground is separating!"

"This is it!"

Shudder after shudder came and all they could do was hold each other and be terrified.

"Everything depends on the abrasive strength of the terrain—how much it will tolerate," Isabella added.

"It'll settle until it becomes stable again—maybe here or maybe at the ocean bottom," Enrique said.

"But we survived!" Ben said incredulously.

"The mountain is not finished," Isabella cautioned.

More shuddering and tremors. They couldn't hold onto the metal bed and ended up sprawled on the ground. The quaking vibrated over and over making moments feel endless. Smaller rocks and dirt rolled under the bed's tail, which was not as high as the front.

They thought they were facing their final moments when the ground at their feet groaned.

"It's separating!" Isabella yelled. Potsbury scrambled out. The only light came from the truck's headlights and Enrique's flashlight. A gap was opening at their feet. They heard a quick long painful wail just barely audible above the rumble and tearing of ground.

"Sergeant!" Ben yelled. "Wait! Come back!"

Ben turned the others back towards the tunnel and they just managed to scramble over the debris past the truck. Potsbury was not with them.

"This way!" Enrique called out and ran towards the interior of the tunnel. They tried to follow but bodies went in one direction and feet elsewhere as if drunk. They stumbled towards Enrique's voice. Rocks rained down and hands went up to protect heads but gashes were formed that bloodied.

A slowing of the rumble gave them a moment. They ran and could hear nothing except the earth groaning. Dust swirled violently as if wrung by a huge fan. Then a bright white light appeared that could have been the light at life's end except it reflected on dust and resembled the spray writhing around a waterfall.

Ben was back in Afghanistan under a helicopter immobilized by its huge spotlight. His training told him to make sense of his environment as quickly as possible and he turned around. He sought the edges of the brightness to get his bearings but the whiteness blinded him and he made out only shadowy forms and borders.

"What happened?" someone asked but nothing followed.

The dust became a maelstrom and rushed past him in a whooshing sound as if being sucked away. Then he felt a cold blast of air in the face and he knew something peculiar had happened. *Was he alive? Could he feel anything? Was he still in the physical world?*

He tasted dirt, and felt the wind but the air was surprisingly cool and fresh. Reflections and brightness came at him from the sides and he was seeing the walls of the tunnel in astounding detail! He struggled to understand.

He blinked and tried to see the light but could make out little. He thought he'd gone blind. He looked back. The tunnel was there but dust was rushing past him and he whirled back around and now saw a white haze tinged with blue stretching off into open sky.

Amidst all the destruction and chaos, a section of the mountain had sheared off and revealed the sky as blue and eternal as ever. The white haze of daylight and of sun shone unscathed and unaffected by the geologic turmoil occurring on the mountainside. Ben was spellbound trying to make sense of what had happened.

He stepped forward carefully and found himself at the edge of a precipice. He felt a hand grab his and he turned and saw a face covered in dust but recognized the eyes; Artemis was looking out next to him awe on her face. The sun was at 45 degrees in the sky, yellow and unaffected. Dust and smoke passed between sun and Ben. Finally, he looked down and saw a writhing mass of earth, trees, and debris rolling over itself and moving closer towards the ocean a kilometer and a half below. Among the dirt that slid and rolled in a convulsing plastic mass, he thought he saw a toy truck being tossed about.

Ben and Artemis stood mesmerized by the collapsing mountain and could not see the gas ventings and ash colored smoke that lifted into the sky from the burst volcanic throat off to the left. Nor did they notice the helicopter hovering in the distance high above the churning ocean.

85
Disaster

La Palma

In the lava tunnel at sea level, the eLRAD sonic weapon had sent pulse after pulse up into the rock deep into Cumbre Vieja Volcano. The beam of energy was focused at a geologic fault left over from a landslide of 400,000 years ago. The earth that had eroded or slid down the volcano had left millions of cubic tons of debris, ruble piles, and a scarped and terraced landscape behind. If these masses had been looked at by ground penetrating radar, they would appear as large blocks of earth stacked atop each other in layers and distinct from the rest of the mountain. The terrorists had no way of knowing that the fault everyone thought was four to six feet, the one they now targeted, was a surface offshoot of a 500-foot fault line deep in the mountain.

The many previous eruptions on La Palma had deposited earth atop of earth making Cumbre Vieja the steepest mountain in the world. Sections of earth strained against each other and would reach a critical point following some unknown geologic timetable. But now, events were conspiring to force the blocks to scrape past each other and release the energy built up over thousands of years.

Despite its name, Cumbre Vieja is not an old volcano but young and active and erupts on average every eleven years. Lava is pushed from the planet's molten interior towards the surface; on its way, it fills crevices branching off from the main throat and sometimes breaks through weak mountainsides spouting debris, ash, and lava. Cumbre Vieja is further prone to collapse because it is made up of volcanic soil, which is mostly ash and pumice, which are light and porous and hold huge quantities of rainwater. Water is so plentiful on La Palma that it runs freely down the sides of the volcanos amply supplying towns and farms but also saturating, weakening, and leaving the earth susceptible to collapse. Magma and other pre-eruption activities heat the water, which expands and may lead to a violent ejection of a kilometer-high section of mountain over island and ocean.

As Isabella feared, the list of events that could trigger a loosening of the hold of earth-on-earth was long: internal lava pressures reaching critical levels; lava-heated water turning to steam; the fault being much larger than previously thought; the eLRAD sonic waves loosening the hold of layer on layer; and the ANFO detonation destabilizing Cumbre Vieja in Smythe's tunnel.

The height and steep incline of Cumbre Vieja compounded the violence. Gravity pulled on the separated masses and accelerated their slide towards the ocean. Debris rolled and cascaded, and, in a domino effect, dislodged previously stable sections. Old ash deposits, porous volcanic rock, and water-saturated soil behaved like lubricants and turned blocks of rock and earth into a cataclysmic flow.

In Smythe's tunnel, Selim, Amir, and Mahmud had initiated a series of small explosive igniter charges. The ANFO detonations instantly pulverized the men and trucks. The main charges on the backs of the flatbeds went off. Explosive gasses expanded into the tunnels and the adjacent natural caverns maximized the effect of the ANFO; the weak bond between the island's soil and rock broke, and the extreme height and grade separated sections of mountain. On its own, the ANFO did not have the power to start the landslide but the series of events together were devastating.

The tunnel ends blew out like cork stoppers. The debris was only five to ten feet thick and no match for the expanding gasses and pressures generated by the detonated ANFO. Outside the tunnel, smoke and dust spewed upwardly in convoluted clouds. Swirling torrents moved past the vegetation of the hillside. Below, boulders rolled away from the entrance. Shouts and cries of pain rose from the police and locals that were hit by airborne missiles. In the chaos, no one imagined that the danger was only beginning.

The explosion appeared to have no other effect for the moment. The terrain absorbed the force waves. For a few seconds, all was quiet and some hoped this was the extent of the danger. Then a low and almost indiscernible hum was heard in the background.

In the other tunnel, Ben and his team felt the blast in their bones as the walls shuddered and debris rained. The few moments of stability gave them time to reach the end of the tunnel and find refuge under the truck's dump bed.

The landslide began with rocky outcroppings and loose sections of earth separating from Cumbre Vieja's sides. These were the first signs of the massive geologic turmoil occurring deep in the volcano. As the earth moved downward, it broke apart and settled on itself. Seen from a distance, the movement appeared slow because the block extended deep into the mountain and it took time for one section to effect its neighbor. Then a section subsided like liquid and blended into the surrounding terrain; it began sliding and sweeping everything in its path. The topography changed leaving behind scoured deep channels. Levees appeared but collapsed a moment later as large blocks and faults jostled, combined and sought stability. Existing terraces and footings gave way and became mush in the turmoil.

The landslide turned into an avalanche. Houses and entire towns turned on themselves and disappeared. As the earth convulsed and turned, whitewashed walls, terra cotta roofs, power grid pylons, and automobiles surfaced, rolled and were quickly swallowed again.

One volcanic throat on the side of the mountain breached and flaming debris and churning smoke poured out. It was, however, a small, localized event that would peter out over the next few days.

If this were the extent of the destruction—terrible though it was— the landslide would have remained of moderate interest to the rest of the world. La Palma was a small remote island in the middle of the

Atlantic and less than a thousand had perished. Air traffic was diverted and the whole incident would soon be overshadowed by events of more interest to the rest of the planet. Only earth scientists would recognize it as the rarest and largest geologic event of the last several thousand years.

The forces that had been unleashed categorized the catastrophe as a Global Geologic Impact Event. The landslide and tsunami left La Palma in near pristine condition compared to the distant coastlines that it would decimate hours later.

A cycle of increased volcanic and seismic activity had started months back on the edges of the African tectonic plate. On the plate's other end in Eritrea, Nabro stratovolcano erupted. That, in turn, had been preceded by a swarm of earthquakes in the Gulf of Aden farther along the African fault line. A month later, a seismic swarm shook La Palma's Canary Island neighbor, El Hierro, raising concern and calls for evacuation. Spikes were recorded on the volcanological station on La Palma but they'd not been alarming enough to force evacuations. On discovering the fault line in his grandfather's cave, Enrique worried that the increased tectonic activity might affect Cumbre Vieja but he never got the time to gather enough data or formulate a case to present to his colleagues.

"This is the first recorded eruption of Nabro," Isabella had said, "so we know the African plate is *sovraccaricati*—how you say—over stressed. Iceland has been *molto attivo* also—active eruptions and lava emissions. Remember the *aeroplano* diversions over Europe last summer?"

La Palma and the other Canary Islands lay on offshoots of the Mid-Atlantic Ridge, which separated the African from the North American tectonic plates and stretched from Iceland to the South Atlantic. The edge of the Eurasian plate was close and ran under the Gibraltar Strait where it met the Mid-Atlantic Ridge at a right angle.

The 50-200 meters thick section of mountain that slid amounted to 200 to 600 cubic meters of material. Isabella had mapped several debris deposits in the ocean—evidence that landslides had occurred at La Palma several times in the past. Due to previous debris, the current slide found resistance in its descent and it barely made it half a kilometer into the ocean.

Regardless, during its descent, the mass of earth displaced huge amounts of water and sent a force wave across the Atlantic. It weakened as it radiated but still traveled thousands of miles. The power it held, and how much it would still have when it reached the North American coast were unknowns. The wave would hit the continental shelf and having nowhere to go, would compress, lift and increase power and speed. The shallow coastal shelves and populated coastlines of America were in the way and would be overrun.

Thankfully, the explosion in the west-east tunnel never happened because Ben and Artemis stopped it. In the east-west tunnel, Renato de la Pena and Smythe had no chance. With only one explosion and only one eLRAD, the section of mountain that sheared off was much smaller than it could have been. Ben, Artemis, Enrique and Isabella had saved North America from a greater catastrophe, but they'd lost Potsbury and Smythe.

The massive force-wave that left La Palma weakened and only reached 15 feet when it hit the eastern coast of the North American Continent. Coastal cities across the seaboard were partially destroyed and thousands of people died from the tsunami and the panic that followed. Too many lived too close to the ocean and did not have enough time or the means to evacuate to a safe distance.

Thornaksen was right. The tsunami's aftermath was worse; it brought disease, chaos, and the breakdown of sections of society.

Massive relief efforts began and, as in past disasters, the American Heartland responded.

Elsewhere on the planet, in La Palma, Cyprus, or five miles inland from America's Atlantic coasts, nature took no notice and the sun shone as impervious as ever.

Epilogue

86
The Little Things

Three Months After The La Palma Tsunami
Thornaksen Estate, La Palma

Ben and Artemis stepped out of Thornaksen's chopper and happily hugged Thornaksen, Enrique, Isabella and Manolo who were waiting on the flag-stoned tarrazza. The two couples hugged and kissed on both cheeks. They'd not seen each other in three months.

Thornaksen ushered everyone through a portico and they found themselves beside a pool and a table set with pastries, scones, a variety of local foods and dried meats. Thornaksen sat everyone and then walked about offering juice and passing platters.

"I am so glad to have everyone together again," Thornaksen said. "I think we should make it an annual event." His face beamed. "Really glad. It would have been a shame to lose you just as we met."

"Mr. Thornaksen, I've never thanked you in person for saving us. We owe you our lives. Thank you," Enrique raised a glass of juice to Thornaksen.

"Yes, *grazie mille,*" Isabella added.

"I've been meaning to ask you," Enrique continued, "how did you happen to be up in the air above the collapse?"

"You see…some days away from work is good for everyone…I'll tell you," Thornaksen said obviously happy. "When the terrorists sealed off the entrance and you left in the Mercedes, there wasn't much I could do. I called for the chopper and just lifted off when the mountain collapsed. Imagine my surprise when a black hole opened and you four were standing there."

"I think we were more surprised that we were alive," Ben added.

"The next few days will be the reunion we never had," Thornaksen said. "We catch up and you get some rest. I know you've all been busy. My home is yours…the most amazing thing I've ever seen, you standing there in a hole on the side of a mountain and the island collapsing below."

Thornaksen paused. He looked at his guests, the ocean in the distance and the mountain above in appreciation.

"…nothing like home…It'd have been a shame to lose all this after getting all my little comforts just so…you know that in all three of my homes I have two identical rooms? Care to guess which?"

"Office and bedroom," Artemis volunteered.

"Not bad, Ms. Nelson. Office, yes—down to the computer and security system: increases efficiency and eliminates the mundane. No. The bedrooms are furnished by local artisans, so they're all different. Office and kitchen—down to a stone stove—it's a weakness and an indulgence. Having the proper tools is like having all the right weapons to fight a war—and we know how those turn out, don't we, Huntley?"

"That, we do. That airlift was something," Ben said.

"Of course you know now that Jorge is retired Canarias Search and Rescue."

"Great pilot. I did lose you the Mercedes and the M4."

Thornaksen laughed deeply and heartily as if he enjoyed giving into the release of emotion.

"The least of our worries. Know who makes the M4? Colt. Know who owns Colt, and Browning, and Winchester? FNH in Belgium— friends of mine. Lots more where that came from."

"What's next, Enrique?" Ben asked.

Enrique hesitated and looked at Isabella. As he was about to answer, Artemis jumped in and with a smile that spoke volumes said, "The two of you make a great couple."

Enrique accepted the complement obviously happy and in love. "Isabella and I have a lot of work at the volcanological station. Data, measurements, field studies, conferences, and scientists from all over the world…" His smile was pure joy.

Artemis looked at Isabella, "We should do a little shopping."

"We'll go to Santa Cruz! Go see Blahnik's new *modelos*."

"Manolo Blahnik? That'd be wonderful!"

"Anything good to eat on the island?" Ben asked.

"Absolutely. Dinner?" Enrique asked.

"We'll meet the women later."

87

No Man Is an Island

Thornaksen Estate, La Palma

"Whatever happened to the young woman that passed the flash drive to you?" Enrique asked.

"Her name is Nivit—I asked the Head of Station in Cyprus. It would have been so much worse if not for her."

"You have to admire the young lady," Thornaksen said.

They were in Thornaksen's conference room. There was some minimal furniture about but its sleek straight lines drew little attention to it. Its subdued nature was intentional for the opposite wall was glass; a spectacular view of the open sky and the Atlantic Ocean stretched off as far as the eye could see. The sky's light blue starkly contrasted with the dark blue of the ocean below. It was nature at its most pristine; it was serene and elemental and the bright crisp light made the colors sharp and lively. Thornaksen's contribution consisted of a frame of canary pines, dragon trees and smaller local flowering plants that added yellows, pinks, and fire reds to the edges. The center of the room was dominated by a long dark conference table with a tapered and rounded midsection. The table-ends finished in squares and the oak top reflected the grain of the wood.

"Nivit proved to be very resourceful. After she passed Sam the flash drive, the Mossad put her under house arrest in Cyprus. That was a mistake because, turns out, she had a backup plan. When she missed her check-in with her brother in Israel, he posted messages and some documents on Wikileaks and Facebook. Bypassed everybody and got leverage in the process. Ended up a sensation and even got expedited entry to the U.S."

"She went public? Just like that?" Enrique asked.

"It's a new world, young man," Thornaksen said. "The internet's changed the Middle East more in one year than the diplomacy of the last 100 years. Power has truly passed to the individual."

"She laid out Israeli surveillance on Cyprus, the Mossad keeping terror threats to themselves, their false flag operations, and the killing of Americans to keep support flowing," Ben explained.

"That must have made interesting reading in the Pentagon...the *U.S.S. Liberty* all over again," Thornaksen smirked.

"Bottom line, she wrote her own ticket. Put the Israelis on the defensive for years. Their official line is that the Mossad Unit on Cyprus went rogue and Sam's murder was unsanctioned...maybe it's true. Who knows? Everyone blames them for the tsunami regardless. We'll never know if they knew La Palma was the target or about the sonic attack from below. "

"You said she ended up with her fiancé?" Artemis asked.

"Just like us," Isabella contributed and took Enrique's hand in hers.

"'*Love triumphs,*' after all," Artemis contributed and looked at Ben with a knowing expression.

Ben glanced back at Artemis who looked beautiful in a comfortable cotton dress that gave her the look of a classic beauty. She had taken advantage of Thornaksen's amenities and bathed. Her hair was done casually and its simplicity gave her a relaxed and elegant look.

"If she did all that, then anything is possible. Maybe the days of the nation state and the haves and have-nots are numbered," Thornaksen said.

"Thousands still died. Not to mention all the destruction," Ben said.

"It's not on you; I told you before. The intelligence community failed —from CIA down to National Recon and Geospatial. You were flying solo on this one so don't blame yourself." Thornaksen looked at Enrique and Isabella. "Besides, the scientists all tell me La Palma's collapse was imminent and nothing any of you could have done would have stopped it."

"We're at about 535 thousand dead."

"But, Huntley, if you hadn't stopped the detonation in the tunnel, we could be looking at tens of millions. You minimized the damage. If you're going to wallow in self-pity, maybe you should go back and work for Langley."

Ben laughed heartily. "No, no. I'm happy working for you." He looked at Artemis.

###

Over dinner that night, Thornaksen was buoyant. He waltzed around and personally poured a local wine he raved about.

"It's an opportunity," he was saying, "for change. Yes, lives were lost and, yes, it's a setback, but the West has the institutions and bureaucratic traditions to weather the chaos, and, now, even the chance to improve its foundation and come out stronger than before."

"It's very difficult," Ben added. "People are overwhelmed with basic necessities, diseases, law and order…they're not thinking about systems of government or political or economic foundations."

"That's why someone has to. Capitalism is obsolete—not because it doesn't work but because it works too well. It concentrates wealth and power in the hands of the few and their priority is self-perpetuation. Capitalism has become a pyramid scheme. The few control or create wealth by printing money and lend it to governments they control. They keep people in check by putting them in debt. It's easy now because, like Ben said, they're preoccupied trying to meet their basic needs."

"But capitalism defeated communism," Artemis said. "America came out on top."

"Actually capitalism bankrupted communism. Capitalism has had a major setback and its wealth and resources will be strained for a long time. On the other hand, it still has talented people and rampant optimism going for it."

"You think you'll be able to change anything?" Artemis said.

"Ben and I are trying," Kal answered. "Even before the tsunami, America had reached the point where more Americans were consuming wealth than producing it. The middle class was almost gone and debt was at an all-time high. The current strain will make disparities worse. India, China, and the Arab World can easily eclipse the U.S. And, no matter what all the think-tanks in Washington say, democracy never caught on in the rest of the world. If anything, this disaster may weaken the cause of democracy. So, yes, we need to be vigilant, even overhaul the system. What's the alternative? The chaos of Africa and Russia? The desperation of China? Is that any way to live? Not for me, thanks."

"You sound pessimistic, Kal," Artemis ventured.

"Democracy values the individual and only in the West do individuals matter," Ben added. "Kal is right; it's a dangerous time to be an idealist."

"I'd like to think I'm realistic, Ms. Nelson. The West is resilient, I'll grant that but it has its weaknesses. Capitalism has appropriated democracy for its own ends—the reverse should be true—capitalism should serve democratic ideals. Corporations were created to benefit the state but they've morphed into self-serving entities. They need to be reined in. Nothing's better than democracy, but we don't have a democracy—we have a republic—people have given their vote to two-party political machines. That's too bad because democracy is the most revolutionary system ever devised. Capitalism has put people into debt. They've lost hope and become demoralized—and that makes them easy to control. If masses ever figured out who had their best interest in mind and turned out and voted for them…that would be a revolution."

"Look what the internet did for Nivit. She stood up to the Mossad and won," Ben contributed.

"What, you want the internet to be the new ballot box?" Artemis asked.

"Why not? That would be great. A fruit vendor in Egypt started the Arab Spring…why not elect presidents online…"

"The revolution just might show up."

"Got to be careful," Thornaksen said. "The masses have the attention span of a twit. Reality is a bummer; they don't want it. Corporations will make tremendous profits from the tsunami and will be formidable opponents. Our only hope is levelheaded idealists for leaders. We'll probably never have an opportunity like this again. Like I said, Ben and I are trying."

88
The Moon Brings Dreams

Thornaksen Estate, La Palma

Enrique was gazing at Isabella across the room. She was wearing her khaki cargo pants with the pockets on either side.

"There's always something in those pockets. Do you do that on purpose?"

"My notebook comes with me always. You know, I was wearing these pants when we first met at the station."

"Oh, I remember. You look great in them."

"My lucky pants. I got them the day I arrived at grad school—I was so ready for fieldwork. Of course, it was five months before I actually got out to the field. I wore them every day. They're so comfortable."

"I approve."

"And you get to take them off," she gave him a seductive and reassuring smile. Nothing could compare to a smile like that from a woman—it told Enrique that she found comfort in him, and that she wanted him.

"My lucky pants, too," he said and approached. She took him in her arms.

########################

Enrique stirred and a surge of anxiety raced through him. The angst wasn't in his mind or in his heart but deeper—a long linear sensation that started in his loins, extended through the uneasiness in his stomach and reached the thumping in his chest. But, Isabella was there next to him and he relaxed.

It was early—twilight really. There was light somewhere in the sky but it had not yet descended to earth. The day was beginning but the sun would not cross over the mountain tops to La Palma's west side until after ten—just as it had when he'd been a boy. He'd only seen the sunrise a few times before going off-island to university. It'd be nice to wake at dawn next to Isabella and see the sun come up together.

These thoughts took two to three seconds. He looked in wonder at Isabella's uncovered back. Bangs of dirty-blond hair lapped over each other creating dark and light shades and giving her hair a natural unruly look. He smiled. He knew it wasn't intentional—she would never go for the artificial waves that appeared as if made in a mold and was never to be touched. Her waves of curls went where they wished naturally—she just ushered them in the general direction. The results were attractive. She had had no qualms about him running his hands through her hair the night before. A self-absorbed and less-giving woman would have held that part of herself back, but Isabella had accepted his touch for the intimate caress and loving touch that it was— similar, say, to a long uninhibited look into each other's eyes or a touch of the lips.

The giving from both sides was honest, true, and total. Perhaps they knew innately that their individual parts where so much less than the sum of what their potential whole could be.

He followed the line of her shoulder and took note of the tan freckles. There was no bra line because—he remembered from the first meeting—she wore none. His eyes moved slowly lingering over every inch of her tanned skin until he reached the dip of her waist. A sheet covered her lower half and accentuated the curves of waist and hips making her more desirable and mysterious. A breeze entered through the open window and the crisp morning air wafted over the light cotton sheet and gently caressed the two of them.

She stirred and moved closer to a fetal position. Enrique pulled the sheet over her shoulder and felt her relax. Seconds later, she nudged slightly until her torso touched his. He put his left hand over her and squeezed her close. She turned and looked over her shoulder.

"Good morning," she said.

It certainly was.

89

The Wonders of the World

Thornaksen Estate, La Palma

"Did you hear Thornaksen and Enrique? It's time you let it go. We did what we could—we *saved* civilization," Isabella was chiding Ben.

"Enrique is a hero in the land he was born with a girl that loves him."

"You're jealous!" Artemis announced.

"What's not to like. He's young, just starting life…"

"Youth has its perks and pitfalls."

"Is that cynicism, I hear?"

"You thought you had a monopoly? And, it's not cynicism; it's perspective."

"You think they'll make it? I mean as a couple."

"You never know, but they seem grounded enough to weather pretty much anything that life throws at them. Like us," Artemis added.

"That's what I'm talking about! I, too, got the girl."

"Nivit, the whistleblower—she came out O.K. too. Pretty good for a 20-year-old. Stopped Armageddon all by herself," Artemis said.

"The terrorists got what they wanted," Ben added.

Artemis snapped and stared Ben down. He was serious.

"They died how they wanted," he answered sheepishly. "How many can choose the time and cause for which to die? You have to admire it."

"Don't you dare say that in public! You'll be crucified."

"I'm old enough to say it."

"You're romanticizing things. Don't expect me to agree with you. They killed thousands. There are better ways of changing the world."

She reached over and kissed him, slowly, affectionately, deeply.

"I told you everyone got what they wanted," he smiled. "Lots of people just don't recognize it when it happens."

"Let it go, Ben. Let it go." She took his hand and they walked around the grounds of the old villa. Around a corner, they entered a side garden.

"This is heaven," Artemis stared in wonder.

"Thornaksen said you'd love this place," Ben answered beaming. They had entered a small piazza surrounded by low stone walls. Taller tree shrubs were in the background against the walls but directly in front were rows and pockets of multi-colored flowers. Just enough of a pattern to indicate that the garden was cared for but not enough to give it the ordered artificiality of an ornamental garden.

Her happiness was contagious. *It's true. Happiness and contentment come to those that do for others,* he thought to himself. He felt giddy and excited like a child that was barely controlling the floodgates of anticipation. He was more energized than he'd been in a long time.

"These freesias—never smelled anything like it." She had bent over a series of white starred flowers with yellow centers.

She looked good. She and Isabella had gone off to Santa Cruz the day before. They had returned in the afternoon with two shopping bags and looking gorgeous. Her hair and features shone. With every move, bangs jostled on her cheekbones right where Ben's fingers had tenderly caressed her on the conveyor in Morocco seemingly an age ago. Her face was radiant and her dark eyes sparkled.

"You look…elegant," he had managed.

Today she had the same fresh look. She was rested and less tense. Her eyes danced and were lively and she was light on her feet as if the ground could hardly hold her.

"Hibiscus," she said pointing to a pinkish flower sitting amongst hundreds of small green leaves. "That's Strelitzia, also called Bird of Paradise. This variety blooms every three years. We're in luck."

She walked over to a large yellow flower with thin reed-like petals that was reminiscent of a sunflower but smaller. "This is Epiphylum," she said. "And so is this," she pointed to a white bud with white petals underneath. "That's bougainvillea," she pointed to two huge mounds with hundreds of flowers, one purple and the other a dull orange.

"Now I know how little I need," she said ebulliently. "Remember the dust in Morocco? All I'll ever ask for again is a bath and clean clothes. You know what Katie, Aph's five-year old told me were the Seven Wonders of the World?"

"Tell me."

"To touch, to hear, to smell, to see, to feel, to laugh…" she stopped.

"That's six," Ben prodded.

Artemis turned, and Ben saw that her eyes were moist.

"The seventh…is to love," she said.

He wrapped his hands around her and squeezed tightly.

"I love you," he said tenderly.

PETER THORN

HAND OF GOD

WOLF'S MOUNT

Appendix

At 6000 feet, Mount Fairweather in Alaska is the highest coastal mountain in the world. From its sides and from the sides of the other peaks of the Saint Elias Range, several glaciers flow towards the ocean three miles away. In parts, the glacial ice has melted and retreated leaving behind a scoured landscape, loose bedrock, and masses of rock perched atop steep fractured hills that surround and overlook the bay on the coast. Weathering has weakened the exposed earth leaving it vulnerable to shifts caused by the grinding of the Pacific Tectonic Plate against the North American Plate.

The hillsides around this particular bay are peculiar because three distinct horizontal zones, layers really, are clearly recognizable. Closest to the water is a zone of exposed bedrock devoid of all topsoil, which means it was forcibly washed away leaving only naked earth behind. A second with trees begins above this layer, but its lime-green color identifies it as young growth meaning it is a recent replacement of the older destroyed and uprooted trees. The third zone lies higher still and is characterized by the dark green of old evergreens—the original inhabitants of the area. These older trees escaped a major alteration of the ecosystem that affected the two lower zones. On close inspection, evidence of the catastrophic event that altered the landscape can still be seen.

Geologic activity in Southern Alaska is frequent and obeys a tectonic calendar determined by convoluted forces deep in the earth. In the Lituya Bay area, the strain of one tectonic plate pushing against another passed a critical point. Huge sections of the earth's 20-mile thick crust slid past one each other at weak contact points and sent out three-dimensional force waves that shook the landscape. The earthquake was measured at a catastrophic 7.9 on the intensity calculating Richter scale.

It was July 9, 1958 and the earth convulsed for three minutes. The colliding tectonic plates deformed, subducted, and otherwise adjusted until they found new more stable resting positions. Even though the epicenter of the friction was 13 miles south of Lituya Bay on Alaska's southeastern coast, thin coats of surface soil and bedrock sections slid 21 feet at the Fairweather Fault. The San Andreas in California, which is a southern cousin, also adjusted, but its movements on this occasion were barely discernible and did not arouse any concern.

In the hilltops of Lituya Bay, however, 25 million cubic feet of gravel and rock loosened, became a landside, and hit the water with enough force to displace enough water and glacial debris to create the tallest wave in recorded history. The upsurge reached 1720 feet, unleashed unprecedented devastation, tore nine-foot diameter trees from their roots, and created a new tree line on the opposite hill. The resulting tsunami was eight times higher than any other wave previously known. Fortunately, the bay was uninhabited but out of six people anchored in nearby boats, two died.

In contrast, the 2004 Sumatra-Andaman earthquake that caused the landslides in the Indian Ocean generated tsunami waves of barely 100 feet. However, the affected areas were populated, and over 230,000 died in locations as far away as eastern Africa. The wave permanently altered the ecosystems it struck. Worst of all, it poisoned freshwater supplies and agricultural areas with layers of saltwater deposits making the arable land sterile and incapable of supporting most life, including human, for many years. Seven years later in 2011, the Tohoku Tsunami in Japan killed about 20,000 people and set off worldwide alarms because it caused nuclear meltdowns. Considered the costliest natural disaster in history, the tsunami that struck the mainland measured only 133 feet.

The debris that slid into Lituya Bay dropped about three-quarters of a mile. A landslide on La Palma will start from about 1.5 miles above sea level—twice the height of Lituya Bay and may started by volcanic eruptions, erosion, or earthquakes. Due to the steep vertical angle, the slide down Cumbre Vieja may continue for an additional four miles until it reaches the bottom of the Atlantic Ocean. The falling land mass will likely range from 200 to 500 billion tons—about 8 times the size of the Lituya Bay landslide.

The possibility of a La Palma landslide is additionally worrisome due to several other factors: La Palma's terrain is prone to erosion and is already home to the largest erosion crater on the planet; La Palma also happens to be the steepest island on earth. Its most precarious volcano, the Cumbre Vieja, has been the most active in the Canary Islands for the last 500 years. If a major volcanic eruption does take place and the massive amounts of water saturating the island's porous rubble interior are turned into steam by rising lava, the western part of the island could separate and become a massive landslide. In fact, telltale debris of several immense landslides in La Palma's past are located around the island. The effects of giant waves, including rocks native to the Canary Islands and other geologic evidence, have been discovered in the Bahamas, further proof that tsunamis emanating from La Palma have already crossed the Atlantic Ocean in the distant past.

Scientific attempts at understanding the mechanics of past and future events in La Palma are ongoing. Predictions of the size of the resulting tsunami due to a landslide range from as few as seven to as many as 2100 feet high. The exact size of the waves will depend on the volume of the earth mass that separates from the mountain, how fast it slides, and how far it will travel towards the ocean floor four miles below.

The Lituya Bay wave grew to immense proportions due to the hillsides and bay that were near and held the water in check. In effect, the area near the landslide bore the full force of the debris that slid. In contrast, waves from a La Palma landslide will travel long distances of over the ocean. Many predict that La Palma's waves will fan out and dissipate in the open waters of the Atlantic and may not reach destructive heights. However, as the Sumatra-Andaman and the Tohoku tsunamis showed, even 100-foot waves cause massive destruction to infrastructure and disrupt the lives of millions of coastal residents. A wave of 100 to 1,000 feet will have a mass of water so large that it would hit the North and South American continents with unprecedented force, destroy all human activity in the affected areas, and likely cripple the U. S. for a long time. It would certainly be a wretched end to one earth epoch and the murky beginning of another.

Eruptions have occurred on La Palma in 1971, 1949, 1712, 1677, 1646 and in years going back to prehistoric eras. Remnants of several giant landslides, involving hundreds of cubic miles of mass, have been mapped on the ocean floor around La Palma and other Canary Islands. The only question is when another landslide will occur and how large it will be. Atlantic tsunami hazards are underestimated or even unrecognized by most people because they are rare. The intervals between landslides stretch into eons and another landslide may not occur for hundreds of years—except, of course, due to a volcanic eruption, earthquake, or simply due to gravity. A landslide caused by human hand as postulated here is unlikely.

If a massive tsunami does strike the Americas, particularly devastating would be the irreparable damage inflicted on the struggle to unfetter the human spirit championed by Western Civilization over the last two and a half millennia and absent from Earth's other major cultural traditions.

AUTHOR'S NOTE

The landslide scenario fictionalized in this book has been the subject scientific research and speculation for decades. The events of 2004 and 2011 alerted the unsuspecting public to the very real tsunami threat. Atlantic Ocean tsunamis are considered rare but indisputable geologic evidence has been found at La Palma, whose coasts are littered with debris fields from volcanoes and landslides, that they have occurred in the distant past.

Stories of violent floods and their history-altering after-effects are part of the histories of many cultures. Japanese written accounts of tsunamis, including pictorial depictions, go back 1300 years to 684 A.D. Thucydides mentions a tsunami in Greece in 479 B.C. and prehistoric tsunamis likely include the inundation of the Black Sea by the Aegean.

Current theory attributes the destruction of Santorini and the advanced civilization found there, which may have been the legendary Atlantis, to a volcano-generated tsunami, and which likely caused the demise of the Minoans on Crete. Even if Santorini and Crete were not Atlantis, a volcanic explosion and tsunami from Santorini destroyed thriving civilizations on both islands.

Earth masses falling into bodies of water are classified as Impact Events and generate mega-tsunamis, which are among the most destructive forces on the planet. The only forces causing greater destruction are asteroid strikes into the oceans, which—surprise—cause even larger mega-tsunamis.

The likelihood of a man-made event setting off a landslide on La Palma is remote. The likelihood of a volcanic eruption doing the same, however, is plausible. When a slide happens, large chunks of earth, already at a precipitous incline, will loosen and plunge into the ocean. Scientists fear this scenario because the loss of life and destruction on both sides of the Atlantic will likely be large enough to alter history.

Threats equal in magnitude to mega-tsunamis (slower and less evident), are already in play around the planet. Human contribution to the decimation of the planet is increasing and may be impossible to reverse. The population explosion, industrialization, and consumer pressures—intensified by the "flattening" effects of readily available information via the World Wide Web—have altered oceans, landscapes, and climate. Increasingly, extreme weather spasms and man-made alterations of the ecosystem upset the planet's geophysical balance.

It is unlikely that man can undo the environmental damage he's caused since the advent of the Industrial Revolution. Politicians have no vision or, more accurately, their electorates do not permit the visionary and expensive solutions needed. Admittedly, politicians have rarely been the instrument of real change—least of all the revolutionary moral shift that humanity now needs. The changes that are occurring in the Middle East, the liberalization of China, and the rise of the Third World demand standards of living and consumer goods that will only further strain the planet. The nation state system, self-serving corporations, and humanity in general have been poor stewards of the earth's one environment.

There is hope. Fifty years ago, the world was made up of approximately 130 nations and numerous repressive regimes. Today, over 200 nations testify that change is possible when individuals and disenfranchised populations pursue common ideals. In a world of instant access and communication, anyone can bypass intransigent bureaucracies, politicians, and corporate interests. A conscientious individual can promote dialectic and solutions, which, increasingly, he views from a global perspective. Today's dreamer or hero will use the internet as the medium for the adventures and the ideals that fulfill him, and he can easily share the methods and rewards for the benefit of all.

Humanity faces huge obstacles but on the bright side, knowledge and education are now exponential. Man now has the ability to store and use knowledge critically; the more than eight billion intellects on the planet are now able to consider their actions and learn lessons better than any time before.

In the 1960's and for the first time, man was able to see his planet against the backdrop of nothingness. After the initial fascination, the sobering realization struck him that perhaps he was alone, that perhaps God had other affairs to tend to, that perhaps man was not the end all and be all he thought he was for millennia, that perhaps he was responsible for his own world. Perhaps he matured a bit and, for the first time, perhaps he developed a planetary conscience. Equality, peace, ecology and a plethora of similar movements began. It's quite clear that developing a planetary psyche will benefit earth and all its species.

—Peter Thorn

Glossary, References, Characters

Abdellatif Ferroukhi - Head of Moroccan cell of plot; previously responsible for the terror attacks on London and Madrid with 'the Doctor' (Abu Nur al-Din).

Abu Nur al-Din - Also known as 'the Doctor'; Egyptian terrorist mastermind previously responsible for the terror attacks on London and Madrid with Abdellatif Ferroukhi.

Ahmed - Teen who scales the anchor chain of the research ship *Pytheas*; idolizes Rafiq Al Jabiri.

Amiantos Mine - Asbestos mine, now closed, in the Troodos Mountain Range; part of the ancient geological ocean floor known as the Troodos Ophiolithic Complex; Cyprus was created with the subduction of the African Plate beneath the Eurasian Plate; the two tectonic plates meet at Troodos.

Amir Shobeik - Terrorist who becomes radicalized when his father, Elie, is assassinated by his former allies, the Israelis.

Anarchist and Antisky - Joint project of the NSA and Britain's GCHQ intercepting data streams of videos, pictures and GPS data from Israeli jets and drones, among others, operating at Golf Section. Antisky is the software tool used to unscramble the data.
http://www.theregister.co.uk/2016/01/29/israeli_drones_and_jet_signals_slurped_by_uk_and_us_sigint_teams/

ANFO - Ammonium nitrate/fuel oil is a bulk industrial explosive mixture. It consists of 94% porous prilled ammonium nitrate (NH4NO3) (AN) that acts as the oxidizing agent and absorbent for the fuel and 6% number 2 fuel oil (FO); used in the 1995 Oklahoma City bombing.

Ari Ben Amin - Israeli Mossad agent who with Ido Wietzman monitor the terrorists on Cyprus; arrested by Cypriots and sentenced to 8 years in prison.

Artemis Nelson - Diplomatic Security investigator; Ben's partner and love interest.

Barnes - Rick Barnes – Flight Lieutenant Squadron Leader of 84 Squadron flying Bell Griffin HAR2s; volunteers as community liaison on Cyprus.

Ben Huntley - U.S. diplomat in Cyprus who investigates Sam's death; Regional Security Officer (RSO), who is haunted and disillusioned by his experiences in Afghanistan.

Bishops - Group Captain Evan Bishops, head of British intelligence base of Troodos RAF also known as Golf Section.

Boyce - British commando member of Rapid Reaction Force.

Burj Khalifa - The tallest building in the world beginning in 2010 at 163 floors with a height of 829.8 meters.

Brubaker - Randy Brubaker—chopper pilot on Alhuceima mission.

Charlie Fui - Dr. Charlie Fui—program manager of Dragonfly MAV program, on loan to Wright Patterson from DARPA, head of DARPA's Biologic Systems and Platforms and part of a DARPA Forward Cell (DFC) which provides immediate combat capability of DARPA systems.

Carstens - Col. Rob Carstens, against use of SEALs for Alhuceima harbor mission.

CLV – Command Liaison Vehicle; British version of the Humvee; a 4WD tactical vehicle by Iveco and in service in several countries.

Cumbre Vieja - A volcanic ridge on the Isla de La Palma in the Canary Islands which in the 20th century erupted in 1949 and in 1971. Scientists disagree whether Cumbre Vieja's collapse will trigger a tsunami. Whether the resulting tsunami travels far from the island is another point of debate.

Cyprus - Island country in the Eastern Mediterranean Sea whose earliest human activity dates to around the 10th millennium BC. Cyprus was formally annexed by Britain in 1914. Today Cyprus is partitioned into two main parts; the Cypriot Republic comprises 59% of the island's area, and the north, which is administered by the self-declared Turkish Republic of Northern Cyprus and recognized only by Turkey. The international community considers the northern territory of the Republic of Cyprus under occupation by Turkish forces (today numbering around 40,000).

DARPA - Defense Advanced Research Projects Agency. An advanced-technology branch of the U.S. Department of Defense, which researches and expands technology and science beyond immediate military requirements. DARPA has had a full-time presence in combat environments in Vietnam and Afghanistan through its Forward Cell program.

Dick Higgins - Veteran DEA officer in Cyprus recently transferred to Italy.

DPD - A Diver Propulsion Device (or underwater propulsion vehicle or underwater scooter) is an item of diving equipment, which increases divers' underwater range and is often used in military operations.

ECHELON - Originally a code-name, now used to describe a signals intelligence (SIGINT) collection and analysis network operated on behalf of the UKUSA Security Agreement (Australia, Canada, New Zealand, the U.K., and the U.S.) A European Parliament report concluded that the name referred to a signals intelligence collection system that intercepts, inspects telephone, fax, e-mail and other global data traffic by intercepting satellite transmissions, public switched telephone networks (which once carried most Internet traffic) and microwave links.

eLRAD - Enhanced Long Range Acoustic Device (speculated). LRAD systems are used by maritime, law enforcement, military and commercial security companies to send instructions and warnings over distance. LRAD systems are also used to deter wildlife from airport runways, wind and solar farms, nuclear power facilities, gas and oil platforms, mining and agricultural operations, and industrial plants. The use of sonic cannons to search for deposits under the ocean floor by shooting sound waves 100 times louder than a jet engine through waters shared by endangered whales and turtles was approved in 2014.

Enrique - Enrique Alcretan—geologist who discovers a massive geologic fault on La Palma.

Erica - Head of Logistics for the Alhuceima drone mission.

F83 - NSA Base in England; see Menwith Hill.

False Flag - Any covert operation that deceives and appears as if carried out by entities other than those that actually executed them. Refers to acts carried out by military or security personnel, which are then blamed on terrorists. The name "false flag" originates in naval warfare where the use of a flag other than the belligerent's true battle flag was a ruse de guerre. The deception was discarded before opening fire on the enemy.

Focused Foiling - Also known as "targeted prevention." Israeli terms describing targeted killings by the Israel Defense Forces (IDF) and used in the Israeli-Palestinian conflict to describe the targeted killing of persons accused of carrying out or planning attacks against Israeli targets. The Israeli army maintains that it pursues such military operations to prevent imminent attacks when it has no discernible means of making an arrest or foiling such attacks by other methods. On December 14, 2006, the Supreme Court of Israel ruled that targeted killing is a legitimate form of self-defense against terrorists and outlined conditions for its use.

Foley - Col. Frank Foley, Navy man; is for use of SEALs on Alhuceima harbor mission.

Globemaster - The Boeing C-17 Globemaster III is a large military transport aircraft, which commonly performs strategic airlift missions, tactical airlifts, and medical evacuation and airdrop duties.

Golf Section - British Signals Intelligence Station officially known as RAF Troodos atop Mt. Olympus, Cyprus.

Hand of God - Plot to use a landslide to create tsunami from La Palma to attack America.

Hank Randall - Lt. Col. Henry Randall—head of operations anti-terror taskforce, overseeing support for Huntley; supports use of nano MAV mission.

Hansen - Andrew Hansen – U.S. Secretary of State who is offered information on "Hand of God" in exchange for release of Israeli spy.

Hertz - Matt "Hertz" Herzenstahl - flight engineer on Alhuceima mission.

Houssaini Brothers - Abdelfattah and Mohammed Houssaini blow up in internet café; based on real suicide bombing on March 11, 2007 in Casablanca, Morocco.

Human Trafficking - The trade of humans for the purpose of sexual slavery, forced labor or commercial sexual exploitation. It includes providing a spouse in a forced marriage and the extraction of organs or tissues. Human trafficking is a crime that violates the victim's rights of movement through coercion and commercial exploitation. Human trafficking represented $31.6 billion in international trade per year in 2010. It is one of the fastest-growing activities of trans-national criminal organizations. In 2016, the estimated victims numbered 35 million.

Ido Wietzman - Israeli Mossad agent who, with Ari Ben Amin, monitor terrorists on Cyprus; arrested by Cypriots and sentenced to eight years in prison.

Impact Event Impact - Events are collisions between objects such as earth, water, or heavenly bodies that will likely cause the greatest destruction known to man.

Indian Ocean Tsunami of 2004 - The Indian Ocean earthquake occurred on 26 December 2004. The event is known by the scientific community as the Sumatra–Andaman Earthquake. The resulting tsunamis killed 230,000 people in 14 countries, and inundated coastal communities with waves up to 30 meters (100 ft.) high.

Isabella - Isabella Giannini; volcanologist, from Milan Italy, Enrique's love interest.

James - James Schreiber; operator of d-fly MAV on Alhuceima drone mission.

Jonathan Pollard - The only American to receive a life sentence for passing classified information to an ally of the United States. Israel has made repeated attempts through both official and unofficial channels to secure his release. He was granted Israeli citizenship in 1995. He was imprisoned in 1987 and his release was finally negotiated for November 2016.

Kal - Kallinikos Thornakson; wealthy powerbroker living in semi-retirement on his La Palma estate; Renaissance man; member of Bilderberg Group.

Keryneia - City on the northern coast of Cyprus noted for its historic harbor and castle and populated since ca. 5800–3000 BC. It is traditionally accepted that the city was founded by Achaeans from the Peloponnese after the Trojan War. Now under the control of the self-declared Turkish Republic of Northern Cyprus.

Khalid Mohamed - Decoy driver who denies killing Sam Johnston but reveals that terror target is La Palma.

Kishon - Avner Kishon – Israeli ambassador who offers terror info in return for U.S. support for Israeli Prime minister's reelection.

Kyle - Operator of d-Fly MAV on Alhuceima drone mission.

Landslide - The failure of a slope. The primary cause of a landslide is gravity although many factors build up specific sub-surface conditions that make the area/slope prone to failure including: groundwater destabilization, loss or absence of vertical vegetative structure, soil structure, erosion, earthquakes, liquefaction, volcanic eruptions, rock-falls, steepness, vibrations from machinery or traffic, and blasting. A landslide often requires a trigger before being released. Underwater landslides and those that impact water can generate tsunamis including mega-tsunamis, which are usually hundreds of meters high. Mega-tsunamis and asteroid impacts are the most destructive forces on earth; an asteroid impact in water will cause a mega tsunami.

La Palma - One of the Canary Islands; has both the steepest mountain and the largest erosion crater in the world; its shores are replete with evidence of several large landslides due to past failures of its steep slopes; it is widely considered the source of past tsunamis and of a devastating future Atlantic Ocean tsunami.

Lefkosia - Capital of Cyprus; also known as Nicosia; its airport is unusable as it is divided between the self-declared Turkish Republic of Northern Cyprus (which is recognized only by Turkey and rejected by the UN) and the Republic of Cyprus.

Len Blinkman - State Public Affairs Officer U.S. Embassy Cyprus.

Lituya Bay – A bay in Southern Alaska and the location of the highest wave in recorded history. An earthquake on July 9, 1958 caused a landslide at the head of the bay and generated a mega-tsunami that measured between 100 ft. (30 m) and 300 ft. (91 m). Accepted as the first direct evidence, including an eyewitness account, of the existence of mega-tsunamis.

Mahmud Mahduni - Palestinian miner with expertise in ANFO; turned extremist at Somali prison; bomber in tunnel.

Maria Andrikou - Cypriot cleaning lady at the U.S. Embassy.

MAV's - Micro Aerial Vehicles, also referred to as drones and nanos in this story, are a class of Miniature Unmanned Air Vehicles that are size restricted and may be autonomous. Modern craft can be as small as 15 centimeters and allow remote observation of hazardous environments that may be otherwise inaccessible.

Mega-tsunami - A tsunami with an initial wave amplitude (height) measured in tens, hundreds, or possibly thousands of meters. Mega-tsunamis are caused by giant landslides and other impact events such as meteorites hitting an ocean. Underwater earthquakes or volcanic eruptions do not normally generate such large tsunamis, but landslides next to bodies of water resulting from earthquakes can, since they cause massive water displacement. If the landslide or impact occurs in a limited body of water, as happened at the Vajont Dam (1963) and Lituya Bay (1958) then the water may not disperse and one or more very large waves may result.

Menwith Hill - Field Station F83 begun in the 1950s' by the NSA. Provides communications and intelligence services to Britain and the U.S. It is considered a communications intercept and missile warning site and has been described as the largest electronic monitoring station in the world. Alleged to be an element of the ECHELON system.

Meron - Meron Ran; former F15I pilot and refusenik presently an Israeli reconnaissance pilot.

Metsada - An Israeli intelligence unit that specializes in sabotage, including "false flag" terrorist attacks and assassinations.

Milhaus - Thomas Milhaus – U.S. Ambassador to Cyprus.

Mt. Olympus - Largest mountain on Cyprus; not to be confused with Mt. Olympus in Greece; Golf Section's location.

Neharin - Ehud Neharin – prime minister of Israel; offers the U.S. terror info in return for support in his reelection.

Nivit Keret - Israeli Mossad agent on Cyprus monitoring terrorists; she reveals terror plot to Sam for which he is killed; Nivit is in love with Ari Ben Amin; Yarden turns her in.

Palm Islands - Dubai's Palm Islands are land reclamation projects designed to double the size of Dubai and add 520 kilometers of non-public beaches. Three were initially planned in the shape of palm trees topped by a crescent but only two were built while the third was named Deira Island.

Plazas de Soberanía - Places of Sovereignty; Spanish controlled areas and islands off the coast of Morocco including Islas Alhuceimas and Islas Chafarinas.

Potsbury – Flight Sergeant Thaddeus Potsbury; young British analyst.

Ramsey - Pilot of Globemaster; British commando.

Rafiq Al Jabiri - Leader of assault on Pytheas and the sonic attack below La Palma, original 1960's terrorist.

RSO - Regional Security Officer Regional - title given to special agents of the U.S. Diplomatic Security Service (DSS) serving overseas. The RSO is the principal security attaché and advisor to the U.S. Ambassador at American Embassies and Consulates.

Sabra and Shatila – The Sabra neighborhood and the adjacent Shatila refugee camp were the location of the killing of between 762 and 3,500 civilians, mostly Palestinians and Lebanese Shiites, by the Kataeb Party (Phalange) a predominantly Christian Lebanese right-wing party from 16-18 September 1982. The Phalanges were ordered by the Israeli Defence Forces (IDF) to clear PLO fighters out Sabra and Shatila. The IDF received reports that the Phalanges were committing atrocities but did not stop them. The Israeli Army stationed troops at Sabra and Shatila exits to prevent residents from leaving and, at the Phalangists' request, fired illuminating flares. The perpetrators of the killings were the "Young Men" gang recruited by Elie Hobeika who was a Phalange leader, the Lebanese Forces intelligence chief and liaison officer with Mossad. Most "Young Men" had been expelled from the Lebanese Forces for insubordination or criminal activities. In 1983, a UN commission concluded that Israel, as the camp's occupying power, bore responsibility for the violence and that the massacre was a form of genocide. In 1983, the Israelis appointed that Kahan Commission to investigate the incident. It concluded that Israeli military personnel, aware that a massacre was in progress, had failed to take serious steps to stop it. The commission judged Israel indirectly responsible, and that Ariel Sharon, then Defense Minister, bore personal responsibility "for ignoring the danger of bloodshed and revenge." Sharon was forced to resign.

Sam Johnston - U.S. diplomat murdered by Israelis in Cyprus thus allowing a terror attack to proceed which would increase American support for Israel and further entangle the U.S. in the Middle East.

SBA (Sovereign Base Areas) - Akrotiri and Dhekelia are British Overseas Territories on Cyprus retained by the British under the 1960 treaty of independence, which was agreed and signed by the United Kingdom, Greece, Turkey and representatives from the Greek and Turkish Cypriot communities. The territory is important as a Signals Intelligence station and as a UK communications gathering and monitoring network in the Mediterranean and the Middle East.

Scott Bailey - Assistant Army Attaché, subordinate to Sam Johnston and Ben Huntley.

SEALs - The U.S. Sea, Air, Land Teams, commonly known as the Navy SEALs, are the U.S. Navy's principal special operations force and a part of the Naval Special Warfare Command and United States Special Operations Command. The SEALs conduct small-unit maritime military operations, which originate from, and return to a river, ocean, swamp, delta, or coastline.

Sjaak - Pytheas crewmember who transports the ELRAD.

Smythe - British commando and head of Rapid Reaction Force.

Stanwell - Leslie Stanwell - Commander and Administrator, British Sovereign Base Areas of Akrotiri and Dhekelia, Cyprus.

Taburiente - Caldera de Taburiente (Taburiente Cauldron) – the largest erosion crater on earth. It is surrounded by La Palma's highest peaks, several of which are over 2 km tall. The terrain drops steeply into the crater in almost vertical cliff faces of over 800 meters. Taburiente was originally a volcano, which collapsed 200-500 thousand years ago due to its height and steepness and then eroded into a crater.

Taqo - Eustaquio "Taqo" Sanches; joystick operator of d-Fly MAV on Alhuceima drone mission.

Tolis Apostolou – tavern keeper and former Cypriot commando during the 1974 Turkish Invasion of Cyprus who uncovers Israeli spies.

Tōhoku Tsunami - In 2011 a megathrust earthquake off the Pacific coast of Tōhoku registered a magnitude 9.0 (Mw). The earthquake is also often referred to in Japan as the Great East Japan Earthquake. It was the most powerful earthquake ever recorded to have hit Japan, and the fourth most powerful earthquake in the world since modern record keeping began in 1900. The earthquake triggered powerful tsunami waves which reached heights of 40.5 meters (133 ft.) and which travelled 10 km (6 mi) inland. In 2015, a Japanese National Police Agency report confirmed 15,891 deaths resulted from the quake.

Turkish Invasion of Cyprus - Launched on 20 July 1974 and followed the 1974 Cypriot coup d'état. The coup had been ordered by the military Junta in Greece and staged by the Cypriot National Guard in conjunction with EOKA-B. In August 1974, a further Turkish invasion resulted in the capture of approximately 40% of the island. The ceasefire line of August 1974 eventually became the United Nations Buffer Zone and is commonly referred to as the Green Line.

Troodos - Mountain range on Cyprus; may also refer to RAF Troodos (the British Spy station located there); juncture point of the African and Eurasian Tectonic Plates.

Tsunami - Also known as a seismic sea wave or as a tidal wave; a series of waves in a water body caused by the displacement of a large volume of water. Earthquakes, volcanic eruptions and other underwater explosions (including underwater nuclear devices), landslides, glacier calvings, meteorite impacts and other disturbances above or below water can generate tsunamis.

"Vi" Revelley - Graduate student picked for execution by Rafiq.

Vondel - Captain of research ship *Pytheas* whose sonic device is stolen by terrorists.

Wartel - Danny Wartel, SEAL team leader on Alhuceima mission.

Whale Deaths and Noise - Whales and other marine mammals face human-caused noise in the ocean from subs and ships emitting sonar and from air guns used in oil exploration. Sonic devices are used to search for petroleum, to initiate earthquakes and avalanches, to control crowds, and are installed on seagoing vessels to repel pirates. Sound waves can drown out the noises that marine mammals rely on for survival and cause serious injury and death. One example: the death of 40 dead pilot whales on India's Andaman coast in October 2013 was attributed to a military sonar system described as "the loudest sound in the sea" which is used to find submarines but kills whales and dolphins.

Yarden - Yarden and Nivit Keret are Israeli Mossad agents on Cyprus monitoring terrorists; Yarden turns Nivit in for betraying Israel.

Yonatan Meir - Yonatan Meir; spy that Israel wants pardoned; based on Jonathan Pollard who spied for Israel against the U.S.

PETER THORN

HAND OF GOD

WOLF'S MOUNT

www.ingramcontent.com/pod-product-compliance
Lightning Source LLC
Chambersburg PA
CBHW071155100726
47908CB00002B/393